"In *Broken*, Travis Thrasher improves again on his gifted ability to write severely flawed characters and place them in suspenseful situations that keep readers turning the pages."   —*CBA Retailers and Resources*

"Each time I read a novel by Travis Thrasher, I close the cover and tell myself that was his best. But I find it hard to imagine that Thrasher is going to be able to surpass *Broken* easily...the story literally drove me to tears... The action is intense, the pace breakneck, the aura of mystery palpable, the sense of the supernatural mysterious...In the vein of *Isolation* and *Ghostwriter*, Thrasher gives us *Broken*, one of his best stories to date."
—The Christian Critic

"Full of the creepiness that Travis Thrasher does so well. Mixing a captivating suspense story with ghosts, demons and a Christian message is truly an art."   —FaithfulReader.com

"Thrasher just keeps getting better."   —*Publishers Weekly* on *Ghostwriter*

"*Ghostwriter* twists like a corkscrew. It's a page-turner and I didn't see the ending coming."   —Meg Gardiner, author of *The Dirty Secrets Club*

"Travis Thrasher is truly one of my favorite authors. Here he creates a new twist on the classic ghost story, blending elements of the supernatural together with real-life horror. *Ghostwriter* is a moving story about love, loss, and the creative forces that drive people to madness."
—Sigmund Brouwer, bestselling author of *Broken Angel*

"*Isolation* proved that Thrasher has what it takes to scare the wits out of his audience while challenging them at the same time. *Ghostwriter* takes Thrasher's writing to a whole new level of terror and heart...*Ghostwriter* is the kind of gem that comes along far too seldom, displaying the kind of writing that deserves to be devoured by the masses."
—TheChristianManifesto.com

"Thrasher...demonstrates considerable talent for the horror genre. Like Stephen King, Thrasher pits flawed but likable characters against evil forces that at first seem escapable but gradually take on a terrifying ubiquity."

—*Publishers Weekly* on *Isolation*

"If you thought Peretti and Dekker's *House* was scary, it's time to read a novel that goes much deeper into the characters and deals with some real-life challenges."
—TitleTrakk.com

40

A NOVEL

TRAVIS THRASHER

FaithWords

NEW YORK   BOSTON   NASHVILLE

FaithWords
Hachette Book Group
237 Park Avenue
New York, NY 10017

www.faithwords.com

Printed in the United States of America

First Edition: May 2011
10 9 8 7 6 5 4 3 2 1

FaithWords is a division of Hachette Book Group, Inc.
The FaithWords name and logo are trademarks of Hachette Book Group, Inc.

Library of Congress Cataloging-in-Publication Data
Thrasher, Travis, 1971-
    40 : a novel / Travis Thrasher.—1st ed.
       p. cm.
    ISBN 978-0-446-50551-2
    1. Terminally ill—Fiction.   2. Death—Fiction.   3. Life change events—
Fiction.   4. Faith—Fiction.   I. Title. II. Title: Forty : a novel.
    PS3570.H6925A614 2011
    813'.6—dc22
                                                              2010050667

For Mackenzie Grace Thrasher
and
Brianna Joy Thrasher

PART ONE

—

Achtung Baby

1

An End Has a Start

He waits on the corner like a child at the bus stop in front of your home and his name is death.

I know his face and know it well. He likes to smile and show off bloodstained teeth. They're sharp, ancient, and remain very busy.

He waits for everyone in the shadows. Unseen and unwanted and undercover. Yet he knows the exact place and the exact time and he only answers to one.

I can see him from the deck, peering around a tree in the forest below. Every day, his shadow grows longer, his head more apparent, his dark holes for eyes more visible.

He whispers all the things you could have done.

He laughs at all the things you should have done.

His middle name is regret, his last name finality.

When I see him again, I realize I'm back to where this all began, knowing every end has a start.

I also know I only have two more days to live.

2

What Difference Does It Make?

I feel watched when I turn onto the dirt road leading to the dead end. I can see this desolate strip in the dark of my dreams, the wild growth of untouched Appalachian wilderness, stifling on all sides. The hanging branches blocking the sun can't block the gaze of God. His face has always shone on this small stretch of land. Why, I don't know.

The house resembles an uncle I haven't seen in years. A little more gray, a few more wrinkles. It would make a pretty picture on a postcard if I hadn't lived here for a chunk of my life.

The shape by the window I park beside is surely Mom waiting for me. The front door of the quaint log cabin opens and she smiles. There is nothing rooted in that smile except love.

"Make it okay?" she asks after I hug her small frame.

"The plane had to crash land in Asheville. Otherwise I was headed to Aruba."

"A little color might do you some good."

"How's Dad?"

"Come into the kitchen for a while. He's fine—just went down for a nap. Want something to drink?"

"How about a shot of bourbon?"

"Stop it."

Her accent is polite southern, sweet southern, the kind the movies never seem to get right. There's more character in that tone than in a bottle of some outrageously expensive vintage wine. She makes me a glass of sweet tea and I'm once again reminded how there's never a good substitute for the real thing.

"How's work going?"

"I'd be fine if I didn't have to deal with temperamental artists." I stand at the kitchen table and look into the family room. "Good to see you got it replaced."

Mom nods but doesn't appear like she wants to bring it up. I sent them the check for the window. I guess I never really thought that the bookend I threw would actually go through two panes, but I wasn't really thinking about much of anything when I threw it except how much I hated my father. I didn't want to break glass; I wanted to break his face.

That was the last time I'd been here. The last thing I did before going out the door and driving away and vowing never to come back to this place.

Mom remembers but I'm sure Dad doesn't.

I don't even know if he remembers who he is anymore, much less the curses I hurled out as I chucked some big block that looked like a remnant of a Roman sculpture from the New Testament.

That was over a year ago.

The older I get, the more I discover how ruthless and uncaring time can be.

His eyes are see-through glass, his face curled up in a joker-like smile on only one side. I'm a moving picture to him, as meaningful as cable television or blowing rain.

I'm ready, and I stand and swallow.

"Hi, Dad."

It's easy to say those words with this tone and this security when there's nobody looking back. When there's nobody listening on the other side, demanding an apology or demanding anything.

I see him shift forward, then back, in the wheelchair. So slight, steady, like the twitching hand of a clock with a dying battery.

"It's Tyler," Mom says behind me, speaking in a way I've never heard her speak to my father.

She's no longer a servant. She's now his interpreter.

Hearing her words moves me more than seeing him here like this, here but not here, alive and breathing, but not really.

He looks feeble and frail. The heart attack might as well have killed him. It took that strong, seemingly unbreakable backbone and snapped it in half.

"Why don't you sit down?"

I follow my mother's advice and then watch as she slips away.

He coughs and sounds like an animal. I study the face.

Then I just sit there for a long time.

I hear myself take a breath. The things we take for granted.

It's remarkable. Really. This life.

I want to ask God why He didn't just take him. What purpose does this shell of a man in front of me have?

God's timing, I hear Charles W. Harrison say.

You can't speak to me, you're a vegetable.

Want to know what Hell is, son?

Don't ask me that question again.

I see you and hear you, TW.

My father's the only one who's ever called me TW, and only at selective moments. Teachable moments. The moments that count, Charles liked to say.

Every moment counts, doesn't it? Doesn't it, Dad?

I look at the library surrounding us. His fleet of battleships against the evil one, our own Sauron that wages war against us daily. My father chose to fight back with words.

The Word, Son.

Afternoon light slips through the blinds, casting my father's shadow over the wall. I see several frames in its wake. Pictures of my mom, Kendra, Kendra's boys. Nowhere do I see my face.

I wonder if he took down my mug before the incident or after.

It's chilly in this room, the smell of cut wood in the air, perhaps just in my mind. Can memories contain scents?

"Everything okay?" Mom asks on her way to their bedroom, which is another door down.

I am ten or twenty-two or thirty-four years old and the answer is the same as always.

A wrong and a fake and a hollow *yes.*

• • •

Before I leave, I take hold of my father's hand. It's not cold and it's not hard and it doesn't shock me. I want to say something.

The moment calls for something to be said and I'm the only one here that can do it.

I can't think of anything.

"How long did they give him?"

"I didn't ask."

"What did Kendra say?"

"She's Kendra. Thinks she's a surgeon and a scientist and Mother Teresa."

"Yeah."

"Are you hungry?"

"I was before the dinner you fixed an hour ago."

"We never had dessert."

"Mom, please."

"You're not around enough for me to fatten you up."

"I have beer to do that for me."

The sliding glass door facing the table we sit at opens onto a deck that overlooks the valley below. The sun floats like a bright beach ball in the distance.

"Remember that tree that used to block the view?" Mom nods toward the bright glow.

"I thought something was different. You can actually see the sunset."

"Pretty, isn't it?" Mom looks out behind the shield of her coffee, lost somewhere way out beyond the rays.

"I told him for years to cut it down."

"He finally listened."

"For once."

"He wanted to cut it down himself. I told him, 'over my dead body.' He got one of the local workers around here to cut it down."

"Probably would've killed him right then and there."

"He listened to you more than you know."

This is the part of being a son I'm not so good at.

The moment when I fail.

I have nothing to say.

I'm embarrassed by the stockpile of emotions in this room. Ashamed that I can't find the combination to open the door and let a few of them come out. Just a few, like dusty tools in a forgotten shed somewhere. Maybe even just one.

"You know he loves you."

I nod. Of course I know that. That isn't the question. How he loved was. I note that Mom isn't using past tense like I am.

He's not in the past tense, not yet.

Yet to me he's always lived in the past tense. I am always and forever in fourth grade and can't ever move on.

The voices sound stronger in the silence than they were when they were spoken.

"So what do you want out of life?"

It was a simple question my father asked last time I was here.

"I haven't really had much time to think about it after being stuffed with your guilt and loathing of this life, *Dad*."

"Seems you've done a pretty good job of living your own life these past ten years."

"Don't."

"Don't what?"

"Don't bring her up."

"You know my feelings on this."

"Yeah, and every single time I see your face you bring her up."

"Which seems to be less and less often."

"People get divorced every day. *Christians*, even."

"A man is known by the fruits of his spirit."

"So what are you saying? Or what are you trying to say through these nice little quotes?"

"That a man is known by his actions, his life. Are you like the barren fig tree?"

"I don't even know what a fig tree is."

40

"The Bible says that if salt loses its flavor, how's it supposed to be seasoned? That it's good for nothing except being trampled upon."

That's what did it. I didn't want to hear it anymore and I didn't want him suggesting that I was still not quite right, like a car he brought in every week but that still had some strange and distant clinking that sounded every time he took it out for a drive.

I wasn't a damned fig tree or some spreading salt for the sidewalk.

A son shouldn't be talked about like something worthless, like something dying, like something that doesn't matter.

What doesn't matter is what I said then or what I might have said now.

In the pit of night when the noise is gone, all I can hear are voices.

His remains the loudest.

It's here that I can't lie.

I don't question Heaven or Hell.

Yet I still sometimes question which one I'll arrive at when my time has come.

3

The Killing Moon

The wind breathes through the open window. I hear the slight fluttering of the outside and shiver. This place continues to scare me.

Fear doesn't have to come from terror. It can come from loneliness. From memories of confinement.

I always thought it was interesting that a man chosen by God to proclaim the gospel decided to live in one of the most isolated parts of the country, where neighbors were a thing you could only see in the brilliant lawns of slumberland. Sure, Dad had his business trips and speaking engagements and his books, but home is where the heart is, right? Dad kept his in hiding.

I'm in my old bedroom, which is now a guest room designed by Cracker Barrel. My iPhone doesn't display any service, Internet or phone, but I'm trying anyway. I'm desperate for some kind of connection. Maybe Dad will send me a text from wherever his mind is hanging out.

I pull out a book, *the* book in fact, from a shelf. I wonder what it's doing there, to be honest. If I were invited to Paul McCartney's house, I doubt he'd have *Abbey Road* on display. Billy Graham probably wouldn't have one of his books either. It feels like a partially eaten mint left on my pillow.

Maybe someone visiting put the book back on this shelf after reading it at night. Or maybe Dad put it there before his heart attacked the rest of his body.

The Grave After the Grave.

40

I know this book well.

The picture on the back is of my father from thirty years ago. He resembles Robert De Niro. The intense De Niro, the one that was able to make *Taxi Driver* and those early Scorsese movies, not the *Meet the Parents* guy, who seems to have mellowed and grown softer with age.

This version says "International Bestseller."

Books don't start out like that. It takes time to build a bestseller. Lots and lots of time. Time away from the family, time to promote, time to pontificate, time.

"Translated into 40 languages."

I know the passages, some almost by heart.

Not by having read them, but by having sat and heard them recounted over and over and over.

A living and breathing sounding board. With pimples.

The simple black cover with the red inscription. An apocalyptic title in a font resembling scratched blood. The notable "Dr." before my father's name. I scan the pages but don't read any of it. I'm almost waiting for it to starting humming, or maybe even begin heckling.

Dad had had only three books published while he worked on what felt to be another hundred. Maybe someone will discover them in storage one day.

It won't be me. Unless I'm looking for kindling.

This book is his life's work and his legacy about the Great Below. About the place people wonder about and joke about but seldom take seriously. The place of fire and brimstone and, my favorite: gnashing of teeth.

Seems like I spent a lot of time gnashing my teeth in this very room.

Dr. Charles William Harrison.

It's a four-word brand I don't want to buy. A bio I don't want to be a part of.

Coming back here reminds me of things like this. These are a few of my not-so-favorite things, Julie Andrews. This place and this book and this feeling of complete and total inadequacy.

I wonder if there really is a whole host of them waiting in the dark. Beautiful creatures, wrecked with the weight of their eternal decision, their eternal damnation. Hideous harbingers who stand in wait, preying on every helpless feeling out there. I wonder if they wait outside this very door, watching in the shadows of night, sneaking in when I'm asleep to drip bloody drool on the floor by my bed.

I'm twelve again, petrified by the notion of death and Hell, by the pictures and portraits of demons delivered by the tongue of the man I call Dad. Fathers are supposed to give their sons the gift of baseball, of camp stories, of exploration and courage and light.

Mine gave me a window into the everlasting side of darkness.

Almost three decades later and I'm still haunted and hounded.

If they do stand outside watching and waiting, they're surely laughing too.

Everything in me wants to reach and bash their ugly faces to obliteration.

I swallow, sigh. Restless. Haunted. Guilty.

The tension isn't from whether I believe in these fallen angels out there. It's my ambivalence toward it all.

When you believe something, you act on it. Right?

I haven't gotten much further than I was when I lived under this roof under these rules under this regime.

Maybe I should have gone to Guam to be a missionary. Maybe I should've become a Christian music singer or a youth pastor or at least volunteered a little more at a children's hospital. Maybe I should've done a lot of things.

Maybe the demons watch and laugh and know I haven't done a damned thing since leaving here.

Something rolls. I can feel the floor outside my bedroom door vibrating. Something's moving on the wood floor, the one my parents have still never bothered to carpet.

I get out of bed and open the door, turning on the light. My eyes take a moment to adjust, and after they do I still can't quite make out what I'm looking at.

Blue and yellow.

It's a blue and yellow roller skate.

"Mom?"

40

Nothing.

I'm about ready to say, "Hello anybody?" but then wonder if maybe Mom is playing a practical joke on me, so I don't. Not that Mom would be doing this in the middle of the night.

Maybe it's Dad, having one last laugh.

I pick up the roller skate to make sure I haven't lost my mind. It's lightweight and dusty.

I can hear the wind gust outside.

Yeah that's outside, not in here, and you know that the wind didn't just cause this thing to roll, and you know you heard it roll; it woke you up.

This used to be my roller skate a long time ago.

Not that I ever did much roller-skating in this house or on the roads around here.

So why is it in the middle of the hallway and where's the other and why am I holding it as if I've found the missing piece to my childhood?

I think of the Talking Heads song I was jamming to on my iPod as my plane landed today.

The famous line that speaks to so many about so much.

"Same as it ever was."

Exactly.

4

Fragile

Mom walks around like a frazzled woman late for a wake. She's looking for the keys that are in her hand. I tell her to slow down, to relax.

"Thank you for coming."

"This isn't charity, Mom. I would've been down here earlier."

"I know you're busy."

"I'm not busy at this very moment. I'm not going anywhere."

"But I know you're busy with your job."

"He almost died," I say.

"God answers prayers."

"You think *this* is an answer to prayer?"

"He's giving us a little more time to spend with your father."

"That's not my father. That's like—that's some kind of lab experiment. It's a mannequin in the window. We're looking, but nobody's looking back out at us."

"Don't say things like that." She looks down at the floor.

"I'm just being honest."

"He can hear us when we talk to him."

"You really think so?"

"I know."

It's Saturday and I've been here for three days and plan on leaving tomorrow. Mom is feeling guilty for leaving me here with Dad, and I'm telling her to stop being ridiculous. Even prisoners get a chance to take a walk outside and breathe in fresh air.

Mom touches my arm.

"Don't," she says.

"Don't what?"

"Carry your anger around with you. It gets heavy after a while."

"I don't."

"I know you haven't always understood your father."

"No, I understand him just fine. It is what it is."

"You want to know something funny? He brought up the strangest thing to me not long ago, before the stroke. Something I hadn't heard him mention in years. You probably don't know this, but when you were a little boy he always spoke about wanting to take you canoeing on the French Broad River. He said he had a dream about it and he said it in a way like it was some deep regret."

"Good."

"Tyler."

"I was around for eighteen years for him to carve out some time for a nice little canoe trip, Mom."

"Your father didn't control all the different—"

"Yeah yeah yeah—we've been down this road before."

"Doesn't mean we can't go down it again. Maybe you're missing something."

I grit my teeth together. "I'm missing nothing."

"It was his place in life. Your father knew his place."

"Yeah? Well, it would've been a hell of a lot easier for me if he'd helped me find mine."

"Maybe he still can."

I walk away from her toward the kitchen and stare out the window by the sink. "This just pisses me off."

"That he had a heart attack?"

"Yeah." I turn and face her. "'Cause I never got to tell him what I really think."

Mom is unruffled. After a lifetime spent carrying the baggage and playing the supporting role, this isn't new. As my anger has intensified over the years, she has grown more mellow.

"I have my cell with me if you need anything," she says.

"We'll be fine. Take your time."

"Thank you for coming down."

She knows what I'm thinking simply by my look.

"I'm just saying—I know that last time—I wasn't sure you'd come back."

"Didn't want it to have to be this way."

I study her posture, her face, her eyes. They all feel weighed down. I wonder if I look the same.

"How are you feeling?" I ask.

"I'm fine."

"Would you tell me if you weren't?"

"Would you?"

I raise my eyebrows and smile.

The restless tides grow stronger as the years number. Sometimes I think it stems from age. *Any chance I can get a 2.0 version? Steve Jobs, reinvent me, please.* Other times I think it's from here—from this place I'm visiting—this suffocating little burrow, this box full of memories. I never slew the dragon in my innermost cave, thus I'm stuck and always have it lurking in the recesses of my dreams.

Silence makes me suspect. I grow leery of the stillness because it's here that I begin to hear them. Voices. Self-doubt. Whispers. Longings. Could-have-beens. Regrets. Questions.

Is this God's spirit prompting me or Satan's minions pricking?

No question why I have the job I do. It drowns out the void of silence.

I'm looking in the kitchen to see if I can find anything with caffeine or maybe a stash of vodka—*Mom, I never knew!*—when I hear the crash coming from my father's study.

His office looks ransacked and he's hunched over, looking dead. I pull Dad up and see a faint shadow of a grimace on his face.

Tears are in his eyes.

I look down in his lap at the soiled khaki pants.

"You okay?" I ask as I feel his forehead, hot and sticky.

How long was he wallowing around like this as I was having a woe-is-me jam session in the kitchen?

40

I curse, not at my father but at myself.

His body tenses and he seems to want to fight this, to fight me off.

He's embarrassed. The man took a dump in his pants and reeks and he's ashamed, and he was trying to clean it up himself.

"It's all right. It's okay. Mistakes happen. Come on—let me wheel you to the bathroom and get you cleaned up."

He sits in the chair, unable to look in my direction. I unbuckle a belt and then pull off his pants and see white hairless legs, lined with veins and smeared with his mess. I hold my breath. Even his socks are stained. In trying to clean up after himself, he made things a lot worse. I guess this hasn't happened before or else he'd be wearing diapers.

I put his clothes in a heap by the bathtub, then start it up.

I find some bubble bath that obviously belongs to Mom.

The stench is raw and unbearable.

I soon help him up and out of messy underwear that will never be worn again. Then I sit him down in the bath, thankful that the bubbles cover most of his bony body.

His bones shiver.

"It's all right. The water will warm you up soon. It'll be fine."

Soon I'm wiping him down, no longer the boy bemoaning his lost youth, no longer Tyler William Harrison attending to Charles William Harrison.

I use a wet cloth and pat down his face.

"God answers prayers."

I shampoo his hair and see my hands shaking as I rub the lather in.

"It gets heavy after a while."

When he's clean and the water is half gone, I help Dad stand up and then dry him off. I find some clothes and take a while putting them on. Soon he's back in his wheelchair, his body shivering a bit, his eyes still remote, his spirit defeated.

I move past him to find a hair dryer and feel the grip of his hand on my arm.

I can't believe how strong it is.

When I look down, there's nothing there. He lets go.

Rubbing my wrist, I remember something else Mom said.

"He can hear us when we talk to him."

That look in her eyes, the look of absolute belief.

"*I know.*"

I tap him on the shoulder.

"It's gonna be all right, Dad. It's gonna be fine."

I leave my father resting in his bed and then make sure Mom isn't somewhere in the house, and then I weep for a few moments. I'm in a dark corner of the house. I try to make it fast and forgettable.

But tears never forget.

5

Once Upon a Time

The world is a set of snapshots gathered together by Google. It's a series of beautiful faces and beautiful bodies living a beautiful life, an unattainable life. The world lets you peek in like a passenger staring out of a plane at the glowing Earth below, but it doesn't let you get out. The glowing, glistening allure soon vanishes, turning the world below to black, your seat belt still is strapped on, the turbulence still ahead.

Flying makes me melancholy. Always has. I once knew a guy I worked with in the studio who ended up dying in a 767 that went down in a Nebraska cornfield. The guy wasn't even twenty-five years old, with his whole life ahead of him. Half the people on that flight ended up living, but not this guy. Even though that happened back in 2003, I still always think of him anytime I get on a plane.

What if I die today? What will I be leaving behind?

Maybe it's the fact that I'm stuck in a seat and it's an evening flight and I'm ready to be back home. Maybe it's because coming back to see my parents always messes with my mind.

Maybe it's because I'm still carrying the same fears I carried when I was a teenager.

I open my case to get out my laptop and do a little work. Nowadays you can work anywhere if you have your computer and some decent headphones. As my hand digs into the bag, I feel something peculiar.

It's some kind of wire—a cable almost. It's thick and heavy.

I examine it under the cone-shaped glare of the light above. It's a small coil of white wire. And it's covered with blood.

I slide it back into my bag, like a murderer hiding evidence. Thankfully, the guy next to me is sleeping, his mouth opened wide enough to see his gums.

I try and think where that could have come from.

I need a drink. Maybe a sleeping pill too.

I eventually order the former as my mind does handstands and flips but gets nowhere. The gin and tonic tastes good. Bigmouth next to me catches his tongue on his throat a few times, making me get my iPod and press *play*.

Music helps. It always has since I was a child.

If someone ever arrested me and went through my iPod, they'd probably have a few questions.

First, they might wonder why I have all those Pet Shop Boys *and* Erasure albums. Then they might ask me if I have a boyfriend.

Second, they would surely want to know why I have this assortment of photos on here.

Just like those fabulous synth-pop albums, the pictures are a guilty pleasure. They are something I know I should get rid of, but something that reminds me that I'm human. They mirror the reality of my life: that I am thirty-nine and single and pretty much alone.

Once upon a time I was that guy in that photo, with the 90210 hair and sideburns, holding the beautiful blonde bride. I was naïve, with unbridled passion and promise. I thought I was grown up, but I didn't have a clue. I thought I could control where life was about to go, but I didn't know I wasn't in the driver's seat. I was that guy playing the keyboard on stage, dreaming of something I really had no talent to dream of. Thinking that I could be twenty-something all my life, rocking and rolling.

Once upon a time I was the guy working with that set of people at the record company, trying to sell something I wanted to create, trying to learn something I wanted to master.

The photos are in chronological order. Snapshots from another time.

There is the picture of me with Brian Eno, the man I wanted to be.

There is a picture of me with Laila, the woman I wanted to be with.

40

There are assorted shots of the life I have now, drunken laughter at some bar in the middle of nothing and nowhere.

A plus B plus C plus D doesn't always end up getting you E.

Sometimes you go to Q with a big fat question mark over it and you wonder how you got there.

Compromise.

That's not all, I think. I got there from a series of compromises and chance encounters and failed promises and selfish desires.

What if I die today?

I hear that voice again, and think of the guy named Simon who died in that plane crash.

What would they say at your funeral and who would show up?

I need to put on some Arcade Fire and crank it up and shut these voices out.

I'm almost through the photos when I see one last shot I don't recognize.

At first all I see is the blurry image at the top. Then I notice the face. It's a head shot of some guy—slightly out of focus, as if it was taken at night at some bar. The man is laughing, his face scruffy, his mouth slightly open.

But the eyes are clear.

They're clear and looking straight ahead and they look red and angry.

The blurry gray smudges at the top of the image are his hands, as if he was trying to reach at the person taking the photo.

I've never seen this man before, but I know that face.

His eyes and the wrinkles underneath and the dark beard and dark eyes.

I feel nauseated with fear. Like I'm falling.

I shut off my iPod, but the image stays in my head.

In the parking lot at O'Hare, I put my bags in my car and then check to see if that wire was really in my bag.

It's there. Still coiled up and splattered with something red.

21

6

Paranoid Android

I've spent a lifetime flirting around with things that aren't so good for me.

Like Angie, for instance.

I think in her case, it's because she knows me a little too much for my own good.

"Something's up," she says before the rest of the partygoers arrive at my place.

"What?"

"You." Angie slides a not-so-subtle finger across my chest.

"I'm fine. Really."

"It was going home, right?"

"It's nothing."

"You've got that—that look. That aura."

I smile and shake my head. "So you're an expert on me, huh?"

"I watch when others don't."

"Should I be frightened?"

"Only if you want to be."

I stare at her round and fantastic lips as if they are still talking.

"Tyler!"

I'm not sure if the scream from the new arrivals saves or stifles, because I'm not sure exactly what I want with Angie. She smiles and slinks away, knowing I'm watching her. Men can't play games like women do, because we're so transparent. Especially after a few beers. We're simple in what we want, even if we try hard not to show it. Women, however, don't seem to know half the time what they want.

Angie looks back and I know exactly what she wants. I've known for some time.

Angie's right. Something *is* up, though I don't think it's just the fact that I'm back to real life after my trip to memory lane with the folks. Something feels different and slightly off.

I feel this as I drink another beer and wonder when I'm going to start feeling a buzz.

I feel this as I glide through the people at my condo, both on the fourth floor studio and on the rooftop.

I feel this as I press *play* on one of three carefully constructed playlists on my iPod, my one source of pride at parties.

I even feel this after we run out of beer and I receive enough cash to buy ten cases. Guess that's one of the hosting favors of a party like this.

Alone and away from the crowd, the uneasy feeling doesn't go away. I walk down the sidewalk and think that this neighborhood *used* to be dangerous at night. It's becoming trendy now, a bit overstated. I prefer the place I live to be misunderstood rather than discovered. Most of the time I tell people I live in Wicker Park, because they don't know where East Village or East Ukranian Village actually is. It's close enough to say Wicker Park, and East Ukranian Village sounds like somewhere in the Czech Republic.

Even though this place is safe and comfortable and cozy, there's some deep part of me that says otherwise. That says everything is different now, that everything has changed.

I just don't know how. Or why.

There is a guy holding a gun at my forehead, cursing in another language while he holds a six-pack in his other hand. I imagine it's my first brush with death, but something inside tells me I'm soon going to learn how absolutely wrong I am.

People have been stabbed in this liquor store. Doesn't mean I won't buy beer when I need to, especially after running out at dusk on my July 4th party. Doesn't mean I won't wander in and pick up a couple of cases and ignore the commotion going on at the cash register.

I hold out the cases of beer and then the guy points the gun back at the clerk, who looks undaunted, like he's seen it before. My cases fall to the floor as the door opens and someone comes inside and I bolt out.

Coward.

I run.

A glorious, ecstatic, horrifying kind of run, the kind that Tom Cruise does in every one of his movies. Sprinting as if I can outrun death, hauling and trying to avoid the sound of a gunshot cracking and the feel of my brain being blown out the front of my skull. I run and run and soon I'm leaning over, throwing up and spitting out the grilled cheddarwurst and the combination of snacks and beers that just turned over like a tornado in my stomach.

My eyes water.

Call someone do something be somebody.

I'm panting as I call 911.

Be all you can be, Ty.

The night can't be over because it hasn't even started yet.

When the voice comes on the other line, I tell them what happened. When they ask if I'm okay, I don't really know how to answer.

Somehow after some amount of time, I begin to move forward to my condo. After my life-and-death experience buying cheap beer.

Should've gotten the Amstel Light.

When I get in, my buddy Cole asks where the beer is. I don't answer, because I'm still in shock. I also know Cole well enough to know that he won't be sympathetic, that he won't believe me, that he'll simply still wonder where the beer is.

Did that all really happen?

I know it did.

I make up some excuse and Cole acts like I'm hammered and not making any sense.

The gloves are off now, Tyler.

What happened to me feels as real as these ghosts surrounding me feel, these "friends," half of whom I don't recognize. A building full of strangers who say "nice place" and "beautiful night" and "where should I put this?" and "good to see you again" when I don't ever remember seeing them in the first place. I see them through jaded glasses: the cluster. This is a tradition and something of legend, this party, and I'm not even the host, but more like the emcee and the party-favor guy.

When I reach the rooftop and see Angie as the sounds of the Editors float away into the clear evening sky, I tug her blouse and bring her lips to mine and kiss her out of need and fear and want and relief.

I taste her surprise and it feels real and reminds me that I'm not dreaming and I'm not dead.

Not yet.

Not yet.

PART TWO

——

Strangeways, Here We Come

7

Enjoy the Silence

The sound of laughter wakes me up.

I open my eyes to darkness and listen.

There it is again.

Sounds like one of my buddies sitting at the bar, reacting to a comment someone made about the Bears or the Cubs or maybe some chick walking past.

Maybe the television is still on.

My condo is on the fourth story of a brick building west of Ashland and south of Division. I've been here since 2004, a couple of years after becoming a full-time single man again, a couple of years after saving enough money to buy it. It's got the vibe of a studio loft when you climb the steps and reach the living area, a large open and airy space with high ceilings. Stairs near the back take you down to a guest bedroom and office, while another set takes you up to my small bedroom. A third set brings you up to the roof, the key that sealed the deal for me.

It's plenty of space for one. Sometimes, I think, too much space.

Sometimes I think of selling it, but after the market tanked a few years ago, those thoughts have lessened.

Especially since I haven't gotten a check in, oh, half a year.

Being an independent producer comes with perks and quirks.

I walk down the short set of wooden stairs and reach the kitchen. No lights. No television. Nobody home.

Across the unlit room, I see the sliding glass door cracked open. I open it more and step out on the deck, leaning on the thick stone wall to look at the street below.

I listen for the laughter again.

Was I dreaming?

An SUV drives down the street below. In the distance, I hear the sound of more vehicles.

I love the city because it reminds me I'm not alone. There is always something to do, somewhere to go, somebody to be with. You're a text away from hanging out with someone.

So you tell yourself.

The cool air against my bare chest feels good. It's still humid, even this late at night.

I hear the cackle again.

Coming from inside.

Coming from my bedroom.

It sounds throaty, strained, almost sickly. Like a man laughing as he's bleeding his guts out.

I'm suddenly wearing a coat of goosebumps. I go back inside and then turn on the lights. I turn on ones I normally don't use. I check my bedroom and then the guest bedroom, the office, the bathrooms.

Nothing.

It would be easy for someone to slip inside a door I might have forgotten to lock one day and then stay in hiding until I decided to look around the place in the middle of the night. It would be easy for them to sneak up behind me and put one hand on my mouth as the other hand takes a ten-inch hunting knife and guts my throat like a dead fish.

These are the thoughts I have while looking around my house.

Maybe I need a dog.

Moments later, all silent and dark again, inside the thin security of my blanket covering me, I hear something.

Maybe I'm dreaming again. Maybe I'm half-asleep or half-awake.

40

I hear words.

"I'm watching you."

They're clear, but I don't get up again.

I move under the covers to seek solace, but instead find myself lost in the vastness of this bed and this life that belongs only to me.

8

No New Tale to Tell

W hat we're looking for is something that's going to be a surprise like *Blue and Bluer.*"

I nod at the A&R guy and can't help watching the hands moving in the air like a symphony conductor, a pastor preaching away.

Got it, my face and body say.

Yeah right is what my mind thinks.

This is like someone saying in earnest business-art-soul-speak, "Let's try and do *Dark Side of the Moon* again," or *Pet Sounds,* or *Joshua Tree,* or *Nevermind.*

Never mind is right, because it's never happening again.

Very few artists ever have a chance to take people's breath away with something groundbreaking and surprising. If, and that's a very big if, they ever do, that's their one and only shot. Not in terms of sales or artistic growth, but in terms of excitement and expectation.

The rest will forever be after the fact.

They'll be chasing the beast forever after.

Some will morph and change and evolve. Groups like U2. Others will cave under the pressure and the anticipation and the demand.

Rick MacLellan is the new A&R rep from the record label. His job is to manage the relationships, between both the artists and the producers. He's my link to Jupiter Records. Which is big, but it's bigger since they're owned by Universal Music Group.

40

This is the fourth time I've met with Rick MacLellan, and once again I'm wishing that Lauren hadn't left. She helped bring a lot of artists my way and helped my dreams become a little more of a reality.

Like all the women in my life that have meant something to me, Lauren moved on. Guess that's part of the deal with me.

Now Rick MacLellan is trying to get his scent over anything and everything he can. He likes to utter clichés like, "This is *OK Computer* mixed with *Exile on Main Street*." Things like, "He's the new Bob Dylan of our day." Things like, "We need the album out in a month, even though we don't have any songs."

He says them with such conviction that I almost wonder if he thinks he's being original.

I nod at Rick MacLellan. I have to. That's part of my job. The same way it is to listen to the strange babblings of some artist going on about their brother's pet snake. That has nothing to do with recording a song, but then again maybe it has everything to do with it.

The guy in front of me, the one who is twenty-four years old but looks fourteen, just can't help sounding so corny.

"Sean's finally on board," Rick MacLellan says.

I nod, glance at the other guy in the room. His name is Gavin, and he's with me.

Sean Torrent, the artist, isn't here.

He's supposed to be here.

Rick MacLellan said he was going to be here. Rick MacLellan said that Sean was going to show up for this meeting in this fancy high-rise that overlooks Lake Michigan and probably is owned by UMG or someone that really, really likes UMG.

It's Sean's album that Rick MacLellan is talking about.

I like saying Rick MacLellan's full name because he's a full name kind of guy. A guy who takes himself and his work and his wardrobe way too seriously. A full name kind of guy like James Bond or Ralph Lauren. Me, I like one-word guys, like Sting and Bono.

"He's wanting to energize the troops, you know? To give fans what they've been wanting ever since *Blue and Bluer*. He's not going into any artistic crap, not on this one. That's why he wants you to produce."

I nod, not sure how to take his last comment, but not caring.

It's a big job, even if it's with Sean.

Maybe I should have the words BLUE and BLUER tattooed on my forehead, etched out on my tombstone. Is bluer even a word? I don't know.

Right place and right time. That's what I tell people wanting to make it in music, or really, in any kind of artistic endeavor.

A girl bouncing around in a disco just like any other girl happens to be at the right place at the right time in the right city in the right decade.

She goes for a one-word name and calls herself Madonna.

Yeah, that woman has talent, but she also has quite a lot of blonde ambition and a whole lot of good fortune.

The right place at the right time.

The way I was at the right studio at the right time, serving as a part-time engineer when Sean Torrent just happened to come out of nowhere and make his breakthrough record. I managed to help and will forever have those helping efforts attached to my résumé.

Rick MacLellan rambles on about the new album I'm supposed to produce, about the songs he hasn't heard, about the artist he hasn't seen. I'm on board and I shake my head and I watch his hands move and I take a sip of my water.

I don't want to bring up the rumors, but they're out there because they're true.

I don't bring them up for the same reason Rick MacLellan doesn't bring them up.

I need this job. Rick MacLellan needs this job. A lot of people need this job.

They need the industry that is Sean Torrent.

Sean, he doesn't have to worry about his industry and brand.

But we do.

After the meeting, after Rick MacLellan leaves me with an iron hand-shake and the scent of highbrow full-name cologne, I sit in this multi-room palace where we held the meeting. I look out the window and see the boats and wish I was on mine.

Gavin's so quiet that I almost forget he's behind me. He shuffles as if he's ready to go.

"So when do we start again?"

He speaks quickly, the way most Brits do. I give him a look that probably says way too much. "Supposed to start after Labor Day."

"Does Sean even know about that holiday?"

"He probably doesn't know what planet he's on."

"So who's going to babysit?"

I look at Gavin and laugh. "You're looking at the day care right here."

He rubs his red goatee and curses.

"One day, just think," I tell him, urging him to look out the windows. "This place could be yours."

"No way. Not me. Maybe people like Rick. Or Sean. Or *you*."

"Hey—that's Rick *MacLellan*. Did you get his card?"

"What a little prat."

"He's going to help us get paid."

"Can he help with drug addicts?"

"Let's go get a drink," I say.

Sometimes that's the only good solution I can think of.

Gavin's been working with me for almost ten years. We met at Component 4, a Chicago recording studio where I learned the craft by starting as a studio runner and working my way up. He was a geeky tech guy who'd migrated to Chicago from England because of some tragic Nick Hornby love-gone-bad story that I still don't know all the details to. There is nothing in a studio that Gavin can't do. He's listed as the engineer on the albums we've worked on together and technically he's the studio engineer. But Gavin does everything I need him to, especially those things a producer should be able to do but that Tyler Harrison unfortunately never learned.

He's on his second pint of dark beer, which he's miraculously figured out how to avoid transferring to his waist. We're at the Clough, a place with cheap beer and cheap lighting and cheap women. They know us by name here, which can be good or bad, depending on how you look at it. This is the place we go after long days or nights to celebrate our successes or more likely drown our sorrows. It's also somewhere between our two residences; Gavin doesn't live too far from Electrical Audio, the studio we've done our last couple albums at. It takes ten minutes or maybe a little more from my place to the studio.

Even in the poor lighting I can make out Gavin's short and spiked red hair.

"You look surprised," he says.

"I'm not sure if I'm surprised by the studio wanting me to produce Sean's album or surprised that I'm willing to do it."

"It's work, mate. These days it's good to work on anything."

"Yeah, guess you're right. I'm still paying for our sessions with ABBA."

"We finished a month ago."

"Yeah, but going over meant that came out of my paycheck."

ABBA is my nickname for a big pop band that acts like they're the Beatles but sound a little more like Ace of Base. They're wildly popular and the job was supposed to pay well, but it turned into a nightmare.

That's exactly why I'm afraid of producing Sean Torrent.

"It all depends on which Sean shows up, you know?"

"Yeah. I know too well," I say.

"We might have a lot of time on our mitts."

"No. They're not going to allow that. The heyday is over. They'll let us sink with this one. I promise you. And I can't sink any further."

"The only thing worrying's going to get you is wrinkles."

I take a sip of beer. This place still has a jukebox, and it's eclectic, playing everything from Irish songs, which it should play, to ones by the Human League. On some nights when there isn't a game to watch, it goes on autopilot and comes up with the most random stuff. That's part of the Clough's charm. I laugh as a song comes on.

"Man it's been a long time since I've heard them."

"Who's this?" Gavin asks.

"Love and Rockets. Great late '80s stuff. The guys from Bauhaus. Brooding souls. Used to dance to their stuff at Medusas."

"The underground club for teens?"

"Yep."

"Anna used to talk about it. We'd go to these clubs after turning twenty-one and she'd always say how they never compared to Medusas."

"They didn't. That was when I still wanted to be Robert Smith of the Cure. Have my own band. Invest in hair product and makeup. Sing about the misery of life."

"Ah, but alas, you found love," Gavin says.

"I found love but love left me dry."

"Sounds like a Sean Torrent lyric."

"Maybe it is."

"Write it down," Gavin says. "We might need it."

"What did you want to do when you were back in your homeland, speaking with fellow *mates*?"

"I've told you, don't try and do the accent. You sound confused when you do it."

"Confused."

"Yes. It's a bit English, a bit Pikey, a bit Japanese."

I laugh and admit that he's probably right.

"What do you mean, what I wanted to do?" he asks.

"When you were young? What did you dream of doing when you grew up?"

"I never thought of it."

"Never? You never wanted to be a musician or a painter or someone famous?"

"Should I have?"

"I guess not."

"Never thought much of it."

"You're my age."

"I'm not *that* old."

"Okay, a year younger," I say.

"And what's that supposed to mean?"

"I don't know. It's just—the older I get, the more I wonder if I chose the wrong path."

"You think you had anything to do with it?"

"Meaning?"

"Meaning you're dealing with everything you've got, you know? Some people are born beautiful. Their life is set."

"You calling me ugly?"

Gavin laughs.

"A person's life isn't always set," I say.

"Some people can play football. Some can act the part of Elton John and have the voice to match. Some people have fathers who work in construction."

"So what about us?"

"We like beer and share a common history."

Sometimes it's hard to know when Gavin is being witty or when he's simply being his normal analytical self.

"Our common history, huh?"

"Failed love."

"Yeah. You can say that again."

Gavin raises his glass to toast. "To marriage and to the ever after."

I toast and drain my beer.

"Guess we're married to Sean Torrent for the moment, aren't we?" he says.

I'm not thinking about Sean. It's easy to go back in time. Songs do that to you. So do other things, like toasts, or locales, or Chicago nights.

"Worried?" Gavin asks.

"Just thinking. Remembering."

"Those are two things I try my best not to do."

"I asked two people to marry me. One said yes, the other disappeared. Both broke my heart."

Gavin gives me a reflective smile, then punches me in the arm. "Mate, if I was a girl, you'd have me at 'both.' But I'm not, so shut your piehole and get us some more beers."

I laugh.

Empathy is for losers.

9

Darkness

That night, my daughter calls me.

This is strange, since I know how much she doesn't like to talk on the phone.

This is even stranger since I wonder how I know something like that, considering that I don't have a daughter.

"Daddy," she says deliberately, with a toddler's foreign tongue.

"Yeah," I say back.

"I miss you, Daddy."

"I miss you, too."

I miss her even though I don't know her name, even though I don't know what she looks like, even though this is all just a dream caused by the hops of the beer I was drinking.

"Daddy."

"Yeah?"

"Don't go by the scary man."

"Okay, I won't."

"Can you tuck me into bed?"

"I will in a minute."

"Now?"

"Okay."

But I can't see a thing in the darkness of my room.

"Are you scared, Daddy?"

"No."

"Don't be. I'll be here. And so will they."

"So will who?" I ask.

"They know, just like you. Just like Mommy. Just like all of us."

"Sweetie?"

"They know and it's okay."

I move the phone next to my ear but find my balled-up fist instead.

It's late and even though I'm awake now, realizing this was a dream, I feel irked.

I wish I had told the little girl on the other end goodbye.

10

Saw Something

One of the perks of my profession is the free stuff. I get a lot of freebies.

I can't remember the last CD I purchased on the day of its release. The last ten concerts I went to were tickets given to me. Sure, I spend a lot of time adding to my record collection, a hobby that's increasing, as the sale of vinyl is actually going up. But there's an inevitable sadness when you work in an industry you love. It loses its mystique. You can't listen to an album anymore and allow it to stand on its own merits. You study the sounds to learn and judge and sample. You don't just *listen* anymore. Especially when that album was given to you for free.

It's something that I have to fight daily. Especially when the business drags me down and talented artists like Sean Torrent force me to be reminded of the business and not the music.

But yeah, I can complain and then I have to be reminded by people like Cole that I get Lollapalooza tickets for free. A three-day premier pass.

"Yeah life is pretty rough, Ty," I can hear Cole saying.

I'm heading toward the fleet of Porta-Johns tucked under trees that don't really provide protection from getting wet. Somewhere behind me in the rain-soaked herd of cattle standing in the afternoon monsoon that doesn't stop the music is Cole. He is my constant companion to things like this, to events where the masses mingle. It can be a Cubs game or a Bloc Party concert or a streetfest. Doesn't matter to Cole.

As I move slowly toward the edge of Grant Park, I can't help notice the kids surrounding me.

This generation doesn't need a soundtrack. They've never known the silence and the still of a life. These twenty-somethings have a playlist full of tracks chosen for them. They spend more time looking for a connection to connect. The beat goes on for this group, hour after hour after hour.

This is my industry, but once a fan always a fan. I recall going to an early Lollapalooza when Ministry played. They'd just released their album *Psalm 69* and we'd listened to it deep into the night and I'd been persuaded to try acid and the proceeding few hours were as hellish as the album we were listening to. I can still hear my friend's words loud and clearly as he stood on the deck of his fifth-story porch saying "I can understand now how somebody could kill themselves."

The next day, the metallic, empty aftertaste of that night remained with me. So did the loopy, twisting world I'd been in. I wondered if I might be permanently brain-damaged, some Syd Barrett vegetable left to wander concerts like this with a haze in my head.

I was a kid and I was stupid. First off stupid to try acid, then stupid to think a little drop might mess me up for life.

Or maybe you're STILL brain-damaged, and that's been your problem ever since, Tyler.

Staring at the mass of bodies around me, I assume that there are a few more brain-dead kids roaming about.

Lollapalooza has come a long way since 1992.

Yes, but have you, Tyler?

I see a young girl, probably a teenager, in tiny shorts and a top barely there, not an inch of her dry. She's standing under a tree with a set of tall, awkward boys surrounding her. She's smoking a cigarette, the center of attention.

Not a care in the world.

Not one care.

I bet she didn't have to pay for her ticket either.

I open the door to exit the Porta-John and the rain squeezes down on me. I squint my eyes to see and then prop the hood of my rain parka back over my damp hair. Then I notice it.

40

The girl and her bodyguards are gone.

I sense something else.

The lack of movement.

The lack of anybody.

You're wrong; they're still here, they're still all around you, just open your eyes.

A guttural pounding throbs in the distance, like an industrial symphony warming up. I'm wondering who's playing and what happened to the last group that was just on the Budweiser stage we're near.

I scan my rainy surroundings and see the heel of someone's shoe. I follow it up to see a figure face down in mud. His entire face, including nose and mouth, are making an imprint in the ground.

I rush over toward him but then see a figure in yellow lying next to him. Another sprawled on the sidewalk. Another stopped in the middle of trying to do a snow angel in the grass.

Then I see the girl—the skinny clothes-barely-there teen I saw.

Her body is crumpled, her face resting on the edge of a grimy puddle, the dark liquid surfacing to her mouth and nose.

They're all lying on the ground in a perverse and insane manner like the aftermath of a World War II battle. Some with eyes open, like that young girl with her dead gaze toward the tops of the trees she's underneath, others with them shut.

I run to the girl and then step on a guy's chest and don't hear a whimper or moan or anything.

I touch the girl and she feels like a product, like a cold and bloated thing pulled out of the ocean.

She's dead. They're all dead.

The guy face-first in the mud.

The girl over there.

The kids over there.

They're all dead.

Meanwhile, the beat goes on.

I'm surrounded by hundreds—

No, thousands, there's thousands here, all dead, all exterminated, a genocide right in front of your face, Tyler.

All of these kids around me, these lifeless soulless bodies strewn about. I feel woozy and sick.

Then I hear something—someone.

A figure walking not around but on top of the bodies, approaching me. A figure in boots and jeans and a T-shirt showing off the cover of Depeche Mode's *Violator*. His arms are wet with blood—no, not blood, just dirt and grime.

This is not real.

He laughs. He's maybe twenty yards away from me, but his laugh is right there in front of me.

I smell him and bite my lip.

That's wrong.

It smells like something bad. Death bad. Sickness bad. Sewer bad.

"They're all lost souls, Tyler. All of them. All graves before the grave."

I shut my eyes and open them again.

Still there. All of it. The bodies, this man, those eyes.

His long, wavy hair is plastered to his cheek and he swats it back. He looks like a construction worker on a three-day binge.

I don't recognize the bearded face that stares at me with glee.

"Look at you."

I can't say anything. It's almost as if my vocal chords have been ripped from my throat.

"Look how scared you are."

He spits something as he steps on someone's face, then I hear him laugh.

It feels like someone pouring warm jelly down my ears and nose and mouth.

Then I feel a banging against my head and turn and see that I'm still in the Porta-John, someone knocking on the door behind me.

Once I'm out, things go from bad to worse.

I'm listening to some group I've never really paid much attention to when the lines of everything start to lean over. Everything starts to smear, like a kid playing with paints spreading it around with his hand. The music seems to do that as well, echoing with the wrong notes and off-key wails. I'm standing in the middle of the crowd with Cole and the others around us and I feel like passing out.

Someone slipped you something.

I'm trying to remember everything I put in my stomach today. Nothing stands out. I'm not dehydrated because it's been raining all day. I'm not drunk either.

This is like that first Lollapalooza where you couldn't get your head out of water, where you couldn't stop the waves from wrapping around your cheeks.

I look at Cole and he's in another world. Nonexpressive, oblivious. Everybody else looks the same.

It's easy to lose yourself at these functions. Just one part of a seventy-thousand-piece jigsaw puzzle of bodies crammed together to move and shout and sing and listen.

The girl in front of me has long brown hair that starts to move over her head and shoulders and back. It moves because it's a hundred small snakes all biting into her skull with the blood spreading like a waterfall down her legs.

I shake my head, trying to get rid of the awful thought.

Lights play tricks.

It's just dark wet hair and mud.

I'm staring at the stage and see a haze of smoke and then see the twirl of something dark, like a plume of birds festering over the crowd, coming at me.

They're not birds.

They're bats.

Hundreds of bats swarming like insects toward us, toward me.

They dart down and I fall to my knees, shielding my face and my head.

Nobody around me does the same.

Because of course nobody sees what I'm seeing.

Nobody is having a hallucinogenic nightmare like me.

Cole grabs my shirt from behind and yanks up. I'm wiping the mud—*blood it's blood we're on, blood we're soaked in*—from my hands as he gives me a look.

"I'll be back," I tell him.

He nods and doesn't ask. Before I'm gone, he shouts out for me to buy some more beer.

It's nice to know I have such supportive friends.

As if a beer is the best thing for me right now.

11

Morning Glory

I t's amazing how much I love my iPhone yet how much I detest talking on it. It *is* a telephone, right? Yet I try my best to avoid talking on it and keep it to avoid interruptions, even though all it seems to do is assault me with e-mails and social network updates and app afflictions.

It's mid-morning after the concert and I'm in my car, heading to the docks, cranking Elbow and trying to wake up, when I hear the tone go off. I answer it, hoping it's Nate with some good news.

Instead it's someone confirming the dates we have the studio time set up for Sean Torrent. It's as if they need to hear my confirmation and get it recorded if they end up needing to sue me in court and send me to jail when it's all said and done. I give a subdued affirmative even though I haven't spoken to Sean yet in person. Some things you just need to have faith in.

As I park my car and head down to the boat, I realize that I'm not the best at putting my faith in others. People, religion, family, friends.

Sometimes I think that if it was up to me, I wouldn't have to rely on anybody.

A few minutes later I'm staring at one of the reasons I was hoping that call would be Nate.

Nate's my manager, the one who oversees contracts along with helping with project supervision. He also helps promote me, which is something I'm not particularly wonderful at.

The last year for Nate and me has been . . .

Well, let me just say that if we were a married couple, we'd probably be talking to our respective lawyers.

In my defense, I would tell about two jobs which have gone by the wayside.

The Sean Torrent job, that's been a given for a couple of months now. Nate had nothing to do with Sean picking me either. I haven't received any money for it so far, and prospects of reaping financial awards due to working with Sean are looking slimmer as each day passes.

The two jobs that fell apart are the ABBA job, the one with a pop band called Overdraft, and another job with the American indie group Yeah Yeah Yeahs. The former wasn't that big of a deal since the band flaked out on me, but Nate should have seen that coming and helped out. The latter, however, was a backbreaker, a land mine in a career. All because Nate tried to overnegotiate with the record label.

Producing Yeah Yeah Yeahs' next album after their breakthrough *It's Blitz!* could have opened dozens of doors. Amazing doors.

Let's just say I got caught up in the moment and the momentum a few years ago. Too bad there wasn't a lot of money accompanying those two things. I assumed it would eventually start coming. I assumed that I could risk buying a 34-foot boat with the inheritance money I got after my grandmother passed.

Yeah, I know what they say about assumptions. I'm feeling like a big one.

Behind the wheel, I don't have to rely on anybody or worry about anything.

So I keep telling myself.

I thought that I could outrun the fears and guilt that I tried to leave behind when my life was unraveling years ago. This boat seemed like the perfect piece of equipment to do the job. It seemed natural that just around the time my ex-wife was remarrying while my life was still going nowhere, I should buy this cruiser for Lake Michigan. It was either that or get a dog or make a trek to climb Mount Everest. Something illogical and life-changing.

I didn't have children, so instead I adopted a Bayliner boat that could fit twelve people and make you forget about the rest of your problems in life. I named it *Precious* based on the Depeche Mode song. For a while,

40

it worked. That along with the help of a woman named Laila, who would soon be long gone.

Now the boat has become a problem. Anything related to money these days is a problem, because I have to still pay when money isn't coming in.

Sometimes when I'm coasting along the crossword puzzle of skyline that's Chicago, I wonder what I was thinking when I bought it. I realize it wasn't just the fact that Julie was gone and I needed someone or something to replace her. It was also the fact that I've always believed and always expected to succeed at whatever it was I was going to do.

Maybe I set the bar too high too soon. But isn't that what the great ones do before they ever get awarded that status?

I'm taking this boat out for a drive simply because its days are numbered.

Sometimes I wonder if the same can be said about my producing career.

There's an Arby's I pass on the way to the docks and everytime I drive back home. I wonder how soon it's going to be before I'm asking customers what kind of sauce they'd like to have with their roast beef sandwich.

I glance at the phone and wonder when I'm going to get that call that's going to relieve the stress and allow me to steer this boat without a worry in the world.

I had grand plans to get this all in order for the new year. I had a dream of buying a small house and transforming it into a studio. But 2010 brought surprises, including a couple jobs I didn't get and a couple other financial surprises.

Just like the rest of the world, I guess.

Amazing what a little success brings. Visions of bigger success. Visions of coffee table books with my quotes on producing, and three million followers on Twitter. Quotes behind your statements as if you're suddenly some genius and the tag "produced by" on the reviews of the big-name albums coming out.

Dreams.

Maybe Ecclesiastes and Bono are really right. Maybe we'll never find what we're looking for, not down here, not here and now.

Hell is wanting something you'll never have every day for the rest of your life.

Thanks, Pop. Thanks for that little subconscious reminder. Thanks for the encouragement.

I crank the V-8 engine to life, yet still hear those familiar echoes on Lake Michigan.

The dream is still alive. It's just been tapered a bit.

When I'm back on land, my phone rings again, and this time I check caller ID to see if it's anybody I want to talk to.

It's someone else from one of the record labels.

I take the call. That's what I'm here to do, to take the call, to monitor the process, to oversee and make decisions. Yet these people I talk to, most of them don't understand about dreams. They understand about deadlines and dollar bills.

Before getting to my car, I glance up to the clear sky.

Heaven won't have deadlines or dollars.

But it will have music.

Sweet music like the sip of an unearthed gem of a Chardonnay. Soulful music that will only inspire more dreams.

Music that doesn't need producing or manipulating, the kind that lives and breathes on its own.

Once I'm off the phone, having given an update to those who need updating, I climb in my car, restless and ready to think about something else. I toss my phone on the passenger side seat and see the large glass bottle on its side.

What is that doing here and when did I put it there?

For a second I remember this.

But then I realize that I haven't had Smirnoff vodka in years. The memory of the taste still makes me ill.

I pick it up and see that it's empty. There's dirt crusted on one side of the glass. The bottle looks old and dated. I haven't seen one like this in a long time.

I glance around but see nobody. I get out of my car and look around. I even walk around the parking lot.

I call out for someone.

Again again again.

Someone's toying with me.

40

Someone's messing with my mind.

I call out but the birds and the swollen sky and the surrounding lull all call back.

Someone's laughing at me. Mocking. Taunting.

I retrieve the liter-sized empty bottle and go back inside to throw it away. Last thing I need is for a cop to wonder what that's doing in my car.

"I couldn't tell you, officer," surely wouldn't be believable.

I don't believe those words myself.

12

Three Days

The boat ride earlier today has swept away the cobwebs but still has left spiders crawling around in my head. It's the afternoon before the inevitable raging party tonight, and I can't help but think about that last party. Not the one held a month ago to celebrate July 4th but the one here on April 21 for my 39th birthday.

The memory of my birthday makes me wince.

Not because police actually had to come and quiet things down, something they really don't like doing around Chicago, but because of the number it signified.

Maybe the volume was turned up so loud for the same reason it's always turned up loud. To forget. To block out the distractions and the doldrums.

To take the emphasis off the here and the now, the here and now saying that you're one year away from turning forty. One year left of pedaling uphill, one year away from starting that inevitable downhill journey.

I never really bother to take note of the symptoms, but they're there.

A full head of hair, thank God, that gives off tiny reminders with a sudden gray strand. *It's just blond* was what I always thought, because my hair sometimes lightens in the summer. *But gray like Gandalf the Grey is not blond and you know it, Tyler.* Those lines in my skin under the eyes spread out like spider webs upon further examination. The difficult love handles that are becoming impossible to get rid of. The moles on my body.

These are a few of the physical reminders.

40

A 39th birthday is a big fat bow strapped to your head like a parachute right before someone kicks you out of the plane with a laugh and a "Happy birthday, old man."

At my party, I was surrounded by twenty-something-year-old beautiful people.

Just like I probably will be later this evening.

I'd share these thoughts with Cole while we're playing bags on my roof deck, but he would stop the conversation at the point of entry. He'd stop it with his usual square-faced reticence, with an uncanny ability of not going deeper, of not even going slightly below the surface. Oh, it's there and I know it's there just like it's there with most people. I know because sometimes after drinking a lot, Cole will dive under the surface. That's the beauty of those "I love you, man" commercials. They tap into this superficiality of the new modern American male, brought up on ESPN and Budweiser and video games. The modern man who is incapable of feeling unless he's had half a case of beer and now is slurring the sentimental feelings he keeps strapped inside.

"Your turn," Cole says.

Maybe Cole is talking about my time to share.

I'm not sure what I think about turning forty in eight months, because I thought there were certain things I was supposed to have by this age and I don't have any of them. A wife? Nope. Kids. Nada. A 401K? Not a chance.

These are the words I might choose to say if I could.

"Come on," Cole says again.

I pick up my bags with the Cubs emblem and go first.

We're listening to the latest album by the National and drinking Sol beer and eating chips and salsa while the sun reminds us it's August. Another five months or so and this will be a barren white land of snowdrifts up here. The rooftop is lined with a wooden floor that I had installed when I moved in. Waist-high walls surround the edges. There's a table with an umbrella along with chairs on one side. A wall lined with outdoor sofas you can easily fall asleep on. A grill, a hammock, some plants and trees that may or may not make it. The other edge, where we're playing bags, has another large lounge bed with plush white cushions.

You can get fifty people up here if you're trying.

And tonight, we probably won't even have to try.

I should be in a good mood, a great mood, but something's bothering me.

"You're quiet today," another friend might ask me.

Not Cole.

Sometimes I love the feeling of talking to myself.

"Sometimes I wonder if I made a mistake letting Julie go," I might say.

"John Mayer is overrated," Cole would say back.

"My father is almost dead," I could say.

"Lindstrom's new single is wicked," Cole would reply.

"I'm going to jump off this rooftop and end it all," I should say.

"Throw your bags first," he'd say back.

It's nice to know where you stand with the people in your life.

There is something freeing knowing you don't have to get deep with some people. When you know the depth of a conversation will be about the depth of the Chicago Bears line. Maybe some people live their lives completely at the surface, in the shallow end, never going under, never knowing there's a deep closed-off portion they can swim around in.

Then again, maybe it would be good to stay over in the shallow end, not worrying about the deep darkness of the sea, not even giving it a second thought.

Instead of talking, we listen to the music and let it talk for us.

Music can feel for you. A singer can be unabashedly romantic and you can sing along. A singer can blatantly curse God and you can move your head to the beat along with him. A band can talk of life's fears and woes and travesties and you can agree in the confines of your Honda or on the way to your work in your khakis. Rock and roll feels and confesses and speaks truth. But most people, like Cole and I, just listen to it and let it feel for us.

Some might wonder what I'm doing here and yeah that makes sense because I'm wondering that myself.

These people around me aren't wondering. They're wandering nomads that pop up in the night where they can't be seen, where the sun can't beat down on them. They sneak in and sip your wine and slide beside you and cause you to look down and wonder who in the world they are.

40

Why is someone this old still acting so young?

Why is someone who knows better acting like he doesn't know anything at all?

I wonder about that all the damned time.

I drank too much and said too much and now I'm feeling tired and feeling lost in my own condo.

It's not going to heal the pain.

I know this but keep on going.

One day you're going to have to grow up.

Who says this is childish; this is what the world does.

You know better. You know better, Tyler.

I know too much and sometimes I want to drown that knowledge.

The noise, those nasty words, the night sky breathing on my skin, the laughter of fools, the neglect of tomorrow and all it brings. This is the *now* I'm living in.

The now when I see him.

Tall, dark T-shirt and jeans, a mass of wavy hair falling over his face. Sitting on the concrete ledge, looking out toward the city, leaning as if any second he might fall.

Grab him, the drunken stupid idiot.

Jane's Addiction sounds better when you're half gone, and that's the key.

I walk toward this figure, through the insanity around me.

I pass a girl in a yellow dress that looks like spring now, but who knows what season she'll look like tomorrow.

The man on the ledge faces me.

The face and that hair and I'm suddenly transported back to Lollapalooza, but I'm not sure why.

Where's Cole?

That grin.

I feel like someone's peeling away my stomach and stripping the muscles.

I can't walk and suddenly can't move.

The world spins.

The noise. Stop that noise. Turn it off—the racket, this ringing in my ears—they're bleeding, they're hurting.

He stands.

Then I see him laugh and drink something from a cup and then he moves behind a group that stand talking.

I feel like a bamboo spear is cutting under my skin and working its way through my spine and then my neck onto my skull.

Can't move, can't say anything, can't think.

The crowd moves and the girl in the yellow dress dances across my path, but the guy I saw, the same one from Lolla last night, is gone.

"Slapping yourself in the face," the song goes, the racket, the madness.

Wake up, I hear a voice say amidst the song and the sounds all around me.

Two seconds until you see, the voice says in a horrific whisper.

Two seconds.

13

Wrapped Around Your Finger

Some of the things Angie says frighten me.

It's in the abyss of night and the high is descending and she's on the cushion next to me, whispering things.

"I can see us here in ten years."

Whispering things.

"Tell me what you want me to be."

Whispering things.

"Nobody knows you like I do."

These things scare me because I don't see us here in ten weeks or maybe even ten days. I don't want to be her anything. She doesn't know me and never will.

Yet she acts like she does and I'm immobile enough to let her go on acting like it's true.

The last person and perhaps only person who knew me and knew me well decided to leave for no apparent reason. Laila Torres left my life without a forwarding address or a simple e-mail. She left me alone.

I don't want to be left alone in this place tonight.

Whispering.

"It's okay when you cry, there's nothing wrong when you do it."

I don't know what nonsense she's talking about.

"It's okay, you have to let these things go."

I don't know what she means.

Whispering.

The stroke of a cheek.

"Let go and let me."

I shiver.

Then I think of the man I saw, or imagined I saw, and I move closer to her warm body, curled up beside mine.

14

Where Is My Mind

A blanket of glass covers my couch like ice on a screen door during a blizzard. I look at my hands and arms right away to see if they reveal any cuts. It's not the first time I've had a wild night full of cloudy pockets of recall. If I did this, surely my hands would tell the tale. But they're fine.

I pick up a piece and examine it. It's thick, like the glass from a windshield. Yet if these are the shards from a car crash, I think with drunken amusement, then where's the car?

For a moment I think of cleaning it up, then scan the rest of the place and feel overwhelmed.

Sunday morning and what are you doing this morning, Tyler?

I decide to call Cole to get a report on what happened after I left planet earth behind last night.

"Why would I spill glass over your couch?" Cole's already in his gear for the concert later today: camouflage shorts, a wife-beater black shirt, and a sombrero. "If I was going to put glass anywhere I'd put it on your bed."

"You're the only one who has a key."

"Not the *only* one."

"Laila wouldn't do this. She's long gone."

Cole opens up the fridge and finds a beer tucked away behind the condiments.

Maybe the saddest thing about him opening it is the fact that I don't think it's odd for him to be drinking around ten in the morning.

"You never know with chicks."

"With some, you do," I tell him.

"Yeah, well, when I left, Angie was still here."

"And where was I?"

"You were asleep on the couch up on the roof."

"Tell me something."

"Yeah?"

"Is Angie crazy?"

Cole takes a sip from the bottle and just looks at me.

"'Cause sometimes I get this feeling like she's completely psycho. I don't know."

Cole is still looking at me.

"I don't know, it's just a feeling sometimes."

Cole hasn't said a word when he grabs the iPod and starts playing some music.

"You think she would do this?" I ask.

I just get a shrug.

I look at the shredded glass sprinkled over my sofa.

I still don't get it.

If it's supposed to be funny, I'm not getting the joke.

"These guys are supposed to be playing in the afternoon," Cole points out.

We've moved on from the windshield glass in my living room and the question of whether Angie is crazy and would do this.

I'm jogging back to the outdoor sitting area with a plate of huevos and chorizo and the world's best Bloody Mary tumbling around in my gut. I forgot to leave a tip and Cole didn't bother to ask. The waitress knows us and I usually tip her well because she's cute and knows it but doesn't act like it.

I put a twenty on the table that still has yet to be cleared off and I see something in the seat I was sitting in.

A baseball bat.

I lean in toward it and glance around to see if anybody is looking at me to claim it. The people sitting outside couldn't care less, not about me or the bat or the fact that it's as red as the tall drink I had a few minutes ago.

I pick it up and hold it. The sucker is heavy, a regulation bat. Not that I really know what a regulation bat is, having never played or even bothered to try to play. This is so heavy I can't imagine swinging it. And just below the top is a smearing of red stain like blood.

I put the bat back down.

Someone's messing with you.

Again, I look around. The waitress with the foreign accent walks by to ask if everything is okay.

"You know who this belongs to?"

For a moment, I expect her to look down and shake her head, as if she can't see the bat, as if the only thing batty around here is my head and my mind.

"No. I thought it was yours."

I shake my head.

"I can bring it inside in case someone comes looking for it."

"Yeah, that'd be great."

With that big old bloodstain, I'm doubting someone's going to be looking for it.

I watch her walk away with it and wonder.

One of my friends is up to something but I still don't get the joke.

I hear Cole's voice calling for me. They've got a cab waiting for me to bring us to Grant Park.

My skin already feels crisp from the sun.

I scan the area outside of the restaurant, then down the sidewalk, across the street, down the other sidewalk.

"Ty!"

Nobody is around.

Nobody except Cole.

Whoever is playing games with me must have an explanation.

Whenever they're ready to appear, I plan to ask them. And to tell them that the joke is over.

15

Compulsion

Any good groups out there?"

"Too many to count."

I'm standing by Buckingham Fountain in the center of this sprawling epic circus talking on the phone. I wonder what the water would feel like. I'm dizzy, but the sun doesn't seem to care, having already chased off the clouds that were hanging around only a couple of days ago. A hot, wet blanket covers everybody.

I wish I could see Nate here. He always *looks* the part of the music guy but sometimes I wonder what he's like when it's just him and he can do anything. Does he kick back and drink a beer and listen to the latest album by Arcade Fire? That's the impression he likes to give off, but frankly, I don't buy it. Because if he truly were that guy, he'd be here right now instead of "on the road" for "business meetings for a couple of the labels." I think that when it's just him, he puts on the radio and lets it do the talking for him. He irons the latest Interpol T-shirt he just bought online, then he colors his hair and carefully plucks out his ear and nose hair, makes sure his shoes aren't too shiny and that his teeth aren't too white, and that his musical palette isn't too Top 40s.

I don't know. This is just a hunch about Nate.

Then again, I want a manager who is good with contracts and numbers and lawyers and all that stuff. Stuff that bothers me. Stuff that gets me off track from the music.

40

"Look, I have to go," he says in an accent that sometimes sounds New York and sometimes sounds English and sometimes sounds something else. "Have you thought any more about Nicole?"

My body goes limp for a moment.

I now want to dunk my head in the fountain for another reason.

"I've been trying not to think about it."

"I need an answer to give them," Nate says.

"It just doesn't seem like a right fit."

"It's a job."

"It's day care."

Nate laughs. Yeah, *he* can laugh. He doesn't have to choose. He can pass, and it's no skin off his back. But if I say *yes* he gets a cut all by doing what he's doing now—talking on the phone in some other city in some other world. He won't have to sit in the studio with some Pop-Tart and spend every single second wishing he could be doing anything else.

"She's supposed to be charming."

"I'm having nightmares of Britney Spears gone bad."

"She's nothing like that."

"Aren't they all like that?"

"She's got that Christian thing going on. You're into that, right?" Nate says this like it's a phase or a fad, like I'm into Pilates or early Bob Dylan or wine collecting.

"Why me?" I ask.

"Because you're one of the best."

"You're really awful at flattery."

"I'm being honest."

"That's great and all, but really. Why?"

"She wanted you. The label wants to make it happen."

I stare at a group of teenagers who don't seem to care about the heat or the black clothes they have on or much of anything.

When did I grow up? What was the moment that officially did it?

"It's a job," Nate says again. "I want to be able to get you these to keep some money coming your way. Especially since we're still trying to get your money from you know who."

"Yeah, I know. And I know who."

"Then keep thinking about it. Give me an answer tomorrow."

"Yeah, okay. But—why can't it be Radiohead or someone like that?"

"One day," Nate says. "We're working our way up to that."

"Having Nicole Lawson on my résumé isn't going to help."

"Make it help. Every album is an opportunity. You said that yourself. One day, Tyler. One day."

Why is it that I don't believe anything anybody ever says about me?

"So, like, what do you do again?"

Mort's wandering eyes, which never stay in one place, barely make connection with mine. We're standing in line waiting for beer, and I'm having a quasi-conversation. I'm guessing that Mort's his last name or at least part of it but I haven't asked. He's a friend of a friend of Cole's and somehow I inherited the job of trying to make sure Mort doesn't get lost. He's already gotten lost twice today. Cole told me to tag along and get us some beer.

The question is one of those I get often, and glancing at the unfocused, wisecracking Mort, I can already guess where this one is heading.

"I'm a music producer."

That line can come out a thousand ways. Add a British accent like Gavin's and a tight upper lip and it can come out pompous. Add a southern accent and they'll ask if I know Carrie Underwood. It can sound like I invented a job to sound cool. Most of the time people ask what that exactly means.

"You any good at playing drums?"

Not quite sure where this line of reason is coming from.

"I don't really play much," I tell Mort, who is lighting a cigarette.

"I used to play drums all the time. Pretty good too. You know anybody who needs a drummer? Any band?"

"Not currently."

"Well, yeah, well keep me in mind. I mean I can wail on them, you know. I'm like the Edge. Wait, that's the guitarist, right? Who's the drummer from U2?"

"Larry Mullen, Jr."

"People say I kinda look like him."

"Hmm, yeah, maybe."

He doesn't look anything like Larry Mullen, Jr. And I'd bet my boat that he doesn't sound anything like him, either.

"I'll get you a beer, what do you want?"

"How about a Bud Light?"

They have two types of beer.

"So, music producer," Mort says as we walk back to where our gang is camped out. Finding people around here involves texting multiple times and knowing landmarks and seeing waving hats or shirts. "So does that mean you get to go to the Grammys?"

"Haven't ever yet."

"But you're pretty good at mixing."

I laugh a little. "I'm not Sir Mix-A-Lot."

"Sir what?"

You know you're getting old when references like this don't make a connection.

We're listening to Minus the Bear and I can feel that itch. That slight bothersome buzz that remains with me, as Cole Porter wrote, night and day.

It's probably the reason that Julie finally left me.

The twitch. The gnawing tension. The angst.

The battle uphill to become Brian Eno never ends. Because there is only one Brian Eno. Only one Beatles. Only one Bono.

Only one Hemingway and Picasso and Brando.

Yet I aspire and try to learn and understand and grow and dream.

You have such a cool job others might say.

Yeah, sure. But I'm still in the minor league.

What do you do again?

You won't get it, I usually think.

So you, like, play around with knobs all day?

You're an idiot.

Have you met Beyoncé?

Yeah, I had dinner with her last night, moron.

People don't get it. Most of my friends and family don't get it and never will. They have vague, simplistic impressions and ideas of what it is. "I need more cowbell." That's what half of them are thinking, really. But that's okay, because the people in my world understand. Yet in this world, I can't see over the backs and shoulders in front of me. I'm just a boy, a guest with a name tag, a listener, a follower.

How do you carve a chunk of the world you are in and make it solely your own?

So you, like, uh, make the songs better and stuff?

That's the goal.

To take rough gems and polish them to perfection.

And to make a mark.

Because it's the only mark you know to make.

Standing there in the masses, I feel like I still haven't left any mark. And time is running out.

16

The Day I Tried to Live

Soundgarden lacerates the lit-up night as I lead with my shoulder and arm through the crowd. This isn't a group of people anymore. It's a swarm, squeezing in a little more, every song. Fences and walls barricade the entrance toward the stage. The biggest guys around with the brightest shirts are security.

I'm trying to find Mort to somehow guide him to where our group is, a little left of the center of the field facing one of the big stages. He disappeared again and it took us several texts before getting hold of him. It'd be easy to just say forget about it until the end of the night, but Soundgarden is his favorite and he's been talking about them all day. Plus, well, the guy makes me laugh. I kinda like having his odd sense of humor around. Even if I know I won't be able to hear anything except the wailing of guitars and Chris Cornell.

There's a tent marked with "VIP Only" on the door and I see a face that turns around and looks at me.

What's Mort doing over there?

He sees me, nudges with his head, then disappears through the doorway.

There's nobody preventing him from going inside.

I reach the open doorway and glance around, but don't see anybody checking for IDs. I enter the tent, which turns out to be more of a hallway that leads behind the wall and around the side of the stage. The sound is more muffled back here, yet it's still loud.

I better get Mort before he ends up getting arrested or thrown out of here.

The tent opens up to a street that's being used as a parking lot for the big tour buses. I can hear their engines running and smell the exhaust as I walk between two of the mammoth, tinted blocks. I'd call out for Mort, but the pounding echoes of one of grunge's finest bands would slap down my voice the second it came out.

I turn the corner and see a light reflecting off glass, like one of those lights set for the stage suddenly turning and being a foot away from me. I'm blinded as my eyes burn and shut, and my hand goes up in front of them. It's gone, whatever the light was, because then I see the side glass of another tour bus.

The door opens with a swoosh and a sucking sound.

I stand there, the vibration of drums and bass rumbling in the ground.

Nobody sees me but I know if they did they'd be wondering what I was doing.

I wait for someone to get out of the bus. Like maybe Aerosmith or Lady Gaga. Because, you know, that would fit the insane moment I'm having, having disappeared behind the curtains looking for the wandering Mort and coming across...

Across what? A piercing light that makes me a bit nauseated.

I still see spots every time I blink.

I don't know how long I stand, waiting.

Something inside—either inside of me or the bus or this area—something seems to be whispering in a soft voice I can barely make out.

Go inside, take a peek.

Maybe it's the beer or the lack of sleep or the thought that maybe Mort's playing around with me.

Or maybe it's the fact that you've been seeing things lately, weird things, crazy things, ever since you went to see your parents, and you know it, so maybe this is another one of those things, Ty, maybe this is the explanation.

I take a breath and climb up the steps.

There's no driver sitting in the seat behind the massive panorama window and the steering wheel the size of a hula hoop.

"Hello?" I call out, my voice a little more audible inside.

There's a curtain right behind the driver's seat. Black and thick. I move a hand through it like a magician.

40

A sliver of sunlight cuts my eyes and I feel like they're being slit with a razor, the soft clear jelly oozing out down my cheeks in a bloody pus. I scream at the attacking light, my knees buckling and my hands grappling over eyes that are numb and closed and blind.

This is where we meet and where we come face to face. After all these years, after all this time, it's finally here, and finally you get to see.

I'm lost and the music is gone and I forget where I am.

A needle is pricking at my pupil and then making tiny little dots, then being plucked and stirred like a spoon in a cup of coffee.

I feel like I'm falling.

"Do not be afraid," a voice says.

It's the most terrifying thing I've ever heard.

The voice sounds familiar, tough but not angry.

I'm in too much pain to recognize it.

I don't dare open my eyes.

"It is okay, Tyler Harrison."

I know that voice and I know what's happening but my mind and my heart are two miles back, stranded on the edge of the highway in flames with the pounding in the head and the grinding in my mind.

My mouth is dry and my back and hands are covered in sweat and I groan and feel weightless and feel like I did before walking down the aisle or after hearing the news from my mother about Dad almost dying.

"Stand."

I do what I'm told out of necessity, without a thought.

I've never been this attentive and this orderly in my life.

I climb up and feel my legs still underneath me and then I open my eyes, fearing that there are none to open.

The world still spins.

I'm still in the bus, if that's what this lounge of sorts is called.

It takes a while for everything to formulate, for color to fill back in, for the shapes and scenery to finally unscramble.

Then I see the man sitting on the couch in front of me.

I know this man and know him well.

I've known him for thirty-nine years.

17

Wake Up

Sit down, Tyler."

I've been in some of these buses before, but this is the most extravagant yet, with burgundy leather couches facing each other and dark framework and marble tables. I rest at the edge of the couch and face this man across from me. My body shivers with dread as I try and keep my eyes on him. Everything in me says that this is another nightmare, another one of those hallucinations like the one I had the other night at the show.

I look and see it. That expression—I've seen it before. I know it.

He's not exactly smiling. The glance is intense and focused, yet strangely calm at the same time. Those blue eyes seem to flood the bus with ocean water that I'm swimming in. He looks like a thirty-year-old Paul Newman.

"It is time to tell you," his voice says. Casual, unhurried, nonchalant.

What was with those blinding lights I just saw? Where'd the spotlights go?

"There will be many things that you see from here on out that you will not understand. Some of these things will never be understood, because that is not their reason for being shown to you."

I shake my head, wondering if I just spoke something aloud but didn't realize I was doing so.

"My name is Matthew."

I want to look around to see if anybody is there, but I can still feel my heart beating and can feel sweat lining my back. I need to breathe because I'm forgetting to do so.

Something about this man across from me, a man wearing dark jeans and a white polo shirt and speaking without a care in the world…something about him terrifies me.

If I could—if I knew I wouldn't be harmed or my eyes wouldn't be torn inside out again—I'd get up and get out and get far away from this guy. From "Matthew."

"You do not have to be afraid."

I nod and feel like I'm trying to say something but I can't.

What is happening to me?

"It is common to be afraid, because you have never seen me like this."

"What—who—?" My tongue feels like a rock in my mouth rolling around.

"I am Matthew and I watch over you."

Right.

I swallow and taste the beer in my mouth. I'm wondering if someone slipped something in my Bud Light. Maybe it was the guy I initially came here looking for, the guy who kept getting lost, the guy…I can't remember his name.

"His name is Mort and he did not do anything to you. Mort is fine. A lost soul who is curious about so many things."

I want to ask.

Of course I want to know but then again I don't *need* to.

"Of course you do not need to ask me. I can hear them as clearly as I see you. The sentiments in your soul speak louder than mere words."

This is another one of your nightmares, Ty, and you know it's about time to get your head cleaned out by a shrink.

Something strange happens every time I look at Matthew. When I look away, his shape and shadow seem to grow larger, like some hulking beast, yet when I look back on him, he resembles a guy my size, a guy my age, a guy like me.

Yet those shadows and that specter hovering perhaps only in my mind boil my fears over.

"I have watched you since you were born, my friend. There have been times, out of necessity, that I could not be at your side, but not for long."

Who are you is what my mouth and my tongue and my heart want to say. Yet I know better.

No you don't. You don't know jack and you're telling yourself you know to cover up the lie, to cover up the fear.

Matthew takes his hand and holds it up and suddenly the world grows silent.

Nothing.

Still. Absolutely still.

And those voices—the turmoil, the rage, the bile, the never-ending never-ending never-ending cyclone of voices and doubts and fears and laughter and nonsense and nonsensical thoughts and feelings and emotions that turn like a top in my head—

They are gone.

I rub my forehead as if I'll find residue covering it.

"He likes to try and sneak in."

"Who?" I ask.

My voice is normal. I can talk.

"I have come to give you a message."

I nod. Then wait for him to keep going.

I've never heard a space, a room so quiet.

It's like I'm in outer space, talking to the lone other person out there.

"You have been watched for thirty-nine of your years, Tyler Harrison. I have been there for most of them. There are things I have done for you that would be too daunting to explain. You have seen me, sometimes every day, yet you have not seen me like this. But today you see me as you can because today I will deliver the message of when you will die."

I'm not looking for hidden cameras.

I don't need to.

Something's changed. I'm not doubting and not wondering and not asking.

I know.

"Die?" I manage to ask.

"You have been given one final gift, Tyler."

"What's that?"

"It is knowledge."

"Knowledge about what? My death?"

"You will live to see your next birthday, but not a day longer."

Those voices piling up in my head like a dam at the bottom of rushing rapids gathering branches and trees and debris are no longer there.

It's strange, too. Living an entire life full of noise and then being able to hear the sounds of silence.

The stillness allows me to be focused. I am able to ask the big question. "Why?"

"The answer to why you are being told this is an answer you already know. It is because you are loved."

"But why—"

He waits for me to finish but I can't.

"You have two hundred and fifty-six days," he says.

"For what? To do what? Why are you telling me this?"

"You may go now."

I look at Matthew.

Normally I'd question if this was a dream, or if he was really an angel. But the doubt and cynicism I carry with me at all times is no longer there.

All I'm wondering about is why.

"Go where? For what? What am I supposed to do?"

"Things are different, Tyler."

"Meaning—what's that supposed to mean?"

"I cannot be there like I have been."

I am suddenly cold and covered in bumps and chilled as I hear the door open and the music in the background start playing again.

The sound scares me.

I smell gas.

My hands tremble.

The man in front of me is still there. He hasn't left. Neither has his expression.

"Is there . . ."

But I can't finish it.

I'm too afraid to know the answer.

I stand and start to walk out of the bus. I've never been so compelled to do what I've been asked—told—to do.

I turn around and look at Matthew.

"Will I see you again?"

"Only if you must. You will not want to see me again, because I will not be coming to help you."

"Why then? What will you be coming to do?"

"You do not want me to prove my point. You have enough. Now go."

I wobble down the stairs and out into the humid evening and suddenly everything about this place and this city and this life feels wrong and half empty and half lived and half everything.

The door behind me shuts like the cell of a prison.

18

Little Man, What Now?

I haven't said a word to anybody.

The lights shine bright and I remain in the dark.

The songs swell and I stay quiet.

The afterglow in the park hovers as streams of sweaty, exhausted strangers disperse into the night. I play my part, even running around in the water at Crown Fountain and getting a nice cool shower with giggling girls half my age. Our group convenes at a bar, but I'm thankful, because part of me thinks that Matthew will be waiting for me on my love seat at home with another declaration for me to behold.

So this is a little insight into the human soul that is Tyler Harrison.

I am one hundred percent certain what I've seen.

I don't question that he was a messenger from God.

I don't even doubt his words.

But I go to a corner bar and hover in the darkness, surrounded by friends, many of whom are mostly strangers.

Someone created before the beginning of this world comes to tell me a message from God Himself and I hole up in a bar, doing nothing and saying nothing, and drink by drink, feeling nothing.

I don't question the truth.

But I don't do anything with it, either.

Not a damned thing.

I really am a little man with little left to give.

PART THREE

—

Black Celebration

19

Wake Up, Stop Dreaming

Work gives you the illusion that you're not going to die.

I've spent the last three days in a home studio that's been loaned out to us working on mixing a track. It's a pretty good one, a song from an Australian band called Cut Copy. How can I describe their music? A tropical drink sipped on the beach. The neon lights of the disco. Bright pants moving on the dance floor. An unabashed '80s sound and vibe that make the '80s seem cool again.

The really cool thing about this track is the voice. It's one of the quintessential '80s voices in my opinion, one of those that sang to me many days and nights. Bernard Sumner from New Order has lead vocals on the track, even though he probably sang it in England after the boys in Australia wrote the song. Now producers all around the country are working on the song. One of these versions might end up on the album, or perhaps on the single as a mix. Or perhaps the work I put in will only be done for some friends who don't share music.

There is no such thing as track one anymore. Everything is stand-alone. Everything is separate and single. The magic of a dozen cohesive tracks is lost on the young, just like their youth. Records are making a comeback simply because they're antiques and collector's items. But bands these days don't think in terms of albums anymore. A band can write and even produce a song and put it on their Web site in the afternoon and offer listeners the option to pay what they want. This is the quickly changing universe I live in.

I'm getting to work with my hero, while my hero still doesn't have a clue who Tyler Harrison is.

Yet it still beats working for Dunder Mifflin.

Gavin left a little while ago while I was tweaking and noodling. Sometimes I have to do this to get something right, the way my ears feel it's right, and when I'm doing so Gavin and I both know it, and he eventually waves the white flag to give me some space. The perfectionist in him knows it's better this way, since I have final say.

The sun is starting to shrink in the west when I walk outside and head down the street. It's been half a week since Lollapalooza and I'm beginning to stop thinking about it. The parties, and the drinking, and the guy waving a gun in my face, and Angie, and the broken glass, and, oh yeah, the bright strobe lights that felt like tacks in my eyes arriving right before seeing a guy named Matthew who said he knew exactly when I was going to die.

A lot of people start Monday morning trying to forget all the mistakes they made over the weekend. The week allows you to accelerate in traffic and get lost, and be overwhelmed, and overworked, and, hopefully, overlooked when it comes to harbingers of death.

The chirpy, groovy sound of the track I've been working on the last few days is still in my head and my feet move to its beat.

But the music always stops, always, and it stops the moment I see my newfound friend standing across the street, facing me.

"There's no place to go now," Bernard Sumner sings in the song, and I suddenly know that he's been singing about me, to me, for me.

Thank you, buddy.

I stop, look, listen.

Stop, drop, and roll, moron.

Then without a thought, I sprint down the sidewalk, the opposite way I was headed.

The opposite direction of Matthew.

I run and don't look back.

I am eighteen again on the track team, with the ability to sprint without keeling over and needing to suck in air with dots floating around in my head and my mouth holding back the need to puke.

I dash around the edge of the building at the intersection and then blast down the sidewalk past a lady walking her dog. The only thing on me is my wallet and my iPhone in my pocket. We live in a modern world and this is my briefcase, baby, all 200,000 apps at my disposal.

Cement is hard on my feet but I run.

All roads eventually lead somewhere and I'm finally a few blocks away and I pause and swallow a blast of breath and then I turn around.

He's nowhere to be found.

So you think that means you outran him, you idiot? Come on.

I look at the intersection and head across the street.

When I get to the edge of the curb, I see him again.

He's standing in the entryway to a clothing store.

That same look, without any heavy breathing, without any real true knowable expression, with just those blue eyes boring into mine.

I don't realize how badly I'm gasping for air, sweating, delirious, my head swirling around, my mouth tasting the onions on the sub I had for lunch.

I swallow, then take off again.

A hundred-yard dash down the side of the street.

I run and slow down a bit to look back.

What good is looking back when you know that he's going to be ahead of you whenever you stop, wherever you rest?

I keep going, moving across the street and past windows and past strangers who don't seem to care that I'm trying to outrun death, and past lights both green and red and around parked cars and west then north then south then west again.

The oxygen on this planet has suddenly disappeared.

I'm no longer eighteen but eighty-two and someone stole my walker and my oxygen tank.

I'm no longer on the track team but rather part of the psychiatric ward and I've escaped after taking off my hospital gown.

Breathing in and out, I pause for a moment on the side of the road.

Matthew is nowhere to be found.

Sweat trickles over my lips.

He's nowhere.

I think I might have just done a nice 5K run.

I try to wave a cab, but barely have the strength to do even that.

Inside I collapse and feel my heart heave against the back window of the taxi like the guy with the chestburster in *Alien*.

"Where to?"

Far away from that guy—you see him, right—right—right?

I manage to give my address in between sounding like an ad against the dangers of smoking. And I don't smoke.

Then I feel the bulge in my pocket.

Why's my iPhone suddenly feel bigger and bulkier?

I grab for my pocket but realize that the phone is in the opposite one.

I pull out something.

It's four or five inches, black and silver, a heavy metal.

For a second it takes me a while to realize what I'm holding.

Then I pull out the wide and sleek blade, four inches long, the size of my hand.

It's a pocket knife.

A pocket knife for a hunter, a killer, a dangerous individual.

How it got into my pocket is beyond me.

Just like everything else.

I drop it on the floor of the cab and leave him the surprise gift when I reach my condo.

When I get inside, Matthew is sitting on the couch waiting for me.

20

The Other Side

This time I don't run. I can't. There's no time.

Matthew is up off the couch with a speed that terrifies me. His face seems to tighten just like his fist as he grabs a clump of my hair and then sends my head and body down against the side of my table.

The pain erupts in my face and I feel like I almost might pass out.

"You need to stop running and pay attention when I am here," he says.

Then he takes his hand and grips my T-shirt. He drags me across the wooden floor like I'm a mop. The side of my face bangs against the edge of my couch.

His hold is normal but it feels like it's some vise that could yank down a tree or a car.

He tosses me in the corner and I look at my T-shirt and notice it's forever ruined.

"You can buy shirts anywhere you want, but I will not be coming around every day. I cannot do that anymore so you must listen and pay attention."

I prop my body up on my shoulders. My head is throbbing, my jaw feeling like it's already swollen to the size of a cantaloupe.

This is definitely not your mother's version of *Touched by an Angel*.

Matthew rests against the side of the couch, looking down at me.

"What are you doing?" I ask.

"Nothing has changed except your memory of our last conversation."

"You didn't tell me what I was supposed to do." I'm holding the edge of my lip that feels like it's bleeding.

"I said you would not want to see me again."

The room is still twirling around me. "What do you want? Why'd you just do that?"

"I came to warn you, Tyler, yet you seemed to think it was a better idea to run away from me, even when that in itself is impossible."

"What do you want?"

I'm a track on repeat, playing over and over and over again.

"If that is truly what you want to know, then why are you running?"

I sigh and wince and shake my head. "I don't know."

"You do know. It is because you are afraid. It is because you do not want to hear what I have to tell you."

"I heard you loud and clear the first time in your bus."

"If you truly understood what I told you, why has nothing changed?"

"What am I supposed to do? What?"

"You have convinced yourself that I did not happen, that I did not show up and say that you were going to die."

"Maybe. But what am I supposed to do? Enroll in a death-in-a-year club? Become a monk? Go feed the hungry?"

Matthew stands back up and plants his foot on my ankle. I howl in pain and see black and red for a while.

"Do not mock your Father, Tyler. Do not spit in His face with your contempt."

I mumble and wail out and curse and then try to keep my mouth shut.

"I can make that tongue of yours cease to talk if you continue with that."

"What is it you want from me?"

Matthew goes to the kitchen and finds a glass, then opens the fridge and finds the water container. He pours me a glass and brings it to me.

"Sit down and drink this."

My hand is shaking when I take the glass. My jaw feels immovable and I limp on my now bruised and aching ankle.

What happened to funny, quirky angels like Clarence from *It's a Wonderful Life*?

40

All this guy wants to do is inflict pain.

"I am here to help you."

"Yeah, well, excuse me if I tend to be just a little cynical about your 'help.'"

For a minute I expect him to take the glass and splinter it over my head and then do some jujitsu, but instead Matthew just sits across from me and waits.

I drink my water and try to stop my hand from shaking, but it seems like the shaking has moved to cover my whole body.

"You need to understand that our time is drawing to a close."

How long has passed? A minute? A year? I'm running around as if I'm on a treadmill except that treadmill is a turning globe and as soon as I stop I'll fall off.

"You need to know that our time here is valuable."

"Okay."

My voice sounds weak. The words evaporate as soon as they're uttered.

"There are things I need to show you, since you need to be shown in order to believe."

"Wonderful."

"The sarcasm needs to stop."

I nod. "I'm sorry—it's just a bad habit."

"Yes, it is."

"What do I need to see?"

"How are you feeling?"

"Awful."

"Drink. It might be good to eat something as well. You have been working hard."

"You've been watching?"

"I've been watching for a very long time. But not for much longer."

"Why?"

"A full stomach might be better for what you are about to see."

"And what's that?"

"Go ahead. I think it's best."

Something tells me I need to do what Matthew says. Or else something bad might happen. Or he might just decide to beat me up again.

85

"I did that so you would stop and pay attention."

I'm rubbing my jaw. "If I knew you would've done that I might not have run away."

"You say that, but even if you had known, you would have run away."

"What are you going to show me? Are we going somewhere?"

"Yes."

That's all I'm getting.

I want to find some hard liquor but I know that Matthew probably won't like that or allow it.

I'm half waiting for him to comment on the thoughts I'm having as I walk across the room.

I glance at my hand and it's shaking like some kind of addict's.

If I slowed down and stopped to think about everything going on—all of this—I think I'd be more scared than I already am.

"Eat, Tyler," Matthew says.

I find half a chicken sandwich and I eat it cold.

It tastes delicious.

"Are you ready?" Matthew eventually asks.

"For what?"

"You are going to see the other side."

"The other side of what?"

"Come on over and let us take a walk."

He starts to walk up the stairs to the roof.

Not a lot of walking can be done up there.

Yet I follow him.

I know I'll be in trouble if I don't.

21

Living a Boy's Adventure Tale

The bullet can be seen from five feet away. It's sitting in the middle of the table, the gleaming silver contrasting with the dark paint over the wood. Matthew stands behind it against a wall, looking out at the skyline of Chicago.

"What is that?"

He turns but doesn't answer as I pick up the bullet.

When I touch it, I discover it's all intact, a regular round in its case. But in my hand something happens. It morphs into something else.

It changes and burns my skin.

I drop it on the deck next to my feet.

I glance at it and it looks distorted, squashed.

It looks like someone just fired it.

"What—"

Matthew doesn't appear surprised. I wonder if he even has the ability to give off that expression.

"He is playing games," he says.

"Who?"

"You will learn soon enough."

"What's going on? Did you put that there?"

"No."

The searing sensation in my hand is very real. I look at the red marks where I was holding the slug.

"You will understand in a minute."

"I'll understand what? I don't get this. I don't get you or that or any of this."

"Tyler."

"Yeah?"

"You are wasting time."

"So what, are you going to show me how I'm going to die?"

"There is a tinge of sarcasm in that question. I can see it in your heart."

"Sorry."

"Do you know why you use sarcasm?"

"No. Not really."

"From the moment you stopped stuttering as a child and finally got through your speech impediments, you have used sarcasm."

"You've really seen everything, huh?"

"It is easy to break the silence with a laugh, but at what cost?"

"I don't even realize I do it."

"There are many things you do not realize, Tyler. This is going to simply be a small glimpse."

I look down at the bullet and still see it on the ground.

Matthew walks over to the edge of the building.

"You're not going to make me jump, are you?"

He smiles at me, then shakes my hand. "No."

Then he grabs my arm and with a force I could never even begin to describe, yanks me from where I stand and thrusts me over the concrete edge.

Before I have time to scream or yell, the world changes before me, like a roller coaster ride diving into a rainbow at full blast.

I can't even breathe because my breath is taken away, left behind on the top of the building I live in.

Soon I find myself standing again, not feeling the effects of having done whatever it is we just did.

"I did not want to waste time with you. I know you do not care for heights."

I glance at Matthew. I'm not sure whether to thank him or try to run away again.

40

"That house right there," Matthew says, pointing straight ahead.

"Where am I?"

But you know and you ask the question like a child asking Mommy for a blanket that's already covering him.

"You know."

And yes, I know.

This is weird.

This isn't some dream where the streets are like jelly and the walls feel like marshmallows and the White Rabbit hops on saying, "follow me, little boy, follow away." No, this is real.

I feel the shudder of wind as a truck drives by. The car next to us is an old Saab and it's real, because I touch it and feel the smooth paint finish.

I think of the '70s.

Barry Manilow and *Star Wars* and Munich International School.

"That is right."

"It is?" It's a little weird to already have grown used to someone reading my mind.

"You are in Steinbach."

"Germany."

"Yes."

"I don't get it—how did this—how'd we—?"

"Do you believe God created the Heavens and the stars?"

"Yeah."

"Then coming to this place is not that difficult to fathom, right?"

I'm about to say that *all* of this is difficult to fathom, but my verbal skills aren't quite keeping up with everything else. Matthew opens a gate and we walk down a brick path surrounded by tall bushes. A few steps lead to a porch that slants upward, while the concrete path continues downward along the side of the house.

On the porch sits a boy.

I stop breathing. If, in fact, I was breathing.

This time I don't have to ask.

It's me.

I'm nine or ten.

No way.

Tall and skinny with thick messy hair I haven't yet bothered doing anything with and more freckles than I remember.

He's alone—or, well, I'm alone—sitting on the porch near the front door, a full story over the walkway below that's heading toward the basement.

This is our house in Germany and that's me. I'm looking at myself as a boy.

I try to swallow, but something hard and rigid is stuck in my throat and I can't.

I know this and know what happens, but why am I here?

I try to say something but I can't.

Matthew is right behind me, standing, watching just like I am.

The boy is sitting with one roller skate on his foot and another in his hands. He moves to try and put it on.

I try to move a hand, but can't. A leg, but can't. I'm immobile but I'm here. I know this because I can feel my heart beating, racing, pumping pumping pumping.

The porch has black metal grills along its side that are more for decoration than for anything else.

I realize this now and then.

The boy leans back against the nonexistent railing to prop himself up as he pulls up the roller skate.

I stare up at him, then quickly glance down at the path.

A large rock the shape of a pyramid and about the size of a bowling ball is right beneath the boy.

It must have been placed there for decoration.

And then.

Yes.

Dear God, no, don't let this happen, don't.

But I can't do anything as I fall—as he falls, the boy that is me—and he plummets down on the path with his head landing squarely on the rock letting out a dull crack

no no no no no

like something heavy and wet splattering sickly over the pavement.

I can't move. I cough. I'm sick.

40

I try and close my eyes but I can't.

The boy's body is shaking.

He's dying, I'm dying. I'm there, right in front of me, dying.

I see shaking hands grabbing the head and then one of those bloody hands reaching down at the roller skate that's crumpled beneath him and trying to take it off, trying to move it.

I want to scream.

I can finally move so I get closer to the boy.

But I'm not really here, am I? 'Cause my feet, 'cause my head, 'cause . . .

"Look," Matthew tells me.

Thick and dark liquid like the inside of the earth pools around my skull that's been wedged open.

A red carpet not only covers the sidewalk and the boy that I once was, but also begins to filter into my picture frame.

"Stay with me," he says.

The images around me are skipping and I'm lightheaded, not to mention feeling woozy and nauseated.

"Stay with me, Tyler."

He obviously wants me to stick around for the climax of this wonderful moment, this highlight, this yesteryear from hell extravaganza.

A door opens and footsteps sound above us.

Then . . .

She is young—how young I don't know—and beautiful.

Pictures don't do her justice and never have and never will.

Mom stands above me and the other dying me and calls out our name and then she howls.

I force my eyelids to clamp shut and yet can't block out the heinous sound.

Take this before you go to bed, Tyler.

Then I open my eyes again and I'm standing on my rooftop, looking out to the skyline of Chicago with nobody around.

For a moment I just stand there, breathing in, holding onto the edge as if I might fall.

Then I take my shaking hand and feel the back of my head.

I didn't die then because that rock was never there. I didn't hit a rock when

91

I fell. I just hit the concrete walkway and got a concussion and walked around the rest of the day with a huge knot on the back of my head.

The wind rustles.

I glance around.

Matthew is nowhere to be found.

22

You're Not Alone

My hand reaches over and scoops up cool water and I feel an urge to let it scoop me in. The city stretches and curls in the distance, the night lights pulsing as Chicago drifts to dreamland. I'm alone and wish I didn't know it.

This is my refuge, but this isn't an ocean I can escape to. An immense lake drifting out to the horizon is still just a lake. Even an ocean is confined. A world is still a spot in the sky of some boy gazing a galaxy away.

Water is restless and is always moving. Maybe that is its comfort, its commonality. The movement feels natural like the thoughts in my head and heart and soul. Ripples splashing and spilling over the sides of this boat, never orderly, always random, always restive.

When my mother's mother passed away and I received a small part of the inheritance, I did the most practical thing, in my mind. I could have bought a house. But by then I didn't have anybody to buy it for. I didn't need a house or a lawn. Families need those. So I bought this boat instead. Yes, the dream of building a studio would come later, making the *Precious* look more and more silly and stupid, but I still don't regret the decision. I bought it from a guy going through a nasty divorce who wanted to get rid of it quickly.

It's been a day since seeing Matthew, and I'm almost convinced that he can't make it out onto the water. Almost. I've almost stopped thinking about him. Almost. The beer I'm drinking has almost helped. Almost.

Life is full of almosts that get you nowhere.

I scan the skyline and feel lost in the vision.

You've held it at bay long enough.

Far enough.

Fast enough.

The glass between myself and the rest. There are cracks now, holes, bleeding in rain and dust and snow and cutting the skin.

The world out there, just beyond, just beyond reach.

It's seeping in like flooding water.

No going back now.

Have you been wrong this long? Have you tried so hard for this?

Water. Rocking. Soothing. Rock me to sleep. Sway to the music. Wrap yourself around me and let me move on and let me forget.

The wind knows. So does the sky. So do the Heavens. So does God.

They all watch and they grieve.

This stillness in the current. This silence in the stirring.

They blow but I keep staying still.

23

Killer

I know the moment I wake up that I'm not in my own bed. I'm not in my own place either. It just feels different. There's a smell—a smell of some kind of meat casserole that's hovering in the air. It's warmer than my place. The covers over me are stiff and smell musty. They're heavy, too. Like the kind of protective garb a dentist puts over you when you're getting X-rays. I pull them off and sit up and look around.

A picture of a family of four glares at me. A bald guy and his blonde wife and two girls.

Maybe if I close my eyes and put the body armor back over me, I'll wake up in my own reality.

But I'm not remotely tired, not anymore.

Today I was supposed to meet with Nicole Lawson for the first time.

Not sure if I'm going to be able to make that preproduction meeting now.

I glance at the picture on the wall again. Something about it seems familiar.

You know them, Tyler.

I see curtains over the windows and pull them back.

I'm on the second story of a house and the windows are dirty. The outside world is both bleak and bright. It's a gray day, but snow covers the landscape out there. It's the kind of snow that's been around for a few days, like stubble that's becoming uglier by the day. I can't tell if it's morning or afternoon since there's little light coming through the haze of clouds.

I see the kid in boots and jeans and a coat that doesn't look warm enough. He's got a cap on and hands in his pockets. He looks lonely.

He's walking down the sidewalk over icy snow toward the corner.

I don't see anybody else around. There's a black truck on the other side of the road that turns and heads down another street.

For a second, I see the red lights of the brakes, then they vanish as if let go.

The boy stops for a moment and leans down, as if seeing something he wants to pick up. His hat falls off—it appears it's windy out there—and he scoops it up.

The brown hair and the face.

Not again.

I don't recognize this place, but I do recognize the boy. He's me. I'm older—maybe in sixth grade.

Where was I living in sixth grade? Most people probably can answer this question, but not me, not with the roaming nomad family, not with the gypsy band I toured around with.

The snow, the suburb, the flat ground.

I'm in Illinois. We lived there a couple of times. This is our first stint. When Dad was teaching at Trinity and working on some kind of really important paper.

I'm afraid of what's going to happen. Especially after having seen the cantaloupe cracking of my skull not long ago.

Yet there's nothing noteworthy in this scene. I'm walking down the street. I try to think where our house is. It's certainly not this one.

Magellan.

The name comes like a meteor from the night sky.

The Magellan family.

I remember them because of their two older daughters that were strange. One was a year older and liked me and always wanted to sit by me on the bus.

I'm not planning on having a play date with the Magellan girls, this I know.

I watch myself walking.

The black truck suddenly moves and turns around as if it's a race.

It begins driving down the street, heading toward the boy.

40

Heading toward me.

No.

Yet the vehicle slows down and then stops on the edge of the street, across from where I'm walking. I let out a sigh, because I didn't want to see myself get run over.

I don't remember this happening.

The window rolls down, but I can't see who the driver is from this angle.

I'm still walking, oblivious. It looks cold outside. I can hear the hum of the wind.

The door opens now and something jumps out of the truck.

It's a dog.

Not a big dog—a small kind, like a poodle. It runs across the street to where I'm standing now.

I pick it up and lift it to my face and then seem to be talking to the driver of the truck.

Don't talk to strangers. Come on Tyler.

The driver doesn't get out, but his door remains open.

I think back to the scene at the house in Germany, about falling and cracking my head open.

That happened but this never did.

The kid starts walking over the edge of the grass parkway and then onto the street and next to the truck.

The boy—me—gives the dog to the owner of the truck.

Why is the door still open?

He's talking, saying something.

Then everything changes...

The boy seems to freeze and awkwardly step back.

A big man steps out. All I see are black gloves and a coat.

He grabs the boy by the arm and yanks down.

No.

I can't tell if I shouted out or not.

Nobody can hear me in here, not unless someone else is here.

Another hand grabs the boy's face, then his hair. With both hands now pulling at the boy, the man rams him inside the truck, shoving him and then continuing to move him with his arm.

The man slips back in the truck and closes the door.

Then he closes the window.

I feel sick.

Once again I feel like I might throw up or pass out.

I remember the thing I found in my bag on my trip back from North Carolina.

The bloody white wire.

The truck drives off.

I suddenly dart out of the room and down the staircase and out into the freezing cold. I'm screaming. The truck is gone.

I'm gone.

I stand there shivering. Outside, everything is different. Now I know where I am. My house is just down the block.

A car heads my way and I move out to the middle of the street to flag it down and get some help.

Then I see the driver.

Matthew pulls up beside me and tells me to get in out of the cold.

"What was that?"

"Get in and we can talk."

My chest is pulsating and my mouth tastes like battery acid might.

"What just happened?"

Matthew seems comfortable behind the wheel of the Volkswagen Rabbit he's driving. He changes gears and slows down.

I glance around. "Is this our old car?"

He nods.

"What is this?"

"I cannot explain every little thing to you, Tyler. The few things I have tried to tell you get ignored or overlooked."

"What just happened to that boy?"

"That boy is you."

"That never happened."

"It just did."

"Is this some vision of things that might have been or something like that? Or another alternate world? Am I supposed to go back and change the past or correct something in the future that will then force me to change the past? I mean—listen to me. I'm not even making sense. It's like trying to explain an episode of *Lost* to someone. I don't get half the stuff myself."

"The man driving that truck is Cornelius Sampson."

"Is. You said is."

"It is January of 1983. You are twelve years old. You will be the third boy that Cornelius Sampson takes and rapes and kills."

"No."

Matthew is as calm as if he's ordering a burger at a Sonic.

"What do I do?"

Matthew looks over at me and then slows the car down. He pulls off the side of the street, then faces me.

"You watch, Tyler. You pay close attention. Every question will get you nowhere. You watch and listen."

"But what am I supposed to do when . . ."

I am suddenly mute.

As mute as Joseph must've been when the angel silenced him.

"You watch and listen. And you remain quiet."

He's not trying to be helpful or encouraging. I see his face that seems slightly tanned and devoid of wrinkles, yet still so real. All of this seems real.

Suddenly I look back out and the car is at the edge of the corner.

Of the city.

I see a brand new Lexus SUV.

That's not from 1983.

Matthew looks at the door handle and nods.

I open it, trying to say something again, but feeling like my lips can't open. I swallow. My tongue is still there; that's good.

Then as the car drives off—this white Rabbit that I haven't seen or thought about in years—I'm finally able to open my mouth. I inhale a gulp of heavy exhaust and then cough.

Should've remembered the Volkswagen was a diesel.

24

Canvas

The minor songs on this album are the ones that matter the most."

This is the first thing Nicole Lawson says that makes me finally hear her instead of just listening to the conversation going around the room.

"And I know that we have to have the pop singles and I have those, but to me this isn't about them. To be honest, I didn't really like my first couple of albums."

Replying to her statement is dangerous. I nod and let the expressive, passionate young girl in front of me continue talking.

For all the times I've seen her on television or in videos, laughing and running around and bouncing her blonde hair back and forth as she dances like just another Miley Cyrus wannabe, it's amazing how serious Nicole Lawson is.

I'm supposed to be selling her on working with me, but it seems like she's trying to sell herself on me.

"I mean, they were good, they had some strong songs on them. It's just—they didn't sound different at all. They sounded like so much of the stuff out there. The stuff that *American Idol* is running through their machine. Overproduced to a point where the personality is gone."

I couldn't have said it better.

Half an hour into the preproduction meeting with the twenty-two-year-old singer, I'm already impressed. First off, there is no discernable annoyance at my missing our first meeting yesterday. Nicole is charming and vivacious and extremely down-to-earth.

"So when you think 'unique,' what's that mean to you?"

The two other people in the room are letting us talk, another surprise. Sometimes somebody from the studio won't shut up, nor will a manager, but in this instance it seems like they're listening, wanting to hear more. Her sales have earned her the right to be heard.

"I know this will sound crazy, but something I've been listening to a lot—an album that I downloaded and got swept away in—are you a Fleet-wood Mac fan?"

"Sure," I say, feeling the smile on my lips that I can't conceal. "I wasn't expecting that."

"I know—and I'm not saying that I'm wanting to do a Fleetwood Mac album. Who could? I mean—Stevie Nicks—she's a legend. I've been listening to *Tusk* a lot."

"Which one is that?" Donald asks us.

"Their follow-up to *Rumours*, the one that wasn't *Rumours 2*."

Donald, the A&R rep, nods in a way that tells me he hasn't heard *Rumours*.

"Some people say it's their best," Nicole says, her pretty, flawless face once again animated now that she knows we share something else in common. "It's beautiful, some of those songs. Simple, haunting."

"So what do you feel is 'unique' about it? Besides the fact that it has three extraordinary songwriters on it?"

Nicole thinks for a second, this sweet little earnest look on her slightly freckled face.

I can understand why the world has fallen in love with her. It's hard not to.

"Everything today has *the sound*. Turn on the radio and you hear *the sound*. That's why some of these groups that come along that don't sound like everything else do well. But I'm not trying to be different, or eclectic. I know what I've built—I'm not stupid. I know we can't go out there and do something, like, vastly different, and destroy the momentum. I just feel like—sometimes the songs can speak for themselves. A simple song that has a piano and a drum with a certain—sound."

"A certain sound."

"Your sound."

"My sound? I wasn't aware I had a sound."

"You do. You totally do."

Donald shifts in his chair to talk. We're in a hotel suite in Chicago and the furniture is uncomfortable. The food on the table remains untouched.

"There are unique things that you do with the artists you've worked with," Donald says. "And not just Sean Torrent. I think we feel that a more simple and straightforward album is necessary. It's a good career move at this time. Everybody is doing peppy and overproduced."

"I can underproduce," I joke. "I can do that quite well. I'll just say *yes* a lot more."

"It's about choices, not gadgets," Nicole says. "The song 'Sara' or 'Storms' or 'Gold Dust Woman.' The Stevie Nicks songs. So deep, so simple. I don't hear songs like that much these days."

"Those are all remarkable songs," I say.

"And haunting. But done in a way—have you heard 'White As Snow' by U2? Done in this way. Of course, just some of the songs. Because I know they can't all be that subdued."

A figure springs into motion. "We have a few demos we can listen to."

I nod as Patrick, the manager, takes out an iPod and connects it into the speakers.

"Nicole—do you have any other examples of artists you like? Of a 'sound' you're going for?"

"It's not even a sound. It's the use of the sound—the silences, the subtleties. The unexplainable, you know. Sometimes it's the things that don't get put into a song that works. An addition of some random instrument halfway through the song. You do those little things. I can't say that I'm wanting it to sound like X or Y or Z. My voice doesn't sound like Stevie Nicks and I don't write songs like her but I love the spirit and the soul."

"I get it."

"I love *Boxer* by the National."

"A somber work."

"Yeah."

"You've mentioned two albums that I hold dear," I tell her.

40

She smiles and I can see a dimple. "I'll admit—I did read up a bit on you online."

"That's okay. I'm the one that's supposed to be flattering you."

"The songs are there," Donald says.

"The last album only had about four songs of mine on it. This time I want them all to be mine. With help, of course."

I ask them to hold off playing the demos. I don't want to let the rough songs tamper with my perceptions.

"Nicole, let me ask you something. Look ahead thirty years at your career. You have a dozen albums out there. Where do you see this being? A minor gem? A shift in a new direction? A bold statement?"

"A major work in minor keys."

I chuckle and glance at Donald. "That's a pretty good line there. Did you give that to her?"

"She came up with it herself."

We proceed to listen to the demo tracks that Nicole has created. There are six that they play me.

With each one, I see where she's coming from and can also see why they want me.

There's a lot of room to breathe on each song.

A regular producer out there would put each through the wringer and it would come out sounding the same.

It would lose that magic about it.

Sometimes, being complicated isn't being creative. It's just lots of colors thrown in for no reason.

Sometimes it's nice to be black and white in a rainbow world.

"What do you think?" Nicole is bold enough to ask me after the last song is finished. "Your absolute honest, off-the-cuff reaction."

"I'd fight to work on those songs with you."

Something seems to surge over and through her.

It looks like joy.

"I think it could be a lot of fun," Nicole says. "You're the boss—make me work hard."

"You will," I say. "Trust me."

25

A Night Like This

What is he really wanting to say and how can he do it in the most creative way?

These are the two questions that burn inside my gut with every project I take on. Sometimes the artist doesn't have a clue what's really going on inside of him, in the dark recesses of his heart and soul. Trying to find it is like chipping away a little each day. Along the way, you figure out how the artist can deliver those feelings and emotions in a unique way. Everything becomes potential. Voice and sound and arrangement and mood and melody—it's all a chance to choose something that will have meaning and impact.

It's late and I'm by myself, surrounded by ten thousand artists from yesterday and today and tomorrow. All on my iPod singing their little hearts out to me.

I've been listening to Nicole Lawson's first two albums, along with listening to Fleetwood Mac and the National, and then half a dozen other bands she referenced as well.

I'm trying to pinpoint a connection, trying to connect the dots.

This sound. This chord. This theme.

I believe everybody in life has a soundtrack, has their top ten albums, has their top one hundred songs. Not based on a critic's criteria, but based on their own life experience. The girl who got away. The sunset seen on vacation. An unpreventable move in the middle of childhood. A loss. A victory. An episode. A love. A life.

40

What is Nicole Lawson's soundtrack?

I'm working now, taking mental notes, drinking a little too much vodka as I do so, feeling a little more buzzed as time dissipates.

It's hard to turn it off. I tell myself I will when . . .

When I land a big one.

You've done that.

When I go full-time.

You've done that.

Okay, then, how about when I don't have to worry about financial things, when I'm my own boss, when I win a Grammy, when artists have me on their cell phones, when my name is synonymous with elite.

Get over yourself, Tyler.

Nobody ever really truly shares their goals. "Hi, my name is Fred, and I want to do as little in life to make as much money as I can." I'd shake that guy's hand. Then run far away from him. "Hi, I'm Brenda, and I'm better-looking than most of the women out there, and I'm going to use this to make my life far better than yours."

Nobody ever comes right out and says what they think. Except movie producers. And musicians on drugs.

The world disintegrates a little more every day and I'm worried about being the biggest someone in my tiny bubble.

Yeah, but that bubble's about to burst, isn't it Tyler?

I turn up the music and drink a little more.

I want to change it all.

But then again, I don't want to do a single thing. I want everything around me to change but I want to remain the same.

Louder.

Blurrier.

Louder.

Blurrier.

Then darkness.

The sound of the crack is a hand striking my cheek. Not tapping but slapping the way a tree trunk crashes to the forest floor after being chain-sawed apart.

I jolt up and look around thinking I'm dreaming.

If only.

"Time to wake up."

I get up and know it's Matthew talking, and I feel the world underneath me squish in a soft and unsteady way. I can't make out anything around me.

"Watch your step."

"Where are we?"

"Remember that field behind your old house?"

"Which one?"

"How many fields have been behind houses you have lived in?"

My mind is groggy. "I don't know."

"Come on."

I see his figure in the darkness. So far, no wings. We emerge from the tall grass onto a small patch of lawn that's indistinguishable from the neighboring plots lining up around it. I see the small one-story house.

That's the little one we rented when we moved back up here my junior year.

I can hear music and voices and laughter coming from inside.

"Around the side," Matthew says.

He leads me into the garage that's open. Several skinny kids are there hanging out. They don't act like they can see us, though they're not paying much attention to anything. Matthew can't walk through walls and neither can I. He opens the door leading inside and then we walk in a hall a lot more narrow than I can remember it being to the bedroom at the end of the hall.

It's locked.

"Try to open that door."

"How?" I ask.

"You've done it before when it was locked."

I jangle the handle. The handle is flimsy, the door lightweight. I've pounded through it before.

The sound of the Cure plays in the background.

"What's behind this?"

"You are."

"What am I doing?"

40

"You are in your bed, Tyler. You are dying."

I step back and then launch a kick that cracks apart the lock without any hesitation.

The room is dark and smells awful.

I don't remember where the light switch is. It takes me a while to find it.

The first thing I see is myself.

Not teen Tyler but thirty-nine-year-old Tyler, standing there looking awfully rough around the edges. I don't see Matthew with me in the frame of the three-foot-tall mirror.

That's because he's a vampire and you're a ghost and both of you are going on a road trip to Hell, Tyler.

"The bed," Matthew says behind me, as if he's interrupting the rambling thoughts going on in my head.

The pungent smell of vomit is all around, making my eyes water. I see a figure underneath dark covers. I pull them back and see the mess that's been made.

All around his head. All over his pillow. Caked like damp crumbs in his nose and mouth.

I go to reach but Matthew stops me.

He's an unmovable force, this creature holding me.

My arm begins to burn and I resist and stop.

"You cannot do anything to him now. He is already dead."

"I'm not dead."

"But *he* is."

"That's me. This is my house and I lived here when we moved up to Chicago my junior year of high school. And we moved—I know we moved again so that can't be me because I *never died.*"

I glance down and remember how lanky I used to be. The boyish face that people say I still have really looked boyish, even stuck in a glossy coating of puke with skin beginning to turn purple.

"Please," I tell Matthew as my body shakes and I begin to cry.

"You cannot do anything."

"Then what—what is this? What are you doing to me?"

"This is alcohol poisoning."

"I never got poisoned."

"I know."

"Then what kind of freak show is this?" I curse and don't care if he suddenly ties up my tongue in a hundred little tiny knots.

I glance around the room and am too freaked out to be nostalgic.

The life-sized Depeche Mode and New Order posters hang on the wall, just like they always did in those John Hughes films. My desk has a corkboard of photos on it. Photos of my old friends that I'd just abandoned and new ones I would abandon in another year, once I graduated and went on to college.

This little room used to depress me and it didn't need music to do so. Or a dead body in the sheets.

"How did this happen?" I ask.

Matthew's eyes move to the base of the bed. I glance down and stare at the white bottle—the family-sized bottle of Smirnoff vodka—lying on the ground, empty.

I've seen that before.

I shake my head and mumble something incoherent and violent and want to break something with that bottle.

"Why are you doing this to me?" I tell this thing next to me.

I start to touch the body but then I can't. I won't.

I'm feeling sick myself.

"Why?" My voice sounds weak and scared and exhausted.

"I did not do this," Matthew says. "You still see only half the picture, even though I continue to give you the whole. You still only see with half the vision you have been given."

"Then why don't you enlighten me?"

"That is exactly what I am doing."

I shake my head and look down. I need to get away from this.

In the background, the Ministry song blasts "Every Day Is Halloween."

Now that Matthew has shown up, I'm beginning to think that is the case.

26

The Stairs

Denial takes determination. With enough will power, one can reject anything.

The crowd at Rodney's new place is promising for a weeknight. The guy has guts to open a restaurant in this economy, especially an eclectic high-end one like Torchlight. The wine alone is steep, but I'm single with money to spare. I want to help Rodney because he's a good friend and a great chef. Plus I like knowing about Torchlight when the rest of Chicago hasn't discovered it just yet.

Angie's loud tonight. That happens when she drinks vodka, and she's drinking vodka tonight.

Enough of that stuff can kill you, and I know because I've been there.

Ah the sweet taste of denial.

I'm watching her across the table and listening to her talk about politics and she laughs and I have this thought.

I'd never in a million years bring her somewhere to meet my mother.

So what am I doing with her, besides fighting her attempts to take me to bed?

Why do I feel a need to invite others every time we get together?

Really, Ty, what are you doing with her?

I see the moving lines of her dress and the little straps over her tanned and toned shoulders and the curving smile of her revealing front.

Angie's bright and cheery, like the highlights in her hair, and she makes me laugh and she makes my senses tremble when she's near because we both know.

The longer time goes by, the longer we both know.

Yet I can't say there's anything more.

It's so shallow that my feet are barely even wet in this murky puddle I'm standing in.

Why is it that even though I believe I'm watched, that I know in my heart that I'm followed intently just like anybody else, I still am prone to wallow in the mire of my own making? To do something against my body and my spirit and my soul that I know I'll probably regret tomorrow and the next day? Yet like a determined and deliberate toddler, I still go ahead and do it.

"I can do it," the toddler in my soul says, and I go ahead and do it.

I sip my wine and glance at Angie and she knows what I'm thinking.

I want to leave this world behind and for a moment be a child doing what *I* want, what *I* need.

Amidst the conversation with friends, I see Angie's red lips whisper, "Want to leave?"

And I nod and can't take my eyes off her.

"Tyler?"

"Yeah."

"We're not fourteen, you know."

"Yeah, I know."

"Then what's wrong?"

"Nothing."

"Something's different."

"It's nothing."

"Maybe we should've taken a cab."

"It's a ten-minute walk."

"Ten minutes is enough for whatever's going on inside," Angie says.

The street lamp above us plays tricks with the shadows and makes that glowing, gorgeous woman in the restaurant minutes ago look like someone else. Like something else. Older and darker. We're standing outside my condo, where Angie stopped before going inside.

"I thought you wanted to leave."

"I did."

"Your eyes give you away," she says.

"I'll wear shades."

"I want the same thing and have for a long time."

I stare down the street corner.

I suddenly not only feel watched. I fear that someone is going to come out of hiding.

Perhaps at the most inopportune of moments, the most awkward of situations.

Angie's blonde locks look almost a sheek white when she moves up to me.

"I wanted you when you used to show up with that model, Laila. Even then."

Talk about buzz kill.

"I'm glad she's gone."

Wrong words to use, lady.

She slides against my leg. "Let's go upstairs and let me tell you all the thoughts I've had these last few years. Let's just see what happens, okay? No pressure. Let's see what comes naturally."

"Not tonight."

She has no idea that the train has left the station and she's standing in a plume of chalky black smoke.

"What?"

"Not tonight."

"What's wrong?"

"Nothing."

"I'm sorry—I didn't mean anything. I didn't mean to say anything bad."

"It's fine."

"I'm sorry for bringing her up," Angie says.

"Yeah. Me too."

The light saturates the steps and the walls and splashes over the wooden floor. I hold a hand over my eyes. They hurt. It's like looking in the sun for an extended time with no break.

My body shakes. Warm. Light-headed. Dizzy.

And I didn't even drink that much tonight.

I had just walked into my condo when the strobe lights blasted on. Now I'm hearing music upstairs on the roof.

Don't go up there. Run away. Get away.

I stand, stuck, debating what to do.

Should've brought the lady up with you, Tyler. Maybe then you wouldn't be seeing your brain cells smearing their way across the floor.

The burning light goes away, yet the music continues to play.

I open the refrigerator and grab a beer.

Like I said, denial can be powerful when you decide to give it your all.

I hear Depeche Mode blasting and singing that death is everywhere.

This is your nightmare and it's unfolding with your soundtrack and with your playlist and with your directorial vision.

I drain the beer in three gulps. Practice makes perfect.

For some reason I wish I had a dog I could snuggle with.

I wish I had someone's hand to hold.

You had Angie and she'd give you a hand to hold.

I sigh. Then I start up the stairs to the rooftop like a kid in trouble, wondering what death scene awaits me next.

27

Inside

The world is moving. And moving fast.

I open my eyes and no longer see Matthew sitting across from me on the couch upstairs on my rooftop.

Of course I don't.

Why that would be so easy, wouldn't it?

Beware of the cynical sarcastic thoughts, Tyler, because who knows when they'll come back to haunt or even hurt you.

My eyes reveal something that doesn't make sense, but when does life make sense anymore?

When did this happen and how did it all start and how can I swallow a pill to get back out of this matrix of my mind?

I feel the surge of movement, the weightless feeling your stomach gets, the slight loss of my breath.

I'm buckled in.

In the backseat of a car.

I stare ahead and see myself driving. If that's what it can be called.

Matthew is sitting next to me, behind the other me.

It reeks of beer a couple of hours old, that bad sour smell that gets stuck on your breath and your skin after a long night of drinking.

The car drifts over into another lane and then corrects itself.

I can see myself, the eyes heavy, then closing, remaining closed for a long second, then another.

Oh dear God please no.

I remember this.

No, make that *I remember the results.*

Laughing, still half drunk on campus the day after, making jokes about living to tell.

I shiver.

I don't want to see this.

I grip whatever I can with my hands.

"Matthew, please, I can't—"

I try to reach the driver but I can't.

The seatbelt is suddenly over my arms like a straitjacket.

I turn to say something to Matthew, but he is no longer there.

The driver—the drunken fool of a driver, the stupid and irresponsible idiot of a college student—fumbles with the tape player and again the car veers into the other lane, the lane with oncoming cars.

Thankfully it's late. A clock says three something.

I smell something else.

Ah, yes, the scent I know well.

Why can't I see a few good things I've done, because I've done a few of them, haven't I? Haven't I?

Steak burrito no beans and sour cream with lots of carrots and peppers on the side.

Yes.

A nice fat twenty-minute drive to get there.

Yes.

This is supposed to be a four-lane street, two lanes heading north and two heading south, with no barrier between them.

But for me, some wasted wreck of a fool coming back from an early morning meal, this is my speedway, my Nascar race, my Daytona 500.

Trent Reznor comes on the radio. Yes, the younger and wilder and meaner Trent Reznor.

With heroes like this, it's no wonder what I'm doing.

"Matthew!"

But he's not there. He can't hear me. Nobody can hear me. The wail of Nine Inch Nails covers us.

40

No.

I feel my

his yours

heart beating.

I pull at my arms and the searing pain burns.

I cannot move.

The eyelids on the idiot drip and dip and close. The car edges left, into the second lane, into the other lanes.

The beams of the approaching lights are unmistakable.

No no wake up wake up Tyler wake up wake up.

His—my—head actually droops.

I curse, but that's not going to help. I want to scream and shout, but nothing I say makes a sound.

I want to beat myself senseless, to beat some life into that kid.

But that happens too, doesn't it, Tyler? Doesn't even get your attention. Nothing does. Nothing ever does. Why is that, Tyler? Why do you want to run and hurt and cause so much heartache?

Lights oncoming and horn honking and then I see something else moving.

The grill of a big truck.

Then, slow-motion.

The original car with the lights veers off to the side. But the truck in another lane behind it swerves the other way, straight at us.

This cannot be happening, no, please.

My head—the college student's head—is slumped down and will never see the impact.

He's—I'm—not wearing a seat belt, not up front.

The head and the shoulders and the body eject through the windshield, blasting shards of glass all over.

Bone is crushed and blood is splattered and skin is peeled back and a body is savaged as it catapults toward the front of an unbreakable unmovable force, all while I sit in the back and watch.

Before blacking out, I see my lap covered in red-speckled chunks of glass.

28

Mad World

Where were you?"

It takes me a moment to recognize Gavin's voice on my cell phone. "I covered but there wasn't a lot to cover with. Nicole looked like a third-grader who got her lunch stolen. Poor girl. Her manager got on the phone with me afterwards and demanded an explanation. The guy's a wanker."

It's Tuesday and I was supposed to meet with Nicole in the studio this morning. The schedule is on a fast track. The final nitpicking on the production deal with Nicole and me is still being worked out between my manager and hers. I'm sure this isn't going to help.

"What's the deal?" Gavin asks. He shares how the A&R guy showed up to see everybody sitting around wasting time and money.

How can I begin to explain when the words won't quite fit in the gums of my mouth?

"Man, I'm sorry."

"I'm not the guy needing an apology. Just some bearings. You okay?"

"I'm fine."

"Tell me this. You're not on drugs, are you?"

"No."

But maybe you are and that's the problem. Maybe you got into some crazy drug stuff working with you-know-who and you've been blocking it out like so many things in your life, right?

40

"Does this have anything to do with a girl?"

"Gavin."

"Look, mate—I'm just shooting it straight with you."

"No girl stuff. Who's sounding like a third-grader now?"

"I just want to know if I need to suddenly bail or watch my back."

"I missed a meeting."

"You know how much the studio costs for a day?" he asks.

"I got an idea."

I bet nobody ever says that to Rick Rubin.

"Ain't coming out of my check."

"Don't I pay you?"

"I don't know," Gavin says with enough of a trace of sarcasm. "Do you?"

I shake my head and seriously think about asking him what day it is. I look across the room and see a photo of my sister with her boys. At least I know I'm in my bedroom.

"What are you doing tonight?" I ask him.

"Oh, the regular. Hanging with the family, watching *American Idol*, having a few pints."

"Shut up."

"The usual."

"Care if I stop by?"

"Something's up. I know it. You get a girl pregnant?"

"Where do you come up with this stuff?"

"Well did you?"

"I'll be around in an hour or so. I'll bring the twins I just adopted from Africa."

The city is alive and reminds me that I'm going to die.

I don't know why I suddenly think of this now in the taxi cab, with motion and a mirror of lights around me. The window is cracked and the evening is cool and life is all around us.

How long has it been since Lollapalooza, since encountering Matthew?

My iPhone says it's August 17, but I don't believe it. I'm beginning not to trust much these days. That's why I'm heading over to hang out with Gavin. I always know where I'm standing with him, and I usually feel a little more stable when he's around. Not just in the studio, but anywhere. I don't want to call him my anchor, because he's not and because that would sound a bit weird. Gavin might really wonder about the state of my mind if he heard me say that. But he's something normal in a life that's increasingly becoming everything but normal. He's the guy in the studio who always finds a solution to any problem.

Maybe he can manage to do that for me now.

"If you were losing your mind, how would you know? You think you'd have any idea?"

Gavin is staring at the screen on the wall that's playing a Cubs game. I'm a fan, but he's something else. He's on the ship of fools who root every year and then get their hearts broken. I always think the worst and that's exactly what happens with our team.

"Drugs," Gavin says without glancing down at me.

"How would you know? I mean—do people that really go insane start slowly, and just live in denial for a while until it goes full throttle and they're gone?"

"What are you talking about?"

"Insanity."

"Yeah, you're looking insane to me all right."

"I'm not kidding."

"What's going on?"

"You ever have crazy things happen to you, stuff that you can't really explain?" I ask.

"Yeah. My ex. She was a ghost of things to come. A demon in a white dress. She was a vampire who didn't want blood but money. She made me stay in America. She forced me to become a fan of baseball."

"Good one."

"You going insane then?"

"How would I know?"

Gavin is checking out the game again, not paying attention. He didn't ask me again about my absence from the morning. I really want to tell him, but then again I know the abuse I'd take if I did.

"You ever think about death?"

40

His eyes track mine and I realize I've had his whole attention. Guys aren't supposed to be able to multitask, but Gavin is the master of this. His brain is a high-speed computer full of compartments like creativity and logic and discipline.

"Death? As in my own?"

"Yeah."

He nods. "I'm a Cubs fan. I think about death numerous times each year, especially come October."

"Seriously."

"Having premonitions?" Gavin asks.

"What if you knew? What if you knew the exact date you were going to die?"

"Then I'd say watch out. I'd take a big loan and have a month-long party. Maybe I'd go shoot my ex right before I went."

There are probably better people in this world I should be talking to. People who, for one, actually believe there is an ever after to wake up to.

"What are your plans?" Gavin asks, nonplussed, as if he believes me.

"I don't know. Should I make any?"

"You could show up to work tomorrow, for starters."

"I could challenge Sean Torrent to a bingefest."

"Early death right there."

"I don't know what I'd do."

Or rather what I will do, because of course it's going to happen, right?

"What's on that bucket list of yours?" he asks.

"Don't have one."

"Maybe you should get one."

"I don't have specific goals, like climbing a mountain or anything like that. It's always been career goals. Getting to a place where I didn't have to work so hard to find projects."

"Seems that's already the case."

"With what?"

"Nicole Lawson wants to work with you pretty bad. You should hear how she talks about your work. That pedestal is pretty high."

"Just because I make an album sound a little better doesn't mean I'm the artist."

"Think she knows that, mate."

"Some people forget."

"Not a bad thing for you, though, is it?"

"I just don't feel like I've—I don't know. That I've accomplished the things I wanted to."

"With what? Music? Or the wife and the kids and the picket fence?"

"All the above," I say.

"You know who one of my favorite all-time musicians was? Lennon. Yet before he was shot and killed, he was wasting his talents. The reports were that he was struggling. He was forty and just think of the songs he had left to write and sing. Was he losing something? Had he lost something? Who knows."

"But he had already made his mark."

"Sure, of course. Yet don't you think he was probably having doubts? What about all those talented beacons of brilliance who decided to kill themselves, directly or indirectly, at an early age?"

"Sometimes when you're that brilliant you need to douse the flames."

"You really believe that?" Gavin asks.

"I don't know."

"Why the death talk?"

"I don't know."

"I think you do."

I curse because I have nothing better to say or do. "I think you'd think I'm crazy if I even tried to explain."

"You're already crazy in a lot of ways, so don't go trying to add on to it."

A rumble goes through the small bar as the Reds batter hits a grand slam. Now it's Gavin who's cursing, though he has a very good reason.

"The Chicago Cubs haven't won a World Series since 1908," he spits out with another juicy expletive. "What have *they* accomplished? Is it ultimately about the accomplishment? Or is it all about the journey? If they'd won seven World Series, would we care as much?"

"Maybe we'd care even more."

Gavin looks and me and laughs. "Yeah, probably."

29

Headhunter

I feel followed, but this is nothing.

I've felt this way as far back as my memory can take me.

What would therapists say? They might say that having a father educate you on the evils of Hell before entering kindergarten might do this to one's psyche. Others might tell me it's true, that I'm being hounded by evil spirits for some hidden sin or negligence. Some might say it's all the music I listen to. Probably one or two might just say I'm stressed and need a little rest and relaxation.

I don't find it strange to think I'm being watched.

All I want to know is, why now? Why after all this time has *this* started happening?

I walk the Chicago sidewalks because I'm not eager to go home. I'm definitely not eager to climb into bed. And if sleep could even come, I sure as Heaven and Hell am not eager to find out what's on the other side.

Even though I lurk in the shadows of the side streets and between buildings and sidewalks that cut beneath large trees, I find myself safer than at home. I feel watched but untouchable.

None of this makes sense.

I think of the other random things that have popped up in the middle of nowhere.

A baseball bat. A pocket knife. The bullet.

Are these clues to something bigger? Am I supposed to take all of this and do something with it, like some strange puzzle, like an unraveling Da Vinci code?

I reach my condo with no answers. The building hovers toward me like the leaning tower of Pisa. I expect someone to be waving from the roof, or maybe the light to be on, with a figure in the window. Maybe the glow of a red bulb with the outline of a noose hanging there. Yet there's nothing to see or hear but the sound of a dog barking in the distance, a soothing sound that reminds me I'm in a neighborhood with people and life.

I climb the steps and reach the second floor where the frat boys live. They're not really frat boys, maybe never were, but they still look and act like a couple of them. They're names are Harvey and Blake and I constantly get them confused, so I always just call both of them "man." When we pass, it's "Hey, man!" or "What's up, man?" I have to fight the urge to call them Hans and Franz. They're probably too young to get the reference anyway.

The frat boys' door is slightly cracked open, and while this isn't unusual, the noise behind it is.

Something's happening.

A scuffle or a fight.

I hear knocking around and the floor shudders and then it sounds like something crashes against the wall. Then I hear a howling that makes me crouch down a bit because it's almost coming from above me. It's a hoarse, penetrating sort of scream. The kind that makes you cringe.

Then I hear and feel more pounding.

I go to touch the door handle.

Don't.

The door swings open before I can touch it.

Before the entryway isn't the frat boys' condo but rather a long dark shaft of a hallway. It's muted red with black carpet, faded mostly gray. About twenty yards away from me, two figures stand over something in the middle of the hallway.

For a moment I think it's Hans and Franz, but then I notice these guys are actually bigger than they are.

Something is being waved around in the air.

You know what that is.

40

Then I see movement. One of the guys is moving, up and down, as if dancing on top of the thing on the ground.

No, not dancing.

Kicking.

And that thing—that thing is a someone. A crumpled, crippled someone being attacked.

The wails come again and then it feels like the floor is whimpering and shivering.

I start to close in on the sight.

A long cylinder being waved in the air comes into view. It's a bat.

I hear the voices speaking, cursing, spitting.

"You think you're really tough, don't you," one voice starts, then continues to mock and rail.

Now I'm running.

Now I'm racing toward that long piece of wood, ready to take it away.

Ready to stop it from occurring.

Yet I run straight through them, just when it happens. Just as the bat swings a 180-degree arc and lands with its bulging side against the already swollen cheek of the figure below.

I can hear bone crunch and see the jaw suddenly vanish.

That's your imagination. You can't see underneath the bat. You can't see through it.

I feel a gasp of air, let out like a coughed sigh or a wheezing death.

"Enough, man," the other voice says.

"Shut up."

The bat is raised again and . . .

Can't won't don't let me no.

I hear it instead of see it and perhaps that's better, or worse.

A sickening chunk of a blow, the kind I can feel deep inside of me.

The one without the bat curses.

"Mike!" he says.

I know who these guys are. Mike and Jay. At least I knew of these guys back in college, back when this happens.

Jay keeps cursing and keeps saying Mike's name over and over and over again.

A scene that was already bad went far worse in a matter of seconds.

Where did that bat come from? They never showed up at my apartment with a bat.

They start walking away and soon they're sprinting down the hallway.

The bloodied and misshapen face of the college student on the hallway carpet, who is now coughing up dark liquid, used to look a lot like my face. I reach down to touch his cheek, but my hand goes through it.

I try to follow the guys who did this, ready to find my home again, ready to get this nightmare behind me.

As I head toward the wall that was the doorway I just walked through moments ago, I hear laughter down the stairs.

It's a sick, mocking laughter.

It doesn't belong to Matthew. I know this.

This comes from someone—something—else.

I reach the wall and stand there. Then I start pounding on it. Again. And again.

Until the skin on my knuckles is red and pink and raw like hamburger meat.

30

Come Undone

It's me. But that's obvious by now.

I don't know what to say.

I guess I just want to know why.

If it's this clear—this totally clear to me—then the reason should be too.

Right?

I'm sorry for everything.

I have no right to ask for anything more, when I haven't in such a long time. When I've even spoken more to Julie than you.

You know my heart, God.

And that's what I'm afraid of.

That's why I never ask and never pray and why—

That's why.

The table is long and the faces above the glasses of wine and the full plates are those I know, yet I can't name them. They laugh and glance and whisper to each other while I sit at the end, watching and wondering, with an empty belly and an empty appetite.

"Tyler."

I look up and see my father. He holds a knife and sticks it carefully in the turkey.

"Tyler."

My sister, Kendra, shakes her head in shame.

"Tyler."

It's Julie, and her mascara is running and it looks like she's been crying for a long time.

"Tyler."

It's Gavin waiting for his glass to be refilled.

"Tyler, man, come on."

It's Cole staring at me upside down.

"Ground control to major Tom."

Cole is speaking again.

Ah, twice is nice. Twice breaks the cycle. Twice might mean I haven't become certifiable just yet.

"What happened to you?" Cole asks.

I find myself sitting in my armchair in the family room of my condo. For the first time since buying it, I notice how uncomfortable it really is. "How'd you get in?"

"Frat boys let me in. Your door was open."

"You saw the frat boys?"

"Yeah, one of them."

"You sure?"

"Can I still get a ride with you?"

"A ride where?"

"You said you could drop me off at Reese's place this morning."

"Oh yeah."

"You mind?"

I shake my head.

I think of Gavin, then I think of Nicole Lawson, then I think of work and my responsibilities and the studio and the eventual paycheck.

Money doesn't really matter when you're suddenly faced with your own mortality.

"Let me get in the shower for a sec."

"I get paid double for being an alarm clock," Cole shouts back at me as I head up the steps to my bedroom.

40

I can hear him blasting some LCD Soundsystem, which comforts me a bit, reminding me of something normal.

The hot water scalds. It's something I can control with a knob, just like I do in the studio. It's a wheel I turn just like I do when I'm driving.

I control this, not someone else.

You don't have any control over anything. Don't you get it, Tyler?

I move and the knots in my back feel soothed by the scathing water. My hand still resembles a cross between something from *Rocky* and *Rocky Horror Picture Show*. The water burns but also numbs the throbbing.

I think of the day ahead.

You still have two things left, don't you?

I try to wrap my head around the project at hand.

Yes, the project at hand, the project known as the end of your life, the end coming near, the end drawing near at hand.

The fog in the bathroom is comforting when I get out of the shower. I really don't want to see myself in the mirror.

I get dressed and feel a little better.

Two more things.

I need to get out of here and get to a Starbucks and get caffeinated and then get working.

Two more things, Tyler.

In my bedroom, I can't help but think of them.

The knife.

And the bullet.

Bingo.

"Ready?" Cole calls out.

What has the man won?

"Yeah."

I slip going down the stairs.

You can't outrun your own thoughts.

There are other ways to deal with this. I just haven't figured out how.

31

Deep Blue

Three days in the studio can seem like three years. Or like three hours. The experience with Nicole so far feels like the latter. It's refreshing to hear her natural talent and enthusiasm. It's wonderful to be at the start of a project with so much possibility and potential. And as if she's reading my mind, Nicole asks me about this on a Friday evening.

"Do you think this can be good?"

"Yeah, sure," I say as I'm fiddling around with an older synth that we haven't plugged in yet.

"No, I mean *good*. Special. The kind of CD you take out ten years after it's been released on a night when you're by yourself, sipping wine."

I stop what I'm doing and glance at her. She's playing with her messy blonde hair with a nervous energy.

"Well, the songs are definitely a little more for people who aren't necessarily alone, you know?" I say.

"I want it to last."

"To last, huh?"

"To be around for a long time to come."

"Don't you think every musician wants this?"

"No."

I love how she didn't hesitate in answering.

"Yeah, I agree. Look, we try our best. It's hard to know. I do know you've got some amazing songs. I'm not just saying that. The potential is there. Unless I majorly screw it up."

"You'll make them magical."

"I've been listening to a lot of the music you referred to as a starting point. It's been helpful."

"Did you guys know you were onto something special when you were working on *Blue and Bluer?*" Nicole asks.

"Not at all. Sean Torrent came out of nowhere. He was sorta like you—with a Christian label. He always referred to U2 as his inspiration there."

"I wouldn't put him in the Christian category."

"Not now, not after his track history and his music. But at one time, he was at least leaning toward that genre. Writing songs that could be interpreted in multiple ways."

"Was it real to him? His faith?"

I hear something in the other room. It's Gavin playing with drum samples.

"I don't know," I say. "I can't look into the guy's heart, so I don't know. I thought—I think at one point in his life it was. But I don't know. Heroin addicts don't make the most model Christians, you know?"

"They can when they stop."

"Yeah."

"You communicate with him at all?"

I shake my head and chuckle. "No. But I am supposed to be producing his next album. Sometime in the next, let's see—decade maybe. The only way I hear about him is when I receive texts from sources at the studio. Or I search him online to find out what he's up to."

"So you didn't know you guys were recording a classic?"

"I don't think any artist every *really* knows. Except maybe when Quincy Jones was making *Thriller* with Michael Jackson. You never know. I think the mistake many make is to think directly opposite of what you said. They want the big hit now. They want something that's trendy and hot and will play in the clubs *now*. They're not thinking ten years from now. They're not even thinking ten weeks from now, to be honest."

"Do you think that far down the road?"

I used to.

"I'd like to think I do."

"And you're being honest when you say the songs are there?"

"I wouldn't tell you that if I didn't believe it." I move a set of headphones off the desk that has the twin iMacs on it. "You can manipulate anything to make it sound however you want it to sound. Sleeker or rougher or faster or sexier. Anything. But the song—the heart and the soul of the song—*that* comes from the artist. In your case, it comes from you. The writer and the singer. Which is awesome, because you're the one who did it all. You can manipulate sounds but you can't manipulate soul, you know?"

"That's so beautiful," Nicole says. "Can I tweet that?"

I laugh again and shake my head as I resume work on our synth.

I play the track over for the sixth time. It's late but I don't worry about cranking it on my Bose speakers in my living room.

Some of the best moments of my life are those when I'm by myself, away from work and obligations and strangers posing as friends. I'm there by myself, listening. Discovering. Embracing some new song. Feeling the chills as I hear something for the very first time with a fear like one might have with doing anything for the first time. The fear comes because there's never going back after the first. Those first notes and that first melody and the strokes and the pattern and the chorus and the repetitions and the add-ons and the fade in and fade out. When you find something that moves you and breaks you, that first time is forever embedded in your soul.

It harkens back to childhood, when I didn't have an option *but* to be alone. When the music comforted and soothed and when sometimes I'd discover something for the first time while listening to my headphones. Walking across a snow-covered field listening to the radio, or listening to track four on side one of the LP, or playing a cassette in my portable player while working on the mountain.

I wonder if every emotion we feel for the rest of our lives is inspired or tainted by emotions felt in our first eighteen years. Why should the following fifty or sixty or seventy years all be defined by those first couple decades?

You don't have years left but months. Weeks. Days.

I turn up the music because the music is louder than my thoughts.

40

My thoughts spiral and they search and they swerve down.

I wonder and watch and wonder and wait and wonder.

I'm that same scared, sad sixteen-year-old boy, soothed by some melancholy song stretched out by the strains of synths.

I haven't grown up or changed. I've just aged.

With more lines and moles and inches and scars, inside and out.

The distant echoes of yesterday and yesteryear never go away. People drown themselves in work and life and children and booze but it's all the same. They hold those memories at bay but I never do, not now, not when I'm drowning in music and remembering and hiding and consoling.

Don't let go.

I never let go. That's my problem. My anchor is always there in the songs and the music and I never let it go. Ever.

32

Mistaken for Strangers

A red emblem on your shirt. Not an emblem but rather blood, your blood, blood as wet as syrup just poured on pancakes, seeping into the softness.

There's something lodged there.

It's a hazy afternoon outside the seat of this car.

The car I used to drive when I was married to Julie.

Sitting in the driveway, the car is running.

A low pulsing throb begins. The blade of the knife pulls out with a sickening sound that streaks the outside with black momentarily.

Fight it make sure your eyelids stay open.

I know this place, but where? Where am I?

Soon the dull trembling increases and starts to burn.

Sweat and shiver and feel sick.

Search for a phone.

This is a dream, Tyler, this is a dream.

It doesn't feel like a dream.

It is dying.

This is how it feels to die.

Insides ooze out onto your side and your back and your buttocks. Coughing feels like an organ might slip out.

Search for something to press against the wound to stop the bleeding.

40

Manny.

The name comes out from nowhere.

Manny's driveway.

The crazy ex-boyfriend that harassed Julie for several years.

The trembling won't stop.

Back the car out of the driveway, then turn down one lane.

Driving far enough and fast enough can get you somewhere and save you.

"Matthew," your voice calls out, but even that seems different.

I never came to his place, so what was I doing there?

Grip the wheel and accelerate and then the gray falls to black again and then

no, Tyler, no, get up, open those damned eyes of yours

the eyes open and see a kid riding his bike past you. He's looking at you funny and he should because you're practically driving on a lawn now.

I almost went there once, but Julie persuaded me not to.

A hot, piercing pain slashes skin, then your insides.

Let out a gasp.

"Matthew, help me, please."

Shiver and scrunch your body and let the darkness suck you into its sweet mouth.

In so many dreams, I find myself running in the muted light, only to awaken in the still of morning. But for me this time, it's the reverse. I suddenly open my eyes and find myself running down a street I don't recognize with the glow of a city around me. I'm not jogging but rather sprinting, hauling as if my life depends on it. I don't stop, but rather put a hand against my side to feel if it's still bleeding. The only reason it's damp is from my sweat.

The air is thick like hot breath. I look behind me and see someone or something running after me, knocking over someone, running faster than I am. I turn right at an intersection and head down a darkened street with old buildings on each side.

For some reason, I think of Mardi Gras.

For some reason, I think I'm in someone else's story, some other book.

I glance at the darkened glass window of a place I'm passing and see the word "Jazz."

The footsteps behind me are getting stronger, closer.

Then I see a fence ahead with a gloomy, abandoned building sleeping behind it. I see the slight opening and I kick the gate open with my leg, running down the sidewalk and up the stairs toward an open door of what looks to be an old and forgotten church.

If I can just get inside—

The roar of a cannon sounds behind me and I feel something slam down and take a chunk off my shoulder. I howl as I stumble on the last step and go careening, bashing my head against the rotted-out doorway.

One hand goes to my shoulder as I slither across the floor.

I feel everything around me suddenly become piercing bright, a thousand stars I'm starting to float toward.

"It's time—we've been waiting for you," a voice all around me says. *"So nice to have you stop by."*

I stop and feel a cold wave cover me.

Whoever or whatever is chasing me is still better than whatever's in this old church.

"Go ahead, look inside," a voice says.

It sounds like—

No.

Then I hear the steps and feel a boot kick my jaw and press it against the floor.

I see something pointing at me. It's a handgun from a video game, from a Clint Eastwood movie, a massive barrel looking straight at me.

"What's your name," the guy holding it asks.

"Tyler. Tyler Harrison."

A voice inside this church starts to laugh.

It's a different one, the voice that's been following and stalking me for some time.

"What are you doing here?" the man asks.

"What?" I mumble.

"Take a few breaths. Take your time."

40

The air doesn't feel like it's getting to my lungs or my head.

"What are you doing in New Orleans?"

"Where?"

"You heard me. I'm not going to ask again."

"What—I don't—you wouldn't believe me if I even tried to explain."

"Explain what?"

The guy speaking and holding the gun is big and square. I can't make out his face, but I don't have to in order to know he's serious.

"I don't know what I'm doing here," I say.

"How do you know James?"

"Who?"

"How do you know the girl?"

"What girl?"

I feel the muzzle of the gun press against my forehead. "You know who I'm talking about and if I don't get an answer soon—"

"Laila?"

The name comes out of nowhere.

As if my mouth and my heart knew.

But of course it doesn't come out of nowhere, it's the name that's always there, that's always hovering, that's always on the tip of your tongue.

The name that went missing.

Perhaps this was where she ended up.

"Are you trying to be a hero?"

"What'd you do to her?"

The man laughs. "She's dead, just like you are. Or, maybe I should say *thanks* to you."

I shake my head and then grab the gun. I try to move it but he jerks it back and then slaps me over the face with it.

The world turns golden bright again and then I see nothing or feel nothing for a moment. Soon I feel the barrel against my forehead.

"Connor and James. Those names mean anything to you?"

"Who?"

The man waits, the barrel bearing into the soft skin.

Suddenly the laughter comes again. But it's different—a different tone, a different voice.

A voice heckles in my ear. *"It's all gone. She's gone, you're gone, they're all gone, Tyler."*

Whoever is laughing and said this isn't the man holding the gun.

"What'd you do to her?"

He presses down harder.

"This."

33

I Don't Care Anymore

Brian Eno speaks to me through Twitter.

Seriously.

Back in the '70s, Brian Eno and a guy named Peter Schmidt published a set of cards called Oblique Strategies. Each card contains a phrase or an odd statement that is supposed to be helpful in getting past a creative roadblock or dilemma. Lots of bands have claimed to be inspired by these, including the French band Phoenix, who say it helped them create the phenomenal *Wolfgang Amadeus Phoenix*.

Now, thanks to Twitter, there's Oblique Twirps. Every hour a new strategy is shared.

I haven't sold my soul to Twitter yet, but I do have to admit I enjoy seeing these pop up.

Today's message feels like a poignant Chinese cookie: "Don't be afraid of things because they're easy to do."

I'm wondering if I was meant to see this tweet before the eons of time. If Matthew, with the urging of God, put this message here at the right place and right time for me to read.

If so, what am I supposed to take away from this message?

Don't be afraid of what? Death on my birthday? More hellacious visions of how I already died in my past? Reminders of something that almost *became horrific?*

The easy thing to do is not to do anything.

Four days since experiencing myself being stabbed and shot, I'm moving on without having any knowledge of what I'm supposed to do.

I'm waiting for Matthew to show up again and give me the manual.

Yet I don't expect him to show up on the train I'm sitting on.

"Hello, Tyler."

The car is almost empty. I took an afternoon train out to the suburbs of Geneva to do some house-hunting for the studio that I know deep down I'll never construct. Even before Matthew came to start haunting me, the writing was on the wall. This dream of buying a house and converting it into a home studio was just that—a big, fat, shiny dream that sparkled like a melting glacier. I've been doing this for the last couple of years, looking at homes and imagining the studio I'd make. It's a little after eleven as the mostly empty car shakes and rattles through the darkness of the west suburbs.

"Interesting night to be house hunting," he says, moving the seat in order to sit down directly across from me.

"It was something to do."

"I think you are trying to hide."

"Am I even able to hide from you?"

"No," Matthew says. "But that does not mean you are not trying."

"Maybe I just feel like I need to get going with some projects."

He nods, those eyes, the color of the sky, cutting through me.

"What?" I ask.

"Perhaps you need to think of other projects."

"This is not funny."

"I am not attempting to make you laugh."

"This isn't some game, because it's freaking me out and messing with my mind."

"Yet everything in your life is just that—a game. Even now, being on this train, traveling to spend your evening speculating and avoiding everything else. Why, Tyler? Why?"

"What do you mean, why? What are you trying to do?"

"My Father's will."

"With what? Huh? With some kind of twisted, Scrooge-on-acid sort of mind game?"

40

"We are not done."

"Oh yes, I think we are."

My yelling prompts a woman several rows behind us to get up and move out of the car.

Now we are alone.

"What's your point in all of this? To frighten me to do something? To get me to repent? To try and scare me into submission?"

The train shakes for a moment and I feel as if it's going to derail and crash and burn, and once again I'm going to see my life not just flash before my eyes but go out in a brilliant bright light.

"You are a stubborn man."

"Yeah, maybe so. I want to be left alone."

"That is something you do not want, Tyler. I can say that with an assurance you will never understand."

"I woke up with a knife stuck in my heart. Do you know that?"

"Of course."

"Why? What was the point of that? It's just—I don't get it. You come and show up and blind me and then you tell me I'm going to die on my birthday. Why? Beats me. You don't tell me that. Then you keep showing up only to frighten me."

"I am showing you the truth as it could have happened."

"The truth? What truth? What kind of demented truth are you talking about? Maybe you have powers, but maybe you're on the other side. What if you're a demon trying to trick me and fool me?"

Matthew just looks at me and we both know that I don't believe my own words.

Never once have I questioned whether or not this man is an angel. He's terrifying and everything in me knows. Now I can understand why the pictures in the Vacation Bible School classes have the people hiding behind rocks and trees when angels come making their announcements. It's not due to the brightness of their wings. It's because you just *know*.

I shake my head and then put both hands over my face.

I want to blink and have him be gone.

"You have been shown these things as a gift, Tyler. The same gift as the one you were given to tell you of your passing."

"Yeah, then maybe I won't ask for any more *gifts*."

"Do not mock your Father."

"I feel like you're mocking me here and now."

"I am showing you the truth."

"Why'd you show me all those scenes out of a horror flick? Huh? Why'd you show me dying time and time again?"

"I was there every time."

"So what—you saved my life every time? Why? For what reason? To only show up later and then tell me I'm going to die. Damn—thanks a lot."

"Your anger and your arrogance make it impossible for you to see the truth."

"I'm done. Okay? Got it? If it's my time to go, then so be it. Make this train crash."

"Do not taunt me, Tyler Harrison. I will break you in a second."

I exhale and feel a second away from death.

"I have one last image to share," Matthew says.

"What's that?"

He moves his head and I see where he's motioning toward. On the floor of the seat across from us sits a black-and-yellow chain saw.

I curse. Either out loud or in my mind. I guess in the sight of God they're both wrong.

There's another color on the chain saw, isn't there?

"Leave me alone," I mumble under a clenched jaw.

"Do you want to know why that is here?"

I want to reach over and punch him and gouge out his eyes and break his nose and bury my fist into his peaceful and placid face.

"Your hate has a scent," Matthew says. "It is that strong."

"Good."

"One last chance."

"For what? *For what?* To tell me how I could have died? By what? What now? My father's chain saw?"

"In this case, you were not the one who died."

"My father's already dead. "

"Your father is still breathing and still very much there."

40

"Not to me. Not anymore. Look—you can't scare me."

"I am not trying to scare you, Tyler."

"I want you to leave. Now."

"There are worse things out there that will bring nightmares. There are those whose sole purpose is to antagonize and terrorize."

"As opposed to those who bring harmony and warm fuzzy thoughts like you?"

"When I am gone, I cannot help you anymore. I cannot protect you anymore."

I get up in his face. If he wants to smell anger, he sure can now. "I don't want your 'help' anymore. I don't need your 'protection.'"

"Ask why you need it."

"I don't want to know why. I want to be left alone."

"You are never alone. Why do you not ask why, Tyler?"

"I've asked a lot of questions and gotten nothing. My entire life. Nothing. Nothing but doom and gloom. Nothing but hellfire and brimstone and a load of heartache."

"Do not do this."

I curse and nod my head.

I expect to feel my heart explode. I'm daring Matthew—this man, this creature, this angel—whatever he is.

Do it, do it now. Hurt me. GET IT OVER WITH.

Matthew sits there and glances at me.

"What?" I ask.

That look.

That look.

I can't take it.

Leave me alone.

"Time as you understand it is fading."

"Sure," I say. "Great. Fabulous."

He looks again, not angry, not saddened, not surprised.

Strong, stable, steady.

I'm about to say something again but he stands and opens the door to the other car and then he's gone.

That big, bloody chain saw remains here.

I don't want—I can't imagine.

I get my phone out and look for something, anything, to take my mind away from this madness.

On Twitter I see another Oblique Twirp.

Is something missing?

34

Love on a Real Train

Everything leads to the inevitable.

Every prayer.

Every kiss.

Every tear.

Every curse.

Every smile.

Every little thing we do or say or think leads to the end. Our last day, our last thought, our last breath. It's the one thing everyone can agree upon, that no one can debate.

One day we will die.

And I find myself agreeing with Matthew.

It's a gift to know when.

Eight months.

That's all I have left.

The train rattles, the glow of suburbia outside. I'm heading back into the city, but then again, maybe this train is heading somewhere else.

We assume a lot in life. Assuming tomorrow is a given, assuming that today is assured.

I see a young couple get on and sit a few seats in front of me. They're so immersed and so happy and so beautiful in their love. I hear laughter. Quiet whispers. I see their heads turn into one.

I believe what Matthew said.

That's not why I feel disturbed, distraught.

Why?

That's what I want to know.

Why me?

I see my parents. Kendra and her family. Julie and her sad heart. Laila and her broken soul.

Why now?

The people that I love the most are still not here to embrace or hold on to or even share anything with.

I see the love shown several seats in front of me and I want and need that but know it's gone.

Is that why? Because I'm alone and I'm no longer needed?

I don't buy that.

There has to be another reason.

I shove the thought away, the same way I forced Matthew to go.

I'm on my own here and I've grown used to it, and if I only have eight months left, then it's time to live a little.

PART FOUR

—

Substance

35

Crystal

Stuck in a cottage with two kids under the age of five isn't my idea of living it up.

There's a clock ticking off like an episode of 24 in my mind, even though I can't see the time anywhere. The group finishing dinner is loud, with the door opening and closing every few minutes as people come and go. Officially this is Kendra and Doug's second home, but unofficially it seems like this is a catering service to those with even a tinge of Dutch in their blood. Doug's last name begins with Van, and with that comes a welcome mat that says "come on in if you're blond and frugal and work in the garbage business."

I love joking with Doug about the Dutch, because every stereotype out there is one he claims with authority and exhibits with pride. Tonight is no different, as he works on his third piece of cake.

"You sure you don't want any?"

"No thanks." The beer is my dessert.

Even though today is a holiday, I feel restless. I'd feel better if I could be immersed in labor, rather than celebrating it. I'll be back in Chicago after a three-day weekend that feels like a two-week day care program. I'd never say this to Kendra, but she knows as well as I do that I look and feel out of place.

Kendra is three years younger than me, and got all the cute genes our parents had to offer. She was a full-time nurse before becoming a full-time mom. Now she's active in mothers' groups at her church and teaches part-time in a preschool and she also occasionally does some nursing work when needed. I'm waiting for her to cure some kind of cancer in another five years while I'm off adjusting volume on bass levels.

But in another five years...

"You didn't eat much," Kendra says.

"That's because that's all I've done this weekend."

"We don't have a problem with that, do we?" Doug asks as he proudly holds both hands on his stomach.

Everybody is up here at Gun Lake like always—his brother, and a couple of boys. It's the first time I've been here on Labor Day weekend.

I feel my phone vibrate and I check the message coming in. I'm betting that I'm going to get a call or an e-mail saying that Sean Torrent isn't going to make the studio tomorrow morning for some reason. This e-mail says there's a sale going on at Banana Republic.

"Can you put that phone away for a while?" Kendra asks, as she glances over at me from her designated spot at the sink, cleaning dishes.

"I probably should. But then I'd worry."

"What do you have to worry about?" Doug shouts over the sound of Kaden's three-year-old voice singing. "Some pop star not getting her milk?"

"You have to be careful about these pop stars."

Around my sister, I usually don't talk too much about what I do. I can tell it bores her and Doug, and the last thing I want to do is bore anybody. Even when I've spoken about artists I've met or venues I've gone to, there's been a disconnect. But I guess I'm the same way when she's talking about Kaden playing ball for the first time and I barely muster an appropriately enthusiastic response.

We all live in our little bubbles, and some happen to be filled with diapers and trucks and cartoons named Caillou.

Talk with Doug quickly turns into one of his ten favorite topics: business. Any business, just one that doesn't have to do with the buying and selling of art of any kind. He can talk about selling swimming pools or the car industry or the food industry or any kind of industry except the one I'm in. Now he's talking about tires for some reason, about sales and about a guy who makes this and sells that and I listen long enough to act like I care.

40

The bathroom is an excuse to get away and get a break and check my e-mails. My place has more square footage than this three-bedroom cottage. I go to my room and face the mirror in front of me.

For the first time, I notice that the mirror is warped. It's like one in a funhouse, a distorted kind that makes you look different for amusement's sake.

It wasn't like that before.

My face looks bigger, stretched out, my head the size of a watermelon. My eyes look stretched out and blurry. The rest of my body is narrow and thin.

That mirror wasn't like that before, because I know I looked into it. I've looked into it every morning I've been here and noticed how old I'm looking.

Then I notice the image in front of me changing.

I'm suddenly naked, even though I can see I'm still wearing clothes.

I can see the veins on my legs and arms and on my chest and face and neck. They become a deep red.

The blood is racing through my body, pumping, moving, flowing.

Then I see the cracks coming. Gray and black lines like a puzzle, festering across my body and turning the red bloodlines white.

My face suddenly becomes white and frosted over, like I've fallen asleep outside in Antarctica.

My eyelids are open but my eyes are lifeless.

Then I see the chunks begin to fall, like a tree set on fire and finally blowing away with the gust of wind, the ashes disintegrating into the air until finally there's no image left in the room.

I stare at the mirror, but this time all I see is the room around me.

I touch my arms, my legs, then I touch the mirror.

Even my touch isn't shown.

I hear Kendra's voice calling out for me and gladly go in search of it, hoping she will see what the mirror obviously can't.

"I'm surprised you came out, to be honest."

"Really?"

Kendra and I are standing at the edge of the dock as the sky becomes more orange and red as the sun disappears. The water on the lake is peaceful, lapping against the wood we stand on, soothing.

"I always thought we'd see more of you guys. I mean, more of you."

"You probably would have if I'd stayed part of the 'you guys.'"

"You ever see her?"

I shake my head. "I was just looking at houses in the town she lives in, believe it or not. Wonder what Freud would say about that, huh? But no. She's an hour away in the suburbs. Occasionally something comes up. Usually it's a minor question. We were together long enough to start building a life together."

"Have you seen her children?"

"No."

There's a lone boat riding across the water and I wonder what it'd feel to drive a speedboat that smooth and swift.

"Tyler?"

"Yeah."

"Thanks for coming up."

"No problem."

"Mom told me she enjoyed seeing you."

"Yeah."

"Was it hard to go back home?"

"Good question. I don't know. That word—hard. Sometimes I think I've had it easy my entire life."

"What do you mean?"

"Look at you. I'm exhausted from just watching you with those kids. They're amazing but man, they're a lot of work."

Kendra smiles in a way that reminds me of our mother.

"So what's 'hard' mean? I don't know. I think—I think a lot about Julie and about the way we were and all that crap and I think that the hardest thing I could have done—that we could have done—was to stay together. But we didn't. Time moves on. People change, you know. People grow up. Or at least they get old."

"It was hard for me to see Dad like that."

"I think it was easier for me. Because he wasn't going to say anything. He wasn't going to judge me anymore. But, then again, I think I felt guilty for him *not* being able to say something." I glance at Kendra. "That's crazy, huh?"

40

She only shakes her head.

The luminesce shows the lines around her eyes, the edge of her jaw. For the first time in—maybe the first time in my life—I notice that Kendra isn't the little annoying Kendra, she's a grown woman, a mother. Somehow she's hurdled over me in the race of life. The picture I'm seeing on that pretty face is one of maturity.

"I love this time of day," she says.

We seldom say the things we really mean or want to say. Sometimes grief or anger or passion or alcohol fuel our words. But in the quiet moments, the moments like this, when an opportunity is available, we so often do what I do now.

"Yeah."

My word is lost at sea the moment it's spoken.

36

Time

Turn it up.

Louder.

Louder.

So if I know I'm going to die seven months from now, does that mean I can do anything I want today?

It's not a question of belief. It's a question of responsibility.

What am I supposed to do and why?

It's nice to know that Matthew came to show me a triple-feature horror show about my own demise, yet didn't even offer me a parting postcard that said where I could go to get more information. Everything in this life is a click away from more information. Google has made information immediate and intrigue nonexistent. You can find out anything at any given moment of any day. Yet I don't have a clue what I'm supposed to do, now that I know the date.

So I get ready to continue my day as if. As if I'm still going to live. As if I still have a role to fill and a duty to perform and expectations to meet.

Louder.

I think of Matthew and of the words I said to make him go away.

I think of his last words to me.

"When I am gone I cannot help you anymore. I cannot protect you anymore."

40

This new coffee I just bought is strong and I take one last sip as I look out onto the glorious September morning, wondering what's waiting for me out there.

Wondering what I need to be protected from.

"I would've bet my left ear that he wasn't going to show."

Gavin says this somewhere behind me in the studio. I'm glued to the Mac as I'm tweaking levels on the song. I've spent the last two hours working on one of Nicole Lawson's tracks. We're scheduled for a second recording stint with her in a few months, and there's always something to do once you have songs in place. But when the artist and his voice and the music and the melodies are all MIA, then that's a whole other problem.

"I mean, what are we supposed to do?"

"I tried calling Rick," I tell him.

"And?"

I'm moving the mouse and click on something that sends a blast of bass through the room.

"That's not what I wanted," I say.

"What'd Rick say?"

"His voicemail said that he was quite excited not to speak to me. I left two messages."

"He's probably picking up Sean's body off some floor."

"Let's hope not."

Gavin lets loose with a colorful curse and then heads into the other room. He doesn't mind working twenty-hour days or being told what to do or even dealing with idiosyncratic personalities. But don't waste his time. He's content to drink a pint and watch a game and waste his own time, but he doesn't like it when someone does it for him.

I drown out the music and focus on the vocals of the track I'm listening to.

Maybe I shouldn't be working on anything related to Nicole, but we have nothing to start work on Sean's album. Nothing but the good old "make it like *Blue and Bluer.*"

Nicole Lawson has an edge to her voice, a rough texture that no producer could manipulate. It gives the poppy sound a tinge of character. It comes across best when she's singing in low, soft tones, like the song I'm listening to.

"Do you hear me when I speak, do you realize I'm still weak?" she says in a simple and subtle way that breaks my heart.

When she first performed it, we did the song in one take, and that first take was the one I want to go with.

I can do ten thousand things with this song, but I don't want to do anything. I want to keep it stark, stripped, raw, and real.

Maybe it will be the song to end the album with. Or start.

I can just hear the record people telling me to add a symphony or some beats or to make it a B-side.

B-sides don't exist anymore.

There's a simple guitar playing behind the melody. This is basically like a demo.

I think of something and then get up to find my iPod.

It takes me a couple of minutes to find it.

The last song on the Smiths album *Louder Than Bombs*.

I listen to it and remember the notes well.

It's the perfect ending of an album.

"Hey, Gavin!"

He comes into the room.

"Let's get Floyd in here."

"To sing songs for Sean?"

"No—to do the music for 'Happily Ever After.'"

I connect the iPod into some speakers, and play him the song.

"This is a cure for insomnia," Gavin says.

"Shut up and listen."

"You want people committing bloody suicide at the end of Nicole's album?"

"You're from England. Aren't you *supposed* to like the Smiths?"

"Morrissey just whines. Please. I wish he would get on with it and go to sleep."

"But listen—it's simple, straightforward, yet haunting."

"We can try it."

Even if Gavin doesn't like my ideas, he'll go with them. He's seen it happen enough times where an idea he thinks is crazy works.

"Think about it. You know the songs. This is the perfect end track. But it's not like the swelling zenith of an epic journey. It's anticlimactic. The grand gesture ends more simply. It's a quiet little farewell."

"I don't know, man."

"Any better ideas?"

"Yeah. How about Sean comes in and we start making some music."

"Get Floyd in here. Let's use the Steinway for this."

Somewhere the rest of the world sleeps or parties or prays but I'm the only one left in this studio, surrounded by the glow of orange and red dots. I'm ready to leave when I check my phone. I have a text that came a few minutes ago.

Sorry for the no-show. Let's meet at the Control. Just tell them you're here to see me. I'll be there.

I have Sean's phone number, even though I never use it. I'm surprised he's kept the same number.

I'm surprised he's alive.

I'd tell Gavin, but he left a couple of hours ago. It's a little after one. Floyd came in and did an amazing job on the piano, playing a soft and sweet melody for Nicole's song. I can't wait to play it for her.

When I'm outside and in the cab, giving him the name of a club I've never been to, I feel a bit disoriented.

I start texting a message to Sean but then stop. No need to waste his time saying I'll be there. He knows I'll be there.

Late night meetings are part of the job.

In the cab, the radio plays the '80s song "These Dreams" by Heart.

I'm in the backseat, riding to the Christian school an hour away.

I really want to tell the driver to turn off the song. Not because I hate it, but because I can't *not* think of junior high listening to it.

I'm fourteen again and I'm terrified of the world, yet that's all I want to discover. The big bold world.

The cab pulls in front of a nondescript building that looks abandoned except for some trendy hipsters walking in front of us.

"There's something out there I can't resist," the singer says.

The big bold world.

I pay the cab and get out and go into big bold world.

If only I knew then what I know now.

I often wonder if it would change things. If it would change me.

37

Live and Let Die

I was led to a room upstairs in the club and then almost led through a door. Until some other guy came out and said I couldn't come in.

It's like we're talking about the President or something.

I'm told to wait downstairs and that's what I'm doing.

Waiting.

Waiting while the same beat drones on over and over and over and over with only slight changes to the melody. A trance nightmare, that's what I'm in. A monkey could play better songs. Yet the crowd dancing and mingling don't seem to care. Throw in a riff from (insert latest pop craze superstar name here) and the crowd remains happy.

This is a world I always wanted to be a part of. Honestly. Sounds so superficial and sad to say it, but the allure of the lights and the dancing and the hard bodies and the intoxicating elements always made me feel like I'd arrived. Especially to that fourteen-year-old living in North Carolina who moved to Chicago his junior year of high school. From the first time I stepped foot in a club called Medusas that had teen night, I knew this was a fantasy that I wanted to be a part of.

I know now it's all a puff of smoke, a magic show that you pay to see. That's all it is. The music eventually stops and the lights eventually come back on and you realize that you're not in Ibiza with some supermodel, you're on a Chicago sidewalk with a guy who's craving a burrito.

I'm waiting and probably look bored when the man comes up to me.

"Isn't going to happen tonight," the guy tells me.

Everything about the guy seems cut. His build, his hair, his glance.

"I got a message from Sean saying he wanted to meet me."

"That's all I can say."

I can't tell if the guy in the black pants and dress shirt works here at Control or works for Sean. He doesn't bother to wait for a response as he walks away and vanishes behind a group of girls who look like they're attending an award show.

I stare at my drink and take a sip and think about leaving.

There's nothing else I'm going to do here.

Except maybe look at her.

The girl on the floor dancing in jeans and high heels and some kind of semblance of a top.

She dances alone, even though she's surrounded by a hundred others. She's in her own little silk and secret world and she's something to look at.

When you're in a place this crowded and this covert, it's easy to stare.

I guess I don't realize how long I'm doing that.

"What if you did more than just look?"

I'm wondering if those are lyrics to the song I'm listening to, yet they sound spoken in my ear.

"Dreadful, isn't it?"

I turn to my right where the voice came from but don't see anything.

"The music."

A guy is standing next to me, staring out at the dance floor that's moving in rhythm. He's tall, with a square face often and only seen on models.

"Sometimes I wonder why these places get packed like this."

I nod, but he still isn't looking at me.

The man is wearing jeans and a black dress shirt. When he glances at me, I wonder if I've met him before.

"It's easy to be critical when it's your job," he says, his voice deep and his words spoken in a slow, deliberate manner. He's talking loud in order to be heard over the thumping beats.

"What do you do?"

"I'm a DJ. I actually put thought into the music, as opposed to these juniors."

40

As if on cue, a remixed club version of a Rihanna song begins to play. The guy standing next to me laughs.

"I love when I'm proven right." He chuckles and then probably sees the look on my face. "Don't worry. I don't hit on guys."

"Yeah, okay," I say.

"Club-hopping tonight?"

"I was supposed to meet someone here."

"Someone forces you to come to a place like this on a weeknight and then blows you off?"

"Yeah. Sort of."

"That sums up my night. Does yours involve a woman?"

I shake my head.

"I'm telling you, the easiest explanation to anything in this dramatic life is one word: women. That's a noun, a verb, an adjective, even an expletive. You name it, that one word sums up the life-and-death struggle of men everywhere."

He waits for a response.

"I don't see a ring on your finger."

"There was at one time," I say.

"So you know what I'm talking about. The mythical struggle through-out our life to conquer the one thing that will conquer and kill us. Women." He takes a sip from a short glass and clenches his teeth as if he's drinking battery acid. "It's at least smart to acknowledge our weakness, even if we know that will be the one thing that kills us, am I not right?"

There's something a little too slick about the guy, yet the way he talks doesn't sound like a used car salesmen. It actually sounds interesting.

For a minute I wonder if this guy is with Sean. If the singer wanted me to meet this guy by chance. Because this doesn't seem like just a chance conversation.

The stranger at my side continues talking. "That girl you're looking at, she could solve that look of malaise on your face, then go on to make the next year of your life a living Hell."

I laugh. "I don't need her to do that."

"Sure you do. 'Cause it makes the journey a little more enjoyable."

I glance back at the woman and find her looking at me.

159

I can't help looking away.

"I think she likes you," the man says. "You should go dance with her before this amazing song ends."

"I'll pass."

"When a woman who looks like that gives you that sort of glance, you don't pass."

"Yeah, well, not tonight," I say.

"You pass up opportunities like that every day?"

He waits for a response but gets none.

The beat and the music change and the woman slinks over toward me.

Looking at me.

Coming to me.

She smiles and says hi.

I open my mouth and am about to fumble out something when she passes me by and then hugs the guy I'm talking to.

She's as tall as I am in her shoes. Eyes that seem to glow glance over at me and the expression is friendly, familiar.

"Hi," she says, this time intended for me.

This is supposed to be just an illusion, makeup covering the flaws, the lights covering the imperfections. But this close up, I can't find any. This close up, I'm frozen.

She whispers something in the guy's ear, then moves past him through the crowd.

The guy has a know-it-all grin on his face that I instantly want to wipe off with my knuckles.

"I don't know about you, man, but my night is gonna get better," he says.

Maybe he sees the defeat or the anger in my eyes.

I don't know.

He turns for a moment, then turns back to face me.

"Hey, buddy. You can't care all too much about things. They're not worth it. Especially in places like this."

For a second he looks around to see if anybody is around us listening.

"If you want to hear some real music come to Black Mirror this Saturday. Tell them at the door 'You sell it well.'"

"I what?"

40

"You sell it well."

"Okay."

The guy laughs. "I'm never going to see you again, huh? Quite all right. I hate strangers talking to me too. Just listen. Time has a way, you know, to make it clear. If you want to stop playing dress rehearsal, you know where to find me."

Saying that, he leaves.

Nothing is clear.

And I wonder if this is Matthew playing another one of his games.

Or maybe.

Maybe it's just . . .

38

Sweet Dreams (Are Made of This)

What have you done with your life?

Nothing.

What legacy are you going to leave behind?

None.

What good thing have you done today, or yesterday, or last week, or last month?

Not a damned thing.

The voice chokes in my ear, breathing heavily, the warm air giving me goose bumps, sending a cold shiver down my neck and my shoulder.

I stand at a corner of an intersection, looking across and seeing the man. I'm talking but I'm not. Every unspoken thought is answered by another voice, unshared.

Who are you?

I've seen every step you've taken and every mistake you've made and every failure you've felt. I'm the shadow of your shadow and the echo of your echo. I am the lie convincing you of the truth.

Snow streaks sideways, yet I feel hot. I can't tell if I'm a child again or if this is the current day.

Everything feels like a slow-motion replay.

Again.

Again.

The figure smiles and I recognize him.

That look like he wants to break me. The disheveled hair blowing in the wind. The unmoving posture.

What if I wanted to change?

It's too late to change, too late in the game. It's already finished, game over.

I breathe out and see my breath linger like a smoke bomb.

What if I tried?

You will fail.

I put a hand on my face and feel how cold and hard and icy it feels.

There's still time.

That's because your God has decided your time is up.

There's still time.

To do all the things you've been holding back on, Tyler. To do more than just imagine. To do more than just dream.

"What do you want?" I hear a voice that sounds like mine yell.

You make me laugh.

"Tell me what you want."

To watch your anger take hold.

"Take hold of what?"

Then a snowy burst clouds the path across the street, and he's gone, the street is gone, this whole image is gone.

I find myself in my condo in real life and real time.

"You don't have to pay money for a shrink to tell you why you're having these nightmares."

It's day two of the Sean Torrent recording sessions, and it's been the second no-show by the musician. Gavin and I are having a late meal—I don't know if I'd call it dinner or what—at a Mexican restaurant, and I've just finished telling him about the nightmare I had last night.

I've skipped telling him about the nightmares I lived out with Matthew.

"So what would you tell me?" I ask.

"Combination of things. Stress, of course."

"Who says I'm stressed?"

"You were stressed about these recording sessions even before they *didn't* start happening."

"Sure."

"Combine that with a whole lot of things. Your father. Laila disappearing."

"She's been gone for a year and a half."

"Yeah? Well, she still shows up on your face."

"I don't think a counselor would be talking with a mouth full of tacos."

"Nice one. That's what you get when it's free."

"Okay."

"Seriously, mate. Look at you. You've got the family thing with your father. Things on the relationship front. Things on the work front. And financial front."

"And my engineer thinks he knows more than I do," I add.

"Your engineer does know more than you do, and he allows you to bask in his amazing talent and ability like every great producer has over time. He could just tell you to get stuffed."

"Think I need a vacation or something?"

"Yeah, soon as we deliver an album to the studio."

"That might be never."

"Exactly. Hello nightmares."

"This just felt so real."

"They always do." Gavin tosses the bundled up napkin on his plate as if he's already feeling the heartburn that is going to come in the morning. "You know, I had this roommate in college that told me a bizarre story about dreams."

"Your dreams?"

"No. His dreams. He told me this one night when we were both pissed drunk. He probably didn't even remember telling me. He said he used to go to this really strict church. Sometime in high school, this guy started having nightmares. Like night after night. About being chased."

"Most nightmares are about being chased," I say.

"Yeah, I know. I think I told him that too. But he said these were epic dreams, the kind of story that would stop when he woke up and then start back at the same place the next night. Like some television show. He knew what the man looked like who was chasing him. It was always the same bloke too. He'd wake up out of his mind. Sometimes sleepwalking, sometimes doing other weird stuff. So his parents took him to the pastor."

"Why the pastor?"

Gavin shrugs. "Guess they thought it would help him. So he goes with his parents and tells the pastor and this pastor tells him like the bloodiest thing you could tell a kid. He told him that sometimes demons haunted you in your dreams. That sometimes they would literally *go* inside your dreams to terrorize you. The pastor told this kid that that was the first step toward possession."

"No."

"He was off his trolley when he was telling me this. But this pastor told him that he was in danger of losing his soul and stuff." Gavin curses and laughs. "You know me, I don't think we have souls."

"You are pretty soulless."

"So I'm mocking this kid. But he wasn't laughing. He was almost in tears telling me this."

"So what happened?"

"He said the pastor prayed over him and that was it."

"The nightmares went away?"

Gavin shakes his head, his face taut, his eyes unmoving. "That was it as far as the pastor was concerned. But the nightmares—they continued."

"That's a nice story," I joke.

"This roommate of mine tells me this, then adds this as he's looking into the woods we were nearby. He's looking into them as if he's being watched. I'll never forget what he said. He goes on about the fact that we're not alone, that we might think we are but we're not. Then he looks me in the eyes with a completely straight face and says, 'He still comes to visit me.' It was like the scariest bonfire story ever, except this guy wasn't trying to scare me."

"What happened to him?"

Gavin doesn't say anything at first.

"What?" I ask.

"A few years out of college, I heard the guy hung himself."

39

Shout

Hey buddy, you probably should've taken Ashland."

The short driver with the Bluetooth snaggled over his ear ignores me and keeps moving his mouth as if he's talking, though I can't hear anything. This is the problem with taking a cab. You have no control over which direction he goes. Once when I was heading to a concert during the height of rush hour, my driver got stuck in a gridlock mess, forcing me to get out and go by foot.

I'm not sure where this guy is going, especially at this time of night. Instead of getting off the Kennedy at Division, we got off on North. Now we're passing Damen and heading toward Western.

"Hey man, I'm close to Ashland and Division. We're going the wrong way."

He turns his head and slits for eyes glance back at me.

"It's okay, just—you can stop here."

The cab accelerates and pushes me back in the seat. I curse and tell the guy to stop the car and let me out. The driver turns his head and smiles.

He has black eyes.

Come on, not now.

The car continues speeding and I try the door but it's locked. Not like I'm going to climb out, not at this speed. We're going sixty—seventy— eighty miles an hour.

I see the blur of lights. A car passing, another veering off to the side, the

40

honk of a horn, the glow of lights above us turning red, the screech somewhere beside me.

We're in Logan Square and it's moving past me like a horror movie shown in 3D.

I'm shouting now, screaming, saying things that are just stuck somewhere deep inside of me like tools buried in a crawl space brought out only in the darkest of moments. I'm banging on the plastic window between us that seems bulletproof. I punch and jam and slam with my palm, but the driver keeps accelerating.

I move back in my seat, writhing around to get my foot up. I kick out at the muted cloud of a covering. Again. Again.

Nothing.

I try the door handle again. My stomach feels like it's a mile away, my head dizzy, my eyes playing dot-to-dot with the lights and the sights and the visions spinning by.

Get out. Get out of here, get out.

I hear laughter.

Not from the front of the car but from above me and next to me like the most glorious demonstration of THX sound equipment ever. A hellish sickly wet laugh that cackles.

The intersection in front of us is a cascade of vehicles barricading our progress, a moving fence of nightcrawlers and cabs.

The cab accelerates.

This is really happening.

I don't have my seat belt on either.

I glance around quickly.

This little box. This little tiny space. This little tiny black dirty spot.

Then I curl up behind the wall in front of me and I brace for impact.

Something rips behind me, then in front, then in half. I see the door beside me turn into the shape of a shark attacking and I'm out.

You're going to be okay.
    Just don't move okay?
    Are you like the barren fig tree?
    Make a sudden, destructive unpredictable action; incorporate.

Always give yourself credit for having more than personality.
This isn't happening.
Yes it is.
Don't leave.
I can't stay.
There's a place for you here now, right here.
You're going to be okay, just stay still.

A doctor comes to me, dressed in white in a white room holding a white phone and tells me I have one last call.

"One last call for what?"

"One last call, Tyler Harrison."

"What happened to me?"

"You almost died."

"But I didn't."

"Your guardian angel was working overtime."

"I think he took the night off."

"One last call, Tyler."

"For what?"

"You know."

40

Death and All His Friends

Aman almost dying should be able to call his spouse or his loved one. Maybe a family member.

I call Cole.

He doesn't quite get the fact that I almost died.

I guess if a hospital releases you the morning after a multiple car crash, the truth is that you didn't nearly die.

That should mean that yes, your guardian angel is working overtime.

But what if his absence meant that the accident happened in the first place?

"Listen to this, it's awesome. Just downloaded it last night."

Something is wrong with this picture as I get into the car—the same kind of thing *that almost killed me last night* and Cole is playing the latest album he downloaded from Hot Chip.

All I got from him was the customary "What happened," accompanied with some jokes about cabdrivers that are both racist and inappropriate for someone *who almost died via a cabdriver.*

I think in the real world or normal world, people would come by with breadbaskets, ready to hold your hand and ask how you're doing. But Cole—he gets in several car crashes daily on his wonderful Xbox or whatever system he's playing. Why should reality and fantasy be any different when they're seldom not?

"You hungry?" he asks.

I'm thinking of replying with a "Yeah, I'm hungry, because *death* really makes me hungry, a four car pileup at North and Kedzie makes me really freaking hungry, so stop and let's eat some eggs."

But I don't, because you know, Cole came without questions. Granted, he has no job, but he still came and he's still there and he's still asking me about breakfast.

"Yeah, sure," I say.

I think death does make you kinda hungry.

"So the driver died?" Cole eventually asks over huevos loaded with lots of salsa.

"Yeah."

"What was up with him?"

I shake my head. "I've had some crazy cabdrivers, but this guy was whacked."

"That's why I walk everywhere."

"You walk everywhere to save money."

"So the cops came and talked to you."

"Yeah. They kept saying I was lucky. I think I heard that a hundred times today."

"Uh huh." Cole looks skeptical.

"What?"

"Personally, I think you're unlucky."

"Why?"

There's little expression on his square face. "Of all the cabs you could get into in Chicago, you get into that one? What are the odds? I've ridden in ten thousand cabs and never had anything like that happen."

"Good perspective. Maybe a tad dire."

I'm the kind of person who needs to reply or round out a conversation, but not Cole. He's already moved on from the conversation.

Later on, in silence, I wonder.

What if Cole was right?

The clouds shuffle above me like pieces in a puzzle as I lie on a lawn chair, staring upward.

The stuff going on in my head feels as full as the scene I'm seeing.

I have a headache from all the thoughts.

"Keep quiet," the song Cole played me goes.

It rumbles. Deep inside. This restlessness. This foreboding. This unease.

"Keep quiet."

What if I was left alone to fend it off for myself? To fend off whatever it is for myself?

You know who and what it is.

Were all those things that Matthew showed me a sign of his intervention? What if he won't intervene anymore?

Yet he told me when I'm going to die.

Think death is worse than surviving what you just lived through?

I don't know.

"Keep quiet."

Is Hell death or is it living through death day after day after day?

Matthew, where'd you go?

A man died for what? For what reason?

Gray and white ice cream in a sea of blue move endlessly above me.

I'm cold.

Protect from what?

"Keep . . . quiet."

41

Stayin' Alive

I start making a list of songs I'd like to be played at my funeral.

I know, that's probably kind of morbid to start thinking that way, but how can I not? What am I supposed to do? Huh? I don't know. Outside of work on Nicole Lawson's album and waiting to hear from Sean Torrent, I can't seem to do much of anything, so I'm doing what I do best—thinking of music.

I figure that in the course of a funeral—with the service and the whole bit by the grave and then the reception afterwards—one might be able to fit in 100 songs. Maybe that's way too many, but I don't want anybody to have to hear the same track twice. Nor do I want some aspiring DJ to start adding his own songs like they always do at a wedding.

This is going to be my funeral, so let it be done my way, okay?

I'm not going to list them in any order. I don't have that much time on my hands.

But the one that first pops up in my mind is a classic.

The first song to start the playlist for the dead: "Stayin' Alive" by the Bee Gees.

Tell me people wouldn't stop and look at their spouses and fight the grin on their faces if they heard that at a funeral?

Come on.

You're walking into a church and you hear Barry Gibb singing "Ah ah ah ah Stayin' Alive."

40

How awesome would that be at a funeral?

That's what I want. I want smiles. I want uplifting music, the kind people normally hear on the radio or at a wedding.

I want people to feel like dancing when they come to remember me.

They don't have to know the truth. They don't have to understand how it all went down. I still don't know how it's all going to go down. Or *if* it's going to go down.

In the end, I want dancing. I plan to dance a lot myself before that day comes.

Think I'm crazy? Maybe.

I might be crazy.

But I also know the future.

I know—and somehow I believe this—that it's my time to go.

But I still have some time left. Just a little. I'm hoping I learn something more than pain and fear. I'm hoping I learn about miracles. I'm hoping I learn about hope.

The music and the dancing I've got down.

It's the hope that I still have to learn.

It's been eight days since the sessions with Sean Torrent were supposed to begin. Eight days of no-shows and conversations with the label and with managers and with managers of managers. Eight days of groveling to Rick MacLellan. Eight days of waiting and wondering and watching the sun rise and set. Eight days of not having a clue what to do about Sean.

Maybe he's off somewhere with Matthew.

The official word given to me was that Sean came down with a virus. To which Gavin said, "Yeah, the kind that comes from sticking a needle in your arm."

Of course, Gavin and I don't know if that's exactly the problem.

We've spent some valuable time looking online for any good gossip.

There are rumors of some woman that Sean's been involved with, and the two have been seen around Chicago.

"What if he's skipping the recording sessions because of love?" I asked Gavin.

"Yeah, I know what he loves."

There's no convincing Gavin about anything else.

So when I get the text that Thursday evening, I think it's my engineer playing a trick on me.

You home? If so let me in.

It's from Sean's phone. The same one that led me to the club a week ago, only to end up waiting. The same one that never seems to answer or be on when I try it.

I go downstairs to the gate and, just like any regular person, there he is.

Sean Torrent stands there in jeans, a T-shirt, a cap, and sunglasses. He smiles like the prodigal son come home.

"How'd you know where I live?"

"It's not that difficult to find out," he says in a raspy voice.

I open the door and before I know it he's giving me a big bear hug. Except he's more like the skeleton of that big bear.

"Man, it's good to see you."

"Yeah, you too," I say.

His gaunt face says it all. It's like looking at a child's Happy Birthday balloon that's half deflated.

"Let me check out the place you call home, all right? No kiddies running around, huh?"

"No. It's just me."

"Excellent."

Sean looks behind him as if there might be someone.

I'm wanting to know where he's been and what he's been doing.

A part of me fears that there's a reason he's looking behind him.

A reason that I don't want anything to do with.

But I've learned over the years that questions like this will get answered. Artists eventually open up and talk. You just have to be there when they do.

"I got some songs you have to listen to."

No apology, no explanation, nothing. He acts like a teenager about ready to head out the door to the prom. Unfortunately, he looks more like a con just released from prison.

I still can't believe he's sitting there, right there, on my couch.

A part of me is afraid he's going to start singing a cappella.

40

"Here." Sean gives me an iPod to plug in. "They're just demos. A couple I even did in my hotel room. Rough stuff, but they're songs. They're melodies. Best stuff I've written in a long time, too. Just—scroll to new songs—there're a bunch in there."

Didn't we already have the preproduction meeting where we heard his demos? Like a month and a half ago?

I fight the urge to ask him if these are the same songs. I'll learn soon enough. I can feel his eyes watching me as I try to find the songs. I stick the iPod in the speakers and wonder what in the world I'm about to hear.

"Turn it up."

Artists are an interesting breed. They're unpredictable, unstable, sometimes unlikable. But the reason we put up with all of that is because of this.

The art.

A simple drum machine starts with a simple beat. Then what sounds like a piano.

Then Sean begins to sing, sounding like he's on stage somewhere.

"Yeah—we recorded that at the Chicago Theater."

He's a man on fire, singing about lost love and about anger and about loss and death.

He howls and I feel a wave flow through me.

I glance at him and he's still grinning. I can't help but do the same.

Is this what you've been up to?

The first demos I heard in that initial meeting were good, but these are intoxicating.

"It's rough, you know, but you get the point."

The point.

The almighty point.

Life and death. That's the point. That should be the point of any good piece of art.

"What was that song called?" I ask, as it goes off.

"They're all untitled. I'm living the lyrics. Every day, man."

I pause before we go to the next song.

I'm not ready for this. There should've been some warning, some kind of buffer, some kind of space between me lounging around watching ESPN and then suddenly listening to Sean Torrent demos.

"Keep listening," he says.

"How many songs do you have on here?"

He shrugs. Even though he doesn't appear particularly healthy, he's still got a mischievous look about him, a ruggedly handsome look that clashes with some of the pretty boys out there. His hair is long and messy in a haven't-taken-a-shower-in-days way. Sean can pull it off.

"Twenty. Maybe more."

"Twenty songs."

"Yeah?"

"Maybe we should wait to listen to them all."

"You mean you haven't been waiting enough?" His laugh echoes around the walls of the condo.

"I feel like I need to get in a better frame of mind."

"That's the point. I want you to react when you haven't had time to think and process and all that. Like the rest of the world. Man, those studios make someone lose their soul. You stop hearing things. What'd you think of that song?"

"Amazing."

"Seriously."

"I'm being serious," I say. "*That* surprised me."

"So what? So you think you need to be in a better frame of mind or something? How many gin-and-tonics have you had?"

"It's not that."

"Let's listen. Come on. If six of the songs work, I'll be surprised. They might be all crap after that. Maybe I blew it all on that track."

"I doubt that."

"Come on. Press *play*. Sit back and listen. Then let's talk about stayin' alive in this deadly business."

42

A Day in the Life

How have you been?" Laila asks.

Her words are as real as the car I sit in, the vehicles surrounding us, the forest we're parked in front of. I feel a brush of warm air glide in through the open window. Everything is real. Her eyes are real and I feel as if they're really, truly there right next to me. She can put her hand on my beating heart and feel that it still beats for her.

Feelings don't always equate to reality, however.

"Confused," I say.

"Don't be."

"Are you okay?"

I've forgotten the time and the place. What year am I living in? Where are we right now?

"You're going to be okay," she says, ignoring my question.

That was the most beautiful thing about Laila, the way she always made me feel okay, even when both of our lives gave no hope whatsoever that it was okay. It was better because she was there telling me so.

It feels like we're hovering in this cloudy car, in this echoing room.

I know it can't be real, because it's been a couple of years since I've seen her. And a year and a half since I discovered that she had left Chicago.

Yet Laila looks and smells and sounds and feels the same.

She takes my hand. "You'll be okay."

Maybe she'll always be this way. In the deep recesses of my dreams, the kind that confront me at the strangest of times, the kind that surprise again and again, she'll be there.

The e-mail awaits as if the sender knew I needed a bit of hope on this September morning.

```
Hey Tyler.
    Looking forward to our next recording ses-
sion! I've been working on a few more songs that
I think you'll love.
    Just wanted to let you know that I prayed for
you this morning. Hoping that your day is good,
productive, and encouraging.
    Peace.
    Nic
```

From anybody else, I'd probably not only be annoyed but offended.

I prayed for you.

It reminds me of my parents praying for me. As if every time they told me they were praying for me was a reminder of why I needed prayer. "You're in our prayers because you're such a sinner, son," seemed to be the message.

Yet with Nicole, I can't feel any irritation.

Nothing about her is forced or phony. I'm sure that she did happen to pray for me today.

Maybe God will hear those prayers.

I'm beginning to think I need a lot of them.

"We should bring in a really heavy beat, an Alan Moulder, 'Bullet with Butterfly Wings,' sort of propulsive bass in the background."

"Yeah, that would be great," Sean says as we finish listening to the demo.

It's been several days of working in the studio, and we're making incredible progress. Whatever was going on with Sean is done or at least is held at bay momentarily. He's been there as long as Gavin and I have been,

40

doing his part, suggesting ideas and sharing his vision, and working with focus.

This is the fun part, the very beginning. When we're just starting to build and create something. The options are endless. This is when musical history and knowledge help out a lot.

Alan Moulder is a famous producer and mixer with a certain sound he brings to groups like Nine Inch Nails and the Smashing Pumpkins. He also happens to be married to Toni Halliday, the lead singer of Curve, a group from the '90s with a unique sound of electronica and rock, blended with Toni's haunting voice.

Sean knows where I'm going with this, because the song works on that level.

So far, he hasn't said the word "blue" once.

I respect him for not going there.

It's almost like he doesn't want to jinx things.

I hear Sean making a joke and Gavin laughing.

It's nice to see that progress is being made.

There's a long way to go, but we're starting something.

Maybe those prayers of Nicole's are working out.

"Let's go somewhere crazy tonight," Sean tells me.

"Like where?"

It's nine on a Friday and the Chicago night is just starting.

"I don't know Chicago. You tell me."

I think of the last time I went out. It was to meet up with Sean, the night I went to the club, the night I met the guy who said he was a DJ.

What was the name of the club the DJ gave me?

He shouts toward the other room and Gavin answers with a "you won't like the places I frequent."

"So Tyler, what do you say?"

"There's a place called Black Mirror—never been there but I met the DJ."

"Don't worry about getting in," he says.

"Well, yeah. Just don't know how decent the place is."

Sean's already on his iPhone, looking it up.

"I think we've worked hard enough this week."

"Lots more to do," I say.

"Let's go celebrate."

"What are we celebrating?"

"Temporary equilibrium."

43

In Your Eyes

Few things in life surprise me anymore. Maybe that's a sign of getting older. Maybe that is what constitutes wisdom, losing that wide-eyed wonder you held as a child, that naivety you held onto until surprise after surprise burst the bright bubble.

But as I walk into the murkiness of the club, the song playing surprises me.

Not that Moby has never been played before at a club. Moby became a household name in places like this. But it's the song that surprises me. I'm not sure I've ever heard "Alone" anywhere other than on my computer and maybe stuck in the background of some moody scene in a movie. It's a striking change from hearing another Beyoncé remix or some endless trance rant.

It also fits where I'm walking into.

This is a club, sure.

But it's not like any club I've ever been to.

First off, there's no dance floor, at least none that I can see. Nor is there some giant bar with four bartenders working the crowd.

The first thing I see, and I see a lot of them, are stairs.

Stairs straight ahead of me, heading down into some dark tomb.

A set of stairs to my left. Another set to my right. Actually, two on my right.

Sean curses when he asks what this place is.

Scattered throughout the large room are an assortment of seating areas. All different in a soft glowing color, like a high-end furniture store with a variety of couches. I can't see anybody's faces because it's too dark in here. But I see shapes and shadows. Groups of four and five, couples on love seats.

I don't even know if the DJ I met the other night is working. I was ready to use my code words on the doorman, but Sean beat me to it. My one moment of being cool this year, ruined. Sean talked to the doorman and they let us in, not that there was some long line or anything. There wasn't much of anything except a door with the word **Exit** marked on it. I'm following Sean, who slows down by the stairs going down.

"This place is trippy," he tells me.

"No joke."

"You see a bar?"

I see a couple of women carrying drinks, but they don't look like servers. It takes me a few minutes to realize they're exactly that. They don't carry trays, they're dressed in business suits or skirts, and they never exchange money. I can tell they're servers because they bring drinks to a group sitting on one of the sets of couches, and then they smile and walk away.

"We have to sit in order to get one?"

Sean shakes his head as the song changes to another favorite I'd select: a brooding mix of Dave Gahan's "Kingdom."

"Let's go downstairs."

Before I can go, a woman as tall as me walks up in a black suit with a white button-down shirt and says hello. I hesitate and wait for her to ask what I want to drink, but she doesn't.

Sean's head has already disappeared down into the dark.

"Hello," I reply.

"You look lost."

Staring at her, I am. "A little."

"You can't get lost in here. Only found."

I keep waiting for her to ask if I want anything.

Will she take my drink order or is she a patron like anybody else?

"I can't read minds, you know," her dark lips say.

"Is there a DJ who works here?"

"That's what you want to ask me?"

40

"Well—I was wondering."

"Yes, Ellis is here."

It's the first time I've heard his name. "Do you know where?"

"Around."

She walks off, and I still don't know if she wanted to take my order or if she wanted something else.

Some of these ladies—the ones dressed up in business attire—are sitting with men. Some bring a drink and then sit down.

I head downstairs, not sure where in the world we are.

Maybe the gregarious DJ from the other night can explain how things work around here.

I see a man across the bar who probably looks a lot like I do: confused and tired and a little out of place. Thankfully there's a bar where I can do something other than look like that poor schmuck. But when I put the drink up to my lips I realize that poor schmuck is me in the mirror.

God I look awful. I look old.

Maybe the woman upstairs was wondering where I'd wandered in from.

Maybe I'm wondering that myself.

The drink tastes good. I wonder where Sean disappeared to.

The music down here is different. It's instrumental, hypnotic, a dark electronica. Not something you dance to.

The vibe is different down here too.

If the upstairs resembled a room lit by candle, this one looks lit by lava lamps. Colors leak down the walls surrounding me, casting off the only glimmers of light here. The light plays tricks. One minute the bartender looks like a woman, next he's shown to be a man. Mirrors are everywhere, from the floor to the ceiling, to give you an effect as if you're out in space. I can understand now the name of this club.

I see people shuffling, but they seem far away in another world.

Sean Torrent is nowhere to be found.

I check my phone but see nothing.

I've heard this melody before. Another movie maybe. Maybe a television commercial. I have this song somewhere amidst the other forty thousand that I have on my computer.

What am I doing here?

I begin to feel it again.

The uncertainty.

There's ten thousand ways a man might die.

What's going to be mine?

Sip.

There must be a reason I was told.

Sip.

There must be a reason I know.

Sip.

There must be a reason I don't doubt, but I'd rather remain indifferent.

Finish and order another.

Why, Matthew? Why?

I wait for Sean.

I wonder if I was told in order to warn me.

Repent and be saved.

But Matthew told me where I was headed.

Did he? Did he confirm that you're going up and not down?

Maybe that's not the point.

I see a woman pass by and let her stare linger and I wonder what the point of anything is anymore.

I feel my heart beat.

For how long?

I glance away and glance back in the mirror and don't like the face I see.

That guy is a middleman in the middle of his life who has managed to stay in the middle of the pack in the middle of the fray in the middle of everything. One foot in and one foot out. Straddling the line. Middle-marching his way toward eternity.

What a waste, the face tells me. *What a waste.*

I feel a tug and turn, expecting to see Sean.

Instead, it's the man I met the other night.

"You ventured out." Ellis shakes my hand.

"I tried," I reply.

He orders me another drink, which is pushing it, considering my lack of dinner.

40

"I'm Tyler," I say, not sure if I introduced myself officially.

"Alone?" he asks.

"Didn't come in alone. Not sure where he went."

The song changes and he smiles.

"You working tonight?" I ask.

"Never stop."

"Good stuff." I listen for a minute. "Global Communication?"

"Name the track and the rest of the night the drinks are on me."

I don't bother answering. "All the songs on that album are lengths of time. Like 8:21."

"So, guess."

"9:47," I say, knowing it's totally made up.

"14:31. Though I stop a little earlier, to keep the masses from going restless."

"Where do you actually DJ?"

He smiles and I notice how flawless his complexion is in the glow against his jaw. It's a stark contrast to the face I was just looking at, the haggard portrait staring back at me. The guy is probably ten years younger than I am.

"This is a bit of an unconventional place. There is no DJ booth. No dance floor. This is the only actual bar you'll see, and it's more for decoration than anything else."

Maybe that's why I'm the only one sitting at it.

"I can change a song in an instant. Remote control and wireless are beautiful things."

"And both rooms—"

"You haven't been upstairs, have you?"

I shake my head.

"Maybe next time. Take it in slowly. It's always better that way."

"There's music upstairs?"

"There's music everywhere," Ellis says. "The soundtrack never stops."

There's a natural confidence about the way he speaks and moves and looks at me. For some reason, however, I get weird vibes when I'm around him. As if we're part of some David Lynch movie that's just starting.

Or maybe that's because I'm living that movie and he's another actor showing up on screen.

He reaches in his pocket and produces a small phone. He reads the text message, then calmly nods at me. "The drama never stops either. I need to step away for a moment."

"Sure."

"Please let me know if there is anything you need. Anything."

The way he says that last word.

Anything.

Anything.

I'm expecting the hypnotic piano chords of "Tubular Bells" by Mike Oldfield to start playing, the kind made famous in *The Exorcist.*

My imagination is on Red Bull.

I think of those women upstairs. The stairways. The glance. *"That's what you want to ask me?"* The closed conversations. The dim lights.

And the fact that Sean Torrent is missing.

I try texting him again. But after a half hour of waiting and walking around, I realize that he's nowhere to be found.

He doesn't want to be found.

What is this place?

The eclectic music journey continues. Jon Hopkins.

I'm about ready to leave, when a blast of exotic dread fills the place.

Nobody seems to notice except me.

It's Peter Gabriel.

But most clubs, if they'd ever venture into anything from Peter Gabriel, they'd do a hideous remix of "Big Time" or "Sledgehammer."

This is from his album *Passion*, the soundtrack to *The Last Temptation of Christ.*

On a dozen speakers in a large room, the song frightens me.

I feel like I'm being watched, I'm being monitored.

My iPod has been snatched and I'm tugged out, mocked.

Where is he? Where is Matthew? He's going to come out any minute now. Any minute.

But he remains absent. So does Sean. Even my new friend, Ellis, if that's his name, is nowhere around.

All that's left is that guy in the mirror, looking at me. Looking at me with questioning, haunting, piercing eyes.

44

Duchess

At home, much later, I can't sleep. All I can do is press *play*.

This restlessness has been there as long as I can remember.

I've prayed for peace. Yet peace is and has remained a stranger.

The only peace comes in pieces of songs. The majesty, the mystery, and the melancholy of music.

This will sound crazy, but it's like the music understands me. And I understand the music.

It speaks when others can't ever begin to even try. It lifts me up and motivates. It evaporates those dark clouds and the stench of defeat. It rubs out the knots and soothes in the salve.

It comforts.

Sometimes I think I'll forever be fourteen. I'll forever be forgotten. I'll forever be in this lost fog, searching and groping and wandering.

Even my own guardian angel has deserted me.

I'm almost forty now, but I'm still in the fog.

The world whispers. *Just another step.* So I take one. Yet I'm only more lost. *Just another.* I remain let down. *Just another.* I let myself down.

Music understands when the others don't. Music is my wife and my queen.

This mood, this broken and disturbed morning, this stilted noon, the split night.

Just another.

I search and remain disappointed.

But music doesn't disappoint.

45

The Thinner the Air

Your father is back in the hospital."

And so it begins.

Just as September rolls over into another month, I find the nightmare slipping out of my mind and my night to become front and center in the daytime.

It's right on cue with this call.

"He's gotten worse."

Just like my life.

"There's nothing we can do but pray."

But Mom doesn't know that I can't even do that, because I sent away an angel.

"I'm doing okay," Mom says.

But all I'm really thinking about is myself.

Woe is me.

Woe is right.

"I'll let you know how things go."

I say *thanks*, but I don't really want to know. I've got enough I'm dealing with. Of course I don't say that, because that sounds cheap and selfish and ridiculous and I'd never say something to sound like that.

Only God knows I'm that way, deep down inside. And I already know I've disappointed Him.

40

Two men bark and curse in a nondescript office. You're there but really not. You're hovering over the proceedings, and your life has suddenly gone from first person to second. You're not an "I" anymore because you're not really there. You're somewhere else in spirit. Perhaps your body is there and your mind is there and your mouth can open and mumble some apologies, but you're not there and haven't been for some time.

"Where'd he go?"

Pluto, you think, exactly where you're headed after this.

"Is Sean even in Chicago?"

Sean who? you think, wondering about the guy you last saw going down the stairs of some club you brought him to.

"So where'd you see him last?"

Of course you don't say, because then the blame would go onto you.

A producer's job is not only to provide creative direction, but also to help manage the artist, while being a liaison between the artist and label.

"This is a trainwreck, and you know who's responsible?"

They're just voices talking to you.

You're a kid in trouble and holier-than-thou is talking to you, telling you where you're heading if you don't stop.

You're a teen and the principal is telling you what kind of mess you're in.

You're a student and the dean of students is asking you what your point is in attending a school like theirs.

"This is a hell of a mess," he says.

And yes, you know.

You know about Hell very well. No need to tell you about it.

"There is nothing worth salvaging about the first sessions."

You want to say that you weren't ready, that Sean Torrent wasn't ready, to blame it on these men and on Sean and the rest of the world. But you do something you're incredibly good at.

"I take responsibility and I apologize," you say.

One of them curses. "He didn't give you any signs? Any warning?"

"He's probably in Aruba by now," the other says, with another curse.

You want to tell them how strong the demos are and how it can be something special, but you doubt it.

You doubt it because you believe that this is your fault.

"I'll try to get him back," you say.

"Back from where? Back for what?"

These guys aren't exactly optimistic.

The day and age for being patient with artists has gone by the wayside. Bad economy and bad industry equals bad mojo.

"This is just a hiccup," you say.

You realize that April is approaching very quickly.

"They didn't like the new direction."

Nicole doesn't understand, and it's going to be hard to explain over the phone something that I don't get myself.

I'm dealing with the worst artistic trainwreck of my life with the Sean Torrent sessions. Yet meanwhile I have to explain to Nicole Lawson what another record label thought of the first batch of her songs.

"They didn't like any of them?"

"They wanted them American Idolized," I say. "They want something…"

"Something what?"

I sigh. No need to beat around the bush. "They want the generic bland crap that every other artist is churning out."

"They said that?"

"Of course not. They use music speak to basically say that."

"What are we supposed to do?"

"It's up to you. Up to us. Eventually we need to deliver to them a record that they will decide to release or not."

"What if they don't release it?"

"Worse things can happen. There's always the case of an album being shelved that then goes on to some acclaim. Look at Wilco's *Yankee Hotel Foxtrot*.

"I'm not exactly a Wilco. I'm in another universe."

"We don't have to make any decisions now, today. We've got another month to think about things."

"What do you think?" she asks me.

40

I want to tell her what I think of music labels and industry folk, but I hold back.

"I'm just wondering about your fans," I say. "What do you think they'd do?"

"They're not twelve years old. At least not all of them."

The sound of her laugh is an antidote to the profanity-laced conversations I've had the last couple of days.

"If you think your fans will join you down this journey, then I say we continue."

"My hope is to gain new fans."

"Mine too."

"Think that can happen? Honestly? Are the songs strong enough? Is the delivery good enough?"

I think for a minute, staring outside the sliding glass door to the condo building across the street from mine.

"You know that when Radiohead first came out and had their runaway hit, 'Creep,' I didn't like them. Even when *The Bends* came out, I ignored it. *Because* of their hit. Then *OK Computer* came out and changed everything. That album blew up my expectations and opinions. It singlehandedly silenced them. I eventually got their earlier albums, as well as taking the journey down their crazy musical road. But that's the thing. Nobody knows. None of us knows exactly what's going to work and what's not going to work."

"You're talking about one of the greatest albums ever made."

"I'm talking about a band making music and singing songs in a studio. Just like we're doing. Just like a thousand others are doing right now. Nobody knows what's going to work. But if you try to repeat success, I think you'll fail. If you copy and paste, I think you've already waved the white flag. You wanted me to come in for what? To create the same album you just did?"

"I want my own *OK Computer*."

"Then you don't need to think anymore. We keep on this path. And when the songs are all there, we overwhelm them."

"What if they remain unimpressed?"

It's a question I don't have an answer for.

"Make this album like it's the last one you're ever going to make," I say.

"Put everything you can into it. All I can do—all I can promise—is that I'll do the same."

What if?

I've lived enough years avoiding this question.

But lately, it's beginning to squeeze through the surfaces and starting to suffocate.

What if.

A hundred thousand what ifs.

If you float around in an ocean full of them, you'll die on your little raft.

The people who do best in life are those who ignore the what ifs and move on.

Do you really believe that?

Switch to mute. Change the channel. Click the track.

It's not that easy.

The what ifs of today and yesterday start morphing into the what ifs from last year and last century.

Who are you trying to be? Have you already raised the white flag yourself?

I look at the warning of the late payment on my boat. I know that in a few months it won't be just a warning.

Do I even care? Do I worry about Nicole's new album? Do I try to find Sean?

What am I supposed to do now?

I'm up on my roof, feeling the slight chill of night. I'm staring at the familiar skyline and I know I should be somewhere else.

I just don't know where.

I don't know who I'm supposed to be anymore.

The what ifs drift around me like embers from a smoldering bonfire.

I need to leave this all behind and do something and go somewhere and escape.

You're good at that, aren't you? But not this time, not this time.

I need an outlet.

I check my phone for e-mails or voicemails or signs of life.

The only thing I see is a friend request on Facebook.

40

It's from DJELLIS.
With a touch of my thumb, we're friends.
Life in this modern era is so easy.
So easy and so phony and so utterly ridiculous.
Nothing has any substance anymore. Nothing at all.

PART FIVE

The Downward Spiral

46

Let's Go Crazy

The heartbeat rattles the room.

I'm sitting underneath the balcony of the Vic Theatre in the long diner-like booth that I'm not sure I've ever sat in before. Usually I'm standing down on the main floor of the small venue a few steps below. I'm waiting for Gavin to bring me another beer and watching the crowd of hipsters filing in. It's a decent crowd for a Tuesday night for the relatively unknown group called Song of the Day. A cluster in the middle of the floor appear extra excited, as if they know someone in the band and are celebrating their arrival. One of them has a banner that is the sort of thing you see in stadiums where U2 or Bon Jovi are playing, not at the Vic.

The sound throttles, the bass burrowing through my skin and coursing through my veins, clawing at my head and scraping away with deep fingernails. It's just the preshow music, a setlist that the band selected to get the crowd into the mood. It's always an interesting portion of any concert, which I pay attention to. I've been paying attention to them ever since standing front and center next to the towering set of speakers at the Metro during college when I was going to see Front 242. I remember the moment clearly when a song began—a startling and stark song with a haunting piano and droning synth and a simple angry voice. It was the first time I ever heard "Something I Can Never Have" by Nine Inch Nails, and my skin crawled as the song built, like I was watching a horror movie in awe.

These songs are a little less dark than that one, but their theme seems to be melancholy. "Lucky" by Radiohead is ultimately about someone surviving death. The Sia song is heartfelt and sad. "Alone in Kyoto" by Air moves me as much as it did when I first heard it in the movie *Lost in Translation*. Even the Coldplay song isn't obvious—an early song of theirs called "Such a Rush," which begins with a Pink Floyd sort of a spacey vibe and builds into angry pleading to slow down.

But then I hear the eerie chords begin. The guitar deliberately plays.

Then the ancient drum machine starts and so does "A Forest" by the Cure.

The beautiful thing about this isn't just that I feel it in every inch of my body. This isn't the Tiesto remix of "A Forest" but rather the tormented original, recorded around 1980.

The beautiful thing is these skinny, slightly bored hipsters around me are hearing this song. And if they haven't already embraced it, they should.

Song of the Day is spotlighting "A Forest" on their preshow playlist for a reason.

My opinion of them shifts up a notch as the song by the Cure continues.

I stand and turn back to see if Gavin is anywhere around. Then I look back at the stage, where crew members are now setting up.

I see something that causes me to blink.

I squint but see it again.

Something falling from the balcony above. I move closer and see small flicks of something descending to the crowd.

Like rain.

Clustering, then dripping off the edge of the balcony, as if the sky is pouring down on an outdoor venue.

For a minute, I wonder where I am.

Just for a moment.

Then another song begins, with its infamous beat pulsing through my skin, and I shiver.

Of course.

I know this song well.

It's the title track on *Blue and Bluer.*

40

I know it because I helped engineer it.

Sean Torrent is in his holding cell, building up the anger and the reckless abandon that took him one take on "Blue and Bluer." A song that starts like Fleetwood Mac's "The Chain" and ends like Nine Inch Nails' "Closer."

The sound pummels me.

The crowd seems to ignore the drizzle.

Then I see the back of a kid's white T-shirt.

It's spotted with something dark.

It looks like he's bleeding.

The rain coming down and draining off the ledges above is dark rain.

It's blood and you know it.

I move and shove past someone and get underneath the opening toward the dome and I look above and taste something bitter like vinegar. I open my hands and see the crimson drops covering them.

People look at me like I'm crazy.

"Do you see this?" I ask.

But Sean Torrent's voice speaks louder than mine.

The crowd is getting doused.

I scream out, but nobody answers.

"It's bleeding from the sky!"

But the beat gets louder and heavier.

"Everything is blue," Sean sings out.

The crowd gets into it, moving around, the floor beneath us slippery.

"But my heart is bluer."

A girl licks her blood-red lips.

"In a world full of loss."

A guy wipes back his drenched hair.

"Your soul makes me newer."

Then I claw my way out of this crowd and feel someone clock me with an elbow. I suck in air and taste a mouthful of waste as I slip on stairs and scatter to the ground and feel my head land on the side of the seat I was just on.

Then I look up and expect to see Sean singing to me in person, yelling at me the way he yelled in that little room when he was basically detailing his love and his breakdown in verbal form.

I see an image of Matthew in my mind, smiling, shaking his head, looking disappointed.

But then I wipe my face and open my eyes and see Gavin looking at me with curiosity.

His hand extends, not to offer me salvation, but rather to offer me a beer.

47

There Is a Light That Never Goes Out

We sit in La Pasadita, eating midnight tacos to help compensate for the beer we drank. It used to be burritos in college, but my stomach can't do those anymore.

"Man, I thought you were wasted there for a minute. What were you doing?"

I'm not sure what to say. "Losing my mind" doesn't seem to want to come out of my mouth. Nor does "having a breakdown" or "seeing blood falling from the sky."

There was no blood. Not when I stood up and collected the beer from Gavin.

But.

I still believe what I saw and felt.

It was real.

I know it was real. Just like everything I've been seeing since Lollapalooza.

"I just slipped on something."

"Maybe it was the song playing that got you all bothered."

"Sean can do that to me."

We talk about the show and about the animated frontman for the band Song of the Day.

"Didn't you say something about working with them?" Gavin asks.

"The label talked to me about their second album. It's a possibility. They're touring now so it won't be for a while."

"They write pretty decent songs. A bit too sappy for my taste, but not bad."

"Maybe they'll be ready to work on something new after we finish with Sean."

"Yeah. By 2020. Either that or by the time we're sacked."

I nod.

I don't like hearing about the future.

I don't even like knowing what year it is.

It reminds me of the truth.

Is this the same truth as in blood falling from Heaven?

Will I wake up a day after turning forty to see a beautiful blue sunset? To know that it was all a dream or a quasi-dream or some other reality or a testing ground for something?

"Tacos not good?"

"No, they're fine," I say. "Just tired."

"You're getting too old for this, mate."

"Speak for yourself."

Sometime later that night, early in the morning of another day, I look at some early photos. I've kept them to remind myself. Remind myself of something that was once young and promising and hopeful. Something that was precious.

Something I lost.

My ex-wife is beautiful and the longer time goes by, the more I know this.

Beautiful inside and out.

We're so young, so naïve, so trusting, so matched. Me in my tux and Julie in that wedding dress wrapped over such a tiny figure. Me holding her hand in a way that I would outgrow. Me cuddled up to her in a way that I would forget.

I don't forget now.

We loved each other on that day and long before it. And even now, I know that the love exists. I don't know what kind of love is inside of her. It's probably a lone island in an ocean of regret. Yet for me, over time, the love has softened and matured.

40

I look at pictures of Julie and remember how much I used to want her. How intoxicating she was against my touch, against my lips. How I ignored our differences and how I surrendered to "LOVE." The Beatles' "All You Need Is Love." Sade's "No Ordinary Love." I was foolish to believe that our passionate love could weather our differences. I was a fool to believe in a love that we could make and that we could perfect.

There's more to love than an act. There's more to love than chemical and physical attraction.

And as much as Julie knew this and tried to change, I was the one who didn't change.

But she's in a better place right now, so you should feel happy for her, right?

That's my mother's voice and I want to strangle it. Yes, she's in a better place and I'm all the worse for it.

I put the photos down and don't feel like sleeping.

I could call Angie and escape.

I could go on the Internet and escape.

I could turn on the television and escape.

I could drink a little more and escape.

But escape is not want I need right now.

I need to surrender.

I already escaped and look where it got me.

48

Running Up That Hill

Some days, I wake up looking for the side of the bed. Doesn't matter if it's wrong or right, but I don't find either. The bed is missing and I'm floundering, fluttering, a fool who is never going to find what he's looking for.

Days when it rains though it's clear, sunny. Days when the garbage man waves as he passes by my house, even though it's not garbage day. Is it? Days that the coffee doesn't pick me up, that the morning news doesn't impress, that the sound of the door shutting behind me doesn't motivate.

Another life, my friend. Another life.

The squares of the sidewalk are pieces of another puzzle someone else put together. They're not mine. They can't be. That condo I just left behind is empty. Its walls echo with the sound of loneliness, the soft shuffling of a lone somebody.

Another place and time.

I'm heading out like I have a real job with real responsibilities, but those have run away with my time and money. They reside in the back pocket of Sean Torrent.

"Everything is blue, but my heart is bluer."

Damn those glossy pictures and those glossy memories.

I'd rather take another imaginary bloodbath than feel this way.

A car honks as I find myself walking right in front of it.

40

Meet Joe Black, Tyler. Meet death as you find yourself looking behind at the beautiful girl and then get run over by a moving vehicle.

I look back down the street I've walked; it has a crayon box full of colors coating the trees. A red leaf the size of a heart falls down and lands on the sidewalk next to my foot.

For a long time, I'm not sure how long, I just stare at it.

Picturesque, vibrant, and dead.

"You have more information than I do," Rick MacLellan says.

He looks more like a nephew than a business colleague. I watch him sip his bottled water, noting his perfectly pressed shirt under a sports coat, along with the perfectly ripped up jeans. I don't like looking at perfection, because it reminds me of the lack of it in my own life.

"You did see him, didn't you?" he asks me.

"Yeah."

We're sitting at a restaurant that Rick wanted to go to. The lunch crowd is busy.

"We're going to have to cancel our remaining time at Electrical Audio. That's not going to be cheap."

"You think I don't know?"

I wonder if he knows just how much it will impact *my* bottom line. His bottom line will be fine in those two-hundred-dollar jeans.

"Are there any family or friends to call?"

"I've tried anybody I can. It's a short list."

"That we know of," Rick says.

"I know. Trust me."

This A&R guy doesn't even look me in the eyes longer than two seconds at a time. I wonder how old Rick MacLellan is. Twenty-two maybe. Not sure how he got the job, but he got it and the label likes him and that's all fine and dandy. He can schmooze with Vampire Weekend all he wants. He doesn't need to schmooze with me. Guys like Sean Torrent don't want to have anything to do with guys like Rick MacLellan.

One reason to love Sean out of oh so many to hate him.

"This is a trainwreck, Tyler."

"Do you really think so?"

"Completely."

He doesn't get my sarcasm.

My crutch.

"Do you know how to sing?" I joke again.

"Me? No, not really. Why?"

This kid is sad.

"Guess there's not a lot else to talk about."

"Just doing my part," he says.

He still won't look at me. There's no one around us, but he's developed a habit of talking with me and looking to see who else is around.

I want to grab his spiked hair and slam his face against the table we're sitting at.

"Hey—you get a free meal," he adds, with a laugh.

Guys like Sean Torrent—yeah, the one we're waiting and wondering and worrying about—are the same ones that are driven to drink and drug because of Rick MacLellan. This guy has nothing to do with any part of music. He's not even a knob in the process. He's a burp after a fine meal. He's a piece of gravel on the side of a superhighway. He is ambient noise in a studio that's not supposed to have it.

"Smile, man, it's not the end of the world," he tells me.

I want to take every one of those pearly whites and break them in two and then scoop out the soft remainder the way one might do with a lobster.

Then again, lobster has some worth.

I'm at the beach, looking out onto Lake Michigan. I haven't been here in a long time, just sitting outside on the wall staring out and thinking.

"I don't know what to say. What do you want me to say? To do? Tell me."

The wind rustles. I see a jogger pass, a biker, a couple, a woman with a dog.

"What am I supposed to do?" I ask with a voice barely louder than a whisper. "Take care of the father I can't stand? Go apologize to Julie for the one thousandth time? Go to Haiti to rebuild a bridge? What? Tell me. You've told me enough, so what else?"

40

A boat moves on the water. Cars rush by behind me. A trio of clouds do a slow-moving dance in the sky.

"Bring Matthew back so I can apologize. Bring him back. Bring something back besides this—this silence. All of this stuff."

I stare at my hands, the hair on my knuckles. The scar on the edge where I once broke a bone.

Wonder what the heart would look like if I could see it? What scars would cover its surface?

It would probably be bloated and thick-skinned and very aged. Not aged like a fine wine, but aged like uncooked meat left out overnight.

"What is there left for me to do? Sit around waiting to die? Nothing is going right and every day something gets worse. What do you want from me? Please, God, please tell me. I know and you know and there's nothing that I can do to change or undo it all, but I don't know. I don't know anything anymore."

But an hour later, sitting there with the fading light of day, I still don't know anything anymore.

Before starting up my car, I check my e-mails and find a message waiting for me on Facebook.

It's from DJELLIS.

"If you're bored tonight, I'll be at Juncture. Come on by. Bring a lady friend."

The image in his photo box is of a set of headphones.

I stare at the message for a while.

On my way back home, I decide to call Angie.

At least I know there's someone who will answer if I call.

49

Late Night, Maudlin Street

What do you do when you get to the middle of your story and realize it's already done?

There will be no side two. No intermission. No sequel.

What do you do when the story you still expected to take off is only headed toward a short epilogue?

I turn up the music, and I'd like to say that it helps, but it doesn't.

I'm driving toward something that I'd like to say I hope will take my mind off this, but it won't.

God doesn't listen and hasn't for a long time.

So I say.

So I excuse myself.

Why is it that so many people live their entire lives without thinking what Jesus would do except when they see it on a bumper sticker?

Every day, I've thought *one day*. Every day I've secretly planned *one day*.

For almost forty years, I've been *one day*ing every single day and night.

But that one day is never going to come, is it?

Is it, Tyler?

"Get busy living or get busy dying," my favorite movie quote goes.

Yeah, I've been busy dying and haven't even known it.

The music serves to help enrage.

40

The music serves to help exorcise.

If I'm dying, and I'm already guilty, and I have nothing left to give, so be it.

Then I'll turn up the music and tune out the rest of everything else.

Including the *one day*itis.

50

Something I Can Never Have

For the last half hour, I've been trying to figure out which one of the women next to Ellis is his girlfriend. I think I've come to the conclusion that both of them are.

After picking up Angie and waiting for her to get glammed up, as she calls it, we headed over here to this lounge called Juncture. I didn't know what to expect when I got the message from Ellis. Part of me didn't know exactly why I decided to come. Ellis wasn't surprised, however, having saved us a spot in the triangle of sofas that he and his ladies occupy a third of.

It's difficult to not think about the blonde and the brunette sitting next to Ellis. Even as I stare at Ellis and listen to him talk, I can make out the long legs of the brunette, crossed and glowing under the lights. I can see her rub a finger down them as if to accentuate the fact that they go on for a mile. The blonde on Ellis's right isn't any better, with a white tank top that demands attention from anybody within a hundred yard radius.

Both of the ladies introduced themselves and neither seems dippy or arrogant or fake. They might be all three, but, surprisingly, they seem more engaging than Angie next to me. Angie seems a little bothered that she's not as glammed up as the two women across from us.

After an hour of casual conversation that doesn't really reveal anything about the person talking, Ellis stands and suggests I come with him. We head to the bar, where he takes a seat and urges me to do the same.

40

"So you made it, friend," he says.

"Yeah."

The little patch of beard under his lip that I call a soul patch shows a little more clearly under the red light right above him.

"So, Tyler. Are you having a good time?"

The question sounds strange, as if it's my father or an older brother asking me this.

"Yeah."

"'Cause I look over and see you sitting next to—what's her name—"

"Angie."

"Sure. Is Angie a good time?"

I don't know whether he's joking or not, but I laugh anyway. "Uh, yeah."

"'Cause those ladies I'm with are."

"I'm sorry—" I start to say.

"I look over at you and you just look—well, a bit heavy. A bit gloomy. The same look I've seen twice already."

"Do I really?"

He nods, then orders a drink.

"Maybe so."

"Something needs to be pretty serious when you're looking like that, surrounded by beauty," Ellis says.

"Yeah."

"Care to share?"

He asks in a way that Cole never would, in a way Gavin wouldn't need to, in a way that, surprisingly, sounds so natural and normal and caring.

A guy I don't even know who at one moment seems so full of himself and at another seems like a longtime friend.

"I don't know—it's not exactly an easy thing to talk about."

"Talk is easy. Talk is the easiest thing in the world to do. Look at our President. He talked his way into the position and he's still talking now. That's all that man does and yes, he does it brilliantly. I voted for him. But talk doesn't change anything."

I stare at him and figure I have nothing to lose. "I might be dying."

He doesn't do a double take, doesn't blink, doesn't sigh, doesn't change in any sort of way. Ellis replies as if he already knew I was going to say that.

"And what if you are? It's not contagious, is it?"

"No."

"You look great. Do you feel great?"

Yeah, outside of that whole I'm-gonna-die part.

"Sure," I say.

"'Cause here's the thing that you already know: we're all dying. I reached my physical potential not too long ago. So I guess it's all downhill, right? I mean, that's what I'm supposed to believe, right?"

"I don't know."

"I know. And I know something else. Every single day is a chance to do things you really, truly want to do. You're either letting life happen to you or you're living it. It's a choice, and not choosing is a choice. You want to know something? Most people I come across don't do the things they really want to do. They hide. They worry. They remain stuck. Are you stuck, Tyler?"

"Maybe."

"I think you are."

"Are you a motivational speaker on the side?"

"I'm a guardian angel who only wants to free you."

"No, please," I say. "I don't need another one of those."

"You're in the dark and what you need is someone to turn on the light. But I don't want to turn on the flashlight, friend. I want it to be a big, fat disco ball right above you like a glistening halo."

I laugh and order a drink. I look back at the ladies we left behind, who have attracted a couple of men.

"Tell me something right now. What do you want to do?"

I shrug, but deep down I know.

I want to take his spot and sit between those two girls.

"Tell me."

"I want to stop worrying," I say, answering his question in the general and vague peace-on-earth sort of sense.

Ellis glances back at the women, then at me. "What's it going to hurt?"

"What do you mean?"

"Do you live every day in fear like this?"

"Fear of what?"

"Fear of want. Fear of desire. Fear of taking."

40

You have no idea, man.

"Look—who are you?" My question isn't dismissive. It's honest and a bit incredulous.

"That's an odd question."

"No. I mean—I get this vibe—that club you invited me to and now this. Your friends."

"Why don't you say what you're thinking instead of constantly running around the meaning?"

"I get this weird vibe you're trying to sell me something. Or someone."

His eyes light up as he laughs. "Did you actually say 'sell'?"

"You asked what I was thinking."

"I'm sorry, I gave up my pimping days right around the time I started to sell drugs on the street."

He stands to go back to the couch.

"Look, I didn't mean anything by that—"

"I don't want to sell you anything, Tyler. I really just want to help. And when I saw you that night looking lost and even lonely, I figured I'd help out. When I discovered we work in the same industry, well, I thought it was fate and destiny that we met."

"You believe in fate?"

"You know what I believe? I believe that if you want something, you can work hard enough to get it. Whatever—whoever—it might be. That's my fate. That's my destiny."

He walks off and I stay there for a moment, watching as he brushes Angie's shoulder with a hand.

She glances up at him and already seems more enamored of him than she is of the guy who brought her here.

Hours later, I leave behind an occupied bed to go up to the roof. I whisper to Angie that I'm going to get some water, but what I really need to do is to go and repent.

God could hear me in a basement barricaded under kryptonite, but still, it seems like He can listen better to me when I'm on my roof.

In the still of a clear night, I stand against the brick wall. I can smell Angie's perfume on my body.

I sigh.

What do you want to do?

Ellis's voice still echoes around in my head.

I followed his advice.

I don't feel any better.

The everything-he-saw on my face is surely still there and multiplied.

I've failed. Again.

Fail, repent, keep failing, keep repenting.

It's a cycle that starts to become ridiculous.

What do you want to do?

Does God stop forgiving after episode number 7,378?

Of course I know the answer.

Maybe you need to forgive yourself.

That's not me talking. That's Ellis.

Yeah, blame him.

I know that I shouldn't have gone any further with Angie.

You're adults, come on, give me a break.

I still feel guilty.

It's not that this is Mom and Dad talking.

I know what I just did was wrong.

I used to be different. I used to be . . .

Better.

That's not the word I want. We're all sinners and I know that.

Of course you know, Tyler, because it's been plugged into your mouth like a pacifier ever since you were a baby.

"Is this feeling inside because I'm supposed to change?"

What do you want to do?

I want freedom. I want fearlessness. I want—

"Something fulfilling," I say out loud to stress my point.

What just happened wasn't fulfilling. Momentarily, yes. Momentarily it was a need and a want and a necessity. But now . . .

"I feel so alone."

It's a ludicrous statement and I know this even after uttering it.

I just left someone to come up here and feel sorry for myself.

DJ Ellis would mock me.

A lot of people would mock me.

I often rationalize my sin, thinking that at least I'm not doing XYZ. I could be over there doing this. I could be over here doing that.

But rationalizing only makes me feel worse.

I think of my parents, especially my father.

I think of Julie.

Then I think of Laila.

Even when you're here, you're somewhere else.

Which one of them said that?

Does it matter?

"It's true I'm somewhere else, but where? Where am I?"

I'm talking to try and out-talk those voices.

They're always there. Always. Morning, noon, and night.

Yet God—above, around, omniscient, all-everything—remains silent. The only reason I can think of for this is that it's because of something I've done.

Something I have or haven't done.

51

That Joke Isn't Funny Anymore

H ave a seat and let's talk."

God doesn't say this, but a god in my business does.

"Sure," I say, sitting down at the table on my roof.

It's still nighttime but I can see him clearly. Strange thing #1: The world looks almost green.

That's because it's another green world, Tyler.

He looks different than I remember him looking—almost younger, like thirty years younger. Strange thing #2.

"How would you explain this to your parents?" he says.

Strange thing #3 is this:

Brian Eno is talking to me on my rooftop deck.

Brian.

Eno.

I think "The Big Ship" is playing on the speakers around us. Did he put that on? What does it mean? What symbolism does it carry?

He asks his question again.

"Excuse me?" I ask, but don't feel my mouth moving.

"Remove the middle, extend the edges," he says.

"This isn't funny anymore." I think I'm saying and/or thinking this to myself, since this is so obviously a dream.

"Voice your suspicions."

"Okay. You're not really here, are you?"

40

"What is the reality of the situation?"

"That's what I'm saying. Am I dreaming? You're not really here, right? You look like Brian Eno—like the '70s Brian Eno. No offense."

"Think—inside the work—outside the work."

"Are these your tweets I'm hearing—or reading—or dreaming?"

"In total darkness, or in a very large room, very quietly."

"Very quietly what?" I ask.

"Do the last thing first."

Then he's gone.

But the song keeps playing.

52

Airbag

We've already flushed twenty grand down the toilet, and that's all on me. That's the way these things can work when you're a producer. It depends on how the agreement is set up among you and the artist and the label.

That's why you're paid the big bucks.

Unless you incur far too many costs producing an album, which means that your bucks become fewer and fewer.

It's been a couple of weeks since seeing Sean, and our studio dates are now in limbo. No calls or e-mails. No nothing since watching him disappear in that strange club I brought him to.

My manager is dealing with the necessary parties, because frankly I really don't care anymore. I don't. I just want the whole Sean Torrent mess to go away.

I'm trying to work out for the third time in a week because I'm starting to realize that I'm not getting a beer belly, I already have one. It's the one part of me I never bother to really look at in the mirror or in the shower, but it's there. This nice, round little butterball that if left to its own devices will turn into a big fat turkey.

Even as I'm on the elliptical machine, a voice asks me why I'm working out.

Trying to fit into the size 33 casket, my friend?

I don't know.

Maybe if you stopped drinking all that beer, the BEER belly will go away.
I don't have a clue.

I'm sweating and hungry when I leave the gym. That's when I get the call.
It's going to be Taco Bell. They want me back right now.

"Tyler, man, where are you? What are you doing?"

Someone is running and is far more out of breath than I am.

"Hello?"

"It's me. Look, we have to meet."

It's Sean.

I think of maybe the best line that came out of *The Godfather III*:
Just when I thought I was out . . . they pull me back in.

"What's going on?" I say.

"Oh dear God, man, I don't know or can't explain. You won't have any idea. No clue. Not a clue. You've gotta get me."

"Where are you?"

"Where am I? I'm that rabbit in *Fatal Attraction,* man. I'm getting my brains boiled. You gotta come and get me."

I'm thinking that whatever trip or ride Sean has been on has suddenly gone bad. *Magic Mountain* has turned into *Nightmare on Elm Street.*

"So tell me where you are."

His voice quivers, out of breath, hoarse, almost unrecognizable.

Bet he sounds great in a studio, Brian Eno. Work your magic, oh sage.

He tells me in colorful language the kind of madness he's been experiencing.

"Like what? Where are you?" I interrupt when he stops making sense.

"I just—I mean, it's not . . . it's not possible. No way."

"So tell me where you're at."

"I don't know, man. I don't. I'm, like—some stinking suburb. I don't know if I'm still in Illinois or Indiana or what."

I want to ask how and who and why, but there's no telling.

"You have to give me something, Sean. An address, a telephone number, something. Where are you calling from?"

"Some cesspool of a house. This place is disgusting." He curses again. "There are real devils in this place. I swear. They're real. Their faces keep changing. They're trying to kill me, man."

He rambles on and starts becoming incoherent.

"Are you calling from your cell?"

"Hell, no. You serious? They got rid of that."

"They?"

"They've been following me for a while now. You won't believe it. You won't believe any of this. All because of her. She's crazy, man. I'm telling you."

"Look—just—go outside. Give me an address, something."

I hear the sound of clinking, then pounding, then shouting. Sean is screaming.

"I'm locked in here!" Then he says "wait" from a distance and I hear something. Shuffling. A drawer being opened and closed.

"They thought they'd drugged me up good. They shouldn't have left me in here. I've got handcuffs on but there's a phone—here—I got this. Some address. Some piece of something in the desk. Damn. It reeks in here like raw sewage."

He rambles off an address. I'm about ready to try and go inside somewhere when I stop.

"Say that again."

"What—894—"

"No. The city. What'd you say?"

"Gary, Indiana."

"Are you serious?"

He curses at me.

"This is for real?"

"Look, man. I met this chick downtown a short while ago and then—I don't know. I really can't begin to describe what's been happening. Except she left me here. Locked up in handcuffs in Gary."

"This has got to be a joke."

"I wish it was."

"Tell me the address again."

After he does, he tells me not to tell anybody else.

"I can't come there alone," I say. "I'll get killed."

"Listen, man, this is trouble. I mean—my girlfriend is going to flip out."

"Your girlfriend?"

40

"Don't be all high-and-mighty."

"I can't just drive there and pick you up, Sean. That's not going to happen."

"You gotta get me. You can't call the cops."

"Just—look, I'll have this number on my phone. I'll get someone—I don't know who—to come with me."

"Discretion."

"You kidding me?"

He curses and says he's not kidding, that he hasn't laughed at all the last week and a half.

"If you don't come get me, I'm going to die."

"Someone's there?"

"No, smart guy. Because she or *they* took everything I had. I need something and I need it bad."

I'm not going to ask what because I know.

I knew the moment I saw him and I know now.

"Just..."

"Get here as fast as you can," he says before I can be trite and say to hang in there and help is on its way.

I have no idea what I'm going to do.

Part of me thinks I should just leave him there to fend for himself.

53

Disappearing World

Is this part of my story or have I become part of Sean's?

Have the demons harassing me started to do the same with him, or have his and mine combined forces and concocted a grand plan to terrorize the two of us?

Where are you, Matthew?

What do you want, God?

Dare I even utter that thought, that request, that hopeless plea?

"What is it?"

"It's getting dark," I say.

"Doesn't matter. That place is just as bad during the middle of the day."

Gavin, who's driving, seems in his intense world, yet he doesn't seem annoyed. It's almost as if the thought of him playing knight and rescuing Sean the princess suits him just fine.

We're using Gavin's GPS, but we're not believing what it's saying. Twice we circle around the abandoned eight-story warehouse.

"Is that it?" I ask.

"Maybe there was an address there fifty years ago."

A large sign on the edge of the building says "Standard."

"Nothing standard about that," Gavin says as he parks the car in front of it.

The street appears abandoned as far as the eyes can tell. But I fear the things I can't see, like what's in the decrepit property next to us.

40

Any windows that once existed on the first floor are now barricaded with faded eyelids of plywood. We walk down the sidewalk and turn the corner. An unstable-looking black fire escape covers half the edge of the building on one side, starting at the third floor and ending at the top. There's no door on this side.

The sound of an engine can be heard.

"He tell you where he'd be?"

I shake my head and try calling the number. It doesn't work.

We walk back down the cracked sidewalk to the arched entryway. The door is mammoth but appears just like everything else around us. I don't even have to try the handle, since the bolt holding it in has a large chunk missing.

"So should we just go inside?" I ask.

Gavin looks at me. "We drove all this way for a reason, right?"

The sun is setting beyond this forgotten city. I step through the doorway and it immediately feels like a dimmer has gone on.

"You wouldn't happen to have a flashlight?" I ask.

"Nope. Just my little friend."

His little friend is a .38 that he's carrying with him. At first I thought he was crazy for bringing it, but now I'm thinking I'm crazy for not having one myself.

We enter a musty, dim hallway. The walls look like they're growing feathers, the shredded and aged wallpaper wrinkling with time. It's surprisingly bare, as if a cleaning crew came in and removed the debris. Room after room reveals an old office building that was converted into apartments and then remodeled into desolation.

I call out Sean's name. My words get sucked into the surroundings.

I see a square box on the wall with a black tab with the instructions of "Listen" and "Talk" above and below it. Then another button marked "Front Door." I'm half tempted to press *Listen* but then realize I don't really want to hear anything coming through that box from somewhere I don't know.

After a few minutes, realizing that it's going to be pitch black before we've even gotten to the third story, I suggest separating. There's nobody in this building, no fire-breathing hellion waiting around the corner. It's just an empty building in a rundown town.

The sooner we can find him, the better.

Gavin and I take a staircase carefully, the groans underneath sounding like stepping over a sleeping elderly person. We reach the second floor and decide to each take a hallway. I walk down one, the windows next to me on my left looking cloudy and ghostlike, the end of the hallway draped in black, the way a prison corridor might appear. I call out again and the sound of my voice not only helps me keep my sanity but it reminds Gavin that I haven't been abducted by a zombie.

I enter a room with a high, stained ceiling. The stump of what used to be a chandelier is in its center, the round knob stuck like a stopper in a bathtub. I walk a few steps and see a face moving with me, jerking quickly and standing stunned in surprise. The blocks of mirror on the wall show half of me, like a crossword puzzle with missing letters. Even in the low light of the room, I can see how pale and freaked out I look.

The beams on the windows look like the bars of a cell. I walk up to one and look outside to see a city no longer there. The sun seeps into the cracks, but nothing comes out of them. I wonder who looked through this window and what kind of life she had.

Why she?

I wonder what it was like to stare at the sunset from here. Day after day. Hoping for something more, for something different, for something new.

This place doesn't give me the creeps as much as it makes me sad.

I hear a voice in the distance. Gavin sounds like he's on another floor.

The strains of the floor and the scent of awakened dust and the sense of loss all walk with me as I go down the hallway to room after room.

An empty building in the middle of an emptying town.

What was Sean doing here?

That's not the question I need to answer.

What are you doing here?

I reach the last door at the end of the apartment and find it locked.

"Sean?"

I hear a heckling noise behind the slab of wood.

"You in there, Sean?"

A low, brooding laugh sounds.

There's no way Sean could make that sound. It makes me think of something else. *Lollapalooza and the figure I saw there in my dream.*

224

40

I kick down the door in a delirious display of courage and folly. Two lines streak across the room. Otherwise, it's empty.

I move toward a window, this one open, and glance outside.

Walking down the street are two teens, laughing at something as their hands gesture and their bodies appear bored.

That wasn't the sound you just heard.

But I force myself to believe that it was.

I'm heading back to the stairs when I hear a shot go off that seems to bounce all around me.

"Gavin!"

I sprint down the corridor and up the stairs and I swear I think I hear that low rumbling laugh behind me.

54

Until Tomorrow

Good thing that the cat that scampered out of the room across Gavin's path wasn't something like a child. Even though his shot simply became a permanent part of this wonderful building we're in, the thought of his trigger-happy finger is enough to get me out of this building and back on the street.

For a while, we stand by the car, waiting and wondering. I can still feel my heart pounding away.

The sky keeps darkening. And I swear I keep hearing small little bits of life all around me. As if there are vampires watching and waiting. Not swooning heartthrob vampires that want to make love to the new girl at school, but the kind that think blood tastes like wine and that think skin is wonderful to puncture.

"So how long do we wait?"

"I don't know," I say. "I'm just glad you didn't shoot me."

"Bugger off."

I laugh to release some of the tension. When Gavin is frustrated or tired, he tends to sound more English, using expressions from his youth.

Any other time I'd already be in the car going eighty miles an hour to get away from the sound we just produced. But here it's just another day, another echo of a gunshot, another shrugged shoulder in a shrugged-off community.

I try calling the line but don't get anything.

40

"I don't know."

I'm about ready to get into the car when a figure comes out of nowhere and steps in the middle of the road.

Before Gavin has time to reach for his gun and do something stupid again, we hear a familiar voice.

"Hey, guys."

The man we came looking for is hobbling across the street like a beggar. He looks like the building we just left behind.

Gavin curses in a way that sounds like disbelief and disgust. He remains leaning on the side of the car.

I walk toward the man whose *Blue and Bluer* album sold over three million copies, a man who once vacationed at Bono's villa, a man once linked to many of Hollywood's leading ladies, not to mention a couple of Victoria's Secret models.

Sean Torrent is wearing scuffed-up jeans, socks, and a shirt that's missing most of its buttons. I can see the slight hollow cavity of his chest and the outline of bones from his rib cage.

This is the man whose album I'm supposed to be producing.

"We just spent an hour looking for you in that building."

"I know," he says. "I just wanted to make sure nobody else came with you."

Gavin curses behind us.

"Seriously?" I ask.

"This wouldn't look good for us, Tyler. Me and you both."

He walks past and heads to the car as if I'm the chauffeur.

And maybe, probably, that's what I am.

"Do you remember working with Delton?"

"Intense days," I say to Sean as I hand him a beer.

We're on the roof, and I can't quite make out the expression on his face as he stares off toward the city. Ulrich Schnauss is playing in the background, providing some glorious shoegaze softness. It's already been agreed that Sean is going to spend the night here at my place. I haven't pried too far. I figure if and when he wants to tell me what happened, he will. He certainly didn't say anything to Gavin's snide remarks on the trip back home.

227

"I remember not having a clue of what was going on. He would bark orders and I'd pretty much do whatever he wanted."

"Would you do that now?" I ask, wondering if he's trying to give me a message.

"Hell no. That's the problem with success. You suddenly get to a level where nobody can tell you nothing. Where nothing matters. Seriously. And want to know something that's just absolutely—well, sad?"

"What?"

"I miss those days. I miss being a nobody that was always broke and wondering when and if my music would get heard. Wondering when I'd be working the nightshift at an IHOP. Wondering when I'd be taking out the dog with the 2.5 kids and thinking what tomorrow's dinner was going to be. It was always about waiting 'til tomorrow. And about the journey, man. I miss the journey."

He's wearing a shirt of mine that has buttons and it looks like a cape on him. He sips his beer and keeps staring out into no-man's land.

"I miss caring," Sean says to me.

"Yeah."

"I don't think it's something that you just get back, either. I mean—my last album—you heard it. What did you think?"

I shrug.

"Yeah," Sean says, waving the beer and spilling a little of it. "Yeah. That's what everybody did. That album oughta be called *The Shrug*. Nobody gives a damn about those songs. They're meaningless. Do you know one of them was a melody I found ten years earlier that I scratched some delirious lyrics to?"

"It wasn't an awful record."

"It was indifferent. And that's worse than simply being an ambitious failure."

I don't say anything, but let the music drift around us like the swirling wind.

"There used to not be this pressure to be...me. Because *me* didn't exist. It was just Sean Torrent. It wasn't *Sean Torrent,* you know? I mean—look, don't take this the wrong way because I'm not going to go out like he did, but I get Kurt Cobain. I get him. I think when the fame hit and

Nevermind became this, like, game-changing album that an industry and a generation embraced, he was like…" Sean spits and curses at the same time. "I think it was over for him."

"Is it over for you?"

"I don't know. I really don't. I mean—my personal life is just a walking disaster. I should have some good things to write about."

"You have some great songs."

"Yeah. I just don't know if I have the soul to pull them off. The rest of the world doesn't get it. Yeah, it comes down to your pipes and the lyrics and the melodies. But the true geniuses, the ones that have made it work and have left a legacy—they have the soul for it."

"You already have quite the legacy."

Sean curses again and shakes his head. "I got lucky."

"You could say *we* got lucky. I was an inexperienced engineer on that record."

"You helped play matchmaker with Mia."

I laugh. "I didn't realize that was in the job description."

I want to ask about her but don't. It's like someone asking me about Julie.

"We had some fun times making that record, didn't we?" Sean asked.

"Is that why you wanted me to produce this album?"

"The label wanted Delton. But he's living in a shack, dissecting animals, and smoking strange stuff."

"But what about you?"

"Yeah," Sean says. "I guess you're right. I wanted to see if I could—I don't know. It's a load of responsibility to give. I don't want to lump it on your shoulders."

"What happened back there?"

"What?"

"We picked you up in the middle of Gary."

"It doesn't take a genius to figure out what I was doing there."

"Were you in danger?"

Sean chuckles and rubs his face. "Before or after the gun was waved in my face and they took my wallet?"

"Who?"

"Beats me. A friend of a friend. Some chick. I don't know. I mean—seriously. My life boils down to self-destructive behavior. About meeting some girl and then making bad choice after bad choice."

"Do you still want to make this album?"

"What else am I going to do?"

"You gotta work with me then."

"I know. I'm not expecting you to be my babysitter." Sean looks over. "Well, not all the time."

"Do you think you have enough left?" I ask him.

"Enough what?"

"Enough soul to record an album."

"Not the one in my head. Not the one I want to record. What I want is to do something that's just—that's not going to happen."

"If you show up, you can do whatever you want."

Sean sits on the edge of the wall without a care in the world.

"You know—when I was a kid, I lived next to this boy. This kid that as it turned out was getting horribly abused by his parents. His father mainly, but the mother knew about it. It was awful. We hung out all the time. We'd escape our houses and go roaming around the neighborhood. I'd make him mixtapes that he later said kept him from wanting to kill himself. Can you believe that? That's the power of music."

"I can believe it."

"This kid." He sighs. "This poor kid, man. I mean, I just—I think that after everything that happened with him, I carried on his legacy."

"What happened?"

"That's what I want to tell. I want to tell his story, our story, the story of two broken souls. A double album called *The Sun and the Rainfall*."

"That's a Depeche song."

"Really?" He laughs. "That was our song, man. And just—just thinking about that story kills me. Makes me cry. Makes me want to go bury my head in mud and let the worms gnaw at my eyeballs."

"So the songs you played—"

"Yeah, totally. They're a part of it. They're messy. I mean, I don't know. I don't know if I'd call it a concept album…but maybe, possibly it is. It's ambitious. I mean—a double album. Nobody even calls them double albums anymore since everything is downloadable."

40

"Let's do it."

"Of course. Sure. But I think—I mean, I still love Mia. I will always love her."

"Have you seen her recently?"

Sean nods.

"I grew up trying to help my next-door neighbor and you know what happens? Turns out that he goes on to marry Mia."

"What?"

"I think God exists, and he did it just because I've messed up so badly in life. That's what I think."

"That sounds like a bad Lifetime movie."

"A what?"

"You probably don't watch much television."

"There's not a whole hell of a lot that I do except dream of her and write pathetic lyrics and then escape with the help of my best friend."

"Was Gary an escape?"

"That? No way. No, that was trying to follow the white rabbit. But it turns out that the rabbit I followed was rabid and possessed. I almost found that out too late."

"Almost," I say.

"I keep escaping almosts. Maybe that's what Kurt Cobain kept doing too. Until he once and for all made the almost an absolute."

55

Walk On

Do others have grand ambitions in life? Perhaps most don't, making people like Bono seem like strange aliens from another galaxy. A short and larger-than-life Irishman who says things like "music can change the world because it can change people" and "there are many side roads and back streets to rock 'n' roll, and most of us get lost down them at times," all while the rest of the world just smiles and keeps mowing their grass and scrubbing their dishes and washing their cars and living their lives.

I get Bono's language and always have. I'm not an artist in that sense, but I have always gotten it, have always understood, have always dreamed.

It's late and Sean is sleeping downstairs in the guest room. As far as I know. Maybe he's slipped out or maybe he's shooting up in his room. I don't know. Such is the friend I am. Such a good Christian Samaritan. I'll give him room and board, but I sure won't give him any sort of hope of God's eternal glory. Because I guess he's heard enough of that and who am I anyway? Who am I?

What do you want out of life, Tyler?

What I want, what I suddenly want and desire more than anything else, is to produce this new album of his.

The Sun and the Rainfall.

I want to create a *Pet Sounds.* I want to help produce a *Sgt. Pepper's Lonely Hearts Club Band.* I want to oversee a *Dark Side of the Moon.* I want to be instrumental in helping with a *Thriller*. I want to steer my car down a place where the streets have no name past another *Joshua Tree*. I want to guide another *Nevermind*. I want to control the keyboards of another *OK Computer*.

Maybe this is ludicrous, but I keep the lunacy to myself. That's all.

Bono has already proven he's crazy, but he's backed it up. Most don't get a chance to in life.

Brag and win the gold or go out with flying colors.

Julie never got this about me. I'd start to go there—here—wherever this here and there is—and she'd get this look. The look that says that I'm certifiable, the one that says *he might just be off his rocker.*

I don't think anybody has ever understood this.

Laila did.

Yeah, maybe that. Maybe she did. But maybe she skipped town and disappeared into the night with all that wonderfully warm understanding.

I stare at the ceiling fan above me that's moving slowly. I can't sleep.

All I think about is the potential.

I want to embark on this journey because I believe it can be something beautiful. It can be something freeing.

It can be a little something I leave behind.

Will that really matter? Will it?

Bono and company say you have to leave it behind.

But that's easy for them to say when they've already made their mark and produced their footprints in this world.

A blink, Tyler.

Just one thing. That's all I'm asking.

A heartbeat, a flicker, a speck.

I still have time and maybe that's what this is about. About creating something and about leaving something special behind.

Maybe?

Possibly?

What's wrong with that, God?

What?

56

Untogether

I guess I'm going to have to wait for my own personal *Sgt. Pepper's Lonely Hearts Club Band*. After letting Sean sleep in, I finally go downstairs to see if my assumptions are correct. They are. The bed is more evenly made than usual and on the cover is a small note.

> Tyler—
>
> Thanks for yesterday. I'll be in touch after I get things in order. I left you something. They managed to steal my wallet but they didn't bother with this. Guess it just has more emotional value than anything else. I'm not giving you this—it's just a sign that I'll be back. Soon.
>
> Sean

I see the necklace spread out on the bed like a black snake. I pick it up and remember.

I was there when Mia gave it to him.

I don't need to question whether he's being honest. He'd follow me anywhere on this earth to get back this thing that probably cost three or four bucks.

There are no price tags on mementos, nor on the memories they leave behind.

40

• • •

A week later, I'm getting ready to head to Nashville for another recording session with Nicole Lawson. This is where Nicole started and where she laid down roots. Her first album was in the Christian & Gospel category, a box she's been out of but that's hounded her ever since. The same way a country box might hound someone, the way electronica might pester an artist. Boxes are created by marketers for consumers, not by artists for fans. It would be nice if it worked that way, but it doesn't.

The label thought we could get another session in at a friend's house that has a home studio. It should be interesting to see what happens. The label wants something other than what they initially heard, but a home studio and a Nashville setting might not necessarily help that.

Maybe they're wanting a new producer.

I've gotten one message in the last week from Sean. It was from his new phone. He wanted me to have the number and also wanted me to know that things were better, that he was doing better. I'm a little afraid to know what *better* means. Better is one of those in-the-eye-of-the-beholder words.

I pack light as usual and get through security quickly on my way to the gate. I always fly American. It's a big terminal at O'Hare so of course there's always a chance of running into someone I might know.

But.

I'm in the line at Starbucks and two people in front of me stands Ellis.

As I order my coffee and he's off pouring cream in his cup, he sees me.

"Hey, Tyler."

I walk over and put my coffee down to shake his hand.

"Glad to see you made it home okay the other night," he tells me. "You were ready to go."

"Yeah, I guess so."

"So where are you flying?"

He doesn't act like it's an odd thing seeing me here.

"Going to Nashville to do a session with someone."

"Nashville." His eyes get large as if he's thinking *sorry to hear that.* "I'm going to New York."

"Work?"

235

Travis Thrasher

"And play," he says with that perfect smile. "But work is play, right? And playing can be work. I guess it's all how you look at it."

He sips his coffee and shakes his head for a minute. "That'll wake you up. So how long are you gone?"

"Six days."

"Excellent. I've got a party in a week that you need to come to."

I nod and probably show too much of what I'm thinking.

"Look—there's not a big city in America where I don't have a dozen friends. And I don't say that to brag, because frankly friends can sometimes be a lot of work and a real drag. But it doesn't take me a couple of years to decide who I want to hang out with. Some people don't like that about me and some people can just piss off, you know? It's up to you to decide which type of person you are and that's really honestly fine with me."

I nod, about to say something, then get cut off.

"But listen—this party really might work for you. *Especially* you. Considering everything."

"Considering what?"

"Look, I gotta go. Safe travels."

He walks off and I notice that he's only carrying a black carryall.

I sip my coffee and think of what he just said.

Considering everything.

What's there to consider? At least to him?

I settle in for the short flight, in a seat next to the window. I scroll through my iPod and find an album and then watch as the square blocks of Illinois farmland disappear behind clouds.

I think of Julie again.

I don't know why at this moment I think of her.

Maybe it's the song, though I think she was already long gone by the time this album came out.

It's because of the obvious, Tyler. Need a reminder?

I think of our last conversation. It's been ten months.

I awkwardly asked how the kids were. Not our kids, of course, but her kids, the ones she had with her new husband. Julie spoke like an adult, like a grownup who had moved on, who was too busy to spend days and nights

236

pining after something that wasn't there. She had told me the kids were fine and then proceeded to tell a couple of stories about them in a way that never seemed to happen when she was with me.

She never used to tell me stories. Ever. Because I never had time for them.

I change the song to try and think of something else.

But Julie stays on my mind.

It's October.

Six months.

If Matthew is right, then that's all the time I have.

I think about it and spend an hour working on an e-mail to Julie.

Yet in the end, right before we start descending, I get rid of it.

She doesn't want to hear from me. Not anymore. There's no easy way to tell her that I think I'm going to die. Even if she believed me, then what?

There's nothing that can come out of that conversation.

The pivotal moment of choice and consequences came years ago when she told me that *we* were dying and that she wanted to change things.

I was the one who let us die.

So claims of another impending death, my own...

Would it even matter? Honestly?

There will be grief when the moment comes and surely there will be regret.

But divorce, in many ways, is worse than death, because the person is still there and still living and still remembering, yet they're no longer a part of your life and never will be. Whatever love and hope lay in the promises of the wedding day were lost forever. The funeral came and went and we were standing on each side of the casket, looking at one another, dressed in black.

Inside the casket lay all our promises and all our tomorrows.

57

Know Who You Are at Every Age

The problem with striving to be different as an artist is that, yes, you can achieve brilliance. But it's far more likely you'll blow it.

People love hearing about artistic magnificence, but nobody loves hearing about artistic negligence and laziness. Unless it's on an epic scale, where jobs are lost and lives are ruined and artists are imprisoned or banished.

Why I'm thinking of this as I listen to Nicole Lawson sing is beyond me. I'm trying to hear the song without anybody else entering my mind.

She's sung it now half a dozen times and while the melody is unique, the way she's singing it feels a bit...

"How was that?" Nicole asks me.

She's not far away from me, standing behind the microphone. Nice thing about the room we're in is that it has everything we need right there around us. No need to go into a separate little room to record the vocals. I personally hate having to do that and Nicole is going with it.

"Stale," I say.

"Really?"

"It sounds very, very normal. Very safe."

"How?"

I'm thinking for a minute and trying to figure out why I'm thinking that.

"First off, I don't think the way you're singing fits the song. The song is not exactly a Madonna 'Holiday' song, you know? This is about something lost. It's like you're trying to sound sad but you're also trying to sound—popish."

"So how should I sound?"

I spend the next hour telling her what I'm thinking. However she sings will come out sounding the same, in a sense. She's going to be singing the same notes and the same lyrics. I don't want her howling or purring or doing any crap like that.

It's about soul.

I play her songs from women that I respect and remain in awe of. I play her songs from singers that will help me show, not tell. Kate Bush is one. Tracey Thorn is another. Elizabeth Fraser of the Cocteau Twins is yet another.

We are all born with certain abilities, and some of us have more than others. Some can carry a tune and some can make that tune fly.

But I just don't want something in tune and meticulous with the beats.

I want to hear where you're at, the moment you're singing it, the moment you're living it.

Art is the ability to share a little chunk of who you are at the moment it's created. A teen pop star should not only explore the part of youth that's often wasted on the young, but should also cry out about the part of being grown up and yet not grown up in a blistering fast world.

"Where were you when you wrote those words? Do you remember?"

Nicole nods.

"I want you to record a little part of you—right now—the twenty-four-year-old who is singing this song. You don't have to act like you're sixteen nor thirty-five. Be who you are right at this very moment and do it with every ounce you have."

In the movies, this would be the moment she has her out-of-the-body experience and she dazzles the crowd of one in the room.

But actually, the version she sings sounds worse.

Afterwards, Nicole knows.

"That was awful," she says with a disbelieving laugh.

"Let's put that on hold. For the moment."

"You sure?"

"Finding your voice takes time. You can carry a tune, but you have to figure out where it's coming from. Where it's heading toward. This is one of the big songs on the album."

"A single?"

"No—I don't see it being a single. It's an emotional turning point on the record. Wherever it goes."

"Okay."

"You'll get it," I tell her. "It's all there. Just—it's a little intimidating listening to Stevie Nicks and then trying to sing soulfully. We'll work on it later."

Being a good producer is knowing when to push and when to stop and back up.

It's about working with someone and knowing their limits.

My senses are telling me that we need to get out of here for the moment and experience a little more life.

Strange how it's easy for me to realize that for someone like Nicole, yet never realize that for myself.

"Did you always want to do this?" Nicole asks.

She's sipping on some herbal tea while I'm drinking a grenade of caffeine in a large cup.

"I wanted to do what you're doing," I say.

"You never tried?"

"I realized early on I can't really sing. So if I couldn't do it really well, then maybe I could at least help those that could. But it was luck. Getting a job as a runner for a studio and then spending hours there learning what to do."

"You can't learn what you do," Nicole says. "You have to be born with ears that know."

"Maybe. I've always loved music and have always been able to pick songs apart. That part is inside of me. But you still have to be able to enter this industry. You have to get lucky and have the door open for you."

"I think God's always wanted me to sing. I've always felt that was what I was supposed to do."

I chuckle.

"What?"

40

"You sound like my parents."

"Really?"

"I grew up hearing about God's will. His will for this and that. Mainly stuff related to what my father did."

"What did he do?"

"More or less a preacher. A preacher who didn't have to preach every Sunday morning. A preacher without a congregation. Unless you count my sister and me."

"I never knew that about you."

"I never talk much about myself with the people I work with. Well, I don't talk about that side of me. I talk about my love of Depeche Mode and about the time I met Morrissey, but I never bring up my parents or my faith."

"Are they still alive?"

I nod. "Yeah, though my father's not in the best health."

"Sorry."

"You know—I think I always felt that the whole 'God's will' was just a way for them to not feel guilty about dragging my sister and me around move after move. It was for 'the ministry.' I hear that term and my skin crawls the way it might watching a Marilyn Manson video."

"Wow."

"What?" I ask.

"That's quite the perspective."

"I'm not saying it's a good one. Or that I'm even right."

Someone comes into the coffee shop we're in and sees Nicole and recognizes her and the two talk for a while. It's a nice thing to see this—the reality of what we're doing, what she's doing. The connection.

The reality is that what we're doing behind walls—behind buttons and speakers and monitors and computers—all of that ends up mattering for moments like this. For a soccer mom who loves to play Nicole's music on the way to bringing her kids to school.

That's the point, right?

After the woman leaves in an excited manner that says her evening has been made, Nicole looks at me with a lighthearted glow on her face.

"That was sweet."

I agree with her.

"You know—the whole thing of God's will. I don't claim to understand it, but I do know this. I feel God gave me this ability. This voice. The ability to sing and give—to give joy. I know it sounds corny."

"That wasn't corny," I say. "I just witnessed a little piece of that."

"The thing is—I feel that I can do that and keep doing that. I didn't want to stay in the contemporary Christian genre, simply because I felt that box was so confining. Yet I still believe my songs can make people feel good about their day. To give them little moments of hope, of reflection, of joy."

"I agree."

"I can't say I know it for a fact, but I believe that's what I've always felt like I was meant to do."

"It's good you know."

"It's good that I'm fortunate to work with people like you who help people like me."

I nod.

It's good you know, Nicole. But I don't have a clue what God's wanted from me.

I sip my coffee and can't help thinking that I was meant for something different.

That God wanted me for something else, for something more.

Somewhere along the way, I ran away from God and His desires.

And in doing so, I let Him down.

58

Regret

That night, at the Nashville hotel, in the deep pit of night, it hits me.

Why all of a sudden after all of this, I don't know.

That's the way I am.

Always.

In the eye of the storm I'm solid, but then when I'm sitting, already dried out and watching the storm clouds dissipating, I suddenly grow scared.

And that's exactly what happens on October 21.

I suddenly realize that I'm going to die in six months and I suddenly start thinking of everything. Everything. Absolutely everything.

I could fool anybody, making it seem like I don't believe God's messenger. I could even almost fool myself, making it seem like I don't really care what Matthew said.

But I know.

I know myself.

I can run, but ultimately I can't hide.

I know that Matthew was real, and I know that what he said was true.

So why haven't I done a single damned thing about it?

On this night, I realize a few things.

I realize that I've been trying to reject and deny.

But I can't. Not anymore.

.   .   .

I think of Mom and Dad and Kendra and her family. That of course leads me to think of Julie. It leads me thinking of Laila. It leads me to think of everybody that's meant anything to me.

I'm lost because I have no idea what I'm supposed to find.

I don't want to leave them, not this way, not with everything half done and half fulfilled.

I don't want to go, God.

I don't feel I should go.

The music and my legacy—whatever that all means—it doesn't matter.

What matters is the imprint I've made on this tiny little planet during my tiny little life.

It's not even the size of a thumbprint. It's more of a pinkie print. A messy, smudged pinkie print of an existence.

I can't just have six months to try and redo it all, because I'm not going to be able to redo jack.

My life flashes, and I see the important moments that could have been.

Leading me to here, this little room in this town.

I'm alone and if I died right now, it wouldn't make much of a difference to tomorrow.

That really sucks.

And all of this—Matthew coming down to tell me, then to show me, to prove to me—what? Why?

It was like he was rubbing it in my face. This is what could have been, you miserable little turd, and you have less than a year left to live. See ya.

I'm reminded that I sent the angel away.

What was I supposed to do? Wait for the next natural disaster and get a backpack and head down there?

I think of Gavin, of Cole, even of Angie.

I can't breathe. I'm freaking out.

Should I stop drinking and stop cursing and stop checking out sites I shouldn't check out online?

I got the package but I didn't get any instructions.

Then, as if God is hearing me and my questions and confusion, I get the sound of a new voicemail.

40

It's three in the morning.

Who would be calling me now?

I grab my phone and listen to the message.

I half expect Matthew to tell me a place and a time to meet.

Instead, it's a voice in another language. Not someone in a mysterious voice I need to decipher but someone speaking Chinese or a language like that.

I turn off the phone and lie back in my bed in disgust.

Thanks, God. Got the message loud and clear.

59

Me and My Big Ideas

On the plane, one of those with a single aisle cutting through it and two seats on each side, my iPod's battery runs out. This is the equivalent of running out of water in a desert, even if the trek across it is only a couple of hours. I stare out the window at the blanket of bubbly clouds and tap my empty plastic cup that provided a shot of Coke.

"Mine does that all the time," the man next to me says. "Except it's not the battery. It's just one song away from giving up the ghost."

I nod at the guy next to me. He's got a friendly, round face.

"Plus, mine looks about four times that size," he says. "It's archaic, the fossil of iPods."

"What did we do without them?"

"I remember thinking that a Walkman was cool."

I chuckle and agree. I'm not exactly sure if I want to begin a conversation. You never know when the guy next to you won't stop talking.

"You live in Chicago?"

"Yeah." Then I add, much to my own hesitation, "You too?"

"I live out in Geneva."

"Beautiful town."

"Yeah. My wife always wanted to live there. It's nice. A bit out of our price range, but we manage."

Most of the time I would have already tuned out, but this guy seems

40

decent enough. It's either talk to him or talk to myself for the duration of the flight, and God knows I don't want the latter.

"You been there long?"

"Yeah, about nine years. I'm a pastor at a church out there."

"Cool."

There's really nothing about being a pastor that I think is cool, but it's what I say.

"Been a while since I went to church," I admit.

"So you live downtown?"

"Yeah. Close to Wicker Park."

He brushes back thick and unruly hair. "I had a college buddy who lived downtown. I'd visit him all the time."

"You ever see him now?"

"No. He ended up heading north. He's a mess now, to be honest. We had a lot of fun. That was back in the old days. I went through a rebellious streak."

"Really?"

"The prodigal son," the guy says.

"I think I'm still going through that phase."

"When you have three kids it's a little hard to do much of anything, not to mention having a church to take care of."

"So are you like the head pastor?"

"Yeah, for the last few years. I worked with the teens until they asked me about taking the position. It was right before building a new facility that just got finished a year ago."

"Building anything nowadays is a risky venture."

He laughs in a loaded way, as if he could tell me a few stories.

"The building is really a blessing," he says. "The church has really been giving."

"Pretty big church?"

"Over two thousand members."

The number slaps me on the side of my face. "Wow. Big responsibility."

"Yeah. It took me a while not to freak out when I first started. Again, the family keeps me grounded."

I nod.

"You married?"

"For a while I tried the ring on for size," I say. "Realized it didn't quite fit."

"Sorry to hear that."

"Yeah, me too."

"I ask because—it's the stuff like the job or being a father or whatever thing I might feel a bit in over my head with—those are the things that my wife helps me out with. Her name is Stacy and she's this amazing anchor in my life."

"Lucky man."

He nods, then shifts in his seat. The guy looks like he could stand to hit the treadmill a little more. Maybe all that Bible-studying and diaper-changing prevents him from getting to the gym.

"So were you in Nashville?"

I nod. "For work."

"What do you do?"

"I'm a music producer."

"Really?"

"Yeah."

The guy looks and sounds genuinely interested and impressed.

"So were you working with someone down there? A country musician?"

I shake my head. "No. Nicole Lawson. Ever heard of her?"

"Seriously? My wife loves her."

I could really impress him by mentioning Sean Torrent, but I don't want to get asked about Sean's next album.

"I'm working on her next album."

"Wow. That's awesome."

I give a polite smile and am not sure what else to say.

Yeah, it's awesome, and it's also going to be one of the last albums I ever make, so I guess I better make a good one, huh?

"I love 'Hold On.' That's a great song of hers."

"Where's that one from?" I ask.

"Her first album."

"I probably should know that."

40

"It's really such a hopeful message, you know?"

"Will have to check it out."

"So then—do you only work with Christian musicians?"

I want to let out a laugh and a curse and then order a shot of something. "Uh, no. I work with all kinds."

All kinds? This isn't Baskin Robbins 31 flavors, you moron.

"Oh, okay. I was just thinking—since Nicole is in that genre."

"She's moving out of it. Or trying to, at least."

"Really? Can I ask why?"

"It's a box. A lot of people wouldn't buy an album if it fits in the Christian brand. So we're doing more of a simple pop album."

He makes a *hmmm* sound that is full of thoughts and opinions.

Of all the people I get to sit by me, it's a pastor with his "*hmmm.*"

"Nicole wants more people to discover her music," I say instinctively.

"Sure."

"It's not like she's renounced her faith or anything."

I'm not sure where that statement comes from. Suddenly I'm defensive. I don't want Joe Chubby Pastor to get the wrong impression of Nicole.

"She really values her faith."

I say it as if I'm talking about Nicole's new bicycle.

"I just think it's sad that a talent like her needs to sell out," the pastor says.

"She's not selling out."

"Okay."

Now it's the guy next to me looking like he's shutting down.

"Seriously, she's not," I say. "I've never met someone with so much integrity."

"Yeah, okay. I don't mean to say anything against her—I don't know, of course. It's just—that's a hot button with me."

"What?"

"It's like pastors who never preach what they should."

"And what's that?"

His eyes have become more intense, his focus more narrow. "You probably wouldn't understand."

"I go to church."

That sounds awfully weak. And that's really pushing it, since I can't remember the last time I actually went.

"Okay."

This is the second time I've gotten an "okay" that sounds equivalent to someone saying "BS."

"No, I mean, I get it. I understand."

Why can't you just tell him that you're a believer too? That you're a Christian as well?

Maybe you're embarrassed to articulate it, or maybe you're not one hundred percent sure.

"I just get tired of pastors who have an audience—many times a growing audience—and they provide a lot of filler. A lot of fluff. They never give the gospel message."

"But we're talking about a musician."

"Of course. I know, they're different. But still."

"Still what?" I ask.

This guy is really annoying me.

"You probably wouldn't understand."

How dare he say I won't understand.

Maybe I should tell him who my father is.

I get it and I understand and I probably *get it* and *understand* more than his round little face ever will.

"Pretend like I will," I say in probably the most smartass tone I'll ever muster.

He laughs. "Look, I'm not trying to offend here. Seriously."

"No offense."

So why then do I want to jam my fist down his throat?

"It's just sad that someone so talented like Nicole Lawson needs to go out and do what everybody else is doing."

"Does she need to say Jesus in every one of her songs?"

"Come on," the man says.

"What?"

"I didn't say—look, it's fine. No big deal. I don't know Nicole."

I'm not sure why it's such a big deal for me that he not get the wrong impression.

"What about having an album that celebrates love and joy and pain?" I ask. "What if she does something that's beautiful and amazing on its own? Can't listeners discover her earlier music? Her earlier hymns and all that?"

"Look—maybe this is before your time, I don't know—but I remember when U2 was a Christian band. And all of us could embrace them as our own."

How old do you think I am? "Of course I remember."

"Then I remember they came out with *Achtung Baby* and basically seemed to want to disown their faith."

"Are you serious?"

"It sure felt like that," the pastor says.

"They were mocking the whole idea of what it meant to be a rock star."

"By drinking and cursing and all that?"

I sigh, then let out a chuckle.

"I'm just saying," the man says. "That's just my opinion."

"Yeah, well, my opinion growing up is that I always felt like Christian stuff, especially Christian songs, were trying to sell a product and a lie. No, Michael W. Smith, friends *aren't* friends forever. Maybe that sounds nice and sweet, but it's about as real as Winnie the Pooh. Because a bunch of my friends aren't Christians and don't want to have anything to do with Christianity so what's that mean?"

"That's pretty old school, if you ask me."

"If I could help Nicole Lawson do something half as meaningful as *Achtung Baby,* I'd die a happy man."

The pastor remains quiet, surely holding his next thought and next opinion.

"It's not like Nicole is going to develop a persona like Bono's 'The Fly.' It's just a genre we're talking about. It's just a box. A brand."

"Is it?" the guy next to me asks. "Is that all it is?"

Yeah, you're damn right that's all it is.

This of course is what I want to say, but I don't.

I don't say much of anything else and neither does he.

The flight suddenly becomes slower and longer. I can tell he wants to talk as much as I do.

When the flight has landed, he nods at me right before standing to get his bag. Then he extends his hand.

"Look, sorry about judging," he says as we shake. "It's a bad habit I have."

"No, it's fine."

"We all carry baggage from our upbringing. Makes us human. I hope Nicole's album is awesome. I know we'll buy it."

"She would say thanks."

"I'm Will."

I tell him my name and wish him a good day.

"What's your church's name?" I ask, more out of courtesy than anything else.

He tells me, but even as the name goes through my mind, I know. I'll never end up going there.

On the way home, I think of my father and the way he used to argue his point about God the Father and God the Son and God the Holy Spirit. I think of this and remember that no matter what I said, my father was right. He was always right.

I don't know what opinion I ever ended up having, because it always came down to what my father said.

I know I need to call my mom and do it soon.

Who knows how much time Dad has left.

Dad and everybody else.

Later that night, in the seclusion of my condo, my little box of a life, I drink to forget. I listen to forget. But drinking and listening don't make my thoughts go away. They don't make the guilt I have go away.

I've carried this around as long as I can remember.

How's that for our wonderful faith, preacher in the seat next to me?

I've had a bit too much, but nobody except God knows.

It's late and everything around disappoints, including Facebook and Twitter and ESPN and Pandora. Everything.

PART SIX

—

Heaven or Las Vegas

60

Landslide

The bad thing about being alone is that there's no one there to keep you from hitting bottom.

The second week of November, I get a call from someone warning me about my late payments on the boat. There's something in me that really just doesn't care. I want to tell this voice on the phone that I'm going to be taking the boat out for one last ride, kinda like the Jim Carrey character in *The Truman Show*. I'll get on the boat and then come to find out that everything, including the loan I took out for it, along with my whole life, is just one big fat reality show.

This is what I'd like to tell him, but instead I say nothing.

You can't take it with you, can you?

All the dreams and the desires and goals don't mean anything when the paychecks stop coming.

Potential.

In another month, maybe around Christmastime, they'll take my boat. So this guy says.

Merry Christmas.

Maybe I should take it out one last time and then "accidentally" sink it. But nobody takes boats out at this time of the year anyway.

Thinking of the cash situation, or rather, the lack-of-cash situation, makes me think of Sean. I'm still waiting for any word on him.

I still have the necklace and the parting words he left on a note.

It's just a sign that I'll be back.
And when will that be? I'm waiting.
Still waiting.
Soon.
I'm tired of waiting on people and phone calls and e-mails and faxes and sound bites and songs and albums and settling costs and royalties.
I'm in the wrong business.
I miss the days when I worked regular hours and got regular checks and lived a regular life.
Liar.
I miss the days when I had money to blow and things to blow it on.
Now it's 11:07 a.m. and I'm drinking.
Who's going to stop me? Where are you, Matthew? Where are you to beat me up again and show me my own demise over and over again?
I'm ignoring the calls that do come in.
A job here I don't want to take.
Too much headache and not enough money.
A complaint there.
Back to the drawing board with Nicole Lawson. Nobody listens to me and nobody cares.
By noon I'm already buzzed.
Maybe I should go to a confessional. But I'm not Catholic. I can do confessional anytime.
The list is as long as my debt. As full as my failures.
Bottom for me is becoming a pool of my pity.
It's really pathetic, moping around doing nothing, thinking about doing nothing, and having nothing to do.
So the text message I get on this momentous day is welcome.
It's Ellis.
Let's meet up.
I wonder who this guy is.
Where he came from.
He showed up around the same time Matthew came and left.
Coincidence?
He took an immediate interest in me.

40

Chance?

I'm available, I text back.

You forgot to mention desperate and angry and in denial.

I curse myself and wait to hear back from him.

But he obviously isn't as available and desperate as I am.

61

The Devil You Know

The band playing in front of Gavin and me is absolutely unique.

They don't fit into any box.

They also sound like teenagers on acid playing with expensive keyboards, with a lead singer that appears to have been locked up in a cave for a year who is howling about the experience.

By song three we're already standing at the bar, writing this night off.

Gavin looks at me and I know. I don't have to ask because I know.

This is part of the life. Searching bands out. Being open to something out there, something real and honest.

Catnip Stars, the band on stage now, are real and honest. I gotta give them that.

"The guy kinda sings like my ex," Gavin says, in a brutally honest way that sends beer coming out of my nose.

"You think I'm joking," he goes on. "I'm not. Some of us like to reminisce about our exes like you, but not me. I see her in my nightmares, mate. I think of her when I hear things like—like those wankers."

I laugh, and then wonder if he's right. If I really do talk about Julie that often, do I talk about her with fondness?

Maybe it's not what you say but how you say it. The look on your face when you say it.

"How much were those tickets?" Gavin asks.

"Nothing."

40

The lead singer cackles on stage and Gavin shakes his head. "Better have been. Those guys are brutal."

"They're trying."

"That's not trying. That's rubbish."

After a beer he urges us to leave. I make a pit stop before heading out into the rainy November night. The bathroom is more like a closet, with an occupied stall and a narrow wedge for a urinal.

I don't hear the door open, but when I go to wash my hands, a man is standing there. His hair looks longer, his beard thicker, his physique taller and broader. He fills most of the passage between me and the door.

He just stands there looking at me.

The face. The man.

"Hello, Tyler."

He's got an accent.

Australian?

I remain still while the thumping bass continues to blast away.

The man smiles.

I must be wearing a very different look, because he studies me and shakes his head.

"You look like you've seen a ghost."

"What do you want?" I ask.

I'm not going to bother with an "excuse me" or a "do I know you?" or any sort of normal conversation, because this is not normal and nothing in my life has been normal since midsummer, right around the same time I began seeing him.

"Why should I want anything?"

"Are you following me?"

"There, now that's better." His smirk is really nasty.

"What?"

"The color in your face is coming back. That's what anger can do, my friend."

"I don't know you."

"Really?"

I glance at the door behind him, then back at the figure.

"You act like I'm going to mug you," he says.

He wears jeans and some monstrous black boots with pointy tips. His shirt is untucked and I see some kind of pendant around his neck.

"I'd offer you a cigarette, but I know you don't smoke."

"What do you want?" I ask.

"See, that's the thing I love. That everything has to be about you. Incredible. It really is truly incredible."

I look at his arms with the folded sleeves and his big hands. He sees me doing this and then takes his palms and opens them up for me.

"Just hands, Tyler. They're not going to do anything. I don't have to touch you to hurt you. Don't you get that?"

I'm about to say something when the man goes to the sink and washes his hands, moving enough to let me get past him.

I hurry to the door, but then hear him call my name.

"You know you can't run anymore," he tells me.

I hear him chuckle as the door closed behind me.

This is the start of a very bad night.

62

Walking in My Shoes

Sometimes nightmares wake up. They sit up in your unmade bed and take a shot of coffee and a quick shower and then they come sprinting after you with an angry vengeance.

I'm on the sidewalk, having left the club we were just at, and I hear a high-pitched screech coming from somewhere underneath me. It's muffled, and echoes like it's coming from underground.

It also sounds angry.

Gavin is a few steps ahead of me and he doesn't seem to hear it.

I stop and hear it louder.

It's a gnawing eeeeeeeeeeeeeee that sounds like a rat.

A possessed and pissed off rat.

"Gavin."

He's turning the corner so I move to catch up to him. My footsteps sound hollow and flat against the pavement. When I get to the intersection and turn at the store on the corner, I stare for a minute down the road that goes into a darkened street, but I don't see or hear him.

I do hear the sound again.

Coming from above me, from all around me.

Itchy chewy scratchy gnawing little squeaks gabbling and clawing.

I look down the street we just came down. Cars fly by as drizzle begins to fall steadily. No Gavin.

I call out his name again. He didn't just vanish. I might be hearing things and even seeing things, but I'm not imagining him disappearing.

The liquor store on this corner has a glass door with a rusted grill over it. I see a figure inside and wonder if it's Gavin. The figure is bigger, wearing different clothes.

I try the door but it won't budge.

The man inside turns.

It's my father standing there, giving me that look. That look I know well. The look of shame and disappointment, the look that says how guilty I am.

He's not there. He can't be there.

I try to open the door again but can't.

The man, my father or whoever it is, just stands there. Then I see something that is a blur that I can't really comprehend. It happens so quickly that I'm numb with confusion and horror.

Another figure—dark, wet, fast—comes up behind my father and jerks an arm in front of his chest and then I see the slit on my father's neck. A waterfall of blood seeps out and my father begins to cry, his hands clutching at his neck, his mouth trying to scream but unable to.

I'm pulling at the door handle and beating on the glass and screaming to let me in.

The face behind my father shows himself and I already know who it is.

The man I just saw back at the club.

Death. Hate. Fear.

He wipes back his wavy mass of hair and sneers at me.

Those eyes.

That smile.

My father falls to the ground.

Call Mom. Call her right now. Make sure Dad's okay.

I feel something painful and I stop pounding on the door. Something loose is stuck to my fingers.

That's your own flesh, Ty. The bloody mass of your knuckles and the gnawed skin hanging off of them.

My father is a heap on the ground of the liquor store.

The floor of the store is suddenly covered with hundreds of black and

40

brown rodents. All making that same hellish sound. Hungry. Clawing. Scampering. Biting.

The rats devour my father, and the man above him just smiles.

I scream and jerk the handle of the door and finally it gives way and the rats all turn and start coming my way.

Somehow I don't feel the ground as I fall into wet and bloody darkness.

63

Fear

What'd you have to drink, man?"

I'm eighteen again and my best friend is taking care of me.

"Sebastian, man—where you been?"

"Who?"

I feel something cool and soothing against my cheek.

I'm twenty-seven and my wife is wiping my face with a damp cloth.

"Julie—Julie I just saw something awful."

"If I look like Julie then you really are knackered."

I see the red crew cut and the pale complexion and realize that Gavin is standing over me.

"What happened?"

"Yeah, good question," he says. "Here, take this."

I take the rag and keep wiping my face, my neck.

I hear the sound of the cushion of the chair as Gavin sits down. I try to sit up, but the world starts to catapult and my brain feels like a falling rock.

"Where are we?" I ask.

"My place. Mate—you're not having a lot of good fortune in cabs."

"What?"

"We made it about five minutes before I had to let you out. You were throwing up."

That's why my mouth and throat taste like this.

"I was walking—you just disappeared."

Every time I open my eyes, the room starts to wobble.

"I went into the store to get some beer. You were having a bloody seizure at the door. Screaming about rats and your father." Gavin curses, then laughs.

He's holding a can of beer.

"Seriously, what happened?"

"I don't know," I say.

I don't.

"There's no way you could've gotten that sloshed that fast."

"I didn't. I just..."

He waits for me to finish my sentence.

I think of the man in the bathroom.

He slipped me something. Or injected me or somehow got something into my system that made me freak out.

"What?" Gavin asks.

I hear the sound of ESPN in the background. I can smell bacon in this apartment. The couch I'm on feels like it was made a hundred years ago, for short people.

"I don't know," is all I can say.

Something is in my system. But I don't know if it's liquor or drugs or something else.

It's fear. Enough of that can do anything, Tyler, and you don't know—you can't begin to know the sort of terror you can experience.

I want to sit up and get up and start to run, but I can barely move my eyes.

"Hey, come on," Gavin says. "Stay put there. I'm going to call you Sean Torrent."

"Funny."

"Let me get you a pillow. I just want to make sure you're done with all your throwing up."

"I think so."

"What were you hollering on about?"

"What do you mean?"

"Back there—you were on the ground screaming a name over and over again."

"Who?"

"Someone named Matthew. Who's that?"

64

Come as You Are

I hear myself sigh and realize it's a bad habit that I've developed when I'm by myself.

I'm parked on the curb in front of a house that used to be half mine. It was part of a story that was only half told. Part of a picture half there.

Julie and I married in 1996 and divorced in 2002. Six years. That's how long it lasted, how long we gave it. Or rather, how long *I* gave it.

This medium-sized house in Batavia was the place we thought we'd be for a while. Four bedrooms were double what we really needed. Julie wanted a couple of kids. I wanted to produce U2's next album. Guess our priorities eventually split us in half.

Earlier today I decided to head into the suburbs to just drive. Those wonderful suburbs that Arcade Fire did a wonderful job dissecting on their last album. I get the sentiments. Yet a part of me still longs for this strange, safe land with square plots and simple lives.

I start up the car.

It will be the last time I ever see the house, though I don't know it at the moment.

We never know things like that. The last word you ever utter to your friend before he dies. The last embrace you feel with a loved one before you never see her again. The last laugh between colleagues. The last whatever.

In some ways, it would be nice to know. Maybe if you had subtitles under the experience you were going through that would help you know its importance. Or perhaps if you had a director's commentary ringing in your ear, telling you what this scene meant, the purpose of this conversation, the symbolism of this set piece.

It would be nice if our lives had those things, but our life isn't a movie and doesn't come with a soundtrack.

Events and conversations and experiences don't work in an orderly structure. They're not part of some hero's journey. They're not full of symbolism and metaphors and foreshadowing. Most of the time they're random and wacky and ridiculous, and when we step away to see the meaning we can't begin to decipher the meaning because the reality is there is no meaning. Accidents waiting to happen. Mistakes waiting to be made. Life and breath and then one day it's gone.

The leaves and the color are almost gone and I'm beginning to dread another winter.

A winter that could possibly be my last.

At least I'll have work to keep me busy.

I always submerge myself in work in the middle of the Chicago winter. That's the only way to see light at the end of the tunnel.

I'm heading down the street in my car and find myself daydreaming, and I end up turned around.

See. The randomness of life exhibited before my very eyes.

Instead of heading toward I-88, for some reason I was going in the opposite direction. I turn my car around and connect with another winding side street going through woods, heading back south toward the Interstate.

And it's here that I come across the church.

First there's the sign; then I see it on the edge of the street I'm driving on. **Faith Creek Community Church.**

Even though I forgot the name after the pastor mentioned it, I remember it now.

There it is on the hill, right here in Geneva, this close to a closing dream of mine.

I slow down and then turn and drive into the large parking lot.

It's Tuesday morning and there's only a handful of cars parked on this sprawling campus. I wouldn't even know it's a church except for the towering white steeple and the signs that say FCCC.

40

The guy wasn't kidding when he said it's a growing church. Looks like one of those megachurches.

I chuckle at the randomness of life.

A part of me believes and always has believed that life is not random. That there is a purpose behind everything. Even our mistakes. God has a way of using them to show something, to tell us something, to instruct and to give insight.

Of course, if I listened and looked for Him more, I'd probably see this a whole lot more.

So I met a pastor on a plane. Big deal. There are lots of churches in the Chicago area and lots of pastors. So I met one and then stumbled across his church.

"So what?" I say out loud.

I ignore the voice that whispers *maybe he can help you.*

I really ignore the one that says *maybe you should tell him what's happening.*

He's a pastor, not a psychiatrist. He surely can't prescribe the kind of meds I need.

Take two aspirin and put on this Michael W. Smith CD.

I'm parked, waiting, looking at the church, wondering. Should I get out? If so what should I do then? Just tell him I was in the neighborhood and wanted to see how things were going and what his take on Romans happened to be?

I put the car back in first gear and head out of this parking lot.

Maybe I'll come back and hear him speak, or maybe I'll never see this church or hear his name ever again.

Random.

That's what life is about.

There are a lot of churches in this country and they don't do a lot of good and I wouldn't know if they did because I haven't been a part of a church—a real part—since my high school days.

Is it that dark down there, Ty?

I soon find the Interstate and speed home with the sounds of Sean Torrent filling my car.

Can you turn on the light? Oh, no, wait, you can't.

Sean's rage and hate fill the car.

It's because you're in the belly of the whale waiting and watching and wondering and wishing.

The loud music sure doesn't help anymore. It used to. It used to drown out the voices and sorrows.

The sorrows learned to swim.

Lyrics pop up like signs on the freeway. Every day, every hour, every moment.

I wonder what life would have been like if those lyrics had been replaced with something a little better.

Something a little more helpful and assuring and meaningful for eternity.

"I will swallow you whole, I will fill this hole," Sean sings.

Sean's voice and his lyrics certainly don't help my mood.

Once again, I let out a big fat woesome sigh, but that doesn't help anything either.

65

Goodbye, Yellow Brick Road

That sounds like a lot of fun, but I have to work."

This is the text on my business card, the tagline on my home page. This is the line I've used for the last fifteen years. I'm surprised my sister is even asking, but I guess after Dad's close call with death, Kendra is feeling a little more sisterly.

"You can't get off for just a couple of days? Don't people in your industry celebrate Thanksgiving?"

"They're not used to giving thanks. They're used to receiving them."

"I'm serious," Kendra says.

"I am too. I'd love to come visit."

"Yeah, right."

She's right and you both know it.

"Maybe at Christmas?"

"We're going to be in North Carolina for Christmas."

"Seriously?"

"I told you about that when you were at the lake."

"Then maybe I'll come and we can relive our childhood."

"Stop."

"I don't like your Thanksgiving meals anyway. It's harder to lose weight these days."

Hoping to have those six-pack abs while you're lying on your back in a coffin? Huh, Tyler, buddy?

"You could gain a little. Look at Doug."

The very picture of what I don't want to be.

Well hello there, Mr. High and Mighty man.

"Look, I'll see if there's a possibility," I say.

I hate it when people don't get back to me or blow smoke up my rear, so I don't know why I'm doing it with Kendra.

One word, pal.

"You won't come," she says.

Guilt.

"I'll see."

"You have some girl that you haven't told me about?"

"No."

"Ty?"

"I don't."

"You didn't exactly tell me about that last girl. The model?"

"Yeah, I know."

"Are you back with her?"

"No."

She pauses for a minute.

Maybe the way I said *no* made her pause.

Two letters. One word.

But Kendra knows me and knows my simple little "no" wasn't so simple.

No, I'm not back with her and I'll never be back with her because it was her choice to leave without much of an explanation, without much of a warning, with a simple heartfelt goodbye that ripped my world apart, but never mind, so, no.

"Are you okay?"

This is the question people should ask Sean Torrent.

I'm fine.

I'm not taking heroin.

Last time a doctor checked, about three or six years ago, my blood pressure and cholesterol looked fine.

I'm not making millions, but I'm managing to make a living.

I mean, come on—I've got a boat. A real big boat.

At least for a little while longer.

40

"I'm fine. Why?"

"You sure?" she asks.

"Okay, I'll confess. I did buy Taylor Swift's last album. There. I said it. I've been wanting to get that off my chest for a long time."

"You're not funny." But she laughs anyway. "I liked that album."

Matthew forgot to mention another reason I'm sarcastic. I use it as a diversion.

"I'll see about Thanksgiving."

"No you won't."

"I promise."

And I mean that I'll see.

Seeing doesn't mean doing.

Seeing is something you can do from afar.

I've been seeing lots and lots my whole life without doing much.

"I love you," Kendra says, surprising me.

I swear, it's like she knows something.

I wonder if Matthew has visited her, too.

66

The Same Deep Water as You

In my dream, I'm working with a supergroup.

There's Sean Torrent singing away.

Trent Reznor is on keyboards.

Eric Clapton plays guitar.

Paul McCartney is on bass. Yet he looks about twenty years old.

Hold on.

John Bonham is bashing away at the drums.

Wait a minute. That's a ghost playing the drums.

"Yes, and what's wrong with that?"

I look to my right and see Steve Martin, there with his banjo.

"How are we going to work the banjo in?" I ask.

"Infinitesimal gradations," Brian Eno tells me. "Now please leave. I'm the only producer worthy of being here."

They laugh and John Bonham throws a drumstick that bounces off my head.

Then I wake up.

I walk in darkness through an open door and down a hallway.

Where am I?

The carpet underneath my bare feet is wet. Each step makes an oozing sound as I move toward the faint light.

40

A low hum sounds from outside.

I'm on a business trip. I'm staying with some musician at his home in L.A. while I help him with a few songs for his next album.

The open room is empty and who knows where the owner is.

You need to leave. You need to go home.

I step outside in the cool night. A plane flies above me. I hear the sound of static, like a speaker left on and buzzing.

Then I see the pool.

Even in the limited light, I can tell the water is darker than it should be.

"It's time, Tyler."

I turn to see the man talking. Nobody is around. The hum continues, crackling and buzzing, while the water licks at the edges of the concrete.

"Hello? Parker?"

Parker is the musician I'm here to help.

But the voice wasn't Parker's.

Parker's conveniently off with one of his girlfriends.

"It's time for another baptism, Tyler."

I feel cold and see that I'm only wearing my boxers. My body is covered in little bumps.

The voice is his.

The man following me.

The man who knows me and knows me well.

"It's time to swim in the blood, Tyler. Time to sink and swallow. Time to suck it up little by little."

I feel something push me and I suddenly plunge into something warm and wet and thick and chunky.

I try to scream but my mouth is full of hot liquid and I gag and shake and flail away.

I can't swim in this muck, this morass.

One hand, then the other, slowly, with my feet and legs kicking out.

Little by little.

Yet I feel dragged under, the bubbling grime pulling me in.

Say hello to Jonah on your way into the belly of the beast you little—

Then I choke and scream as I reach the surface.

Soon I'm on the edge of the pool, the water around me—and it's just water, cool and smelling like chlorine—moving up and down and glowing off the cold moonlight.

I cough and gag and spit out but there's no one around.

There's no bloody pool.

There's no engulfing mouth beneath me.

I float for a while, dizzy and disoriented.

The buzzing sound is still there, but it's coming from a speaker that was left on a little too loud.

What are you doing here, Tyler?

I rest my arms against the hard surface edge of the pool and stare up at the throbbing moon.

67

World in My Eyes

This world has been telling me I need a better life ever since I was born. A better tricycle, a better pair of gym shoes, a better lunch, a better stereo, a better car to borrow from the parents, a better jump shot, a better complexion, a better girlfriend, a better college to go to, a better set of friends, a better job, a better wife, a better life.

Getting older is about dealing with this friend and enemy known as Better.

He whispers.

He lingers.

He mocks.

He teases.

The more you play around with Better, the more he's going to hurt and destroy.

Since the dawn of cable and MTV and satellite dishes and the Internet, we have had to deal with Better.

The world paints a pretty picture, a far better picture, and then stands on the other side of the raging river, inviting us to come over and check it out.

You too can achieve your dreams.

You too can become a success.

You too can feel the wonder and the power and the exquisite absolute perfection we have to offer if you just swim

over

here.

And you try and he tries and she tries and we all try but we never get over there.

It's a myth, a mirage, a lie.

Wisdom comes in ignoring the voices and ignoring the invitations.

There's still time.

There's still a way.

I deserve to get a little something I want. I deserve to feel good and to be happy and to taste a little taste, just a little, just a tiny little drop.

"What can I get for you?"

Where am I?

In a plane or in a restaurant or back home with Julie?

Does it even matter?

"Escape," I tell the airline attendant.

"Excuse me?"

"No. There is no excuse. There's no excuse for any of us."

68

Life's What You Make It

I can see the building on 401 North Wabash Avenue from my roof. When I tell the cabdriver the directions, it doesn't dawn on me that I'm telling him to drive me to Trump Tower. I watched this ninety-two-story hulking, glowing beast go up but have never set foot inside it, like a lot of places in Chicago.

Until now.

It's eight o'clock and it's a clear but cold evening. I go through glass doors into the lobby and say that I'm seeing Mr. Ellis on the 51st floor. I don't know if Ellis is his first or last name, but I'm not about to say DJ Ellis. Makes me think of DJ Jazzy Jeff and the Fresh Prince.

The square LCD screen right below a **No Smoking** sign in the elevator reveals ghostly floor numbers. I feel weightless, a bit dizzy.

The hallway leads to a door that I knock on. Doesn't seem too different from any other condo I've been in until the door opens and I see a sprawling, glistening panorama of Chicago settling in for the night.

Ellis stands at the door and shakes my hand.

"You made it. Good man."

"Yeah, sure. Thanks for the call."

For a second, it's impossible not to breathe everything in and remain silent.

The soft orange glow of the lights. The massive flat screen television that's showing a poker competition. Stereos seem to be surrounding me from all sides, playing "Rabbit in Your Headlights" by UNKLE as if the knock on the door was set to cue the song.

I know this song well because I love the Thom Yorke–sung haunting chill-out melody.

"Tell me this place isn't insane," Ellis says with a laugh. "Nobody in the world, including Trump himself, deserves to live like this. So I tell myself to make me feel better."

I'm glancing at the floor-to-ceiling windows. The river below us makes an arrow to the lake that seems like a stone's throw away.

"Keep your coat on," Ellis says, as he opens doors that lead to a walkway lit up by a dozen candlelike illuminations.

I step out onto the stone terrace and feel the wind spiraling around me. He walks beside me.

"This is why I bought this place. For this. Look at this. Come here— you have to come over to the side."

I stay put. "No thanks."

"Don't like heights?"

"Not exactly," I say.

"Me neither. But you get used to this after awhile. Trust me. It's a rush. I mean, the whole world can be sucking you dry and making you feel absolutely drained and you step out here and it all . . . goes . . . away."

The wall he's standing beside comes to his chest, but isn't tall enough for me.

He leans over it and then looks back at me and laughs.

"You gotta be here in the summertime. I've slept out here."

I feel dizzy and imagine in horror someone sleepwalking out here.

Ellis walks beside me and heads back inside. I close the door behind me.

"It takes a while to get used to it. You will."

He says this as if I'm going to be staying a while. Or visiting often.

I don't get it with this guy.

"Drink?"

"Sure. What do you have?"

"Tell me what you want. I'll have it."

Like everything about him, Ellis doesn't say this in an arrogant

40

I've-got-something-to-prove manner. I think he's just being completely honest and can't help it.

Some other guys I know might try to be wise guys and make Ellis eat his words. But I don't.

I'm still figuring out why he invited me here, if this has something to do with work or with Sean Torrent or with my industry.

"Relax and take off your coat," he says, giving me the gin and tonic. "So that's got New Amsterdam Straight Gin in it. Cheap and crazy smooth. If you don't like it I'll get you something a little more traditional."

The music in the background sounds like Four Tet or a mix. I sip the drink and feel like I'm in some Brothers Grimm story, just about ready to be poisoned.

I could see Ellis showing me around the rest of his place, but he doesn't bother. He changes the track and puts on something from Tricky's landmark album, *Maxinquaye*.

Excellent choice in music, I've gotta give him that.

He sits, making it awkward for me not to take a seat in one of the three chairs in the living room.

"I've been in this place just about a year. I was one of the few people who actually seemed to make a profit out of the insane housing flop of the last few years."

"I tried," I say.

"Tried what?"

"I thought about getting a place, buying a foreclosure or something like that, hoping to make it into a studio."

"Yeah? So what happened?"

"Life happens."

He doesn't press me, and I like that. Most would ask, not just out of curiosity but out of need.

I'm still trying to attach a need to this guy.

I sip my drink and say something about the muted poker game on television.

"Yeah, bad habit of mine, gotta confess. I know you blow money but I can't help it. You play much?"

I shake my head.

"Smart man," he says.

I glance around, take a sip, shift in my chair.

"Man, you look absolutely awkward and miserable," he says with a laugh.

"Really?"

"Oh yeah. What's up?"

"I'm just—I'm a little at a loss here."

"You came on your own accord, right?"

"Yeah," I say. "I just—what's going on here?"

"What do you mean?"

"Look, I'm not trying to be rude or anything, but I'm just waiting for you to try and sell me a time-share or some pyramid scheme. I don't know."

Ellis laughs. It's obvious he's completely amused. "You think I need to sell you a time-share? I mean, come on."

"Well, no."

"Here's the thing," Ellis says. "I'm a good judge of people, ninety-five percent of the time. I don't wait. Life is too quick to wait. You act on what you want and what you feel. I met you and thought you were decent. I don't know, but I'm guessing you're not one of those insanely rich guys. Those guys are mostly pricks. You're into music but you're not a musician. Most musicians I've met are ridiculous. You're good-looking but not too good-looking. And, well, you're not gay. I'm not looking or asking for anything except someone cool to hang out with and someone who won't talk about politics or religion, but rather music and making music."

"Okay."

"And when I say talking about music and making music, I don't mean selling and marketing music. I mean music, period. The beats and the rhythms and the soundscapes. That all sound *okay* to you?"

Now I feel a bit stupid. "Yeah."

"You sure? Because one thing I don't like is repeating myself. Or needing to question what the person I'm with is thinking. Got that?"

"Sure. Got it. Enough said."

"Good. Cheers."

The thing with this—well, this life—is that most of the time, I've never come across people who get it. Not who get me, because I don't expect that to ever

40

fully happen. Plus, nobody ever really "gets" anybody else, the way I'm talking about the word get. But most of the time, acquaintances leave me unimpressed.

I'm not counting artists. I'm talking about those who I sit back with, talking about life and sports and music, with no other vested interest. At least none that I can detect. This is not Bono I'm talking with, hoping to one day produce. This isn't Brian Eno I'm discussing music with, asking him questions to pick his brain in order to better myself. This isn't Sean Torrent I'm talking with, trying to figure out whowhatwherewhenandwhy in order to make our jobs easier in the long run.

No.

This is a DJ I met who's sitting across from me, leaving me impressed.

Not by wisdom. That doesn't work for me.

Not by wealth. That's like a hot girl walking past before starting to talk and reveal just how full of herself she really is.

Not by wit. There are plenty of people I know that are funny and witty. Someone like Cole in his deadpan dry sense of humor, for example.

No, this guy, he *gets* it.

He doesn't mind talking about a local eatery one minute and then getting deep the next. He seems in touch with his emotions.

I'm impressed because I can carry on a conversation with him the way I used to be able to with Laila.

She was the only one I could really, truly talk to.

Is there a connection between the two of them?

I don't know.

I just know that this is different than talking about nothing with others. About living and breathing and eating next to others without knowing them.

In a span of an hour, sitting there listening to music and drinking, something I do with others, I get to know this guy better than those I consider my closest friends.

Maybe I should find this sad.

Not tonight.

Fueled by standing on the top of the world, I'm feeling liberated.

"Here's the thing. People let you down."

"Yeah," I say.

We're talking loud, above the gushing wind, as close to the edge as I can possibly stand.

"You get that, don't you?" Ellis asks. "I mean everybody does, right?"

"Sure."

"This place is usually so full of people and most of the time it's totally empty. Devoid of that thing, you know. Relying on someone. No strings, nothing attached, just a bud."

"This place is amazing. Really."

"Of course it is. I like it best when I'm by myself, to be honest. I sit on this deck and look out onto Chicago and I just soak it all in. This place is my sanctuary."

"I can see why."

"I've felt like this, here, all of my life."

"Like what?"

"Above everything. Above it all. Ever since I can remember. Not because of any one thing, not really. I mean, it's never been about one thing but it's been just about—about this here."

Ellis puts his palm against his heart and taps it.

"I've always just believed and it's happened. Really." He curses in an incredulous way. "Stuff I've seen would blow your mind. It blows my mind. Still. Yet I sit here at nights and don't have to wonder. I accept it. It's reality. It's reality and it's all this crazy blur."

I nod and look out, feeling the night sigh against my neck and my cheek.

"What moves you?"

"What?"

"It's not a difficult question," Ellis says.

"A lot of things."

"You don't need to think long to answer that question."

"Moments."

"See, I told you," he says.

"Those—those defining moments. Like a music video. Those moments that you know you'll always remember."

"They come often?"

"Not often enough. Not anymore."

40

"What if I told you that I could make a moment turn into an entire weekend? An entire week?"

"I wouldn't be surprised."

"Would you be willing to see?"

"To see what?"

"To see if I'm being honest?"

I'm about to ask again and try and figure out . . . but I already promised.

Maybe I should accept this.

It's about time I just stop with the questions and the searching and just go.

"I'm not saying you're lying," I say.

"But I might be telling a tall tale."

"In your line of things, I'm sure that lots of things can happen."

He curses and finishes his drink, then looks over the edge of the deck.

"I've never been a big fan of showing off or flexing my pecs. I hate guys like that. Seriously. I'm being honest."

"Okay."

"Listen—I'm being totally serious. What I can show you will change everything."

"What? Where?"

"I'm doing a set of club appearances in Vegas in a couple of weeks. You need to check them out."

"I'm busy."

"You already said business was a little—what did you say—spotty?"

"Yeah."

"My manager can't go. Take his seat."

"Just like that?"

He comes up to me and stares right in my face. I feel off balance with nowhere to go.

"Yes. Just like that. Don't sleep on it. *Yes* or *no.*"

Just do it, Tyler.

Don't wait anymore.

Don't hesitate.

"Why not?"

He laughs. "This isn't an invitation."

"Then what is it?"

"This is an intervention, man. You've lived your whole life and you still barely know half."

"Half of what?"

"Half of everything."

"And Vegas is going to show me? I've been there before."

"I could take you to Topeka, Kansas, and fill in the crevices."

"The crevices?"

"If I wanted to hear myself talk I'd record myself. Stop repeating everything I say."

"Sorry."

"And don't apologize." He curses. "I stopped apologizing when I learned my father didn't know how to. Listen. Listen good. What you know and what you think you know is all a big fat lie. It's a mirage. The people that really do know manage to outdo expectations every day. It's not in some mystery pill or some psychobabble, but it's what's inside of here—right here—right there."

He jerks his fist against my chest.

I sip my drink and wonder what this guy is talking about.

For the first time in some time—I can't even remember—I have a strange feeling.

Not fear or anxiety or anger or guilt.

I feel a light-headed release of giddy laughter. As if it's drifting from the street below and floating above and swirling in the recesses of this open deck in the Heavens of Chicago.

If this guy's going to show me something I haven't seen or done or thought about, I want to see it.

I want to prove him wrong. Almost as badly as I want him to be right.

69

Square One

Maybe I should feel guilt for leaving like this, but I don't.

Maybe I should check in with someone before I decide to check out, but I don't.

Maybe I should listen to those voices inside that tell me to be careful and tell me to stay back, but I don't.

I can't remember the last time I felt this...

This free.

Sure you do, but denial is the bag over your head.

Through the airport check-in, I ignore the memories.

Even while I'm waiting at the gate, wondering when and if Ellis is going to show up, I breathe in my own air while the bag of forgetting remains wrapped over my head.

Soon they're checking everybody in and I stand in line with the rest of the passengers in first class.

Maybe I should wait, but I want to enjoy every moment of living someone else's life.

It's only after everybody has boarded that Ellis steps onto the plane, wearing sunglasses, some really cool jacket, expensive jeans, and a T-shirt probably worth more than all the clothes I'm wearing.

"You made it," he tells me, with a bit of irony.

"You're the one who barely made it."

"I was talking to this lady." He takes off his shades and it looks like he hasn't slept. "Met her when I was getting my coffee. I think I've convinced her to come to Vegas."

"On this flight?"

"No. We looked. Another one."

"Who was she?"

"She was a work of art. Flawless."

"Her name?"

"She e-mailed it to me."

He gets situated and I can smell the liquor drifting from his pores.

"Long night?"

"They always are." He smiles, then adds, "It pays the bills."

"Fun way to pay them."

He slips his shades back on as he pulls out his iPod. "Listen, not to be a grinch or anything, but I need my sleep. It's a short trip, but long enough for me to revitalize."

"Yeah, that's cool."

"Here—go through this and pick out some songs."

I hold his iPod. "Some songs for what?"

"Some songs to play tonight. I'm curious to see what you come up with."

Surely he already had a playlist for tonight. Or some idea.

"What if I choose something really awful?"

"You won't find anything awful on that iPod. That's the special one."

"Special how?"

"Check it out. Nighty-night."

For the next three hours and twenty-three minutes, I'm lost. And mesmerized.

A dozen or more times, I want to wake up the sleeping man next to me, but I don't. So I have to keep my surprise to myself.

For now.

I close my eyes and escape.

I'm nudged and I take out the earphones.

"Feel any different?"

"Where'd you get this stuff?" I ask.

"Not because of the music. Because of where we're almost at."

40

I can feel the plane beginning to descend as I hand him back his iPod. "There's a lot of stuff on there—stuff I've never heard. Demos. Crazy mixes. Songs that sound like they're on albums that have yet to be released."

"They are."

"Where—how—"

Ellis laughs. "The thing about this life is that there is always a door to go through. Always. Most people never even bother knocking. They live their whole life just outside, never in, always wondering and looking at it and thinking about it. But never knocking."

I'm not sure exactly what he's talking about.

What do doors and knocking have to do with music?

"You're mine the next few days. And then..."

I wait. But the follow up to the "And then..." never comes.

I'm cold in my seat and feel that lingering little snake of guilt.

I know the first thing I need to do when I land is sliver it in pieces and leave it on this plane.

70

Let Go

I like this place because it brings out the authenticity in people's hearts."

I laugh because I still don't get Ellis's sense of humor. But he's not trying to make a joke.

The world around us is black, with shadows shuffling around and red lights illuminating bare smiles and shoulders. Vegas is outside beyond the glass, just below this hovering sphere. We're in one of the big-name casinos in one of their big-name lounges.

Already I'm feeling lost.

Already I'm ready to wake up.

"People live their whole lives trying to be something, only to break it minutes after coming here," Ellis says.

I watch a woman walking by. Then I look at Ellis and know he's watching me.

"I thought you were supposed to work tonight."

"I am."

It's closing in on ten at night. Ten Las Vegas time.

"How'd you get into all this?"

"Probably the same as how you got into it. Dreams of fame and fortune. And, of course, love of music. The never-ending romance with irresistible rhythms."

"Did you always think you'd become a DJ?"

Ellis laughs. "I've wanted to do it all throughout my life. Act. Write. Sports. Everything. But music—nothing compares to it. Right?"

"Yeah."

"I went to college for a couple of years but dropped out. Lived in Los Angeles for a while. New York. I lived in the club scene. Picked up some nasty little habits. But also picked up some nice contacts. The key was kicking those bad habits to the curb and using those contacts instead. And that's what I did."

"Yeah, but how do you go from—from being at those clubs to then headlining a gig at one?"

"How do you go from being in a studio bringing coffee to Sean Torrent to one day producing his next album?"

I nod. "Right place at the right time."

"Yes, but you have to know what to *do* with that right moment. A lot of people think that life is completely meaningless and pointless and they think they'll never be in that right moment. But they probably have already missed half a dozen of them. Others think everything happens for a reason and if the great Allah of the North decides it will happen, it will happen. It's about fighting to find that moment. And then having the talent to do something with it."

"Talent can be a subjective thing."

Ellis sips his water and uncrosses his legs, then moves over the table we're sitting next to. "Everything is subjective. But with enough determination, you can make the perception absolutely reality."

"What perception is that?"

"Any perception. The Beatles convinced a whole world they were the best and the forefathers of pop music. The same way King James convinced the world that his Bible was the definitive authority. Both were conning people. Because they were just selling something. A product or a faith. It's all the same thing."

"Wow."

"What? Don't believe me?"

"That's a pretty cynical look at things. To say the least."

"I love the Beatles and I read my Bible," Ellis says. "That's not the point.

The point is about building something. A brand. A life in this world. Not *this* world—this place is Narnia on crack. We entered through the wardrobe but instead of talking animals, we got a whole lot of other crazy things. I'm talking about life outside of Vegas, life in the regular world."

I think of Ellis's place in Chicago and wonder what the regular world looks like to him.

"Most people get to a point where they're content," Ellis says. "Content to just coexist. Go to a job, pay bills, go on an occasional vacation, have a barbeque with friends, raise three children, spend their retirement someplace that's warm. Try to get life in order before turning too old. Contentment. That's what most people do. But people like us, we're different. People like us have tried and we've kept trying. People like us look around every single day to be at the right place and at the right time. And we're both too stubborn or too stupid to give up at the end of another failed day."

"I'd say it's been a while since you've seen that kind of day."

"What does failure look like to you, Tyler?"

"Procrastination. Like the house I never bought and the studio I never built."

Ellis curses loud enough for the couples around us to notice. Nobody cares, not here. "So what? Wake up when you're back home and just press the trigger. Just find something that works and buy it. Do it."

"I don't know."

"I get the idea that you worry way too much."

"I blame my father," I say.

"My father was a scared little man who took out his fears on every single person he could find, including his son," Ellis responds. "By the time I was sixteen, I had enough. I told him—I told him one night after he chastised me and verbally abused not only me but my mother—I went outside with him and told him that if he ever did something like that again, I'd cut his throat in his sleep. And you know what? He believed me."

"Wow. Intense."

"You know why he believed me? Because he knew me. Because he knew I wasn't just saying that. I meant it."

"How are things now?"

"What do you mean 'now'?"

"With your parents."

"I don't have parents. That was one of the first things that signaled the end. There were many more things but, hey, when you tell someone you're going to kill them if they don't watch out, they don't have a lot of desire to stick around, huh?"

"Sorry to hear that."

"Why?" Ellis asks. "I don't wake up longing for Daddy. If and when I think of them, I think how good it was to cut the cord. Because it helped me to be here, to be right here right now."

"My father's almost dead. Had a heart attack not long ago," I say.

"Maybe it's time to cut the cord."

I nod.

"I'm just saying. But look around. Man, why the hell are we talking about our failed fathers? You're not a father, are you?"

"No. Thank goodness."

"Me neither. See, we learned. We're smarter than those fools. We're smart enough to know we're not going to fail where they and many, many other fools fail. Again, that's being at the right place at the right time. Or more like not being at the wrong place at the wrong time."

"Yeah, maybe."

"Look, Tyler. Tonight, and tomorrow, and the next day and the next, don't go around with that melancholy baggage on your face and your soul. Lose the baggage. Lose yourself. Because maybe, just maybe, you'll be surprised what you'll find."

71

God Is a DJ

I'm in third grade, living outside of Munich, Germany, and already feeling the disappointment of my father, who obviously has never sinned in his entire life. I've gone with my classmates on a ski week to Italy and not once do I think this is unusual (though the older I get, the more surreal I find that life to be). My best friend, Jacob, offered to pay for it. Or I should say his family offered to pay for it. No wonder I always cheer for the Swedish athletes in the winter Olympics.

It's the end of the day and students from our school have gone into the small town and are hanging out in a disco. A real authentic Italian disco that's having a kids' night. Most of the students are older than Jacob and I, but for one night we're hanging out with them. Nobody's doing anything illegal or immoral—we're a bunch of kids, from twelfth grade down. I just remember the neon lights and the dark shadowy corners and the wood dance floor. We danced to Pink Floyd's "Another Brick in the Wall."

For the first time in my life, I realize that there is hope.

I realize that I can escape from Charles William Harrison. Even for the night.

"We don't need no education," I chant with the rest of the kids dancing and laughing and singing.

Thirty years later, I haven't changed much.

I'm still that boy, marveling at my surroundings. A boy trying to escape

40

his father for the night. A boy unshackled and realizing the world is far more exciting than some lead him to believe.

And a boy who…dances.

Music has a personality and the song playing is like that crazy girl in college that shows up at parties and seeks you out and only wants a little chunk of your soul in return for a really good time.

One word for you, Tyler. Angie.

The thought is lost in the enclosed space of shadows and lights dancing with one another. I can feel the bass of the song rattling off my skin, the touch of strangers against my shoulders, the motion of youth carrying me along. For a while I'm not Tyler Harrison anymore. I'm not thirty-nine anymore. I'm not close to my expiration date anymore.

For a while, I imagine I'm the captain at the controls. The figure in the jeans and the T-shirt, toned and tanned and thrilled to be hovering on the stage behind an electric turntable.

I remember what Ellis told me before departing into the club and leaving me on my own.

The words flicker on the walls and strobe through the strangers.

"In this place we can be ourselves. The person we always wanted to be. Everybody wants to dance and move and be a part of something. That's the beauty. There's no such thing as a clique, not on the dance floor of a club."

Ellis's words are true.

I don't have to worry about dancing with someone, because a dozen people are surrounding me and dancing with me.

I don't have to worry about being on my own, because everybody is attached and a part of something here and now.

We all cling to the beats and move like a well-oiled choir. I see smiles and glances up at the star-painted ceiling and faces lost in movement and fixed in concentration. Hands wave up in the air like a revival as Ellis urges them back and forth. This is our church. Age and fashion and personality and past don't matter here and now in these moments as the massive cluster shifts like waves on the ocean.

A dark-haired beauty moves toward me and for a while remains at my side, then smiles and disappears into the rest of the bodies.

I think of the last time I was dancing like this and I can't help but think of Laila.

I feel dizzy and out of breath and warm and thirsty, but never once do I feel silly or out of place or frigid.

This is all build-up. All foreplay. All forgetting and letting go.

And it almost works.

72

Stairway to Heaven

It's easy to forget what time it is, or what day it is, or who I am.

In this place, it's easy to shut out the noise. There's enough in this city to drown out everything else.

That first night drifts into the rest of the week like blood in water, coloring and saturating everything. I feel like I'm swimming underwater, that I can't come up for air, that I don't want to go up for air. I'd rather stay down here in the dark, submerged and satisfied.

I leave my phone in my hotel suite.

I listen to Ellis talk about his views on life and love and the moment, as he keeps saying. *The moment, Tyler. It's about the moment.*

I find myself stuck in moments from my life. Stuck in that house in Germany and on that mountain in North Carolina and on the in-law's driveway in the suburbs and on a city street in Chicago. Stuck in moments I can't let go.

The past can either prevent or propel.

So Ellis says.

You are the only one that's going to hold yourself back. The only voice that's going to say yes or no. We live life like we're still sixteen and capable of being grounded. Nobody's going to take away your lunch anymore. Nobody's going to cancel recess.

As the days and nights morph into one long giant party, Ellis continues to educate me.

I know that denial usually comes before anger in terms of the stages of grief, but there's no road map for the journey I'm on. I'm at some party with beautiful people serving delicious drinks and there's no reason for me to feel angry at all.

"Having fun?" Ellis says at some point when he catches me talking to a woman.

I nod and he seems to like the look on my face. The way a father might with the gift he just gave his son. The way an older brother might when bringing his younger sibling to a forbidden party.

Then he whispers something to me.

He knows this girl, and he knows what she's like.

In this place, it's that easy.

In this place, I'm not in denial anymore.

It's about the moment. It's about living without regrets.

I drink to lessen the guilt. I drink to stop hearing the voices.

The only voice I hear is Ellis's.

The only sin I know of is not living life the way you want to.

The only words I hear belong to my sponsor, the Chicago DJ who seems to be working on a pet project.

If we make it to eighty-five, what are we going to regret? We're going to regret not taking that chance, not seizing the moment, not embracing the now that we had.

I'm staring at the now and am lost in her eyes and her lips and her long legs.

This is the second day of being around her and yesterday I didn't seize the moment or fully embrace the now.

I woke up sometime this morning wondering why. Wondering why not.

And later in muted light and quiet corners, I follow her down stairs and a hallway.

I pause in the doorway for a minute and she looks back and laughs.

"There are some things I'm not good at, and that's one of them," she says.

"What?"

"The middle ground. The place you've been the last twenty-four hours.

40

The playground. Doesn't work for me. It's cute for a little while. But I'm done playing cute."

She enters the soft crimson glow and the door slides back and stops, shortly before closing.

It remains open, just a sliver, the slit of hazy light inviting me in.

I stand there for a moment. I think about what Ellis whispered to me.

People talk about an eternity, but sometimes a night can really feel better than Heaven ever will, and you and I both know that.

My hand touches the door.

Then I picture someone else and remember her last words to me.

I think of Laila and think of the last thing she ever told me.

This makes my decision.

73

Heaven Is Ten Zillion Light Years Away

The doors remain open.
  The gold glitters.
  The dice fall.
The drinks keep coming.

May I help you? Can I get you anything? Would you like another life? Would you like another soul?

Sleek and long and slender and smiling.

The strangers surround.

What are you doing? Go home. Go somewhere, anywhere but here.

The mirror knows.

The streets swallow.

Hell is this place, Tyler, these people, that desperate smell, the savage desire.

The doors remain open.

Stepping through a fog, a haze, through laughter, through glances, in the early morning light and the setting sun and the beating glow of midnight.

Trying to run to forget, to numb all these regrets. Trying. Trying. Trying.

74

Teardrop

I wake up sprawled over a bed, with the sheets on the floor. Sunlight gashes through the opening where the blinds meet. As I sit for a moment, the room hovers back and forth. My throat is raw and feels like I've been smoking. The aftertaste of onion and garlic lingers in my mouth. I sneeze and release a web of slime onto my bare arm. Then I notice my hand.

The knuckles are swollen and bloody.

I search the data in my brain, going back to my last memory, but everything is fuzzy. I think back to what I remember vividly. Standing at that door waiting to go in, almost going in, almost giving in. But then remembering Laila's words and then leaving and disappearing.

To where? Where did I go?

I stand and open the blinds and get momentarily blinded. I find my phone. I turn it on and see that I have fifteen voicemails.

Then I notice the date. November 27th.

It's two days after Thanksgiving.

How long have I been here? A week? More?

On the desk next to my phone is a wad of money with a clip on it. It can't be mine since I never carry that much cash. And since I've never seen that clip before. I see chips of various casinos. A napkin with the name *Eva* and a number scribbled in ink. Another piece of paper with another number on it.

When I start wobbling, I decide to sit back down.

What's happened here?

A pair of my jeans are on the floor. I can see from where I'm sitting that they're bloody too.

Maybe you don't want to know what's happened, Tyler.

I scratch my hair and it feels greasy and thick. So does the beard on my face.

Then I look around, wondering if someone else is here.

I'm alone.

I sit there for a while, floating in and out of sleep or whatever else it is, before the phone rings.

"Yeah?"

"You're alive."

It's Ellis.

"I don't feel alive."

"Not after that bender."

"After that what?"

The voice laughs. "Next time I'll be more careful when I say to let down your guard."

I curl my fingers into a fist and see them start shaking, the raw skin beginning to bleed again.

"I don't remember the last—the last few days."

"I'm glad you turned on your phone. I haven't been able to reach you."

"Since when?"

"Since Wednesday."

I don't know the day, but that doesn't sound good.

"It's like you're the guy from *Leaving Las Vegas* or something," Ellis says. "You have some sort of death wish or something?"

Yeah. Or something.

I don't know what to say.

"Clean up and meet me downstairs. There's this great restaurant where you can find anything you want. You hungry?"

"I'm a lot of things," I say.

"I'll be waiting."

40

• • •

The hot, scalding water can only do so much. It can steam the bathroom and scrub the skin, but it can't penetrate the soul. There is no bath I can take for that, no baptism I can find for the moment. There is nothing I can do but feel the burn against my body and try and tell myself to move on.

Yet after I put on cologne and clean clothes, I make a mistake.

I listen to the voicemails.

It's my life on audio. A podcast of shame.

First it's my mother asking about Thanksgiving. Then my sister doing the same.

Cole calls, wondering where I am. So does Gavin.

There's a strange and cryptic call from Sean Torrent, sounding like he's on the run. And maybe he is. Maybe he's in Mexico with a few girls and a stash of dope, hiding from the authorities. Maybe he and I could be Butch Cassidy and the Sundance Kid.

A call from my manager. Another from Rick MacLellan. Another from Nicole Lawson's manager.

Next is my mother again. This one obviously came after Thanksgiving. *Where did I eat turkey and gravy this year? Where did I give thanks? The Bellagio?*

Then, last but not least, comes a voice I least expect.

It's Julie.

"Hi Tyler. I just wanted to say hi. Like I usually do on this day. I know that maybe I shouldn't, so it's probably best just leaving a voicemail. But I just wanted to say that I'm thinking about your father and his health. I hope he's doing better. And hope you're doing okay, too. I know how things are between the two of you—how they were—and I just wanted to let you know I'm thinking of you. I just hope it's not too tough. I hope you had a good Thanksgiving spent with your family. Please send them my regards. And—well, just take care, okay?"

I turn off the phone.

I'm thinking about your father.

I spent the last few days in a black hole.

Trying not to think of him.

Without warning, I feel tears streaming down my face.

I'm just tired and still probably half drunk and half ashamed and half famished. It's just the lack of sleep and eats and health and goodness.

I wipe my cheeks and then stare at the guy in the mirror. He looks like someone I once knew.

"Let me get you some coffee."

I feel Ellis pat me on the shoulder as he pours from a stainless steel carafe. I sit down and feel like the kid sitting across from the principal. Only this principal looks tanned, rested, and is wearing a New Order T-shirt and a grin.

"I was going to call the police if I didn't find you today," Ellis says.

"Maybe you should have done that a few days ago." I look at a menu at this fancy restaurant. I still don't know what time it is.

"I spoke to you briefly on Friday. You called me, but I think it was an accident."

"Really?"

"Yes. You were slurring and positively out of your mind. You thought you were calling for someone named Laila."

"Yeah, I was definitely out of my mind then. Sorry about that."

Ellis shakes his head. "No apologies necessary. I do have to leave this weekend, but you don't have to."

"Yeah, I think I do," I say as I clear my throat. "I think I better get out of here as soon as I can."

"I think this was a long time coming."

"What?"

"This bender of yours."

"You think?" The coffee tastes bitter, but it's hot and soothing to my stomach.

"Thing I learned years ago was that alcohol and me don't make a great mix," Ellis comments. "It's like that girl that's fun to mess around with, but you know you can never, ever marry her. She's a trainwreck. So I go out on dates every now and then but I never sleep over and I never leave her my number."

"I think I lost your metaphor midway," I say.

He laughs. "That's fine. It's just—I understand where you're at."

"No, I don't think you do."

"Try me."

"What if I told you that I didn't have much time to live?"

"You already did," Ellis says.

"Really?"

"Sure."

"You believe me?"

"No. But you were already pretty soused."

"So what was your suggestion?"

Ellis smiles and gives me a glance that worries me.

"What?"

"I told you to do exactly what you're doing."

"Are you serious?"

He nods. "Guess you can blame me."

A server comes and I order a couple of different dishes: the eggs Benedict and the pecan waffle. I get a side of bacon. And the largest glass of orange juice they have.

"Hungry?" Ellis asks.

"You really told me to get bombed?"

"I think I put it a little more eloquently. But yeah, sure, I told you to."

"Okay."

"You said the thing you liked was being out of control. Of not giving one damn. Because all your life, you have been in control. Or tried to be, at least. All your life, you have cared. You care and you control way too much, if you ask me. And I'm a controlling guy. But it goes back to our childhood. Everything does. It goes back to the relationship with our parents, what we think of our fathers, how much we dislike our fathers, how similar we are to our fathers. Everything boils down to our fathers."

Ellis pauses for a moment, then articulates his curse.

"You shared what your father was like and I get it. Man do I get it. So I told you to do everything you want to try and rid yourself of his face and his memory."

"I think I went a little overboard on the getting rid of the memories part," I say.

"Did it work?"

"Now I have something else."

"What's that?"

"Guilt."

"Oh man. I got rid of that at a young age."

"It's not that easy for me."

"It still can be. Trust me. It can. When you wake up and realize that all you can do and all you can control is here, right here, right with these two hands, then that's what guides your life. You're serving nothing but these two things."

He's holding out his hands as if trying to catch falling raindrops.

"But when you believe in God and know you're doing stuff that is really not that good for you—"

"Is it God? Really? Is that who you think you're supposed to serve? Or is it that father you told me about who lives and acts like he is God?"

"I don't know."

I drain my large orange juice and wave down the server for another.

"There's no reason to have any guilt, unless those bruises and cuts on your hand are from beating someone's face in."

"I don't know where they came from."

From the look on his face and the laughter coming from him, I can tell the guy across from me is enjoying this.

"Glad to be amusing."

"No," Ellis says. "*I'm* glad to be amusing. See what you could have missed had you stayed in Chicago?"

"I think I already missed a good chunk of Vegas and I'm here."

"Welcome to the real world, my friend. That's the best part of Vegas."

"Please don't spout out the tagline."

He lets go a curse. "I hate taglines. No. The best part of Vegas is leaving it all behind. Money, sin, shame. You sit on the plane and it takes off and you can just leave it all behind."

"Remind me how easy it is when we're up."

"I'll do that. I'm very good at doing that."

75

Unfinished Sympathy

This isn't happening.

Yes it is.

Laila, please. Don't leave.

I can't stay.

There's a place for you here now, right here.

Not when she's still there.

She's nowhere around.

She's a part of you and always will be.

Please.

It's unfair to ask a question I can't answer.

I love you.

What is love?

It counts.

Nothing counts.

You said it yourself.

Nothing counts and nothing matters and nothing is here. This is nothing. *We* are nothing and you need to get that in your head.

I love you.

We're nothing and never will be.

Please.

Stop touching me.

Don't.

No.

Just—

No.

Laila.

I can't be her for you.

I'm not asking you to be.

You don't have to say it to feel it.

What happens tomorrow?

You wake up and go on with life because that's what people do. That's what life does. It steps over you and goes on. You need to go on.

And what about you?

I'll do what I've always done.

Let me help.

Two halves won't make a whole, Tyler, not this time.

Stop.

Not ever.

Some conversations will always be a part of you, like an incision from surgery that will always scar the skin.

I never thought I'd meet someone like Laila. I never thought there was a Laila out there. Yes, there are exotic beauties out there and yes sometimes you can fall in love with them. But the Laila that I never expected to meet was beneath the surface of that exquisite exterior she knew and she used.

I met her at a party. She used to call me shy and that was okay because in a lot of ways I am. At least with women. Laila could see it in my eyes—how I felt, what I wanted—but she could also see something else. The other thing that made me not advance on those desires, the other thing that seemed to single me out from the rest.

Once I found out about her life and the secrets she carried around, at least those that she shared with me, I was hooked. I loved her and wanted to free her from herself and that life. She became an obsession, a challenge, an all-consuming everything. Then she disappeared.

Laila once told me that she was a troubled soul, but the only troubling thing about it was that I was never able to fix it.

Years later, I know it was foolish to ever think I could.

40

I'm not sure why I think of Laila here and now on the airplane, but I do.

I'm weak, sick of my head and living out of my body. I need to go back home. I need to stop running.

Maybe I should take that missions trip I've been putting off my whole entire sad life.

Moving out and moving away, I see glimpses and reminders of the past few days

years

and I find nothing worth remembering.

On your deathbed you're not going to remember stuff like this. You're not going to remember the moments from this blurry week.

What I will remember are conversations with those I loved, and the regrets of never following them up.

PART SEVEN

———

Disintegration

76

The Chain

It's the tenth day of December, and I'm the walking dead. My nose can't stop running, and the mucus coming out of it feels like my liquefied brain. I had a sore throat and fever a couple of days ago, which has gone away and has been replaced by a swarmful of bees and warm honey in my head. I want to sleep but have too much to do.

And in four months and eleven days, I'm supposed to die.

So yeah, life makes a lot of sense.

About as much sense as those gray hairs that I continue spotting on my head. Every now and then I've seen one and rationalized it as a blond strand turning white, but under the sunroof and the cloudy sky I'll see those suckers, especially since I need a haircut. I guess it fits since I'm almost forty, since I'm almost middle-aged.

The number has never really hit me until now, until I'm in my condo, trying to do work on my computer and forcing my heavy eyelids to stay open.

Forty.

Maybe I have never really fully embraced that number because I've never felt like an almost-forty-year-old should. Shouldn't I be married with a couple kids in grade school by now? I'm not even dating. Not really. Many of my friends are in their late twenties or act like they're still in them. I work in an industry that's built for teenagers and twenty-somethings. I'm single and recently got back from a spring-break-like vacation to Vegas.

Yeah, just like every other forty-year-old guy out there.

Maybe this is my midlife crisis. Maybe my crisis isn't that of a life, but that of a soul. A soul that's been in hibernation for so long I can't remember what it looks and feels like when its thawed out. A series of relationships so weak and thin I couldn't spot a genuine one from a foot away. Maybe my crisis is that I'm finally waking up to the reality that I've been in a midlife crisis for a decade now, starting when the marriage deteriorated ten years ago and then continuing when it was officially declared over, in 2002.

What have you been doing since then? What have you built up and given away and lived out?

I don't have much to show except a series of CDs. A playlist of songs PRODUCED BY TYLER HARRISON.

Big deal.

The post-Vegas blues and guilt, wrapped around a deluge of work and sprinkled in with getting sick, is making me start to think and go down.

Going to that place—the one that I hover above, that I hang-glide over, that I occasionally fall into.

Sometimes I've slipped and fallen into the black morass. It's a hopeless place, where anxiety is a thing you can touch and fear wears a smile. I fell into it after Julie and I were over, and it took me a while to even realize it. By then I had set up camp on the base of the dark mountain ledge and had no idea how to get off.

I know I need to just concentrate and work. To get through the hours of this day, to get over this sickness.

But there's something else.

The visions and the nightmares and the strange sightings . . .

They've returned.

As if they were waiting for me at the gate the moment I deboarded the plane from Vegas.

"They're going to get a new producer."

"Fabulous."

Maybe I should care, but I don't.

"They wanted to tell you in person."

40

"You're just as important as I am," I tell Gavin.

He curses and talks about Nicole Lawson's manager. "That guy is an arse. He has no clue. None of them do, really. It makes me wonder what I'm doing in this business. Maybe I should be selling high-end stereo equipment."

"So why? What 'direction' do they want?"

"Nicole wasn't there, you know."

"Yeah, I'm sure she wasn't. She's left a few messages apologizing and feeling awful and all that. She said it was worth it to work with me. It's not her fault. Let her make the damned album she wants to make, you know?"

"They wanted it more upbeat."

I think of a list of poptarts who all have the same kind of sound. Warm, regurgitated earwax.

"They're going to kill her career," I say.

"*They* don't think so." Gavin curses again and finishes his beer.

We've been here before. But in the past, it's only made my resolve tougher. Bigger, stronger, tougher. But not now.

"I wish people would stop wasting our time."

"Our time is there to waste," I tell my friend and partner.

"No it's not."

"Sure it is. We're part of the machinery. The music *business*. Very few are able to make a living in this business, you know? And a rare lot are able to do what they want. We can't. Not yet."

And not ever.

Gavin doesn't agree and says so with colorful profanity, resorting back to a thicker accent and sounding like he came off the set of a Guy Ritchie movie.

"So we have anything to do between now and Christmas?" Gavin eventually asks.

"There's this little-known singer—his name is Sean Torrent."

"I don't want to hear his name. Not anymore."

"Things could be worse." I hand him the letter.

"What's this?" Gavin asks.

"Go ahead and read it."

A couple of minutes later, he's staring at me in disbelief.

"I knew it was risky buying a boat."

"So at the first of the year, that's it? Just like that?"

I nod. "No money, no boat."

"But how can they take it from you so bloody quick?"

"It's a funny thing, being your own boss. It takes everybody so much time to pay you, yet when you owe somebody, they're calling the second it's past due."

Gavin grits his teeth. "This is a tragic night."

"No it's not. The Haiti earthquake is a tragedy. This—this is just part of life. Part of our lives."

"You seem indifferent."

"Not indifferent. Just—maybe just a bit wiser."

"A bit wiser? Seriously? What'd you learn then? Tell me so I can know."

"We go through life thinking it's in our control, but it's not. Not ever. Things are completely random. You can work as hard as you can and not even get paid, not even get credit, while someone sits on their ass and does nothing and gets praised all over the world. Nothing is fair and nothing makes sense."

"Sod's law."

"Sod's what?"

"If something can go wrong, it bloody will."

"Think that's Murphy's law there," I say.

"So what happened to you in Vegas?"

"It wasn't Vegas. It's just—it's just reality."

"Reality, huh?"

"Yeah."

"Sorry, but I didn't sign up for that."

"Yeah, I know. None of us did. But it's just the thing we have to realize sooner or later."

"What?"

That we're all going to die, Gavin.

"Nothing is in our control. Nothing. Absolutely nothing."

40

As we leave the bar, I see his disheveled figure sitting on a stool, watching us.

Watching and laughing.

The specter or ghost or demon taunting and haunting me.

I ignore the laughter as we pass.

I'm not about to ask Gavin if he notices him.

77

High Hopes

I study to try and perfect my craft. Listening for things others don't hear. Listening for the unexpected, the things I wouldn't do, the things that make it unique. I listen and wait and wonder and I get myself tied into a knot over pressing.

Sometimes I wonder what this drive is.

You don't need to wonder. I'm here right beside you, whispering now that I've got a free pass to the Six Flags of your dreams, TW.

Sometimes I wonder why I strive so hard to be like my father.

When I'm immersed in a project, I feel like Frodo climbing up that mountain of coughing fiery death. I feel like I must keep going to my inevitable doom. All for the task at hand. Yet when I'm not working on a project—which is rare, to be honest—I find myself spiraling and lost in a forest full of talking trees, with visions of wizards lurking nearby, telling me I'm not doing anything with my life.

I hear the voice of my father asking, *What are you doing?*

How about building and creating and sculpting? Does it have to have a label to be worthy of something? Does it have to have a ministry and an imprint of Babies for Bono to be something that is born again? Can't I create because God put this in me to create?

You doodle at the sound board with knobs and wires. You play with instruments that can barely be heard by the ears of a trained dog. You shepherd needy artists, hoping for something big and some kind of break, and then you deliver it to greedy salesmen hoping for something even bigger.

The voices don't go away.

At night they only grow louder.

With Christmas approaching they only grow stronger.

I am melancholy Charlie Brown without a Snoopy.

I am bewildered George Bailey without Zuzu's petals.

I am the hardened Captain von Trapp without his music.

I am Scrooge without the courage to call it as I see it and live up to the name.

I don't know how I see it.

The aching grip of winter seizes everything, including my heart.

I long to warm it and warm my body and warm my senses. I long for someone I can talk to about these longings, for someone to take me in her arms and listen to me and feel my heart beat against hers and to know. To know I'm there. To know she hears me. To know that she gets it.

Winter holiday nights are when it's the worst. When I'm the worst. And I try to fight it and combat it with work, but work just gets wearisome.

Work is still just work. And I don't need a voice to wonder what it's all for.

I never used to believe in chance, in the random, in coincidence. When I was a kid, I used to believe everything happened for a reason. But age and the world slowly but surely snuffed that out.

Yet I can't help but think of that as I'm walking down the sidewalk and see a familiar face walking toward me. For a brief second it's déjà vu, as if this has happened before, but as I get closer and see him, I realize this is only the second time I've come across this man's path.

"Hey," I say, for a second forgetting his name, just remembering that he's a pastor.

He slows down but seems unsure for a moment, then makes the connection.

"Airplane, right?"

"Yeah."

The man nods. "Sorry. My head's on another planet. Didn't even see you coming."

"That's okay."

"It's Tyler, right? You live down here."

"Yeah. Not far."

I remember that his name is Will.

"Looks like I made it down right before the first snow of the year."

"Coming from the suburbs?"

"Yeah. But I'm speaking at this conference downtown. At Moody."

"You lost?" I ask, knowing that the college is east of here, on the other side of the Dan Ryan Expressway.

Will shakes his head. "No, just visiting an old buddy of mine who lives down here."

"Cool."

He glances across the street, then down the sidewalk, as if unsure how to break up our conversation. I assume he's going to say something like *well, good seeing you,* but instead he surprises me.

"Hey—look, I'm glad to see you again. I was rethinking our conversation and felt like I came across pretty heavy-handed."

"It's fine," I say. "Really."

"Maybe. I don't know. It's difficult to know the right words to say in circumstances like that."

"They were fine. Honestly. It's no big deal."

"Well, look, I'm saying that because I thought it might be interesting for you to come by the Institute. Hear me speak. In an official capacity."

"Yeah, okay."

"No, I'm serious," he says. "Just wait."

He opens his bag and rifles through an assortment of items until he pulls out a handful of postcards.

"They made up a bunch of these. Here, take one."

His picture is there with a variety of others.

"It gives the times and everything. I know you said it's been a while since you went to church—or since you felt good about going. But don't think of this as church."

40

"And don't think of your talk as preaching?"

His laugh cracks me up. It says a lot about him. It says that there's no ego there, at least none that I can see.

"Yeah, maybe. Well, Saturday night I'm definitely preaching. The other times I'm just building up or wrapping up."

"So if I was to come, I should probably avoid Saturday night."

"Definitely. You won't like what I have to say then."

I nod and he looks at me. "What?"

"Do you use this technique on a lot of people?"

"The postcard?" Will asks.

"No. Telling me not to do something."

"You don't like being told what to do?"

"Does anybody?"

A gust of wind blows down the street and we both seem to duck down, unsure of what's coming next.

"Just think about it, okay? It's good running into you again."

"No problem."

"And, hey—if you do come, stick around to say hi. And maybe rescue me from the other speakers."

A few nights later, I'm on my knees at the middle of the congregation. I feel a hand touching my shoulder.

"Pastor," I say.

Will smiles at me and urges me to stand. I wipe my cheeks and clear my throat.

"Everything feels so different now," I say. "Everything feels so right."

"Okay," he says.

"I mean, suddenly I'm not worried about my bills or my job or my past mistakes and all the people I've let down. I'm not even worried about my own death."

"That's good. Now, please."

He's shooing me away like I'm in grade school.

"I just thought—I thought we could talk. When you gave the altar call…"

"I didn't finish my message, Tyler," he says.

Then I turn around and see an entire auditorium full of several thousand people looking at me.

Staring down at me.

Judging me.

"It's okay. There'll be time for that in just a little while. We need to pass around the offering."

"But—"

Suddenly I see three men in white coming to get me. They're carrying a leather jacket, the kind that you see patients wearing in the funny farm.

Wait a minute. That's not the kind mental patients wear. That's the kind they stuck on Hannibal Lecter. And wait a minute. This isn't an auditorium at the Moody Bible Institute. This is the Chicago Theater.

Of course it is. This is my dream and that's why it's a hybrid of my memories.

Snow falls for the first time of the season, to remind us that's it's woken up and that it'll be coming the next four months. I see it on the deck outside my main room as I sip coffee and wonder what I'm going to do and think about meeting the pastor on the street. I tried looking for the postcard he gave me but it's gone. Part of me wonders if I threw it away last night, but I don't remember doing so.

I think of church.

The last church service I attended was with my sister and her family at Gun Lake. We went to a little chapel off the main road that was packed, where everybody seemed to know everybody else. I kept waiting for someone to stand up and politely ask me to leave during the service, but no one did. The service itself was fine. The message was fine. Everything about it was fine. Nothing was revolutionary. Nothing moved me. Nothing bothered me.

It was...fine.

I think of the last time I visited my church. The one I "go" to. The way an overweight person "goes" to their gym. I'm on the quarterly setting myself. So many things come up—work, trips, forgetfulness, laziness, hangovers.

I'm sure if I told that to a pastor, he would be less than impressed.

It never used to be like this. I enjoyed the church I went to when I was a junior and a senior in high school. The same with the church Julie and I used to go to.

Now, church reminds me of those times. I compare and contrast. I'll sit in a seat or a pew and wonder. What would I have been like if . . . What would life have been like if . . .

If I remained that naïve and optimistic kid in high school. If I remained with my childhood sweetheart.

I don't like going backwards, feeling guilt, feeling like I've done something wrong and that I'll never ever be able to move on. I hate those feelings. So sure enough, I've avoided those by avoiding church.

It's been remarkably easy.

It hasn't even really bothered me. Missing church, that is.

Changing who I used to be to who I am now. Changing who I once thought I'd spend the rest of my life with to who I'm with now. That's what bothers me. That's what I miss.

I stare out the sliding glass doors and lament the coming of winter.

I notice something on the edge of the stone wall.

The postcard.

I open the door and go to retrieve it, but it slips off in the wind and drifts downward into the trees and the street below.

I can't remember the dates or the times of the event.

Then again, I don't need to know. I'm not going to go anyway.

78

Disappear Here

Christmas is a week away.

It's a bit ridiculous to try and find meaning inside this madness.

The store doors and the walls of racks. The credit cards and the round guys dressed in red and white. The obsession of buying and wrapping and giving and receiving.

Meanwhile, parties bring people together, and in my world, proceed to get everybody drunk and high as a kite, declaring the past wonderful and the future sublime.

Snow falls and liquor warms and for the first time in a long time I feel more lonely and I know I can't be on my own this Christmas.

I think of this at Party #1. A room full of strangers with nothing to say. Angie is here with me. So is Cole. Yet I feel more alone than ever.

I honestly think of calling Julie here, but I can't. My days of drunk dialing are long gone. She's probably dressing up one of her kids in a snowman suit as she sips cocoa and watches her wonderful life with her husband.

I've talked about maybe seeing my sister and her family sometime. "Sometime" works because it means nothing and my sister and I both know it. Sometime is that New Year's resolution that never happens. Sometime is that pot at the end of the rainbow. Sometime is the amends needing to be made that get lost in transit and in translation.

The same with my mom. I've talked about going down there to be with her at Christmas. With her and the body she lives with. With her and the caricature of the father I used to have. I should be down there. I need to go down.

I think of this at Party #2. A room full of fakers with too much to say.

The art on the wall grins. The lamps take aim at me. The mannequins in this main room all look the same. Hard, distant, secret, shadowy, fake, false.

He's there.

Of course he's there.

The same guy following me, staying with me, ever since Lollapalooza. My own Ken Kesey, penning his follow-up to *One Flew Over The Cuckoo's Nest*. Taking notes on my downward descent.

The rogue scoundrel scalawag laughing at me.

He's here. Watching.

Gavin is here too. Talking. Mingling. Doing his part. Because he's got a job. And a life. And he's not being hounded by insanity.

I sigh.

I'm supposed to believe that the God and maker of this universe created us all, all of us, every bit. The magic and the majesty—that's what He did.

That's what you claim to believe, right?

And I'm supposed to believe that this God sent His son, His only one, to die for all of us. All of us stupid, silly little sinners. That God allowed His son to die to take on the guilt and the hurt of all to the grave. To fall down and then to rise back up.

That's what you believed in as a young boy, where you put your heart and soul.

Where is your heart and soul now, Tyler? Where is it?

Is it in this room?

Is it with these people?

Is it hovering on the 51st floor of the Trump Building?

Is it speaking at the Moody Bible Institute?

Or is it here, in the middle of this room, disappearing into nothing.

I want to text myself out.

I want to e-mail myself away.

I want to disappear and be someone else. Someone I should have been.

The week leading up to Christmas, where a tiny little heart finally cried out in the dirty wilderness in some distant manger.

This is how you celebrate that birth. This is how you escape.

Bring on Santa. Bring on the schnapps. Bring on the solitary seclusion. The sin. The secrets. The sinking.

I close my eyes and wish for something I know I can't have.

The last half of my life back.

I wasn't always like this and I only have myself to blame.

79

Exile

There is something breathtaking about being blanketed by white. Snow falls and covers the lifeless gray and the world looks brighter and bigger and you can't help remembering childhood notions of eating flakes and making angels and rolling men. In the dead of winter, life comes with every falling star, unique and special.

I'm in the driveway of the house I nearly bought a year ago, listening to music and drinking Scotch and staring at the structure that symbolized so much. This is my Drive-In of Shame. Of Lost Opportunity. Of Failed Expectations. Of Regret.

A part of me nudges my cheek and whispers in my ear, *If, Tyler. If only you'd bought this place and done something with your life and your dreams. If only.*

I'm listening to tracks I didn't even realize I had on my iPod. Ones I produced years ago. Ones I played while making love to Julie. Ones that prompt sadness and hurt and loss in my drunken soul.

It's Christmas Eve, the sun not gone just yet, the snow still falling, and I'm still lingering here. I've already declined to go down south to be with my parents. Ditto with Kendra and her family. Gavin is getting together with some friends that are closer than family and he said we should meet up sometime and drown our sorrows. I decided to do it myself, like I usually do. Do it myself by myself for myself. Me me me.

Merry Christmas.

I play shuffle. Love the shuffle. Wish life could shuffle like the iPod does. Press *play* and you're sixteen again, hanging out with friends, laughing at nothing for no other reason but to laugh. You're twenty-six and you're holding hands with your wife for no other reason but to hold her hand. You're not even thirty and you're helping work on an album that will go on to be one of the biggest and best of all time and all along you have no idea because that's your job.

"Memories of Green" by Vangelis. This was one of those songs, one of my songs, one of *them*.

"Of These, Hope" by Peter Gabriel. "The Sweetest Condition" by Depeche Mode. "The Name of the Game" by ABBA. "The Snowman's Music Box Dance" by George Winston.

Gotta love how things work out like that. The perfect song and the absolutely wrong mood.

"Carrying Audrey" by James Newton Howard.

I remember all of these. A movie here, a sound bite there.

This is my history collected in a little square instrument.

I see my life in segments, like carefully constructed record collections.

I sigh and think of Julie. Of my parents. Of my family. Relatives who often ask about me who I never ask anything back. *Too busy, too important, too full, gotta go.*

I repeat the last track.

The only thing I've been too full of is myself. Nothing else. Nothing more.

I know what this track means. Where it comes from. The scene it depicts.

I'd give anything to go back and shuffle in time. And then stay there. To turn off shuffle and to switch to repeat and then to stay.

It's getting darker. Snow continues to fall. I continue to drink. Good combo. Great timing.

It's just a house.

So many houses in my life are portraits of something.

The house Julie and I used to live in is a portrait of loss.

The house in front of me is a portrait of failure.

The house my parents are living in is a portrait of fear.

They're all the same damned thing.

40

I know that this will be the last time I ever step foot on this driveway or any driveway like this. I'll never come back. That's the way I learned, growing up. You say goodbye and you live the rest of your days with the memories, but you don't go backwards. You don't stay in that moment. You don't revisit to reminisce.

I back up and feel fine to drive and feel warm enough not to need heat. I turn up the music. Shuffle, where will you take me?

Ah, Phil Collins, I haven't heard from you since I was in ninth grade.

I drive down a street that I don't quite recognize, but that's okay. I'll find an adjoining street that I recognize.

It's just up ahead, around the corner, just a few minutes away. Through the white streets and the cloudy intersections and the hazy surroundings.

This elusive friend with its slight smile.

This curious confidante with its playful scowl.

I'm almost there.

I can feel it, taste it.

Hope.

Yet when I get there and turn the corner it's gone. He's disappeared. She's evaporated.

Always and every time.

80

Home

uddy, it's okay. Just hold on, okay? We're almost there. Here, I'm turning now.

I open my eyes and see windshield wipers brushing off the thick chunks of snow as headlights cut through the white night. A sign on the corner of the street we're turning onto says Sycamore. I swallow and feel a throbbing in my temple. For a moment I think I'm driving myself, I see myself driving this car in the snow. Then I realize that it's someone else.

"It's okay—I got a feeling you have a nasty concussion," the driver says to me.

I squint and try to see if it's really him.

When he smiles I know.

It's Pastor Will.

"What's going on?"

"That's what I've been trying to ask you."

I lick my lips and can taste blood, can feel the cut with my tongue.

"You ran into a tree back there off the road. It doesn't look like you were going very fast but—well, things didn't look too good."

"The car?"

"No. What I found inside the car."

It takes me a moment to try and figure out what he's talking about.

"You banged your face and lip a bit, but that was about all. Besides nicking the tree. I moved your car and parked it alongside the road. And I removed that empty bottle."

Now I get it.

"Maybe I should take you to the hospital?"

"No, no. That's okay. I'm fine."

"Are you sure?"

"Yeah. Please—I don't want any trouble. I don't need it. Really."

He glances at me with an indecisive look.

"Where are you coming from?" I ask.

"We always have a Christmas Eve service at the church. The wife and kids left before me."

"Oh, man."

"It's okay. Look—let's just get you inside to relax."

"Not on your—not now. Please. I can call someone to get me."

"It's fine. Really. Just—we're here."

We pull up to a modest two-story house in a neighborhood full of similarly styled homes. I see a white minivan parked next to us.

For a moment, I glance at him as he turns off the car.

"Can I ask you a question?"

"Yeah, sure," Will says.

"Are you a guardian angel? Another one sent down? A new one, maybe?"

He laughs. "I might be a lot of things, but a guardian angel I'm not. Ask my wife. She'll say I'm the furthest thing from that."

"Okay, but—but thanks anyway."

"Come on—let's get something warm inside your stomach. Something nonalcoholic."

In the next hour, my shame and embarrassment turn to surprise and incredulity.

Stacy is an energetic and never-stopping cute blonde who doesn't seem surprised to have me over. She also doesn't seem to have much time for anything with all the kids in this house. There is a ten-year-girl named Madison, then a boy named Brandon who is seven or eight, and the twin girls who are four years old (and whose names I forget). One of the twins—I hear her name as Tessa—is crying over something, so Stacy takes her upstairs. The boy is going up and down the stairs while Madison watches television.

I've cleaned myself up and am having a cup of hot apple cider. I keep wanting to apologize and also say how surreal it is to be in this family's house on Christmas Eve, but I don't get the chance. Stacy shouts down for Will and then he's gone, leaving me with the other four-year-old girl.

"Do you go to our church?" she asks me.

"No."

"Why not?"

"Well, I live in the city."

"What church to you go to, then?"

Yes, it's about time for me to feel convicted around Christmastime. And this year, it will be a four-year-old and missionary in training to do so.

"I like our church. My daddy is a pastor."

"I've heard."

"Do you want a marshmallow?" she asks.

I take one and then she wanders back in the room where her older sister is watching a show.

I feel like an intruder, sipping this Christmas mug, smelling the scents of cinnamon and turkey and dressing, seeing all the cards on their fridge and kitchen counter. A family shot gives me a weird sense of déjà vu as if I've seen it before, but then it goes away.

What am I doing here? How'd this happen?

"Sorry about that," Will says.

"No, really, I'm sorry."

"It's fine. Come on. Our big day is over. Almost over."

"Look—it's Christmas Eve."

"You'd think that'd be the best night to be charitable, huh?"

"I know, and I appreciate it. I just—I'm sure you want to be with your family."

"Tyler, listen. Please. It's fine. This house is and always has been an unlocked revolving door. I actually love it like that. The kids are used to seeing people here all the time."

"Even if they smell like Scotch?"

Will smiles. "They'll think it's for cooking."

We go into the family room and spend a while talking together and being interrupted by the kids and Stacy. I watch one of the girls, Sara Beth, I believe, dance repeatedly to a song she plays on a little CD player. I have this crazy thought that if I was given another twenty years, I could make this girl become the next Carrie Underwood.

My head begins to feel better and the throbbing pain is starting to go away.

When I look outside, it's still snowing.

"You can spend the night, you know," Will says. "We have a pullout in the basement. The house isn't the biggest, but you know—you're certainly welcome to."

"No. No—absolutely not."

"Yeah, okay. Well, I'm not letting you drive for another couple of hours. If that."

"I'm fine."

"Did you have dinner?"

I smile.

"Besides the whiskey?"

"Not exactly," I say.

"One of the perks of being a pastor is that you're given a lot of food. How do you think I got this belly?" He taps it with his hand. "Let's get you something to eat."

I walk through the house and see a picture on the wall. A family shot.

It makes me think of home and of my parents.

"Can you excuse me for just a moment?" I ask. "I need to make an important call."

"No problem. I'll be sampling the food. For you. Because that's the kind of guy I am."

81

Nothing Else Matters

Your father said a few words tonight," Mom says, almost immediately.

I'm thinking maybe I shouldn't be calling.

"He asked about you."

I'm thinking maybe I should still be in my stranded car, hunched over the steering wheel, reeking of Scotch.

"It's a miracle."

And once again, I'm not there to witness it. Once again, I'm doing my own thing.

You should be happy, Tyler, you should be happy for your mother.

I should be a lot of things, but deep in my core I'm not. Deep down I'm really, seriously disappointing.

"I wish you were here."

And suddenly, inexplicably, I do too.

I don't just wish. I know I should be there.

I'm sitting in a living room by a Christmas tree decked out and lit with colorful lights and I hear the sounds of laughter and children in the background.

"I know it's hard to get away at this time of year."

But it's not, Mom, it's really not. It's really particularly easy to get away and I spend every day of my life getting away. Getting away with it and getting away from people and getting away from everything.

40

"When are you coming down?" she asks.

I don't know.

Dad is probably talking more than I am tonight.

"Merry Christmas, Tyler."

The kids are all upstairs, trying to go to sleep. This little family snapshot amazes me. It feels right. It feels so real.

I feel like I belong right here.

I'm sitting on the couch across from Stacy, who's been asking me about my job. I don't mind talking about it but, here and now, sitting in their family room on Christmas Eve, talking about Sean Torrent just doesn't feel right.

"So how'd you two meet?" I ask.

"It was a bit scandalous. He was a youth pastor at the church I went to."

"And you were, what, one of his students?"

Stacy cracks up and shakes her head. "I'm younger than Will, but not that young. I worked on staff at the church too. It was a small church and it just happened."

For some strange reason, I think of my sophomore year of high school, when I got expelled. I think of saying goodbye to the girl on that cold winter day.

"I never thought I'd work at a church, let alone marry a pastor. But then again, Will never thought he'd be a pastor, to be honest. That's probably why he was talking about you."

"What do you mean?" I ask.

"When he met you on the plane. He told me about you."

"Really?"

"Yeah. Because he thought how cool it'd be to do what you do."

I nod.

"What? You don't act like it's anything unique."

"No," I say. "It's unique. And I wouldn't change it for anything. It's just—it's probably like any job. It can be trying. There are parts that I love and parts I hate. The business part of it—that part I'm not a big fan of."

"Same with Will. He can't stand the administrative side of running a church. But, as I always tell him, you have to have that part too. Unless you're just going to preach on a curb somewhere and expect the masses to come."

"What are you telling him about me?" a voice calls out.

Will comes in and sits by Stacy, putting an arm around her like a newlywed.

"Madison is getting so old," he says, then tells his wife a story about her tucking in the twins on her own in a motherly fashion.

For a moment I feel strange, sitting here, listening to something that should be private and personal.

"You need anything?" Will asks me.

"No. I'm fine. Really. Thanks."

"The bump on your forehead is going away."

"That's good, because I have lots of Christmas pictures to take care of."

"What are you doing tomorrow?" Stacy asks.

"I was probably going to celebrate with some friends."

"Any family in the area?"

I tell them about my parents, who live far away, then my sister and her family, who spend Christmas with her husband's side of the family.

"With the church, it's hard for us to see family," Will says. "My mother is living and my sister spends Christmas with her. We feel like we can't go anywhere because of our church family. Which is okay."

"Do you have a service tomorrow?"

"No. Since Christmas is on a Saturday, we had the annual Christmas Eve service and then will have normal services on Sunday. Though I love having church on Christmas, to be honest. It's a good reminder what the day is all about."

"Yeah."

"Our children sometimes have a hard time remembering that," Stacy says, pointing at the Christmas tree with all the presents underneath.

The phone rings and Stacy gets it, then tells Will that it's for him. A few minutes later, Will comes back out looking serious and pale.

"Glenda Barrington just passed away," he says to his wife. "I should go to the hospital to see the family."

Again, here I am, a lump in the back of their throats, just filling time and space.

40

"I can go get my car," I tell him.

"I don't know—a cup of coffee isn't going to get you sober."

"It's been a few hours," I say. "I'm fine. I was just tired. The snow has eased up a bit. I'm fine, really."

They both look at me like I'm their son asking to borrow the car.

"Seriously, I'm fine."

"I'll take you home," Will says.

After about ten minutes of trying to get him to do something else, I have to relent. He might be a nice guy, but he is certainly stubborn. I thank Stacy for her hospitality and apologize for intruding in their Christmas Eve.

"Take care of yourself, okay?" she says, not in a mean-spirited way but in a tone that surprises me.

She acts like she's known me for a long time.

The freeway isn't crowded and is salted down well enough to drive at a normal speed. We make polite small talk, but I'm already feeling sluggish and drift in and out of sleep. Driving home would have been a bad idea.

To stay awake, I find an old song by the Cure playing on the radio and leave it on there.

"That brings me back," Will says.

"Really?"

"I used to love these guys."

"They're still around."

"I haven't listened to them in a long time. I sorta gave up bands like them."

"How come?"

"Going to sound preacher-esque again."

"Try me."

"I got to a point when I realized something. At least for me. I felt like I was surrounding myself with all these people and voices that hated God, or at least didn't want to have anything to do with Him. It made me wonder if it was going to start changing my mind and heart, a little each day."

"If you believe something, music isn't going to change that."

"Really?" Will asks. "It might at least cause one never to grow."

I don't know what to say, because I'm too tired to think of anything to say.

As we near my condo, I look over at the driver.

"Are you always such a good Samaritan or is it only around Christmas time?"

"I try."

"I appreciate it. Really."

"Wish you could've been here earlier today. I would have brought you to church."

"Yeah. That would have been great. A slightly soused visitor coming to your service."

"Why not?" Will says. "It's not a golf club or something like that. I want people to come. I sometimes get tired that it's all the same people—affluent white suburbanites. But then again, they need saving too."

"You sound like my father."

Will laughs.

"So what did you preach on? The Christmas story?"

"Not really. I did a variation of it. I asked this question: 'What if this was your last Christmas ever? The very last time you'd have to celebrate Christmas? What would you do differently?' Of course, I wanted to get people thinking about their family and the holiday and what gift they would give as a last present and all of that."

"A bit bleak for a Christmas Eve sermon."

"Want to do me a favor?" Will asks.

"Of course."

"Tomorrow or even tonight—sometime on this Christmas—go to the church's Web site and download the sermon. You can put it on your iPod. Listen to it. You'll see why I talk about this."

"Okay."

"Seriously—I mean it. Do it for me."

"Sure. Totally. That's the least I can do."

I direct him through the city streets to my place. After he stops the car in front of it, he clamps his hand down on my shoulder and then offers it to me to shake.

"You going to be okay?" he asks.

"I'll be fine. Really. I really appreciate this."

40

"Look, buddy. Whatever caused you to hit that tree—and I'm not talking about what you were drinking—whatever it is, it's not bigger than God. Know that. Whatever you might be running away from or running toward, don't forget about Him. Nothing else matters. It's hard for me to believe that myself at times, but it's the truth."

82

Haunted When the Minutes Drag

omeone is toying with me. Having fun for his sake. Making a mess of my mind.

It's not a guy at my door with a chain saw. It's the grease stains on a counter that I know without question don't belong to me.

It's the stuff in my condo that is missing. Utensils. Pictures. Clothes. Even songs on my iTunes.

I'm not going crazy.

It's subliminal messages that I hear everywhere.

ESPN reporting a trade.

"You have four months left."

ABC evening news.

"You're leaving nothing behind."

The latest album by U2.

"You're going to die alone, you pitiful sorrowful soul."

These don't come from my mind. They're all around. They're in this isolated place.

Whoever is messing with me is having a jolly old time.

I think of calling Mom but I can't.

I think of calling Kendra but I don't.

I think of calling Julie but I won't.

Instead, with Christmas Eve a distant memory, on a night of drinking

40

too much gin and listening to too much of the National, I stand up in my condo and dare him to come and show his face.

"I'm here, come and get me!"

The words echo off the walls.

"If you want to hurt me, do it now!"

The soft glow of light warms the room.

"I want to see your face!"

I want to see the scruffy, sinister sneer of the man who's been following me. But nobody comes. The wind howls outside and I swear I think I hear laughter.

Soft, bubbling, skittering, quivering laughter.

The kind that belongs to a dead man gasping a last breath.

That same night but much later, much drunker, much crazier, I call a number I'm not even sure exists anymore. I still have the necklace Sean gave me.

"If you're there, you listen to me. You listen to me. I don't think you have the guts to do anything else. To do anything more. I think you're content to fade away to nothingness because you had this one shining moment in your career when you really, truly excelled. I don't think you have the courage to try again to put your heart and your soul out there to be judged and critiqued. You're fighting this album because you're scared and I get it. I get it all right and that's fine. That's fine, but don't waste my time because I don't have much time left. You got that? You hear me, Sean? You want to do something meaningful and something original and real, then you show up at my doorstep ready to work. I dare you. I dare you to dream about coming and showing up. I'll do my part, but you need to do your part. And the first thing is getting over your pitiful fears and doing something. I can't do many things in this world and when I leave it behind in April all I'll know is that I could help shape some pretty decent albums and that's all. That's it. But that's more than you know. That's more than your hollow soul can say."

I leave it at that, knowing it will be the last statement I ever make to Sean Torrent, who surely won't give two rips about anything I just said.

• • •

Does God speak to the broken and bruised?

Does He come to those sleeping with a stranger?

Does He knock on the drunken man's door?

Does He watch and wait over the thief?

Does He listen to the beating and raging heart of an evil man?

I don't know.

I don't know anything except that Hell is a place where all your hopes and dreams drift out into an ocean and all you can do is watch from this hot, empty shore.

I don't know.

But sometime that night, restless and warm as the world outside is stormy and cold, I download the sermon from the pastor I spent Christmas Eve with and I listen.

And something happens.

Something happens as the pastor speaks.

Something in me is moved.

I'm crippled and moving with a crutch. I'm without words and without pride.

He says something that never dawned on me. Of course, I haven't been reading my Bible, nor have I been walking the walk.

He compares an eternity in Heaven to the Christmas mornings of our youth.

Then Pastor Will talks about the pain in this life, the pain that bleeds over everything.

"But I also see small pockets of joy," he says. "They remind me to keep going, to keep at it, to remain persistent."

I feel weak and worthless.

I make Sean Torrent look like a man with purpose.

I'm nothing.

"We have to remain persistent in the great hope of eternity. One day those tiny bubbles will pop, and those small pockets will be replaced by a healed world full of joy."

Will's words are refreshing. They offer hope. They actually make

40

me want to believe them. Deep down I do, but I'm just like Sean Torrent.

I'm scared and I'm stuck.

I just don't know what I'm stuck on and I don't have enough time to change the groove in this cracked record of mine.

So it repeats the same sound and lyrics over and over and over again.

83

Praying for Time

Tell me.
>   Listen to me.
>   I'll change.
I'll be a better man.

My nephews and nieces will know my middle name and will know what I prefer for breakfast.

I'll stop drinking. Stop lusting after what's not mine. Stop trying to be important in this little stamp of a world.

Just give me more time.

I can't change it all in four months.

Give me four more years.

Give me them to know myself, the new me, the me I could be, the me I'm supposed to be.

Do you hear me, God?

I believe in you but fear these sins and these scars are impossible for you to ignore.

I beg you for more time.

Time to love.

Time to learn about love.

Time to let the voices rest and let my soul rehabilitate.

I don't want to leave, not with these standings, not with this report card.

40

Please, Father, You can do anything.
Please save me.
Please let me see another New Year's Eve like this one.
Please God.
Please.

PART EIGHT

—

So

84

Shape of My Heart

Remember when you were a kid and you couldn't wait to grow up and get away? Get away from your parents and your house and your miserable little life?

You gotta love the irony of life.

You gotta love the days when you look back and wish you could go back. Back to those days. Back to the days of your youth. Back to the days of your marriage. Back to the rocky roads of whatever time.

Life is one long rocky road. It fools you because it smooths out and the car accelerates and it's downhill and you're coasting and then you hit a pothole and things go to crap again.

The point is believing some myth that it's going to get better.

When is that? When exactly?

I remember thinking that it would probably never get better than that brief stretch of road I drove down with Laila Torres. My hand was held and I felt loved and needed and I felt like it could get better. That the dream was within my grasp.

Just like the dream I had when I went off to college or got married and started a job or produced my first album.

The potential of what? The promise of what?

I believed that the open road could fill the open hole in my heart.

I don't believe that anymore.

And it's not that I've given up hope.

I've given up on the fallacy this world offers. The myth this world tries to sell. Eventually everybody comes to realize that it's just smoke and mirrors anyway. Some discover this early and chart their own path toward happiness. Some battle these desires to the day they die, hanging on with bloody hands to a futile rail.

I would probably think this even if I wasn't going to die in two months.

I would think this because it's true.

Life isn't a hero's journey. We love watching them, but our journeys take different routes and different directions. They're inconsistent. They're odd and full of contradictions and most don't always make sense.

It's February and a whole month has passed and yet nothing monumental has happened or changed or occurred. I'm the same as I was and life moves on and I'm waiting and watching and wondering.

Wondering why God decided to tell me. Wondering why Matthew chased after me and then abandoned me. Wondering even why the dark forces playing with my mind decided to go away.

A hero moves on toward the inevitable. But not me. I'm not a hero. I haven't moved and haven't done anything.

This changes on February tenth when I get an unexpected visitor.

What I will realize is that forty years can be like a blink. And that two months can be like two lifetimes.

The buzzer rings and I let my guest in. It can only be Cole, since that's the only person I've been seeing lately. Gavin has given up and is immersed in another project with someone else. People have to keep working and living, don't they? Unless they only have a couple more months.

I unlock the door and then go back up the stairs, back to my cocoon, back to my television and love seat and comforter.

This room has seen better days. So has this body. So has this face, this hair, this person that glances back at me in the silhouette of the darkened windows shielding me from winter's woes.

I hear the steps coming.

"Where'd you go last night?"

But then I see the face underneath the hat and wonder if I'm dreaming.

"Hello, Tyler."

Matthew is standing at the top of the stairs, his black hat and overcoat spotted with flakes, the scarf around his neck being unwrapped.

"You are not dreaming," he says.

"Are you sure?"

"Yes."

There is no blinding light as he walks into the room, no sprouting wings as he takes off his coat. He puts the overcoat and hat on the arm of a chair.

"You're back."

He nods, looking at me with no noticeable expression and no sign that he's going to look away.

"Why?" I ask.

"Do you know I was there?"

"Where?"

"I was with the others who witnessed the birth of our Heavenly Father. The child in the manger. The question you had about Christmas and its meaning. It's not a question. I will forever remember seeing that baby with his parents, so young and so scared, all while the angels and the stars and the galaxies bowed down before Him."

"You were really there?"

"Do you doubt me?"

"No. Even though—even though I doubt pretty much everything in my life. But no, I don't doubt that."

"There are tiny glimpses and reminders of the glory and the grace, yet most are too blind and too busy to see. This is particularly the case around Christmas."

"So you came back to talk to me about Christmas a month and a half later?"

"God answered your prayer, Tyler. That is why I am here."

I know better now not to rant or be cynical or skeptical.

"I am to finish what I started."

Maybe it's the way I seem to move behind the counter or look at him gravely or perhaps turn green with fear, but Matthew senses my anxiety.

"You do not need to be scared."

Easy for you to say, buddy.

"There are not easy or hard things to say," he says, answering my thought, reminding me that he doesn't need words to have a conversation. "There is just the truth."

I think of Jack Handey from *Saturday Night Live,* who I'm not sure is an actual person, and I think of one of his quotes for some reason: "If God dwells inside us like some people say, I sure hope He likes enchiladas, because that's what He's getting."

Sometimes I can't help the rubbish going through my head.

"You do not need to stay in the kitchen."

I glance at the can of beer on the counter and then decide not to keep drinking it. I walk into the main room and sit on a seat across from Matthew.

"I'm sorry about what I said—about wanting you to go away."

"Before we go on, we have to finish what was started."

But you know what that means, don't you? And you don't really want that, do you? You just want to sit here in silence and solitude drinking away your last days, right Tyler?

"Okay," I force out.

"Do you know what that means?"

"Yes. And no. I don't know. But I'm willing."

Matthew looks at me. "Open your hands," he says.

I glance down and then do what he says.

"Look at them."

But I glance his way and he shakes his head.

"Look at them. Do not look at anything else. Look at your hands."

So I do.

And I can see them slowly change.

As does the light and my surroundings and my clothes and every other thing I can sense and smell and see.

I keep looking at those hands.

Then I hear a voice.

It's my father.

85

Some Distant Memory

Y ou've done enough, look at your hands."

It's Dad, and just by his voice I can tell he's younger.

Something jars in the back of my brain. A memory. Not *this* memory, but a memory with Matthew.

No.

"I'm fine, really," I say, but then again *I* didn't really say it, the body I'm in says it.

What's going on? I'm possessing myself? What's next?

"Look, you're practically bleeding," Dad says. He reaches over and takes one of my hands. "Those are nasty looking blisters. Let me finish."

"Dad," I say.

The chain saw.

But no, Tyler, you're missing a very critical and important piece of the memory. Like all people do who are in denial.

The bloody chain saw.

I suddenly don't feel like watching myself cut off one of my own limbs.

I hear Matthew's voice tell me to finish what was started.

But why was this started in the first place and where is this headed toward?

"I can still operate this thing," Dad says.

Then it dawns on me.

"Are you sure?" the voice coming from my mouth asks.

"I'm not that old."

I see him take the chain saw with his gloved hands. I'm trying to think of what year we're in. I don't need to ask where we're at. We're on the hill below the cabin, cutting wood.

It's cold, I know that. I can feel it starting in my boots and continuing up. My hands are numb, both from the temperature and from the blisters. Yet I can feel the dampness of sweat underneath my cap. We've been out here for some time.

I hear the steps of my dad walking down the hill from me. Then I see the tree.

It's that big damned tree I finally got him to cut. But why are we cutting it ourselves?

I want to ask him how old he is and the year but I can't.

"Be careful," is what I say.

"You make sure you stay away from where it's going to fall. Move over to the side."

Please don't make me watch this.

I try to squint and move and run and rush to him but I can't do anything except feel my body and my legs wander over to the side of the hill.

The sound of the engine and the barking, biting blade against the tree.

I'm staring at him.

This has to be at least five years ago or so. But that was when things were really bad, when I didn't want to have anything to do with him and this place, when I didn't want to deal with the guilt of losing Julie.

The saw cuts into the crevice already there.

Grinding, slicing, digging.

Please God, don't make me watch this, please.

The great tree that blocked our view for years and years jerks and slams out sideways while the engine of the instrument is still on

please

and the chain saw keeps going down, straight down, straight down into the dark limb that happens to be his pant leg, that happens to be his thigh.

The chain saw doesn't subside but rather purrs in excitement.

The sound I hear then...

No please no.

The sound, that horrific sound.

40

Hell is that sound, that noise, that scream.

It only ends as the tree topples over toward me, so massive that I am barely able to get out of its way as it hurls down and shakes everything around us.

I'm running down to where he is. The chain saw is off now, discarded, useless, like a bee after biting.

I hear my heavy breathing and my running and the word "Dad" coming out of my mouth.

I see his hands holding his thigh. Then I see the blood pumping out. I hear his cry and his deep-rooted howling and I feel like I'm going to pass out and that I'm going to throw up, but I reach him anyway.

I hear another voice far above me.

God, where are you? God, why? Please God?

"Charles?"

It's not God but Mom, calling down to us from the deck above.

I see my father's face and look at his hands and then I know. I glance at the chain saw with its bloody chunks and I know. As I grab his leg and feel the wet warmth over my hands, I know. I know.

I'm not here to watch my own death this time but to watch my father's death.

I just don't understand why.

86

Touched

My hands are holding air.

Like my lungs, my heart, my soul, my being.

Empty, invisible air.

I want to grab back time, whatever form it came in, whatever form I just lived through. I want to take it back and fix it, change it, correct it.

Matthew is across from me, the stoic mask still on his face.

"I knew."

He doesn't say anything, waiting for me to continue. I wonder if I need to bother talking, yet he seems to do stuff like this, forcing me to talk.

"I knew I didn't want to see what scene that chain saw belonged to."

"Your father is still alive."

"Barely. How long ago was that?"

"Long enough."

"But that never happened. That whole thing—it wasn't even close to happening."

"In another life it might have," Matthew says.

"Why? Why show me all these things? Why show me *that?*"

"I told you."

"I still don't understand. I don't understand any of it."

"Yet instead of finding an answer, you sent me away. Instead you were left alone."

"That's been my problem my whole life. Wanting to try and do it on

40

my own. Wanting to be left alone. You know that, right? Do I have to state everything?"

"A fallen angel can do many things when left alone, Tyler. They not only hurt and kill, but they worry, taunt, jeer, boast, deflate. They are voices of hatred, voices of anger, voices of doubt, voices of loss. They confuse even those spoken for."

"Am I spoken for?"

"You are."

The two words rip through me like a destroyer on the ocean, leaving rippling wakes behind it.

"I shouldn't be. You know? I probably shouldn't be after everything— after all the things—after what kind of life I've lived. And still live."

"That is why I came."

"But I don't understand. Why was I saved so many times? Does that just—is that just the way it happens with everybody?"

"You have been touched, from the very beginning, more than many others, more than you could ever begin to know."

"Touched? Me? Why? Touched by God? What for?"

"You still do not understand."

"Then fill me in, professor."

Matthew stands. "In a second I could take your heart and send it scattered into the sky."

"But why wasn't I allowed to die?"

"It has nothing to do with you."

"But I'm *touched*. Right? That's what you just said."

"It is called grace. You have grown up hearing about it and witnessing it, yet you still do not understand it."

"Grace? Great. But what I don't understand then is how I was saved from all those deaths. Did you just come in and bat the bad guys with your wings?"

Even before I look at him I apologize. I let him take his time explaining.

"Sometimes it is as easy as capturing a parent's attention about an errant stone lying on the sidewalk below an elevated porch. Sometimes it is much more, like restraining those who inhabit and terrorize. Sometimes it is a gift from someone else. Sometimes it's prompting someone to leave without saying goodbye."

"But I don't understand—all the things I saw. Were those really—could those all have really happened? I mean—the man who shot me—what was I doing? Where was I? Did Laila die too?"

"If Laila had stayed in your life, the answer to your last question would have been yes."

I still don't understand how and why. I still want and need to know the answer.

"I'm asking now. Please, Matthew, tell me."

"She is safe," he tells me.

I almost start to cry. I hold back the tears and restrain myself from showing emotion. If Matthew can see all my actions, then he's seen me do much, much worse.

"Thank you. Thank you for telling me."

"You are loved and protected and yet you wonder, Tyler. You wonder if God even notices. He can take the good and can take the bad and He can build something out of either of them."

"Is it this way with every person? I mean—how protected they are?"

"No."

"Then why?" I ask.

"You were meant for something else."

"Meaning?" I ask.

"You were meant for more, Tyler."

I let out an exhausted sigh. "Wow." Then I chuckle. "I guess when an angel tells you that you should've done more in life, that really, truly means you've failed."

"There have been battles over you that you could not imagine."

"Really? Who won?"

"You were touched and earmarked."

"But we have free will, don't we? I was asked, but like Jonah I ran away. I've been sitting and rotting in the belly of the whale a long time, huh?"

"Even in a shortened life, a man may achieve God's will. The sun can shine even in the shadows of a man's final days."

I laugh. "I have two months. That's it."

"You had more," Matthew says.

I nod.

40

Thanks for the reminder.

"But why show that about my father? That wasn't about saving me. He died. I don't get where that fits into my story."

"You will. In time. Just know this. Your mother and father are reasons why I am here."

87

Right Down the Line

Matthew doesn't give me any more answers. Instead, he gives me an assignment before he needs to leave. I want to ask where he's going. I refrain from making a crack like "working the night shift at the diner?" The assignment he gives makes about as much sense as him saying I'm touched. Yeah, I'm earmarked for greatness. That church I was going to plant in Peru had to wait. Sorry about that, Peruvians.

Matthew would uppercut you if he was right here.

He leaves me and heads out into the dark wintry night. I start working on his assignment. I can't help thinking of my parents, of Laila, of the idea that Matthew has been there all throughout my life watching and waiting and watching and watching more. I wonder if I would have chosen and done all the things I did throughout my life if I had known he was there, watching every move.

You know the answer, because you know God's seen it all, yet that hasn't stopped you, has it?

So I begin.

While I work on my homework assignment, I can't help realizing what this has been about.

So all of this...so everything, all the terror and fear and pain and guilt...

40

It's not been about God getting back at me.

It's been about me giving back.

It's about being given a date and still having potential. Still having a chance. Still having a purpose.

I make lists and compilations.

I feel like Arcade Fire's "Neighborhood #3." I feel like Orbital's "Choice."

I'm going through my iPod and making a list, all while e-mailing and texting and getting my game on.

I can do something in two months.

I can be something.

I can make something more and different and better.

I'm going to try because that's the point, right?

Why else would he ask me for something related to music and songs?

Why else would that even come up, right?

So I get to work. I haven't felt this way, this inspired, this full of a rush, in some time.

Maybe this is a playlist of songs that will be played at my funeral, a playlist I already started to make.

Matthew asked for 100 songs. The hundred songs that mean the most to me. Not the list I'd come up with and give to *Rolling Stone* as my top 100 pop songs. These are songs that hit me at the right time and place, songs that moved me, songs that I never skip over if they start playing.

He also asked for my top ten albums.

Before leaving, he gave me no explanation, no time frame, only telling me that he wanted this list when he came back.

So I start making my list of songs and albums. I stay up most of the night playing music. I'm filling the playlist on my computer in no particular order.

Many of the songs I find are ones that played during my youth, when I wanted to grow up and longed to get out and be my own person.

It's amazing that we spend our childhood longing for stuff we can't have. Then we grow up and claim it as our own, only to realize it wasn't worth much in the first place.

Doesn't change that deep-rooted desire. Doesn't change the place it has in your heart.

Doesn't change the memories either.

I bounce on my aunt and uncle's bed with my cousins as we listen to records in the stereo that's cranked up in the living room.

I roller-skate with my sister in the unfinished basement with the beam in the center as we listen to music off an 8-track player.

I'm in the back seat of the car on the long drive cross-country as the music fills the speakers. It's Mom's turn and she pushes the edge by letting us listen to the Beatles.

I'm at camp, walking with strangers I just met who will become the sun-drenched snapshot of friends in my mind, and we hear the song on in the background.

This is how it starts. How I record my life. Through songs.

The girl I fell for in sixth grade has an accompanying song.

Music remembers.

Notes play for a hundred different purposes. Some taunt. Some tease. Some tempt. Some tell stories nobody else will ever know.

Fourteen again. Pimply and persecuted by upper classmen. Listening to forget.

Twenty-four again. Proud and determined to do it right. Listening to celebrate.

Thirty-five again. Perplexed and searching for meaning in the chaos. Listening to feel.

These are the songs I end up marking for Matthew. The songs I call my fellow friends and enemies. Some whisper as they caress my ears. Others bite as they cackle in laughter.

They know. They remember. They share my joy, my pain, my soul.

Songs are the sound of memories.

88

This Is the Day

Two invitations arrive at my online door on the same day in late February. I wonder if this is the work of Matthew's hand or if it's one of life's great big ironies.

I'm quickly beginning to believe there is no such thing as life's great big ironies.

One is an invitation to some kind of club thing that I initially think is spam before I see it's from DJ Ellis. The header makes me smile: **Songs of Faith and Devotion with DJ Ellis.**

It gives an address of a club named Aura, as well as the time it starts: nine p.m. There are several guest DJs and some other bands or performers listed.

The other invitation is an e-mail that I get from Pastor Will.

It's for Saturday, February 26.

The same date as the club event for Ellis.

Yet this event starts at six at night.

Hey, Tyler, just wanted to pass this event along to you in case you might be interested. Hope all is well—Will

    Join us at Faith Creek Community Church for an evening of opening up some of the controversies in the Bible.

Was there really a literal whale in the story of Jonah? Did Lazarus really die and was he raised from the dead? Is there really a place called Hell?

A night full of frank and honest discussion of some of the Bible's mysteries and hot buttons that turn off a lot of people interested in faith.

I reread the sentences on Jonah and Lazarus.

Is there really a place called Hell?

This isn't coincidence.

Maybe this is a test. One of the final tests.

What will Tyler do? Which friend will he pick? Where will he go, the church or the club?

Yet that's too pedestrian, too clichéd.

Plus, I can go to both if I want, since one is at six and the other is at nine.

Maybe I'm meant to bring Ellis to church?

Cliché.

Or maybe I'm meant to bring Will with me to the club?

What's the point here, Tyler?

I accept both invitations. Maybe this is the day. Maybe there's still a chance to be the person I'm supposed to be.

He shows up at my door, the devil, wearing a grin on his weary face.

"And I thought *I* looked bad," he says, as he falls back onto the couch as if he's going to stay a while.

Sean Torrent looks nothing like the basking personality that contradicted his brooding music and lyrics in his late '90s vault to success. He's the snapshot of what comes after the episode of *Behind the Music* ends.

"I didn't think I'd ever see you again," I say.

"What? With your happy New Year's Eve go to hell greeting? Quite the pick-me-up, let me tell you."

"Yeah, sorry about that."

"Please." He curses and lets out a sigh. I can't get over how pale and

40

thin he looks. "*That* was a wake-up call. Literally woke me up, first off. But seriously. That challenged me. It pissed me off and then got into my head. I don't know if that was your point but it sure did it."

"I had no point," I say.

"Maybe that's why it worked. My last intervention felt like a casting call for a reality show on MTV. I kept wondering where the cameras were. Ridiculous."

"How are you?"

"Your offer still there? If I show up ready to work, will you—are you still willing to do the same?"

I nod.

"What's this business about April? About you not being around? You sick or something?"

"It's nothing."

He looks at me and doesn't believe my words, but either doesn't care or is respecting my privacy.

"Then tell me this," he says. "We have much time to work?"

"No."

"I'm ready to finish what we started."

"It might not be that easy."

"Fame and fortune buys you ease," Sean says. "It doesn't buy you inspiration or desire, but it sure as hell buys you ease."

I don't know what I'm exactly supposed to be doing in my life at this point. But I do know if something like this comes into my living room ready for a second chance, I'm going to take it.

So I do.

The work inspires. It inspires both hope and sadness. The hope is for Sean and his career and what we're doing and what we will leave behind. The sadness is that I'll be leaving this all behind.

Shouldn't I be excited?

But I know what I'm meant to do and it's this, here, right here.

Shouldn't I be doing something more?

I've made my lists and I'm waiting for Matthew to show up.

Meanwhile, the work keeps me busy.

Busy enough for me to ignore my mom's call.

"Your father is talking again, Tyler."

Busy enough for me to ignore my brother-in-law's birthday.

All you have to do is call and talk to him for ten minutes.

Busy enough to not reply to Nicole's text.

You don't have to hide from something that's not your fault.

Busy enough for me to neglect to contact anyone around me.

So it's probably a strange thing that when I get around to contacting somebody, it's Will. I call him to tell him what I thought of his Christmas message. It's been playing in my head for sometime now. I still have it on my iPod and actually *want* to listen to it again. That's unusual. That's downright miraculous.

The phone number I call is no longer in service, however. I realize that I've never tried calling it and I probably typed in the wrong numbers on my phone.

I know where he lives. I know where his church is. I'll see him soon. Very soon, in fact.

The funny thing about life is that you really can't compare it to some highway you're driving down.

You don't suddenly get off at the exit when you're going eighty-five miles an hour, knowing where you're going and what you're headed toward. Right?

But this is exactly what happens. And this is exactly the destination I've been driving to for the last thirty-nine years of my life.

PART NINE

A Rush of Blood
to the Head

89

True Faith

Here."

Matthew sits at my table as if he's waiting for a bowl of porridge. I've asked if he wants anything as I make coffee.

By now this is not strange or surreal. It is what it is. I'm asking an angel if he'd like a cup of coffee.

Of course you are. Why wouldn't you?

My printed-out playlist rests in front of him. All 100-plus songs. On three stapled pages.

"I had a little trouble sticking with one hundred."

They're in no order.

1. "An End Has a Start" by Editors
2. "What Difference Does It Make" by the Smiths
3. "The Killing Moon" by Echo & The Bunnymen
4. "Fragile" by Sting
5. "Once Upon a Time" by the Smashing Pumpkins
6. "Paranoid Android" by Radiohead

The list goes on.

"You said to pick the songs that mean something to me. That have an emotional quality to them. So that's the list. And then I picked my favorite albums too. Again, the ones with the most meaning."

Achtung Baby changed my perception of U2 and showed me how artists can reinvent themselves. *Strangeways, Here We Come* was the soundtrack to my final move in high school, along with being the swan song of the Smiths.

I can go on. But as I look at Matthew, I can tell he doesn't care.

He hasn't even looked at this list.

"You asked for that, right?"

"Yes."

"Can I ask what you wanted it for?"

"There is a reason I'm here, Tyler. A reason why you were granted this gift."

I wonder why death is such a gift.

And why being told is a nice fat bow tied around it. Like a noose.

"It is no noose."

I shake my head, the nerves coming back, the need for a shot of tequila. "That continues to startle me—you reading my head."

"Prayers are like songs. They have a value and a worth. None of them are without merit. None. And your parents have prayed for you for many years. They prayed for you even before you were born."

I sit down across from him and take a sip of coffee. The room feels quiet, open, ready.

"Your father prayed many prayers for you before his heart attack. He prayed for you to see. He prayed for your eyes to be opened."

"For me to see what? For my eyes to be opened to what?"

"To eternity. To the faith inside of you. To everything he has spent time talking about."

"Yeah—ten million things you didn't want to know about Hell."

"All your life, you had an opportunity to learn. To hear and understand. To be given a gift."

"A gift of what?"

"Yet you ignored it."

"My father? I ignored my father?"

Matthew stares at me and I know that means yes.

"And that's why I'm dying then? That's why I'm going to die on my fortieth birthday?"

40

"No, Tyler. That has always been your destiny. The gift is that you have been told."

"Oh really, Clarence? Yeah, well, next time I want to see myself die in a dozen ways, I'll thank you."

"You fool. You still don't understand. You have been given the chance to see the past as proof for a skeptical soul. You have been given the opportunity to be told the future in an answer to your father's prayers. And even after all of that, even after you told me to go away, God answered another of your prayers."

I sigh. I don't understand this.

So my father is right and I'm wrong and this is the way I'm shown it.

Matthew seems to read my mind and he says nothing.

He only smiles.

"You are very much like Thomas. He needed proof too. Consider this, Tyler. He said 'Unless I see the nail marks in His hands and put my finger where the nails were, and put my hand into His side, I will not believe it.' The Lord and Savior came back and allowed Thomas to touch Him in order to believe. Few are fortunate to be given such a gift. Your father and mother were blessed to believe their whole lives, yet never saw nor touched Christ."

"But explain—why—why show me how I died?"

"I showed you how you lived, Tyler. How you were protected. How you were loved."

"But *why?*"

"There is the life you could have lived, Tyler. And there is the life you should have lived. Yet you did neither. You have lived thirty-nine years waiting and wondering. You have watched from the sidelines. You have felt the urging and have resisted it. You have drowned out God's voice and have replaced it with so many other voices. Many voices that have detracted and taken away."

"What's that mean? I don't understand."

"Play these songs for me."

"My list? Now?"

Matthew nods and I find my iPod to start playing the first song.

"Try the next one," Matthew says, repeatedly, as I scroll through the list and play samples from each song.

Travis Thrasher

After half a dozen he nods and then walks over to the stereo. I think he's going to turn it off like my father might, but instead he turns it up.

"Have you listened to these words? Listen to what they're saying."

Depeche Mode is singing "Enjoy the Silence," perhaps one of my favorite songs of all time.

"Yeah, I know," I tell him.

He gives me the list of songs back and the blue eyes bore into mine.

"What are the songs saying? Summed up, what do they tell you?"

"That this life is sad. That people are broken. That we're all going to die."

He looks at me.

"I've been a realist," I continue. "Always have. Depeche Mode sings about faith and sex. And you know what—I get it. Most don't think about the faith part but I do and I have since I could start to think for myself. But it's the other stuff. It's that other stuff that's weighed me down. They seem to know because they're always singing about the sin of everything."

"You have lots of songs in your memory."

"Because I have a lot of memories. Because I have a lot of sins."

"Imagine, Tyler. Imagine the energy and excitement and passion that you invested in that list of yours. Imagine what it would be like if you invested that in eternity."

I sigh and sit against the couch.

Maybe I should be reacting and doing something else but I'm just so damned tired. I really am.

"I don't know what to say."

"Your father had that passion and he lived his whole life with that in mind. He knew Colossians 3 by heart and he took it to heart."

"Would've been nice to have a little of that love for me."

"But he is a sinner like you. Like all who have sinned and fallen short of the glory of God. Your sin is no different, Tyler."

"So who should I have been then? Huh? Who? What was I supposed to do? Who was I supposed to be?"

"You have seen him."

"What's that mean?"

"The person you should have been. And the person you could have been."

372

I feel my point of view shift and watch us from up above.

I feel a tingling, a *you-knew-that-deep-down-but-were-too-dumb-to-call-it*.

I already know but then my mouth moves to ask.

"What do you mean?"

He nods at me.

And he smiles.

"What? Who? What are you talking about?"

"What if this, all of this—" Matthew says, pointing at this list. "What if that energy had been directed into living and in looking ahead at eternity?"

And I thought I couldn't feel any lower.

"This is not about shame, Tyler. This is about opportunity. And you were given a glimpse. Into what could have been. And what should have been."

For a moment, I think of the invitations to the events this night, the men they came from.

Ellis.

Will.

He smiles.

And I know.

"No," I say. "No. No way."

"Tyler—"

But I've already grabbed my keys and phone and am rushing outside to prove that he's not right and that I haven't gone completely bonkers.

And then I hear Clarence, not Matthew, talking.

You see Tyler, you've really not had a wonderful life. It's been actually somewhat lukewarm. Maybe you should've just done us all a favor and thrown it away.

I drive to Trump Tower.

Could've and should've.

I curse, knowing the answers I'm running away from.

90

Alive

Do you ever feel like a toy requiring a triple A battery? The kind a kid leaves on and is quickly drained of any juice?

I'm being toyed with. Like a mechanical hamster.

The woman at the desk of the Trump Tower looks at me like I'm a toy left out in a garage sale, broken and worthless and in need of a Dumpster.

"I'm sorry, but there is no one here by that name."

Ellis. That was all I knew. DJ Ellis.

What was his full name? Was that really his name?

I tell her I visited his condo on the 51st floor and she obliges me the way someone might a handicapped person.

"No Ellis, first or last name."

I hear her words, but I already know them before she speaks them.

Where are you, Matthew? Where'd you go this time? I want some answers. I deserve some answers.

I try for a few more minutes because I'm stubborn and because I'm stubborn.

That's right: I'm stubborn in being stubborn; you didn't read a typo there.

"Anybody that works as a DJ?"

She asks what he looks like and I try to describe him but I'm not really saying much at all. Tall, spiked hair, I don't know.

Kinda resembles me in a way, I guess. A more toned, tanned, better looking version of me.

I don't say this because I'm already two steps from sprinting out of here.

In my car I go online to find the sites I had seen him on. A MySpace page. A Facebook fan page.

He was my friend on Facebook, what do you mean he's not real?

Nothing.

No DJ Ellis and no Ellis.

Think of your father, Tyler.

The voice comes out of nowhere and I try to see if Matthew is sitting in the back of my Audi. Or maybe he's hovering over it like in one of those ridiculous angel movies.

Oh no, it's Nicolas Cage and he's an angel gone bad!

I shake my head as if it's going to stop the voices.

Not a sign. Not a single clue.

I head west toward the suburbs. Toward where I spent Christmas Eve. Toward the church I passed and heard about. To the church I was going to visit tonight.

But you never went there, did you, Tyler? Did you?

My car races over a hundred miles an hour. I'd like to explain to a cop where I'm headed and what I'm doing.

When you're a couple of months away from death, a ticket doesn't seem so daunting.

I remember the address of Will's house.

320 Sycamore Street.

I find it and knock on the door, expecting to find Pastor Will there, holding his daughter and inviting me in. Maybe I'll just ask to stay there permanently. I'll tell him the truth about everything and he'll be able to combat these demons and these crazy visions and all of that. I'll change and I'll become a better person and I'll become a deacon and maybe there's a short-term missions project I can go on in the next month.

I'll be a better person, I'll change, I'll try, I'll really try.

The woman who answers the door is definitely not Stacy.

She's shorter and has darker features and doesn't seem to speak any English.

"Is Will here? Stacy? The family?"

"No," the strong accent says. "Sorry."

I look inside and see different furniture and furnishings. She says something to me and is about ready to close the door, but I tell her to stop. I need to go look inside her house. Then I just shove my way past her to see the inside.

The woman now is shouting at me in Spanish as I look around. I see a little boy about four years old come look at me.

Everything is different.

This is the same house but not the same family.

What is happening to my brain?

The woman is still screaming and the boy looks terrified and I hold up my hands and apologize and get out.

This is a bad dream. When am I going to wake up? Please God, let me wake up!

The church isn't far from here.

I head toward it on the road and of course find what I already know is there.

Twists aren't really fun when you already know what's coming.

This cannot be happening. I saw the cars in this parking lot. I saw the building erected here. I heard the sermon online. I heard about the tremendous growth.

And yet, I never set foot in the building.

Symbolic, huh, Tyler.

I get out of my car, parked on the edge of the street. There was a driveway winding up the hill and then a massive parking lot.

Now it's just a hill with a scattering of trees and an empty field.

The trees are barren from winter. I see a sign that says **Private Property/Keep Off**.

I stare up at the sky. The February day is cold and ugly.

I kneel down and pluck some weeds to make sure I can tell if I'm dreaming or awake. They feel real. This barren hilltop is real. It's real and unused and so full of potential.

"Does it remind you of anything, Tyler?"

The voice startles me and makes me jerk back up to my feet.

"Does it remind you of anybody?"

"Why?" I ask Matthew.

40

"Few men have ever been given the insight you have been given. First you were given an opportunity to see how God protected you. Then, even after you did not believe and only wanted me to go away, you were given the opportunity to meet yourself in two other lives."

"To meet myself? You know how crazy—how utterly bizarre that is?"

"Those were snapshots, Tyler."

"What? How? Were those dreams? Were those men even real? And why didn't I—how could I meet myself and not know?"

"In some ways, you did know. But the obvious conclusion was kept from you to show you the outcome."

"The outcome? What's that supposed to mean?"

I laugh. I am breathing heavily.

"The question has never been where you will spend eternity, Tyler."

"It's been a question to me."

"If you had never come to faith at an early age, you would have become the man you saw in Ellis."

"A DJ? Seriously? Is that a joke?"

"It's no joke."

"But the club he's supposed to be at tonight—it's real. I googled it and it's still around."

"Yes, and they're going to be just as busy as they would have been if Ellis was there tonight."

I'm out of breath, full of caffeine I haven't had, my mind wandering like someone with ADD. "But what's with his name?"

"Think of your father."

He speaks without any anger or *told-you-so* tone inflections, so much so that it drives me crazy.

"What about my father?"

"What did he used to tell you, over and over?"

The jokes keep coming.

"Seriously?"

I know but don't say it out loud.

"A boy who grew up hating his father and everything he stood for, who ended up leaving before he graduated high school, a man who decided to soak up the pleasures this world has to offer. He might take the name of

377

the phrase his father used that he despised. 'Hell is.' He might do it as a joke, as something of a wink and nod. And he might end up stuck with that name."

I think of Ellis and how he had everything he wanted and needed.

There was no remorse in his words. No hint of an apology.

You sit on the plane and it takes off and you can just leave it all behind.

That's what he did with his whole life, leaving it behind.

"How could that have been me?"

"Without God's grace and His change, that could have easily been you."

I think I stand there with my mouth open, thinking and looking up at the sky.

"But what about the pastor I met? I met the guy on a plane. How could I—how could I meet *myself*? I mean physically meet me?"

"Do you think it is so impossible for God, who created the Heavens and the Earth and breathed life into Adam and Eve, to show who you could have been? Or who you should have been?"

"And Will—of course, right. He's who I *should* have been."

I glance back at the hill that *should have* had a church on it. A building of hope and life that I *should have* helped build.

Well, thank you very much. Thanks for the affirmation that my life really truly has sucked.

"But why the name Will? Just trying to have a clever ruse to fool me even though I'd still never get what I was being fooled about?"

"William is your middle name."

"Yeah? So? I never went by it."

"A typo at his college made the professors all start calling him William. All the students got to know him that way and he kept it. He thought that things happen like that for a reason, and when he met the girl he would eventually marry, he continued to let her call him Will."

"So that family—those kids…"

"Yes, Tyler."

"What has this all been about? Why? Why show me? What have you been trying to do to me?"

Matthew laughs. This is unusual, because I don't recall him ever laughing.

40

I wonder if he is truly amused or if he is doing that to make a point, just like bringing me to the barren hill here.

"Why do you continue to miss the obvious?"

"What? How can I miss the obvious when everything around me *doesn't make sense?*"

"This is not about you. Your life is not about you, Tyler. This world is not about the people living and breathing in it."

"Go ahead. Say it. This is the time to say it because Dad sure isn't around to do it for you. Say it. 'Hell is a place with people who only think of themselves.' Or something like that, right?"

"There is still time, Tyler."

"Time for what? Time to realize everything I *haven't* done with my life? I mean—haven't you already shown me enough? Haven't you already shoved enough in my face? You tell me to write up a list of favorite songs, *for what?* Again, to remind me of how pagan and awful I am. How I'm a major FAIL. Man. I thought my father was bad."

"What do you tell the people you work with?"

"Excuse me?" I ask.

"You ask your artists to sing with 'soul,' and you understand what that means so clearly. Yet you do not live your life taking your own advice, Tyler. You do not live a soulful life. You have not lived a soulful life for thirty-nine of your years."

"What does that mean, a 'soulful' life? This—that up there. The building that used to be there? Is that soulful?"

"You know. And there is still time."

"Still time for what? An afternoon matinee? One last martini?"

"There is still time."

He begins to walk away and I call out his name.

Again, somehow I know.

Somehow I realize that I'm not going to see him again. At least not in this life.

"If all of this—if all of these thirty-nine years—if they've all been for nothing—then why am I still here? Why did God save me as you say He did? 'Cause you know, if you weren't saying that I'd begin to really think I was never one of His to begin with and that Hell is going to be a place I'm going to see very soon."

"Again, you think it is all about you. But it is about Him. And it is about what you can do—the choices you have—in the time that is remaining."

"Matthew...why did I see my father die in front of me? Why?"

"Did you hear what Ellis told you about his parents?"

"He hadn't spoken with them in years."

"What about Will?"

"He said his father had passed away."

"That is right. Will had been there at the cabin to help out his father. Bad things happen to good people, Tyler. But sometimes, a person's mistakes give birth to blessed opportunities."

91

God Put a Smile Upon Your Face

You're halfway to North Carolina. You have a quickly packed bag in the back seat. You're not running away from your problems. This time you're driving toward them.

You listen to the songs you carefully spent hours selecting for your playlist. The songs still move you and always will. You think over Matthew's words. The revelations continue to shock, yet at the same time nothing is surprising anymore.

Life is a series of choices.

Julie and Laila. The could have been and should have been.

Choices. Roads. Journeys.

Seeing yourself as Ellis isn't that hard. But seeing yourself in Will is harder. Until you begin to peel back the layers and realize what's inside at the core.

It doesn't feel like a very big leap from sixteen to thirty-nine, but it is.

Moments stream through your mind, snapshots, images, and impressions.

These are the moments you've forgotten about, the memories you've buried.

Praying to a Father that you're hopelessly and desperately trying to separate from the image of your own father. Praying to God that you need help and that you need hope and that you need rescuing. Asking for forgiveness for the sins of a fourth grader. Saying words you don't understand yet, words that are real and that work.

Have you forgotten about those words, Tyler?

The camps you go to where you sit at the fire and pray and wonder what you're supposed to do with your life.

The desire to stand before people and be bold like your father. Bold yet compassionate as well, wanting to help and not hurt, wanting to show love through actions and not fears, wanting to do it in a better way.

Falling in love with Julie and thinking and believing she's the right one for you. For the rest of your life.

There was potential, yes. There was hope. There was a map set out.

So what went wrong? Why did everything have to go so wrong?

You don't know much anymore.

You've tried it your way and you've failed.

You've seen His hand time and time again and you've been sent off in the right direction again and again, and yet here you are. You've barely moved.

There should be more distance between sixteen and thirty-nine.

You have come to realize something. The one who has halted your course and whispered promises and pleasures . . . You know this now. There is no promise remaining. No soul-printed watermark. The devil is a thief, barring all roads home. He doesn't wait by a lake of fire with a gun, but rather with guilt, waiting for an admission, waiting for your blinded eyes to see a sky that will never be blue again. Out of the devil's mouth come lies. He corners you and covers you in isolation, sneaking out like a ghost at night. He waits and watches every breath you take. He smiles, knowing you're eternally broken, leaving you in solitary confinement.

But there is still time left before 40 comes.

Still time.

Still hope.

Still a chance to break his back.

92

Let It Be

There is not enough time for grudges. There aren't enough days for bitterness. The hours number too few to let resentments coat them.

I open the door.

I'm a boy. Scared, worried, wrecked with guilt.

I walk into the office.

I'm a sinner coming before the judge. I'm the color red splashed in a room full of white. I'm all that could have been, facing all that is.

I stand at the doorway and see my father.

I'm the only son and I want my youth back.

Eyes, feeble and distorted, look my way. A dying body moves, a closed mouth mumbles.

That snapshot on the Hallmark card. That holiday movie with the dog. That hug. All those moments I never found.

Let it go.

That sense of security. That sense of hope. All the sense in the world never found, not here, not before this man.

Let it be, Tyler.

I move and get behind my father and wheel him out. Out of the office and out of the house. I sweep him in my arms and place him in the car.

When you're a child you can't do anything about it, and when you're an adult you're too busy and bitter to do anything.

I start the car and drive.

"It won't take us long," I tell him.

Then I put on the Beatles and make sure it's loud enough for Dad to hear clearly.

It's a warm day, but the water in the French Broad River is still cold. It doesn't matter.

It takes a while to get my father in the canoe, but eventually he's in the front while I'm in the back. We're not riding the rapids like he might have one day wanted. He might be ready to go, but not that way. Not with my help.

Instead, we take the boat and paddle out over a shallow and placid stretch of water.

I can't see his face, but I know that he sees where we are. I'm sure of it.

As I paddle gently, the hills on each side of us, the mountains I grew to both love and hate, I can't help but think of where my father is going. Where I'm going.

There won't be apologies in Heaven. I think there will be embraces. Not forced and not awkward and not routine. I think they'll be natural and everyone will make up for a lifetime of ones never given and never even thought of.

I sit and think of this in the canoe with my father.

I'd like to think that he knows what this boat ride means. But that would be too good to be true.

But Heaven—it *is* good, and it is true.

I believe this pales in comparison, because on this boat lies the seeping water of regret. But everything pales in comparison.

All he ever wanted to do was tell others about that good and true thing. He just did it in his own way. His own broken and blemished way.

I know now that you have to try, you have to love, and, if possible, if you have time, you have to heal the hurt carried so deeply in your heart.

I don't tell my father that I'm sorry, not because he might not understand, but because I believe he already knows.

Three days later, on March 24, my father finally goes to the place he's talked about for so long.

93

This Woman's Work

She is a picture of strength I'll never understand.

The faces and the names blur, overwhelm, exhaust. You might have thought my father was Billy Graham with all the people coming and telling our family stories of his impact. I'm detached and distant. Yet my mother remains composed, classy, a picture of grace.

Maybe this is good, since she's going to lose her son in another month. *She's going to need that strength.*

Hundreds of people greet the family at the visitation. I discover relatives I never knew, neighbors I never ran across, men and women impacted by my father's words. From behind the pulpit and behind his desk.

I keep waiting for her to break down, to have that Sally Field moment in *Steel Magnolias* where she just lets it all vent. But no.

My sister has her family with her. I'm like some sad prodigal son. I should have brought a dog to stand in line with me. At least I'd have something to show for my life.

We all go back to the cabin and seem to go about our regular routines. The children don't understand, of course. And the adults seem to have had plenty of time to see this coming.

I don't talk much with Kendra. But I manage to say goodnight to Mom, who I find in my father's study.

She is still wearing her black dress.

"I think I'm going to bed," I tell her.

"Okay."

"I'm surprised you haven't passed out yet. It's going to be a long day tomorrow."

"I was just thinking about something your father used to tell me. Something after one of his infamous sermons he'd give on Hell."

"What's that?"

She smiles, glancing down at one of the trinkets on his desk. It's a compass, and it was something he bought as an illustration for direction.

"He'd tell me what he thought Heaven was going to be like. He'd always come up with a new thought. 'The feel of a newborn against your arms for the first time,' he'd say. 'The sun setting over the ocean. The rain falling on a desert plain after a drought. The sound of applause at victory.'"

"Maybe he should have said those things in his sermons and his books. Maybe then people would have liked what he said a little more."

Mom looks at me, a look of serenity covering her pretty face. "He believed that was his mission in life. To tell those who don't know. To tell those who might think they know but don't. To move them."

I let out a chuckle. Surely a sad and wise-sounding chuckle. "To move them to anger?"

"To move them to do something. He said that we were given glimpses of Heaven all the time. The kiss of a loved one. The emotions and feelings and blessings we have. And yet, we were never able to really truly know what Heaven might be like. And I wonder now—I wonder what he's thinking and feeling at this very instant."

"Yeah."

"In some ways, I envy him."

"Yeah, me too," I say to Mom.

And I mean that. I really do.

The sunlight can heal a broken soul.

It's easy to stare at the shards of a broken heart, but when you look up and see the vast, open, endless blue, punctuated with golden light, it's impossible to give up.

God did that for a reason, I believe.

40

Night reminds us of the darkness and our place, but morning reminds us of hope.

I think of this as I make coffee and stare at the sliding glass door and the opening to the sky in the distance.

Sometimes it's easy to remain in the night. Searching in vain with a flimsy flashlight, trudging through shadowy forests and endless deserts and eternal oceans. Going around and around and around. All for what?

The rising sun reminds us that there is a God and that He hasn't forgotten us.

94

Goodbye

I don't expect to see Julie there. But when I do, I realize that there is no way she wouldn't come to the funeral.

I also realize there is no way I can *not* say something to her before she leaves.

After everything is said and all the prayers are offered publicly and the coffin finally descends into the cemetery close to the cabin, I hug those around me and find the figure approaching slowly and carefully. I know it's Julie because I know how she walks. I know how she thinks and how she cries and how she makes love and how she says goodbye.

"Hi, Julie," I say, wanting to say her name out loud.

Saying it and hearing her greet me back and then hugging her—this is what does it.

This is what makes the tears finally come.

I don't get on my knees and begin wailing. The tears are short-lived, but it doesn't matter. They made their appearance and Julie saw them.

"I'm sorry for your loss," she says.

Ever so proper, ever so respectful.

I nod.

It dawns on me that she's been to this little church before. She came here when we came to visit my parents at the cabin.

She knows this life. And in some ways—in many ways, in fact—she should have been standing with me and sitting next to me and holding my hand all throughout this.

We both know this, of course, but we also realize how life has moved on.

I can't help but notice her husband and their kids walking with the rest of the people back to the church.

"How are you doing?" she asks.

The things I'd like to tell her.

I'm doing fine, considering the last eight months of my life. Let's see, where can I start?

"I'm fine."

"It was a really beautiful ceremony. An amazing tribute to him."

"Yeah," I say in more of a sigh than a reply. "Sometimes I wondered if they were talking about the right man. Then I realized how things would've been different if he'd had a better son."

"Tyler, stop."

"I know. Even at my father's funeral, I make it about me."

She just looks at me. I know there's nothing she can say. She's treading in deep water and we both know it.

"You know something? He adored you. He always believed you were a genuine answer to prayer—a miracle, in fact—when I showed up with you at my side."

"I don't know about that," she says.

"No, it's true. And you know, I think he's right. You were the miracle. It's just—I was the skeptic. I didn't believe. And I just think—I not only let you down, but I let my parents down too."

The love is still there inside of her. It's a different shade of color, a different form, but I can still see traces of it.

"How were things...near the end?" Julie asks. "Between the two of you?"

"They were okay. We don't always know when we are going to have to say *sorry*, you know? When we're going to have to say goodbye. In my own way, I guess I did both."

She turns around and then waves at her family.

"You should go," I tell her.

"Is there anything I can do for you? For your family?"

And right there, as this wind blows against her and streams of blonde caress her cheek and nose and lips, I realize it.

I might never have this opportunity again.

I think briefly about the words I just said to her.

"I've thought about a lot of things this past year," I say. "I guess that's what happens when you come close to hitting forty. And of all the things I've thought about and all the regrets I've had, this is what I know. This is the truth, Julie. If I could do one thing over in this life, it would be with you."

"What? Not marrying me?"

"No. Not leaving you."

Her blue eyes glance at me. They don't look away.

They are older, but they're still those same eyes that loved me and that I fell in love with and they don't change. They never fully go away.

"I have said sorry enough for a dozen relationships, and I don't want to say that again," I say. "But there's one thing I haven't said to you. That I probably should've said every morning and every night when we were together."

"Tyler, please—"

"No, just, please. Just hear me out. I would have told you—what I want to tell you now is thank you. Thank you for the time we had. Thank you for loving me. Thank you for putting up with me."

Those tears have made a resurgence. I can feel them streaming and falling. But they don't intimidate me anymore.

"Thank you for coming into my life, Julie. Thank you for being perhaps the greatest source of joy this flawed life had."

She hugs me again, this time longer.

Like I said before, I believe Heaven won't have hugs of regret or hugs of sorrow.

I believe it will have hugs of grace, just like this one.

When I see her face again, my tears have spread. She wipes them away from her eyes.

"You act like you're never going to see me again," she says.

"You never know."

40

For a long moment, we stare at each other. The melodies of memories drift between us.

"No, I'll see you again," I tell her. "I know I'll see you again. Sometime down the road."

"You take care."

"You too."

95

Live to Tell

I believe some of the most magnificent works of art come from pain, and because we are such flawed and broken creatures, pain comes easily.

I think of this as I listen to Nicole finish singing a song called "Forever." It can be interpreted in a dozen different ways, which is one of the beauties of significant pop songs. Nicole is singing about loss, and I imagine that it has to be a personal loss. It makes me think of my father, then makes me think of Julie. She's singing that loss is not a forever thing, but love is.

During this last take, I can see the tears in Nicole's eyes. I give her space and time to recover from the place she was at.

"How was that?" she eventually asks me.

"Remarkable," I say. "I don't need to play that back to know."

This is our eighth day in the recording studio.

The beautiful thing about knowing you're going to die and when you're going to die is the ability to do things like this.

To bankroll the production for an album that may never see light of day.

Every day, at some point, Nicole asks me about this. She asks me if I'm sure about this, if this makes sense, if anything is going to come from these sessions.

"Maybe this will make a fabulous Christmas gift for your daughter one day," I say.

"You know something I don't?"

40

I laugh. "I don't know much. But I do know that what we're doing here matters. This counts."

Chances are this is our last day in the studio.

We have finished thirteen songs and if it were up to me—if I was the slick studio head that sold and swapped artists like they were baseball cards—I would pick nine.

I know which nine I'd pick.

This track we just completed, the track titled "Forever," would start the album. The completed track that ends with a hush and a kiss, the track called "Happily Ever After," would end the album.

Gavin is working with me and I've told him he's getting his regular pay. *Along with a little something else.*

Nicole comes and sits down in the armchair in the corner of the studio. I love this little cocoon of a world we're in. Surrounded by machines and consoles and guitars and synths and a variety of microphones and wires upon wires. It's dark all the time, making the rest of the world seem asleep, making it seem like Vegas in here. A city that never sleeps. Nicole sips her tea and asks me what's next.

"I think we're done. Or at least you are. The mixing and the final production still will take some time."

She glances at me. "Tyler?"

"Yeah."

"Why are you doing this? After the label passed?"

"Why not?"

"But this is your own money."

"Remember what you told me some time ago?"

She shakes her head. "I say a lot of things. Most of which probably don't make a lot of sense."

"This made a lot of sense. After the label scrapped our wonderful work, you left me this wonderful voicemail I was too stubborn to ever respond to. You thanked me for working together, and you said it was worthwhile because life is about relationships and not accomplishments. Remember that?"

"Did I say that? Sounds remarkably bright for someone so—as the media *always* puts it—young."

393

"Yeah. I remember thinking about that and initially thinking you were wrong. I remember I thought that relationships come and go, but the work—the almighty work—that is what remains."

"And now?"

"Now I think that's a load of crap. Work does matter and work can be good, but you don't take it with you. In the end, I don't believe it matters."

"Yet we're working to produce something that, what? That might never see light of day?"

I smile.

Nicole doesn't know my story. She has no idea that this installment of my story is about to end. But I believe her story has just started. And I believe that what we've done here is not only meaningful, but beautiful.

I'm here because I want to do this for her.

It's a small gift. And it's something that I wish I would have started doing twenty years ago. Helping out and giving back and helping along.

"This will see light of day," I tell her. "I promise you it will. Maybe not in any way you or I can make sense of now, but it will matter. It will count."

She comes over and gives me a big hug.

"What's going on in here?" Gavin asks. "This feels like a bloody funeral or something."

He curses and says that there's a lot more work that needs to be done.

I agree, Gavin.

I totally agree.

96

Right Where It Belongs

I walk along this ocean of regret, with gentle waves of memory gliding across my path. Time only grows, the bottom endless and the horizon eternal. Storms swell and seagulls soar and all I can do is look out and see the sun set.

It's interesting that after moving around so much during my youth, I settled on this Midwest city. Known for harsh winters and strong winds. Known more for disasters like the Great Fire or failures like the Cubs than anything else. This city fits my soul. It's big and brilliant and full of so much potential, but it never quite gets there. Like the Olympic bid. So close. So close but not finishing it out.

I look out at the lake and think back to when I first saw Matthew. It was at Lollapalooza, at the park behind me.

You live thirty-nine years doing things on your own for the most part, and then you have a divine messenger saying you could have done so much more.

I love the people that say "No regrets." Everybody likes saying *no regrets* as if it's a rest stop they neglected to see as they passed by at a hundred miles an hour.

I do have regrets. I do wish I could slow down and get off the Interstate.

I wish for a lot.

Most of all, time.

I've got my iPhone and I'm making out a list. My will.

Maybe this will all be a lesson for me.

Maybe this will all be for naught. Or not. However the saying goes.

What if this is just the start? The start of a new chapter, a new chance, a new change? What if I was going to finally take a turn and embrace the person I should be? The person changed by God's grace and challenged to be someone who challenges others?

What if?

What if I wake up on the morning I'm forty years old?

What if God gives me not a second or a twenty-second, but an infinite number of chances? Chances to start over and try again and make an impact?

Life is full of what-ifs.

That road we coast down can look pretty different when seen in the rear-view mirror. You can see the potholes and the cracks in the concrete. You can see the one-way signs and the closed-for-repair barricades.

What if tomorrow *does* come?

What will I do then?

You spend eighteen years of your life dreaming of what if? What if I get away? What if I find love and fame and fortune? What if?

Then one day you realize that you've been asking the wrong what-ifs.

What if God never came into your life?

What if you were raised without two parents who both loved and feared God?

What if church was a fast-food restaurant to you?

What if you had no such thing as guilt?

What if you had no idea what grace meant?

What if God hadn't loved you and hadn't sent His son to die for you?

Those are the what-ifs that only now enter into my mind and my heart and my life.

It's not about asking "what if I never failed?" It's about asking "what if there was never a chance to be forgiven of those failures?"

Life is all about what-ifs. It's the gift of free will and choice.

I just wish I would've asked different what-ifs earlier.

97

Faith

I'm heading to North Carolina tomorrow."

It's one of those precursors to summer, a warm belly of an April evening that feels more like August. I invited Cole over for dinner and drinks and favorites like Depeche Mode. Just like the other three hundred nights or more. The glow of the sky is perfect, as is the slight sigh of a breeze, as is the mellow mood in my head and heart. Sol beer can do that.

"To see your mom?"

Yes, and to celebrate my birthday with my own death.

"Thought she might like some company."

"Yeah."

There are things I want to say and should say but don't quite know how to say.

This is life, this is what so many grow out of, what so many soon forget.

They stop realizing there are things they need to say and the words drift off into the deep, dark sea.

"Hey, Cole. If I ask you a question, will you give me a legitimate answer?"

He nods, his eyes finally revealed after hiding under giant shades all afternoon.

"Have I been a good friend?"

"Not really," he says without much of a thought.

I know he's being sarcastic, and I know he's being typical Cole.

"I said a legitimate answer."

He shrugs.

"'Cause here's the thing. I've been thinking about life a lot. Especially with the passing of my father. I've tried to think of all the meaningful relationships I have. Or that I have had. And I don't know. I give myself a C-minus, at best. That's at best."

The music plays in the background. Just like it always has for the two of us.

Our friendship was built upon music. That was the bridge. That was the initial bond.

Sometimes I wonder if that's the only cementing factor that's been in my life.

He doesn't say anything and the moment waits. I can see Matthew somewhere, watching. Wondering if I'm going to say anything.

It doesn't matter what I say, not now, not at this moment, because what's done has already been done.

There is no way I'm suddenly going to try and go Billy Graham on the guy, because he knows me and I know him.

It doesn't work that way, not after so much time. Not after so much *wasted* time.

"I feel that in a lot of ways, I've let people down. Including you."

Cole gets us some more beers and then sits on the couch like he's sat many times. "What are you talking about?"

"I don't know," I say.

As if it knows, my iPod plays a song to fit the silence and the mood. At least my mood. We listen to it without saying anything, and I assume the moment has already passed.

"Remember when Liz left me?" Cole asks.

He never brings Liz up, even when I might bring up Julie. He never brings her up ever and this is a first. This is like talking about the dead brother who got mauled by an intruder.

I nod. I still can't believe he's even said her name. He's not obliterated and he's not on any crazy substance and he's not suicidal.

"I remember when I showed up here. Remember that? You didn't say anything and you didn't give me any advice and that's what I wanted. Just a friend."

"Yeah."

"You got an A then."

"Thanks."

"It was pretty rough, you know. And you were cool. It was helpful to be around you. None of the other guys—they understood but they wanted to go get me drunk or they wanted to just try and make me forget. You didn't. You talked about your faith. In little doses."

I chuckle. "Did it do any good?"

"I don't know. At the time it did."

"What about now?"

"That's not my thing. You know that."

Again, there's nothing more I can say.

"I hope you meet someone else like Liz," I tell him.

He's staring off at the skyline of Chicago and has already moved on.

I can't remember when he was ever this open and vulnerable.

The conversation is just starting.

But it's over as soon as it started.

A little while later, the city glows and purrs.

Cole took off a while ago. Maybe if he knew, he'd say more and act differently, but I can't tell him. He wouldn't believe me if I did. And there's a part of me, this miniscule part, that still has hope that I won't be right. That Matthew won't be right.

Midnight moves over and it's still cozy outside.

I look at the city and take in my surroundings.

I've made a nice little nest for myself.

For what?

Really, for what?

I think of Cole and of our last conversation and lack of conversation.

The biggest moments in life are the small ones, the kind not worth remembering. They're the unseen nails holding the building tight. They're the scent in the air and the gust against the sails and the soft, gentle sigh of sleep. They're life, second by second, and can only be appreciated in hindsight.

My breath is heavy. This skyline spins. The world stands still, holding its breath. I look out and I know. I know. I know how much I've wasted and waited and watched and wrestled.

I take in a silent, soft, sweet breath.

"Forgive me, God."

PART TEN

In Rainbows

98

The End

Maybe it's a dream.

I'm still wondering and waiting to see if all of this is a dream. Life feels like a dream, doesn't it? Sometimes? The feeling of being cheered on from the sidelines. Or being beaten up by a bully. Or being interlocked with your loved one. Or holding onto your child for the first time, as I can imagine it might feel. Dreamlike. Wondering when you're going to wake up.

I've been driving all day, heading to North Carolina, back to the cabin where my mom awaits. I'm making a pit stop.

I enter the diner and he's there.

Like in a gangster movie. My own personal road to perdition. He's sitting a few booths down. Smiling. Sipping his coffee. Waiting.

He nods in the direction of the empty seat across from him. I sit down in it.

Is this really happening, or are you just making this up at some rest stop after closing your eyes?

If God did create the sun and the moon and the stars, why not?

If one of his most beautiful and beloved angels decided to spit in His face and go his own way, why not?

Why can't I be sitting across from this creature, this thing, this menace who has spent my whole life trying to damn me?

We are all God's creatures. Both of us here. Flawed and imperfect.

But there is a difference between him and me.

"On your way somewhere?" the man with the dark stubble and dark eyes asks.

He gives me a look that resembles someone just before they're about to attack. The look of Russell Crowe in the arena at the end of *Gladiator*. That's the look that's in the heart of his gaze and eyes. Mean, restless, hungry.

"One last stop before you go see sweet, dear Mommy?"

"Why are you here?"

"I cannot continue to go down the road with you."

"Why stop now? You've been so consistent my whole life."

"You don't have to give up like such a weak, old man," he tells me. "You're in the prime of your life."

Even now, this thing is working. He never takes a day off. He probably doesn't get paid overtime. His life is a job and that job is to bleed.

"What exactly am I giving up?"

"The anger that's deep inside," he says. "I know it's there."

"Have you always hounded me?"

"I have always hounded your name and as long as you have carried it, yes, I have been nearby."

"My parents? My sister?"

"You were the easy one. I could get to you."

A server comes and I still wonder if this is exactly real. Yet the coffee she pours me tastes real. The Willie Nelson song in the background sounds real. Everything appears real.

"Why? Why was it so easy with me?"

"All I had to do was sing you sweet little lullabies," he says.

He grins.

"Why are you here?" I ask.

"I'm here from the very beginning and up to the very end."

"You can't go where I'm going."

He gives me an empty look, a vacant stare, a nothing of a response.

"This isn't the sort of story for a climactic showdown," I say. "I've already gone into the dark cave and seen my soul shattered. The battle's been won. You've lost."

40

"There is a matter of finishing."

"I don't think a few days quantifies finishing well or not."

"There is still time."

"What? What do you want me to do? Huh? What is your name? What name do you go by?"

"You wouldn't know or understand it if I said it."

"Paraphrase," I say.

"Fear. The fear of falling when standing before the new class. The fear of getting in trouble and facing the consequences. The fear of losing what's most important to you over and over and over again. Fear."

"I hate you."

"You hate yourself because you are weak. I'm not afraid but I can see and give fear."

I curse at the thing in front of me.

"Damn your maker. There is still time, Tyler William Harrison. There is still time. There is nothing left to learn and the bleeding will soon be over."

"If I could I'd strap you to the back of my car and drag you to my parent's house."

He seems to like my anger and intensity.

"So much like your father," he says.

"I'm nothing like him. I've come to understand—to wish that I'd been more like him."

"He struggled his whole life with fears."

"Yeah, but he managed to control them, didn't he? He managed to escape them."

"You are a fool. You really are just a child, aren't you?"

"You don't know me."

"In the next few days, think about all those who have abandoned you. Think about friends who don't know you. Think about family who barely contact you. Think about Julie and what could have been. Think about Laila and how she just left you. The door always shuts, so shut the door back, Tyler. You still have time."

"I'm not shutting anything and I'm not renouncing my God."

"Go out on a high. Go out angry and torn. You still have time to make an impact in this place."

"Why? This is a hollow shell."

"Curse God and you will be given more life."

"You can't give life," I say. "You can't give anything."

"Say you'll do anything and you'll be given more time."

I laugh. Shake my head. Squint at the man thing beast creature demon across from me.

"You're really pathetic, aren't you? Why are you wasting time on someone like me when there are so many others that are so much more worthy?" I ask.

He just looks at me.

"Why did you haunt me, only to suddenly stop and leave me alone?"

"Because it was working," he says. "Because you started giving up hope around the time you went to Vegas."

"And you were content then? Just like that?"

"I had more important things to do."

"So then—tell me why. I don't understand, why me? Why?"

You will.

The voice comes from . . . from where?

It sounds like Matthew.

Maybe he's going to come out from the bathroom and they'll have an epic showdown.

There is just silence.

I look down at my coffee cup that's trembling; then I see the empty seat across from me.

"Can I get you anything else right now?"

I look at the server, who doesn't act like anything is wrong or different.

I don't know if I could take another year of this, much less another month or even a week.

"Pie," I say. "I want some pie before I go."

99

Somewhere Only We Know

P eople don't believe in miracles, man, but I'm telling you this is a bona fide miracle, and it's happened right here in my lap in my front lawn in the porch of my memory, man."

This is the start of a rambling voicemail from Sean Torrent.

I think of the necklace I gave him back, the one he promised he was going to reclaim. He didn't break his word. I've got to give him that.

One day I'd like to read the Sean Torrent story to see what happened. I'm a part of it, a rather insignificant part.

My hope is that Matthew plays a role in it too.

"This album is amazing. It's going to be a double album in a world that doesn't do doubles. I'm going to shove it down the throat of Walmarts and Targets that have to find a little tiny box to put things in. I want to give it away for free but, Hell, I don't think they're going to let me. Gotta at least pay for the cost of making this thing. And I'm paying you back. If that's the last thing I'm going to do, I'm going to pay you back and you're going to get that studio, Tyler. I swear you're going to get it. And we're going to make more records and, by God, you're going to be considered as brilliant as Eno. I swear. I swear man."

It sounds like he's driving or something. Who knows what this guy is up to.

"But listen to me, before—I don't know how much time I have left. You just have to know this. I have been the recipient of a lot of generosity my whole life and the part that I'm bad at, the part I suck at, is this. But Tyler. Listen, man. Okay? Thank you. Thank you. We made something meaningful. Something magical. It's as much yours as it is mine. And one day, when—"

He cuts off.

I play it again to see if it won't cut off or if he's going to call me back, but nothing.

I realize these are the last words I'm going to hear from Sean Torrent.

Fitting, too.

I can't help but laugh.

Things like this make me truly think that God has a sense of humor. Not in my crude and cynical manner. But in understanding the ironies of life and educating us throughout them.

I think of Sean Torrent and all I can do is pray for him.

It's a cliché. In this day and age when even those who absolutely have no faith say they'll be praying, that the term *prayer* means nothing.

But I've been in direct contact with God lately. So it means something to me and it means a lot. I know it's real and it can work.

100

Never Let Me Down Again

He waits on the corner like a child at the bus stop in front of your home and his name is death.

I know his face and know it well. He likes to smile and show off bloodstained teeth. They're sharp, ancient, and remain very busy.

He waits for everyone in the shadows. Unseen and unwanted and undercover. Yet he knows the exact place and the exact time and he only answers to one.

I can see him from the deck, peering around a tree in the forest below. Every day, his shadow grows longer, his head more apparent, his dark holes for eyes more visible.

He whispers all the things you could have done.

He laughs at all the things you should have done.

His middle name is regret, his last name finality.

When I see him again, I realize I'm back to where this all began, knowing every end has a start.

I also know I only have two more days to live.

101

Hallowed Ground

Mom?"

"Yeah."

"Do you fear death?"

"A little."

"Really?"

"I don't know anybody who doesn't. Even if we know with assurance where we're going."

"Because we don't really know, right?"

"That's faith. But I believe—I believe there's something more and something better. I believe that we're going to have a glorious inheritance."

"But what about—you ever think of those who don't spend their whole life witnessing and sharing the gospel?"

"Like the apostle Paul?"

"But he was given more time. I'm talking about—the thief on the cross next to Jesus. Or the old man on his deathbed who finally confesses."

"It doesn't matter."

"Really?"

"There's not going to be comparing in Heaven. There will be celebrating. I don't think there will be front rows that you have to pay lots of money for."

"Wow."

"What?"

40

"Your using a musical reference. Just for me."

"I'm not as unhip as you think I am."

"I think that if there's anybody who has showed me the face of Heaven, it's you."

"Hardly."

"Thanks," I say.

"For what?"

"For everything you've done. For being a mom. For praying. For doing the things I never knew or can't remember."

"You don't have to thank me."

"I think there'll be more time to thank you guys. That's what I think Heaven will be."

"That's a good thought for a late night."

Imagine your favorite artist creating your favorite album of all time. You're finally going to see him in concert. And it's beyond incredible. It's more exciting than Zoo TV. It's more thrilling than front row dead center on the Devotional Tour. It's beyond description.

And then you're invited backstage to meet him. He is surrounded by the masses, but at the same time he greets you with a hug and he knows your first name.

He not only knows you but he loves you.

This is how I imagine Heaven to be.

Those feelings deep inside—the feeling of getting closer but still not reaching it—those feelings will finally be quenched.

Maybe I won't have a big mansion, but I don't think there will be any Joneses to keep up with.

411

102

Like Treasure

I open one last treasure and reread it.

The words have stayed with me. They have helped me remember when I truly lost my way in Vegas.

I tried to forget that this letter came because no address or other explanation came with it. But now I embrace these last words.

They're words from another flawed and broken soul, but nevertheless they will follow me to my grave.

Dear Tyler:

Forgive the paper—this is a page from my journal, the one you've seen me carrying around. I figure this works well enough to say the things I need to say.

I know that we've said our goodbyes, but so often in life, when people say them they don't think that they're ever really, truly final. But this one is, Tyler. There are many reasons why, and all I can tell you is that I needed to leave. I can't come back. But things are okay. I'm okay.

I just want to ask one thing of you. And it's this: don't change who you are. Don't conform to this world, Tyler. Keep that little boy in your heart. That's who you are. That's the precious part of you

40

that I never want to die. That will be the part of you that I will always carry with me, no matter where we are.

I still don't know if things happen for a reason, but I do believe we were meant to meet each other and fall in love. That love will never go away either.

Goodbye.
Laila

103

One—40

So what if this is your last day?

What are you going to do?

I'd like to have a party with everybody I know, but I realize that would be one of the worst things I could do. Not for myself, but for them. *He died right after his big party!* They would forever be left with that strange and haunting memory. As if they participated in my demise.

Even now, I think such melancholy thoughts.

I've been able to say goodbye in my own limited ways. And I've managed to set things in motion that I know will either amuse or honor or cause reflection.

Like leaving Cole my boat (as long as he's willing to continue with the payments on it).

Or leaving Gavin my recording equipment.

Or giving my music collection to Julie.

But those are the things that don't really, truly matter. Because eventually, Gavin and Cole and Julie and the rest of the people in my life will be at the same point I'm at. Whether they know it or not.

I think I know and believe. I think the journey is ending soon.

The journey.

I love that term, the journey.

In some ways—in many ways—the journey never really started.

40

The hero stayed at home with his headphones on.

The prince got a chance to meet and marry the princess but then managed to stay clear of the dragon.

Some journey, huh?

The tagline for the *Jerry Maguire* poster said "The Journey Is Everything." But maybe it's never been about the journey. Maybe it's always been about destination.

Right, Dad?

Maybe my journey finally started just now. Maybe I've really, truly just started living. My heart and my soul finally seem in tune. Yet nobody's there to hear them.

But you know what? I'm looking forward to music. Life's turns and corners and roads all come back around to the music and the melodies.

How beautiful are the chords of a musician?

How much more beautiful is the creator of those chords?

If you believe in God, then you have to believe He created everything. Including A minor and B major and the glorious C.

The progression that attracted people from Beethoven to Bono.

The swell and the surge and the silence and the subtleties.

Music is not random, and anybody who knows it and studies it learns about its rhythms and its technical side and its science.

Music is a universe of infinite possibilities.

I like to think that the Beatles haven't in fact written all the songs there are to write, that there are more waiting, that there are plenty more waiting.

They're not all hymns.

They don't all feature harps.

Nor do they need the beat of drums or the vibration of the guitar.

There are instruments we still have yet to hear.

Voices we have yet to discover.

And songs we have yet to sing.

Songs that rejoice that there's no need to be melancholy and no need to doubt and no need to distress.

Songs that celebrate the ultimate songmaker. The ultimate songwriter.

Songs that define the ultimate and the only producer.

• • •

It's a little after eleven and I'm upstairs in my old room, listening to tapes. And I come across one that I remember well and I slip it into the plastic holster. Then I turn it on.

I play the song and find tears running down my cheek.

I rewind and play the song again.

I've discovered that the way God talks to me is not with subtle messages, but with the obvious.

"40" by U2 cannot be any more obvious.

The rest of the cabin is quiet.

I imagine Mom is asleep. Good for her.

Midnight is approaching, and with it come questions. Curiosities.

I wonder. I really wonder what's going to happen.

I can't help but think about my life, all forty years, stuck up on the corkboard for me to look at and ponder.

I wonder why I was the son of a man so hell-bent on trying to get people saved and Heavenbound.

I wonder what kind of courage and grace it took for my mom to remain married to him.

I wonder what my sister is like, what she's really like, and what it would be like to be her friend.

I think of Julie and think of everything I could have done but never did.

I think of those who have been close and dear like the fingers on my hands, those who have touched me and have been there, even when I didn't know it.

I think of Matthew, who watched over me, and I feel humbled and thankful. I don't understand it and don't fully realize it, but I am thankful nonetheless. A guardian angel doesn't feed you platitudes and hand you lollipops. He's entrusted to a mission and he serves.

Why me, I'll never know.

Maybe because of that father and that mother. Maybe because I was meant for more. The more that I'll never be able to see.

What lies beyond today?

None of us knows.

Not a single one of us.

40

We can think we have the answers, but we don't.

We can plan our sunrises but we really can't ever know for sure if they'll come.

All we have is today.

All we have is now.

I feel the touch of grace. And the gentle washing of forgiveness. And the blanket of assurance.

Yet I'm afraid.

I'm afraid because I'm human and I'm flawed and I just don't know.

This is all I believe. This is all I can say.

This is my story and this is all I have.

Everybody has a story, but every story ends the same.

The question is, what will you take with you?

Not surrounding you, but inside of you.

I take with me these memories and these realizations and the grace to carry me through them. The blessed, beautiful grace.

Despite everything I haven't done, and everyone I haven't impacted, I'm still offered hope. That's what I'm taking with me. That's what I'm thinking right now.

Ten minutes till midnight. Until the start of the new day.

It's time to go to bed and wait.

Not wait for sleep, but wait for the story to begin.

To wait. To wait and to wonder how long.

To wait for something new.

To wait for a new song.

Acknowledgments

Thank you to all of those who have played a key part in my writing journey:

The ladies I love—Sharon, Kylie, Mackenzie, Brianna, and Hailey. I'm a lucky man.

My parents—Mom and Dad, and Mom and Dad Noorlag. I appreciate all the ways you've helped our family out these last few years.

My agent, Claudia, for encouragement and wisdom as we continue to wade through these wonderful publishing waters.

My editor, Christina, and my publisher, FaithWords. Thank you for allowing me to write books like *40*.

Scott and Kristen Molenhouse, for providing the setting of *40*, along with many fun-filled memories of Chicago.

My relatives, many of whom I don't get to see as often as I'd like, because of this writing thing.

All the publishing colleagues and authors I've had the great fortune to meet over the years.

And of course, to my continued readers, who encourage and motivate me to keep telling this variety of stories.

Discussion Questions

1. Why was it so easy for Tyler to accept that Matthew is an angel? What does the Bible say about angels?
2. Do you believe in angels and demons? Is it easier to believe in the former than in the latter?
3. If an angel told you that you were going to die on your next birthday, what would your response be?
4. What role do songs and music play in *40*? What is the significance of the chapter titles?
5. What is the significance of the number 40? What does that number signify in the Bible?
6. Why does Matthew show Tyler "visions" of what might have happened?
7. Why do the nightmarish visions stop around the new year?
8. What are your thoughts on the characters of Ellis and Will?
9. The word *journey* is used a lot in *40*. Is life about the journey or about the destination? How does your belief regarding the journey affect the way you live your life on a daily basis?
10. The famous Beatles lyric goes, "And, in the end, the love you take is equal to the love you make." Do you believe this in relation to your life?
11. If you could pick one song to sum up your life and its story, what would that be?
12. What do you think about how *40* ends?

Also by Travis Thrasher

Isolation
Ghostwriter
Broken

Available from FaithWords wherever books are sold.